Deus ex Machina

Deus ex Machina

BOOK ONE OF THE LITERARY DEVICES TRILOGY

Samuel Monte

Samuel Monte

Deus ex Machina

Book One of The Literary Devices Trilogy

By:

Samuel Monte

2020

Deus ex machina, (Latin: "god from the machine") a person or thing that appears or is introduced into a situation suddenly and unexpectedly and provides an artificial or contrived solution to an apparently insoluble difficulty.

- *From Encyclopedia Britannica online*

Chapter One

A dull, low buzzing sound awoke Dex that morning. Doing a sort of push up on his bed, he rolled over to his left side and grabbed his phone from the nightstand. Oh yeah, he thought to himself. I turned the ringer off before I went to sleep. There were fifteen messages from his best friend and roommate, Neil. They started with asking if he was okay last night. Do you need to talk? I will be there with you tomorrow. This was why he turned the ringer off. Of course he knew what today was. He had been dreading it, obviously. It still needed to be done. He quickly threw on an old tank top that passed the smell test and went downstairs.

As he descended the stairs, his nose was accosted with the smell of bacon and eggs. Dex couldn't help but smile. Neil was such a great roommate. Dex had known them since childhood. The two quickly bonded with their love of all things superhero related. As time passed, their friendship became more of a sibling relationship. Neil was loved and accepted as they are by Dex's parents as one of their own. Rarely were the two ever separated. On the night of his parents' death, Neil wept with Dex. Dex knew he couldn't have gotten through everything without Neil and he was more grateful for them than they would ever know.

"Dex! It's about time you got up. I was worried you drank too much last night." Neil smiled kindly at Dex as they scooped some eggs and bacon on a plate for him. "I hope you don't mind. I figured you could use a good meal. I'd make a pot of coffee, but... well... you know. We make it a cup at a time." Neil produced a cup of black coffee. "But I did make you one just like your humor: dark, bitter, and strong enough to keep the existential dread at bay for a bit." Dex couldn't help but laugh as Neil used the joke Dex had used himself a million times.

"So," Neil inquired with a smirk, "what happened last night?" Dex sighed. There was nothing spicy or juicy to report. Dex worked as a tutor for hire for local schools including a college campus. Unbeknownst to Dex, his parents left him a trust fund of stocks that were very well invested. Millions of dollars were invested and reinvested all the time. It was odd to Dex that this was the case. His father worked tirelessly in a power plant all of his life. The family owned a house, but they never spent money extravagantly. There was never any sign that the family was very wealthy. "If you work for what you need, you'll be self-sufficient. Work Hard: live humbly." He had heard this lesson all throughout his childhood, but he never thought of the huge ramifications until after their passing. Dex was able live off of the interest comfortably, having all of his material needs met. He didn't need to work but chose to do so lest he become bored and selfish. Neil worked in the local comic book and gaming shop in town- The Cathedral of Heroes. Dex's nights were filled with tutoring people and proofreading papers. Neil spent his days talking of tabletop games and various pop culture icons. It wasn't much, but it was honest work.

Dex wiped his mouth and swallowed his breakfast. "I was proofreading an interesting sociological paper. This girl was talking about religious conspiracy theories."

"Oh. So, like, is Jesus black and what would that mean?" Neil asked.

Dex shook his head. "No. More like this theory about faith in general. Apparently, there is this theory that the world isn't what it seems. That people of faith can sort of 'see beyond the veil' as it were and see reality for what it is. A huge, massive paper based on the social implications of people who think they can see angels and demons. And then it goes even further and suggests that people have special powers." Dex chuckled and drank some coffee. It was warm and bitter. "Apparently, there is this whole organization that acts as a check to evil in the world."

"So, where did the author land on it all?" Neil asked inquisitively.

"Essentially, her paper stated that it had to remain a secret. Humanity as whole is not ready for the truth of the world. It would be disastrous if everyone knew how the world really worked all at once. So, it's good that this exists and membership into this sort of club is exclusive. They stated that anyone can join, but you have to actively choose to see the world for what it is. Since most people don't want the truth, they live blissfully unaware and the human mind fills in the gaps for them. The doctor who heals a patient quickly uses only science. The mother who lifts the car off of their child uses adrenalin and not angelic help. It's always a gun fight and never energy blasts."

"That's wild, bud." Neil took a drink of their coffee. As they sat the cup down, Dex saw it was a light brown color. Neil was, in many ways, the other side to Dex's coin. Whereas Dex drank his coffee dark and bitter, Neil drank theirs with plenty of cream and sugar. Dex was more prone to flights of fancy. He would describe himself as an idealistic man. Neil was more concrete. Neil lived in a world of facts and figures. They were more concrete than Dex, but used that in imaginative ways. Whereas Dex excelled at creative writing and grammar, Neil excelled at mathematics. Each one complemented the other. This was one of the reasons their bond was so strong.

"So," Neil said, looking nervously at their cup, "are you ready for today?" Suddenly, reality flooded the room. There was no more time of talk for outlandish theories. Dex took another drink of his coffee. Bitter. Dark. Yet now, after the question, the coffee seemed to transform. It was much darker than before. He noted that it seemed even more bitter. Any vestiges of sweetness that would have come from the beans were now gone. His coffee became like his reality: darker and bitter than others. Perhaps this is why Dex never added cream and sugar to his coffee. If coffee was like the world, then why try to change it? Why add stuff to it just to make it better suited to your needs? No- coffee, like the world, should be accepted as is- dark and bitter.

Dex thought for a moment. Was he ready? His parents had been gone for a few years now. Five years ago, Dex had lost his parents to a car crash. He bristled at the thought. His parents, to him, were like gods. They were kind and just and full of mercy yet their wrath would burn through a sun. A car crash seemed an unceremonious way for them to leave this world. They should have gone out fighting some battle of cosmic significance. In the end, it was gravel at the top of a mountain that did them in. Their car lost control on gravel and slipped off a mountain. Hitting another road on the way down at the right speed and at the right angle sliced the car in half longways, killing them instantly. Dex replayed the night over and over in his head. An officer named Gordon came to inform him of the accident. He then had to go and identify the top halves of their bodies. It was one of those memories that, while a blur, was burned into his brain. From the moment Officer Gordon came to collect him, time slowed down. He remembers it now in flashes. Opening the door for the officer. Standing in a cold room. The sheets being moved from his parents for a positive ID. Neil and him crying for hours.

Dex could never forget standing in the morgue. It's cold, he thought to himself. It wasn't the cold of the seasons. It was an artificial cold. The room smelled faintly of chemicals and with every exhale, he saw a bit of steam coming out of his nostrils. The room was a testament to mankind's hubris, he thought. Being in an artificially chilled room surrounded by chemicals and death held dominion over humanity. He approached the tables with someone in a lab coat. The only sounds in room were the reverberations of their footsteps and the dull hum of fluorescent lights. The sheets over the bodies were stained a crimson red where his parent's lower halves should be. One by one, the person in the room moved the sheets.

"That's them," Dex said. This was when the world imploded. Some people describe loss and a massive change as an explosion. For Dex, it was more of an implosion. His world didn't expand, but instead collapsed inward. Everything that he was and knew sort of sucked up into himself. All of his emotions and even his faith became small, nestled somewhere in his brain that Dex couldn't find for quite some time. Yet for every action, there is an equal and opposite reaction. With time and help from Neil, his universe once more began to expand and continued to expand to this day. He was certainly, by no means, "over it" and some days were harder than others, but he was trying.

This was not something one would or could forget. This was a defining moment for him. And so, every year on the anniversary of their death, Dex visited their graves. He and Neil dressed up as if they were going to a funeral. Neil brought flowers. Dex always brought the sword his parents bought for him- a katana that he had named Ruach. When Dex was fifteen, his love of superheroes evolved into a love of anime and manga. He went to his parents with a simple request: he wanted to follow the path of the warrior. Of course, it wasn't worded like that. What he really wanted was a decorative sword that he could slice bottles and occasionally the errant watermelon in the back yard. The only thing odder than the lengthy conversation was their final answer. First, if there was to be a weapon in the house, Dex would have to learn to wield it. This was no problem for him as it meant he would actually learn to use the katana he sought. Second, had to swear an oath that he would only use the blade to kill as a last resort. This was always very odd as Dex never intended to actually fight, but he was happy to oblige. The last condition was that he would trust his parents to procure a real sword for him. They weren't raising some mall ninja. He remembered a bit of sadness in their eyes, almost as if they were fearful that he may one day have to take up arms. Whatever they were thinking and feeling, Dex was just happy he got a sword.

He had agreed to all these terms. After his training, he was presented with a silver sheathed katana. The handle was bound in a white cloth. On the end of it in raised Hebrew letters was the word rauch where the sword would get its name. Taking the sword out, the ripples on the blade were exquisite. Dex would later learn that this ripple was called Hamon. It is a visual effect of the hardening process. Most modern swords made by machines have a false Hamon on them through etching or chemical treatments. Dex was assured by his parents that this blade was hand forged in the traditional way. It was built to be extremely lightweight and still very durable. Since that time, he treated his blade with the respect that he promised his parents- cleaning it and maintaining his practice with it. It was like a sacred object to him given to him by his parents. As a constant reminder of their love for him, he felt it was always necessary to take it with him to the cemetery.

"Neil," Dex said, finishing up his breakfast. "truth be told, I'm never ready for this. It takes a huge emotional toll on me and almost drags me back to The Big Sad." He looked up with a small half smile on his face.

"If I didn't have you to help me, I would never be ready. You're always there for me and I appreciate you more than you will ever know." Neil's eyes glassed over with water.

"Aw beans..." they said with a small chuckle. "You're such a jerk. You're going to ruin my eye liner. I love you too, man." The two shared warm, comforting hug. "Now go get ready. It's probably going to be a long day." Dex nodded and went back upstairs to retrieve his father's suit. Dex didn't own any suits of his own. He never really needed to have one. His father was a bit of a pack rat and kept many old suits. Now that he was gone, Dex thought that one of the best ways to honor him was to wear his suits when he needed to. While cliché, Dex was aware that he truly was his parents' child. From his father he inherited a sense of hard work. Work smarter: not harder. Do what you need to do in the best possible way, but do it in a smart, efficient way. From his mother, he inherited a lofty sense of optimism and dreams. Yes, the world was a dark and terrible place at times, but you can make a difference in it. Be the change you want to see in the world.

Dex selected a simple black suit with a black tie. He typically enjoyed more outlandish, flamboyant ties. His father did not. After a quick shower, he shaved and combed his short brown hair. He looked around "his" room, once his parent's room. After their passing, Dex decided this room should be used. Neil had their own room which left two bedrooms available for storage. He walked over to the dresser and looked at Ruach, shining in the light. He strapped the sword to his side with a clip and drew the blade. Holding in a ready stance, he gave the sword a small but quick downward slash at an angle. The familiar sound of that wind like whistle brought a peace and comfort to him. He heard a knock behind him. Dex turned around to find Neil standing there.

"Ya know, I'm pretty sure your parents got rid of the monsters in house when we were little. Don't you remember your mom's secret word to make them all disappear at night?"

"How could I forget Zotts?" Dex replied. Neil sighed.

"I still miss them, too." They looked down. "Is that weird? I feel like it might be a bit weird."

"Dude, don't you remember your eighteenth birthday? The day you moved in? My mom bought you that vanity you always said you always wanted and it was fully stocked, right? And my dad painted that room with purple, yellow, white and black accents? You were literally the second child they always wanted."

"I know that," Neil said quietly. They ran their hand through their shock of black, curly hair- a movement that Dex learned after many years meant that Neil was being contemplative. "I just... I want you to know that you aren't alone in your feelings and stuff. Like, I'm here for you and I get it. I don't want to make it about me, but I get what you're going through."

"Dude, do I have to repeat myself from downstairs? You really want your makeup messed up again?" Dex said with a laugh. Neil rubbed their neck: an indication that Neil was feeling at ease. This movement was used to show discomfort or ease depending on the situation, Dex had learned. As Neil was smiling when he made the motion, Dex assumed rightly that he was at ease.

"Okay. Point taken." They nodded toward the door. "You ready?" Dex simply nodded a reply. Neil moved to the side and motioned towards the staircase. Yes of course I know the way, Dex thought to himself. It wasn't that he was apprehensive about the whole thing. It needed to be done. Dex felt like he had moved on in a sense. This wasn't necessarily a sad event. It was somber. How should one honor their parents? They gave him life. They taught him how to live and be self-sufficient. They provided for him in the event of their passing. How else was a twenty-five-year-old meant to live their life? Dex felt it was his duty to honor and remember them. He was positive that Neil felt the same way.

Upon reaching the garage, Dex finally spoke up. "I'm driving. We're taking my Dad's truck." Neil had thought that might be the case. There were two cars in the garage: Neil's sensible four door sedan, and Dex's work horse of a truck. It had been his father's truck which he lovingly tended to. Over time, the red, once vibrant and full of life, had dulled. There was no other vehicle that Dex wanted to drive. His mother, though she had always fanned hating the truck, had loved it. In her mind, it was just like her husband: dependable. The night of the car crash, they had been in her car. One vehicle was for work: the other was for pleasure.

They climbed in the truck. It still smelled faintly of cigarillos that his father used to smoke when no one else was around. Try as his mother could, she could never fully get the smell of tobacco out of the vehicle no matter how many chemicals she sprayed in it. To Dex and Neil, it was an instant reminder of Dex's father. Dex placed the key in the ignition. The truck roared to life. He had forgotten what CD was left in the truck. Typically, Neil or Dex simply connected their phones to the speakers and played their own music. When Dex was feeling nostalgic, like last night, he would listen to his parents own CD collection. David Gilmour's voice suddenly filled the cab of the truck as the engine roared to life.

"How I wish, how I wish you were here..."

It was as if it were a message from Dex and Neil to God. They longed for Dex's parents to be near them. In their absence, they longed for the comfort that God could give them. They just needed something- some force in the universe to let them know that they weren't as alone as they felt. Dex especially longed for the closeness to something. All he wanted was some force to reach out to him to let him know that everything was still okay.

The ride to the cemetery was rather uneventful. They listened to Pink Floyd's "Wish You Were Here" album and chatted little. Mostly, the conversation was strictly about the weather and plans for the upcoming week. Neil, however, seemed to have a different agenda. As they neared the cemetery, they asked a simple question.

"So that paper you were proof reading? The one about angels and demons and this whole unseen world- what did you make of it?"

"I'm not sure," Dex answered truthfully. To be honest, Dex thought it was a pretty open and shut paper. After all, the idea of the assignment was to look at some sort of conspiracy theory and how it can affect people. He had read a few other papers on this topic, but those were standard conspiracy theories. He had read about Q and the moon landing being faked and even the idea of a flat earth. This paper, however, jarred him to the core. It wasn't necessarily the scope of it all that bothered him. Should it ever be shown that the moon landing was, in fact, faked, it would not be that big of a deal Dex thought. After all, that was a singular event. It had happened in the past. In all honesty, it makes sense that people would, in a sense, be able to move on from the whole thing. This theory, however, had larger implications. If the world wasn't as most people see it to be, what would that mean for the fabric of society? How would this fundamentally shift everything? Not only that, but the knowledge of people with special abilities would surely make national news. Perhaps, Dex thought, that this was, in general, the answer. Perhaps humanity as a whole wasn't ready for this revelation. After all, the author posited that one had to actively choose to see the world in this way. What did that even look like? Would a person, choosing to see the reality of the world, see angels and demons fighting above them? Would they see people using energy blasts or whatever special gifts people had? How would that change the daily goings on in the world? This theory had a huge implication- not just because of what it could mean visa vi powers and gifts, but the religious implications. If angels and demons existed, then some where there must be a higher power over them, right? If these things existed, then some religion that claimed the ultimate truth must also be right. This could lend itself to more problems in the long run.

On the other hand, it would be the truth. There would be something other than the speed of light that would be shown to be a constant in the world. There would finally be a measuring stick that people could all rally around to see what the world actually is. Finally, there would be some kind of order in an otherwise random and chaotic existence. Yet, again, on the other hand, this would surely ruffle more than a few feathers. As soon as there is some kind of universal truth to anything, people will question it. That is, as far as Dex could tell, human nature. Human beings always wanted more. They desired to be the masters of their own destiny. Religion became another way for people to exert control over people. If there was one objective truth, as most religions claimed, then by that very fact, there were others that were wrong or lies. People don't like being told they are wrong. They fight and they claw for superiority much in the same way prey fights against their predators. The problem, as far as he could tell, was human agency. Even if there was an objective truth of the world, people would twist it and use it to their own ends. In much the same way many adherents to religion felt their faith was co-opted by other forces in the world, this objective truth would be turned and co-opted into something that didn't even resemble the truth.

On the other hand, something that was real and true: wouldn't that be worth preserving? Wouldn't that be worth fighting for?

"I think it's an interesting idea," Dex said instead of all the questions he had been thinking since reading this paper, "and it would be interesting to see how it all played out in the real world."

"Do you think there is merit to it all? I mean, you've read about other theories, right?"

"Oh, most definitely."

"So, which one holds weight? Which one seems the most plausible?"

"Well," Dex said thoughtfully, "I would have to say the whole superpower thing. Everything else seems rather plausible. There are reasons why the United States would fake the moon landing. Like, that makes sense given the space race and all that. Flat earth has been disproven by scientists. This other thing?" Dex shook his head. "It would radically change everything. It's the biggest lie possible. And people will believe a lie that is so huge and earth shaking because they can't believe that someone would have the audacity to come up with a lie that big."

"That's not a real answer," Neil replied. "That's dodging the question. I asked you which one you think has the most merit." Dex sighed.

"I gave you an answer," he said tersely.

"So the world is fake and people have special powers?"

"I didn't say that," Dex said, slightly defensively. "I said that one is the most believable based on the idea of the 'big lie' theory. Look, dude: that's the best answer you're going to get from me." Neil chuckled.

"That's fair," they said with a slight smirk on their face. Neil knew Dex better than he realized. By answering the question in the way that he did, Dex revealed that the answer he gave was not what he thought was real, but what he wished was real. Dex was obviously defensive with his answer. Why? It was because he didn't want to answer which one he thought was real. Neil was reasonably sure that Dex would have viewed this as the most terrifying theory, but also the most hopeful. Dex, at his core, was a hopeful optimist just like his mother. Though he shielded himself through dark humor, like his father, there was no escaping that in his inner most being, Dex was a dreamer longing for something to help him make the world a better place. Neil smiled with a sense of satisfaction. They were sure that Dex had considered all of these points.

The finally arrived at the cemetery at about eleven o'clock in the morning. It was a cool, refreshing spring morning in April. Dex had always enjoyed spring, though not as much as fall. Fall was closing time. Spring was the opposite. It was the beginning of new life. Each spring was a chance for new growth and new life. That and a yearly sinus infection.

They parked the truck and got out, each carrying their offerings. Dex held his sword while Neil brought a bouquet of lilies. There was an odd breeze that began to blow. While not a particularly chilly day, this breeze seemed to say that it should be colder. Something was off as far as the weather was concerned.

Neil let out a sigh and under their breath they said, "Aw beans..." Dex looked confused. Neil only used that in situations that they felt slightly uncomfortable in. As far as Dex could tell, this was a pretty standard day. At least it will until Dex saw what caused Neil to make that exclamation. He looked up toward the spot on the hill where his parents were buried. There was no mistaking it: there were four people standing there. One of them, a figure with a backpack turned and left. The other three started doing something with their feet. It seemed to Dex that it was a similar motion of golfers who are trying to replace a divot with their feet. There was no mistaking it: they had done something to his parents' grave.

"Look we could come back in a bit if you'd like," Neil offered. Always the rational realist, Dex thought. Of course, that was the smart choice. They were outnumbered by one person now. Given that it was early in the morning, Dex assumed that they were some sort of drug users tweaking and they were most likely stomping imaginary creatures of some sort. Had it been another day, Dex would have come back to site later. Today, however, was the anniversary of his parents' deaths. Today of all days,

Dex had a right to not only be there when he wanted, but to defend his parents' graves.

"Yo!" Dex said as he approached the group in a jog. "YO! What are y'all doing here?" As he got towards the group, something felt... off to Dex. The three appeared to be perfect cliché characters: one jock, one cheerleader, and one goth. Yet they appeared to be a similar age to Dex: mid-twenties. Why, then, were they dressed like they just stepped out of a John Hughes movie? It seemed off to Dex. It just didn't make sense. The jock let out a dismissive laugh.

"Yeah, we're pretty much doing whatever we want. Don't worry about it."

"Oh no, see I am going to worry about it, because this is my parents' grave." The three looked at each other and laughed.

"Well what are the odds of that?" the cheerleader said. "Is this fate?"

"Oh, it very well could be fate," the jock replied. He turned to face the goth. "You think this is fate?"

"I think he's Blind," the goth said, eyeing Dex. Dex let out his own dismissive laugh.

"Yeah, okay buddy," he said. "Just go so we can do our thing, okay?" He finally turned and looked. Neil was next to him, but he couldn't help but notice Neil's breathing had become a bit faster. Their face had become a bit paler. If they run their hand through their hair, this isn't too good, Dex thought. As soon as he thought that, Neil, acting almost out of instinct, combed their hand through their hair. Aw beans, Dex thought to himself.

"I would suggest that, if you don't want trouble, you leave now. I'm not looking for a fight, but I won't run from one." It was Neil that spoke. They spoke calmly and forcefully, which added to Dex's confusion. Dex could tell that Neil was nervous. He had this ability to read people. His mother always said he was an empath, like herself. Dex just realized that he could read a person's body language and get to the heart of what a person was feeling. Neil's sudden declaration of intent, while noble, didn't match up with the fact that Neil was, as far as Dex could tell, nervous. This begs the question: what was Neil nervous about?

"Your friend," the goth said, motioning towards Dex. "He's Blind, right?"

"Honestly I think that's for the best. I mean seriously: the whole thing you three have going on? Like, did you guys even try to match up? It's like some terrible mismatch. Like, when a kid has a bunch of doll parts and just randomly puts toys together." Neil gasped. "Oh my gosh: are you guys cosplaying the toys Sid messed with in Toy Story?"

The jock stepped forward and then Dex's world exploded.

No sooner did he step forward than Neil raised their hands. He was holding, what appeared to Dex, to be two old western Colt .45 guns. They appeared to shine in the sun, almost glowing.

"Neil...?" Dex began to speak.

"Not now, Dex. Just go with it."

"You sure you want to do to this with your friend here?" the cheerleader asked, producing what appeared to be dark red pom-poms.

"I don't," Neil responded, "but you're not really giving me a lot of other options here. You won't leave, so I'll have to make you."

Dex was lost. The jock pulled out a baseball bat from nowhere. The goth placed a monocle on his eye for some reason. Dex, not wanting to be left out of whatever was going on, drew his sword. The cheerleader laughed and walked towards him.

"So cute," she chided. She then swung her right arm in a large arc, hitting Dex in the stomach. The reaction was instantaneous. He was sent flying backwards. It was as if some large, solid thing had hit him with an unseen force. That's a hell of a pom-pom, Dex thought. I should probably tuck my chin towards my chest now. He did, and as he rolled a bit down the hill, it didn't hurt quite as bad as it could have. This was oddly familiar to Dex- like a dream he had and forgot. Reacting on some kind of instinct, he knew he had to stand at the ready with his sword drawn.

Neil began running backwards towards him, shooting his guns as he went.

"You good, Dex?" they shouted.

"As good as I can be considering," Dex replied.

"Right. Meet me behind that big tree over on your left." Dex began to make his way there as Neil kept up with the suppressing fire. Neil kept firing round after round. Dex counted to six. Neil should be out, Dex thought. Where did they keep their bullets? But Neil kept firing, keeping the three at bay. The two of them regrouped behind the tree.

"What the Hell is going on, Neil?! Where did you get those?"

"Okay," Neil said with a big sigh. "not a lot of time, so just go with it. You know that paper? The crazy one we were talking about?"

"Yeah?" Dex replied even more confused.

"Assume it's real. Please. Just go with it and we may get out of here alive." Dex had to think for a moment. To be frank, it was all a bit nutty still. However, the alternative was possibly worst. There were several logical inconsistencies that have occurred as of late. The sudden knowledge of Neil having guns and producing them out of nowhere was chief among them. That was further compounded by the knowledge that Neil should have logically run out of bullets by now. The guns should hold only six bullets each. This would give Neil twelve shots before he had to reload. However, Dex was confident that Neil should have ran out of bullets a while ago. Furthermore, there was no logical reason that a cheerleader should have sent him tumbling down a hill with one hit. Sir Arthur Conan Doyle once wrote, "Once you eliminate the impossible, whatever remains, no matter how improbable, must be the truth." Dex reasoned that there was no way for these events to have occurred in a logical manner. Therefore, he thought, it stood to reason that there could very well be some merit into this theory.

That was all it took. Instantly, Dex's eyes felt dry, as if all moisture had suddenly solidified into something irritating them. He reflectively closed them and began rubbing his eye, begging them for some tears of relief. After he opened them again, he looked in his hands. Something like fish scales covered his fingers, glinting in the sun. He would have loved to have study these more, but he was suddenly overcome with the sense of déjà vu once again.

"Neil! Left side! Shoot now!" Several things happened in rapid succession. First, Neil listened. Neil had no real reason to listen, but he trusted Dex and did as they were told. Dex noted that Neil's hands no longer held guns. Instead, they simply shone with a bright, yellow light. Second, the reason that he had to shoot was because Dex knew somehow that the cheerleader was rounding the corner for an attack. Instead of pom-poms, her hands had transformed into oversized humanoid scaley hands. They appeared ashen and grey, an unholy mix of dragonhide and sharp, jagged rocks. While Dex would have loved more information on what he was seeing, he understood an attack was coming now from the left side of the tree. Raising Ruach, he was able to block and hold an attack that felt very cold.

As Dex looked up, he saw the jock holding what he once thought was a baseball bat. It appeared to be an icicle, yet it was attached to his arm. Where his normal arm should be, it appeared to be a cold, dead human arm pulsating with blue veins in time with his beating heart.

"They're Grafters," Neil said. "They don't have any Gifts so they sell parts of their soul to demons for demonic grafts. It gives them demonic powers." Dex realized that Neil spoke as if it was simply a fact. For Dex, this was the most confusing day of his life. For Neil, it was Tuesday. Neil finally landed a blast on the cheerleader that sent her flying into a tombstone. She hit her head and was knocked out.

Dex felt a sudden surge of strength. Acting on instinct, he pushed his blade upwards, tossing the jock off balance. Without hesitation, he brought his blade straight down towards his opponent's head. I must only kill if I have to, Dex thought to himself. The blade began to glow a yellow like Neil's hands. He brought it down straight down on the jock's head. Instead of slicing straight through him, the yellow energy seemed to almost dull the blade, making it a blunt weapon. Dex followed through with his attack as he was trained to do. He drove the jock's head down into the ground. He was not dead, but he was unconscious. Dex put his sword away and looked at Neil.

"I have several questions," Neil said.

"Oh yes," Dex replied, his voice dripping with sarcasm. "you have questions. Of course, you do. Never mind all of *my* questions. Let's do yours first." They started to laugh and move from behind the tree. There was no sound or warning. There was no bang. There was nothing to show that a blast had occurred. There was only a smoking hole in Neil's stomach.

"Ouch," Neil said as they fell to their knees.

"A pity," the goth said, his right eye filled with a blue flame. "I was aiming for the head." The eye that had been covered with the monocle was glowing with a blue fire. Half of his face had been replaced with what appeared to be a grinning skull.

The day his parents died, Dex's world imploded and folded in on itself. Now five years to the day later, Dex stood confused in the cemetery losing his best friend and sibling. Five years of rage and grief and loss had coalesced into this dark, tiny and heavy pit in his soul. Now, with the prospect of losing Neil, there was an explosion inside of Dex.

Acting on instinct, Dex's whole body began to glow with a bright yellow light. He grabbed the hilt of his sword. In a swift, fluid motion, he pulled the blade out. There was a sound like that of a rushing wind followed by a wave of energy emanating from his blade. It traveled with fierce intensity, cutting through the wind until it reached the goth, hitting him. He crumbled instantly, folding in on himself. Dex said nothing but returned his sword to its sheath and approached Neil. There was a slight bit of blood on his lips.

"The good news is I'm in shock, so it doesn't hurt that bad," Neil said with a weak laugh.

"You aren't dying today," Dex replied. He placed his hand over the wound. Energy flowed from his hand into Neil's body. The wound began to shrink until the only the hole in Neil's clothing remained. With this final act, Dex realized he was very tired and fell backwards into a deep sleep.

Behind Neil, there was a sound of footsteps. They turned and looked and they gasped. It was them. There was a red-haired woman, a well-dressed blond man, and a man with a long, scruffy beard wearing a poncho and a conical straw hat.

"Dex Machina," the man in the hat replied. "You have already exceeded our expectations.

Chapter Two

Dex awoke from what he had assumed was a fevered dream. There were bits he could remember: the cheerleader, guns, and something to do with hands. And Neil. Neil was hurt. He had to go find Neil. He had to make sure Neil was okay. He threw the covers off of his bed and stood up. It must have been too fast, because he felt woozy. He steadied himself on the dresser. Ruach caught his eye. He stared at it for a moment. What was it about this sword? In the light, it appeared to be glowing. This gave Dex pause. What did this mean? What couldn't he remember? He picked the sword up. It felt... different somehow. It had a certain new weight to it that Dex couldn't figure out. It had always been a rather light weight blade. There were no discernable attachments to it. So where did the weight come from? Slowly, he removed the sword. It must have been a while since he cleaned and sharpened it. It seemed dirty.

Then he remembered. There had been a fight. He had taken it to his parents' graves. There was some kind of fight. That was the weight Ruach now carried with it: the weight of battle. It all seemed so familiar to him, as if he was overcome with déjà vu. I have to go downstairs, he realized. He wasn't sure how he knew, but he knew for certain that those had to be his next steps. Why not just call Neil? Why not yell for him first? No: something told him he had to go downstairs. He returned Ruach to its stand and started quietly downstairs. The logical place to look first was the kitchen. If Neil was downstairs, chances are that they were in the kitchen.

As he approached the doorway to the kitchen, he caught Neil's eyes. He had just scooped a large spoonful of Fruity Pebbles into their mouth. Neil stood there, wide eyed and slowly chewing. Dex didn't know what to say. He was relieved. He had been so worried that Neil was hurt. But looking at Neil like this, he knew they were worried and shocked. It wasn't just the expression they had on their face. There was something else. It was as if Neil was emanating worry from their very body. Dex felt it. Deep in his inner most being, he could feel Neil being worried.

"Dude: I didn't know when you were going to wake up." Neil sat their cereal down and ran over to hug Dex.

"I just needed some sleep, I guess. Must have been tired. I could go for some breakfast." Neil let go of the hug. Dex knew he was now more concerned than anything else. Again, though it was written on their face, he felt it. "What's wrong? Did you eat all the cereal again?"

"Dude, it's like, five o'clock in the afternoon."

"I slept all day?" Now it was Dex's turn to be worried.

"No. You slept for like, two days." He looked at the calendar on the wall. Neil always dutifully crossed off the days. It was no longer April fourth. It was, apparently, April sixth.

"I think I need to sit down..." Dex said. He made his way over to the kitchen table. Neil rushed over with a cup of coffee and Dex's own bowl of Fruity Pebbles. They grabbed their own bowl and sat down to join him.

"So, what do you remember?" Neil asked delicately. Dex took a sip of his coffee. It was hot, yet it was somehow different. He looked at it. It was still rather dark, but for some reason, it didn't seem as bitter as it once did. There was no sugar or cream in it and it wasn't bad. It. Just wasn't as bitter as what he was used to.

"We went to the cemetery. And when we go there, there were these people around my parents' graves. One of them left. I asked the other three what they were doing. Then you pulled out guns. No," Dex said, shaking his head. "they weren't guns. Your hands: they were... glowing?" Neil nodded.

"What else?"

"The people there: they had inhuman body parts."

"Grafters, yes. No Gift of their own. They sell..."

"...parts of their souls to demons for demonic grafts." Dex finished Neil's sentence. "You got hurt." Neil nodded again.

"Yep. One of the Grafters had half their face replaced with skull demon's face. It allows for powerful blasts of negative energy out of the gem eye." Dex looked at Neil concerned.

"You got hurt."

"And you saved me. You used your healing Gift. Which is what is so confusing." Neil took another bite of their cereal.

"She was right, wasn't she? The girl who wrote that paper."

"That's a bingo." Neil replied. "So, you've got that basics. We can skip over that."

"You feel relieved and scared." Dex said suddenly. Neil sighed.

"And that would be confirmation of number four. Excuse me for a moment." Neil quickly finished their cereal while Dex merely toyed with his.

"So, you're going to explain all of this so it makes sense?" Dex asked. Neil shook their head.

"Oh no. I'm just going to explain it. Starting with The Unveiling. Remember when those scales fell from your eyes? That was all it took. You made the choice to see the truth. So now you no longer look into the mirror dimly."

"Can I get rid of it?" Dex asked.

"Oh, for sure. It would take time, but you could go back. But you won't. I know you." Dex opened his mouth to raise an objection, but he knew that Neil was right. Oh sure: if one could go back, it would make sense that some would want to. Dex knew in his heart he wouldn't go back. He couldn't. If one sees the truth, why would one go back to the comforting lie? It seemed to Dex that the truth, no matter how terrible, was always better than a comforting lie. Everything else would have to work itself out.

"So what happens next?" Dex asked, finishing his own cereal.

"Well, like I said a few days ago, I have several questions. These are even more pressed upon because of who showed up shortly after you went unconscious. So, we have to go to the comic store." Neil spoke so plainly. Yet Dex could feel there was something that they were not telling him.

"So, let's assume that, for some reason, I have become some kind of human lie detector. Want to cut out the BS and tell me why?" Neil sighed.

"Okay. So somehow that lady really hit it on the head. That organization that protects the world? It's called The Order and I'm a part of it."

"Of course you are." Dex said, partly sarcastic. Dex understood that people thought that God literally had the world on the string. God was, to them, some kind of meticulous watch maker putting everything in its right place. If Dex was eschewing everything else that seemed normal to him, why not just let it roll? Now that his memory of the other day was slowly coming back, Dex remembered Neil saying, "Just go with it," several times. So why not? Just go with it. It stood to reason that at this point, if everything else was so crazy, then he might as well agree to the simplest answer: there was some higher power that set all of this in motion. So just go with it all.

"Alright: this could get a little boring but bear with me. Remember that fellow named Jesus?" Neil asked. Dex rolled his eyes.

"Yes: I am vaguely familiar with his work."

"So, before Jesus, the realm of the divine and the realm of the material- our world- were more separated. Jesus, being of both realms, actually merged the two. Peter being the rock was more than just starting the church- it was the foundation of The Order. Some of the Apostles became teachers. Others went on and founded The Order. These were the ones who exceled at one of the four Gifts: prophecy, healing, telepathy, and channeling. Each of these gifts use positive energy in some way." Neil made their hand glow. "I am a Channeler. I channel positive energy into blasts of energy."

"So you're Goku?" Dex asked, trying to make a tense conversation a little lighter. Neil snorted in laughter.

"I wish. I'm more like Krillin." Neil's face shifted into a confused look. "But you? You're confusing. You've shown signs of all four of the Gifts. I have no idea where you fit into it all."

"Ah. So *I'm* Goku."

"To be honest, anything is possible. Which is why we are going to The Cathedral of Heroes to figure out what all is going on."

"Because of course the clandestine organization keeping the world safe is based in the comic bookstore." Dex said.

"Dude, why do you think so many of them have the word 'hero' in the title?" Dex's attempt at sarcasm had failed spectacularly. "Go get dressed. Parking is already going to suck because it is Yu-gi-Oh night." Dex simply nodded and went to get dressed. As he got to the stairs, he turned and looked at Neil.

"What happened to my suit?" he asked, already knowing the answer.

"I didn't want you to be uncomfortable. So, when we got home, I took it off of you and sent it to be cleaned."

"Thank you," Dex replied. He made his way upstairs grateful for Neil. He knew that they knew it was his dad's suit. Because of what it meant to Dex, it meant that to Neil as well. Neil went out of their way to make sure it was well taken care of since Dex couldn't have dealt with it.

Dressing proved even more a chore than Dex had originally thought. There was a fine art, in his mind, to dressing to be amongst "his people." The shirt you wore made a statement about yourself in Dex's mind. It told those in the shop this is me. This is what I like. He had many t-shirts with various comic book heroes and villains on them. Obviously, Dex couldn't wear a shirt with a villain on it. Sorry, Dr. Doom. You'd have to sit this one out. Should he go with DC or Marvel or an independent comic? Looking back on the whole thing, he decided to instead look at his anime and manga t-shirts. There was no other option at all, he thought. He donned a shirt with the cast of Konosuba. This was an isekai anime and manga. The hallmark of this type of anime was the fact that the protagonist finds themself in a strange new world where they must adapt. Now, more than ever, Dex felt this in his soul. Dex knew, somehow, that he had to take Ruach with him. Assuming that it fell under the rules of this brave new world he found himself in, people either wouldn't notice or it would be explained away in some mundane fashion.

As he was going back to where Neil was, he noticed Neil wore a very serious look on their face. Given the events a few days ago, this did not bode particularly well. Were they anticipating more trouble? What was going to happen? And who exactly was Neil taking Dex to meet? For all of Dex's concerns, he sensed a calmness in Neil. Neil believed that what they were doing was the right thing to do. There were no second thoughts about it. Whoever they were going to meet put Neil in a state of easiness.

"So listen," they said to Dex picking up the keys. "two things. First, I'm driving. You literally just got up. Second," Neil hesitated for a moment. "just... just don't tell anyone about any Gift or Gifts you may or may not have. At least not until after we meet with The Four." Dex nodded quietly. These were acceptable to him especially since he had no real idea what all was going on.

They climbed into Neil's sensible four door sedan. The car was Neil's baby. While sensible, it was a sweet cherry red in color. Thankfully, Dex was comfortable with Neil's driving. Too often, he had found himself in positions where riding shotgun made him nervous. Being a passenger meant giving up a certain amount of control. Typically, this made Dex uncomfortable as he liked to be in control of most situations in his life. Neil was one of the few people he trusted unequivocally to drive. As the car came to life, Roger Waters picked up from the place he left off in the song. *"And all that you slight and everyone you fight. And all that is now and all that is gone. And all that's to come and everything under the sun is in tune. But the sun is eclipsed by the moon."*

The car ride was one of slightly awkward silence. What else was there to say? Dex's world had been turned upside down. Everything that he thought was true and firm turned out to be a comfortable lie. To top all of that off, there was some kind of issue with what Gift Dex may have. If Dex understood Neil correctly, the dispensation of Gifts followed the "everybody gets one" rule. Yet Dex had shown all four of the gifts active in himself: prophesy in telling Neil where to shoot, healing by saving Neil, channeling by using energy on his sword, and telepathy by feeling Neil's emotions. It just didn't make any sense at all. Even given how strange the world had become, it didn't make any sense and that in and of itself was saying something.

"I'm not shaving my head," Dex said suddenly. Neil looked confused.

"What the Hell are you talking about?" they asked.

"Usually when you join a cult, they make you shave your head. If that's the case, then I'm out." Neil looked at Dex dumbfounded for a moment.

"Have you not seen my head?"

"Hair grows back," Dex retorted.

"They aren't going to make you shave your head. They are going to figure out what is going on and want to train you."

"Train me for what?" Dex asked. Neil smiled knowingly.

"To make a difference, Dex. To make a difference."

The Cathedral of Heroes was the local comic and gaming shop. They hosted many wonderful evening events such as Friday Night Magic and a weekly Dungeons and Dragons group. For the more competitive and meticulous, they offered Warhammer 40k battles. Being that it was a Thursday night, the shop was filled with people playing Yu-gi-Oh cards in a tournament. Parking was not impossible, however, they had to park about a block from the store. Getting out of the car, Dex hesitated to bring Ruach with him.

"Dude, what if people freak out?" Dex asked Neil.

"I wouldn't worry about it. Anyone who notices won't make a huge deal about it even if they don't have the Sight. Plus, I mean, it's a comic store. Like, why wouldn't there be someone with a sword anyway?"

"I am assuming that's the name for the Gift of seeing, then?" Dex asked.

"Bingo. My guess is there is going to be a lot of information thrown at you very quickly considering..." Neil trailed off, running their fingers through their hair. Dex felt it. Neil had said something they shouldn't have said. He was embarrassed and worried. Going to a comic store that is a front for a secret society of protectors against the forces of darkness should have been weird. That wasn't. What Neil just said, however, embarrassed them: like they almost let a special present for a birthday surprise slip. Dex decided not to point all of this out. After all, Neil had never given Dex a reason to not trust him.

As they approached the door of the shop, the familiar hum of the neon knight battling the dragon greeted them. There was a young boy around twelve years old smiling as he left the store. He held in his hands a small cardboard box of playing cards. In his excitement, his feet became tangled in themselves and he tripped. The cards went flying, and the young boy slide a few inches. Neil and Dex instantly rushed to his side.

"Hey buddy," Dex said in a soothing voice. "it's okay. We can help you." Neil began to pick up the boy's cards. "Anything broken?" He shook his head with tears in his eyes. He and Dex looked down at the boy's knee. A nice sized bit of road rash was on his knee. From the look of it, it had to sting. "Look, buddy: it's okay. I know a magic word."

"Magic isn't real. I'm twelve: I'm not stupid," the boy said defensively.

"Fair enough," Dex replied, "but I'm no ordinary person. Humor me, okay?" Dex had never tried to heal a person before. He was sure he had done it before, but that had been on instinct. He didn't plan to do it. To suggest that he even knew how to start this process was a huge improbability. The problem was Dex had a soft spot for kids. He hated seeing people in pain- especially kids. So if he could help in any way possible, Dex was going to try. He had to think. What was a comforting, almost healing moment he could think of? What did healing feel like? He reasoned that it felt much like the world being fixed in some way. When it comes to physical pain, that would mean an alleviation of that pain. Dex had felt that before, to be sure, but how to best conjure that memory. He then realized that it the core, healing was about feeling safe and whole. There was one memory- one word- that reminded him of what it meant to feel safe and whole. He placed his hand over the scrape, closed his eyes, and said, "Zotts."

The warmth in Dex started in a small place in is chest. He could feel it travel down his arm into his hand and spread across his fingers. The warmth seemed to weigh his hand down, yet he could feel it falling from his fingers onto the knee. The boy sat there, wide eyed and transfixed by what was happening. Dex wasn't sure if he was Blind himself, but he was sure the boy could feel what was going on. In a matter of moments, it was done. His knee was back to normal and no one could tell that he ever scraped it. Dex looked at the boy and placed a finger over his own lips.

"Don't tell anyone. It's a secret, okay?" The boy nodded with a look of disbelief on his face. Neil finally came over to them with an annoyed look on their face. There was no need to feel what Neil was feeling. It was painfully obvious that they were annoyed with Dex. They had told him that he needed to keep any and all abilities under wraps for now. If anyone saw what he had just done, they would assume that Dex was a Healer. This was not necessarily a lie, but it was not the full truth as well. The boy grabbed his cards and ran off, not sure what to make of the whole situation. Neil looked at Dex as if to say you had one job. Dex gave a half smile and a small shrug.

"Hey, Neil." A voice said from the doorway of The Cathedral of Heroes. "Looks like you found a new Healer. Nice sword, by the way."

"Aw beans..." Neil said under their breath. The voice came from a young man. He was about the same age as Dex and Neil. He was a handsome man with the kind of good looks one would describe as having classic good looks. His face was squarish, but it had a certain softness to it. His blonde hair was cut short on the sides. The top was left longer and brushed back into a sort of bouffant. "Yeah," Neil finally said. "This is my friend, Dex. Brought him in for an evaluation." Jude held his hand out to Dex.

"Hi. I'm Jude," he said with a smile.

"Dex," he replied standing up and shaking his hand.

"Don't do that," Neil said suddenly.

"Do what?" Jude asked innocently.

"Dude, you skim everyone that comes into the shop. It's annoying. I can vouch for him. He's not Corrupted."

"What's a Corrupted?" Dex asked.

"Those are people who use their Gifts for various nefarious purposes," Jude explained. "Instead of using positive energy to fuel their Gifts, they tap into negative energy. For example, as Neil so eloquently pointed out, I'm a Psyker. I use positive energy to fuel my psychic powers. If I were Corrupted, I would be using negative energy and dominating the minds of people." Dex felt an odd emotion off of Jude. It was one of pride. He could tell that Jude took a great amount of pride in his Gift and using it. Dex remembered him now. He had seen him before. He was a manager of the shop. No wonder he scanned everyone who came in.

"Well if we are spilling all our secrets in the middle of the street for all to hear, Jude is on The Council. He's part of the cabal that oversees field agents." Neil was now not even pretending to not be annoyed.

"Point taken," Jude said with a kind smile on his face. "Let's head inside and we will get you both on your way." They entered the shop which appeared to be guarded by cardboard cutouts of Batman and Spider-Man. Dex took a deep breath. He felt at peace entering into the shop. Surrounded by stories of the fantastic, Dex could lose himself in a world where anything was possible: a world that could be made better than what it was. Yet now, even as the scent of comics and sweat filled the air, this time was different. This time, as he crossed the threshold, he really was entering into a world where anything was possible and he apparently had the power to change the world.

"Well, I have the Skeleton Key tonight, so if you need to go somewhere, just tell me where and I'll send you off," Jude told them.

"Not necessary," a quiet voice said to their right. The three of them looked to see two women looking at a rack of various back issues. The one had long, dark braided hair and was currently engrossed in an issue of the original Secret Wars story line. She easily pushed up the thin, round glasses on her nose while she continued reading. She was not terribly tall and did not look out of place in the shop. She wore an oversized track suit that was set off by large golden hoops dangling from her ears. "Dex and Neil are heading in the same direction as us. There is an upcoming rush of people coming in after a late college class. You'll need to not be distracted to help out here." She said all of this quietly and without looking up from her comic.

The woman next to her had long, fiery red hair. Dex felt Neil and Jude tense up. These two were obviously important in some manner. The red headed woman was a pair of jeans and a Ramones t-shirt. She sighed.

"Ophelia is right, but being a Prophet is sort of like having an unfair advantage."

"Prophetess." the woman with the braids responded still reading her book. "Representation matters, Rhianna."

"Yes. Prophetess. But the fact remains the same." She turned to Dex and extended a hand. "I'm Rhianna. That," she said motioning to the woman with the book, "is Ophelia. We popped in here to see how things were going. Ophelia said you were coming and there would be a rush, so we figured we would just take you back to headquarters with us since we needed to head there to finish up some paperwork." Paperwork? Dex thought that this did not sound as exciting as he once hoped. Where was the gravitas of what happened the other day? If The Order was supposed to keep peace then how, pray tell, was that accomplished by being some kind of bureaucrat? Jude gave a chuckle.

"Alright. Well you all have fun. Hope to see you around, Dex."

"Yeah, man. Same."

The four of them headed back towards the stockroom. Dex was wondering where exactly they were going, so he began to ask his traveling companions. "So where exactly..."

"No questions: no talking. I'm thinking." Rhianna was radiating concern. She was worried about something, but Dex didn't know what. Her demeanor changed from cool and relaxed to forceful and in charge.

"I'm not sure why you're worried, Rhianna. Everything's fine. If it wasn't, I would have said something by now." Ophelia's quiet voice rang out from behind them. It was rather comforting. She radiated a sort of peace that didn't make sense. Dex felt as if the world could literally be falling down around them and Ophelia would not be screaming. She exuded confidence in some kind of fate. Dex longed for this kind of peace and comfort.

They arrived at the door and Rhianna gave out a long big sigh. This was it: this was the big reveal. Through this doorway stood a new life for Dex. The beginning of his life as a hero was... through a broom closet. Rhianna looked around. There was no one else in the stock room. She pulled out a keychain with a small figure of Bakugo from My Hero Academia on it. Dex looked and saw what looked like a blank key with no grooves and a small sliver human skull for decoration. He assumed that this was The Skeleton Key that Jude had mentioned. As she moved the key towards the doorknob, little cubes of metal started folding up from the bottom of the key. It began to form into a more recognizable key shape. It slid perfectly into the door. Rhianna turned the key and opened the door. It was no broom closet. Rather, it led to a long red carpeted staircase.

"The Skeleton Key connects two doors together that a person has been through. Very effective for fast travel," Ophelia quietly said. Rhianna went to say something, but Ophelia continued. "Dex wanted to know but didn't want to ask. I didn't think it was fair that he was left out of the loop." Rhianna stepped forward and everyone followed. Ophelia closed the door behind them.

"Look, Ophelia: we had a job to do. We went here to nondescriptly pick these two up. Don't draw attention and bring them here. From the get-go, we already had complications because that one," Rhianna said as she pointed to Dex, "already outed himself as a Healer."

"Healing is his strongest power," Ophelia said. "I've already seen that."

"But you didn't see him healing that boy?" Rhianna asked.

"I see what I need to see. You know that. We can assume then that everything is happening how it is supposed to. There is no need to be antsy."

"Yes, I get your optimism, but do you see how this can stress out those of us who aren't Prophets?" she asked.

"Prophetess," Ophelia countered. "Representation matters."

"Oh, you know what I meant," Rhianna snapped. She came to a deep red door after a few minutes' walk. "Right. So here's how this works: Jules and Adrian are here too..."

"Wait, what?" Neil suddenly interjected. Rhianna looked with concern to Neil. Her demeaner changed. It became softer and more maternal.

"Neil, I understand your concern. Dex is your friend and this whole situation is troubling. However, I know you at least trust me. And I promise you that you aren't in any danger or trouble here. Please just relax. At this point, we need you two as much as you both need us." Dex could feel she was being authentic and honest with her concern. She actually really did care for Neil and Dex. What was this business of them helping The Order? This changed the dynamic of this meeting drastically. Suddenly, Dex and Ophelia spoke together at the same time.

"It's going to be fine. Just go with it." Ophelia actually looked up at Dex for a moment. She said nothing but looked at him intently with her brown eyes. She was impressed.

"This might actually work," she finally said. With that, they entered the door into a dimly lit room. It looked like a study with many leather-bound books filling the shelves. There were two rectangular tables. There were two chairs at the one table facing a table with four chairs. Seated in the middle were two men. One was blonde with piercing blue eyes. He was incredibly well groomed in an all-black suit. His jacket was lined with a blood red satin. He sat there; his hands folded in front of him. He regarded no one in the room other than the man seated to his left.

The man to his left had a large, straw conical hat that rested on the chair he sat on. He wore a simple multicolored poncho with a white garb underneath. His hair was long and brown. His beard was wild and unkempt. He stopped talking when the group walked in.

"Neil! And Dex! Welcome! Please, have a seat. Can we get you anything? A glass of water?" he spoke with a kind yet firm voice. Dex was confused.

"I mean, I could go for some water to be honest…" Dex said. The man in the poncho got up and walked over to the built-in bar in the study to get some water. The blonde man sat up and said,

"Please sit down." He was not one to mince words, apparently. He had the look of someone who had no time for formalities or niceties. It was strange, but everyone sat down save the man in the poncho. He brought over two glasses of ice water and handed them to Neil and Dex. As he approached, Dex started to feel better. It was the strangest feeling. He was overcome not with relief, but with strength. He had only partially recovered from the incident a few days ago. Yet now, standing in this man's presence, he felt better than he had in a long time. Just being around this person seemed to make him feel better.

"I'm Jules," he said turning to walk back to his seat. "I'm a Healer, not unlike yourself," he said with a hint of irony in his voice. "Rhianna is our Channeler. Ophelia is our Prophetess, and this is gentleman here is Adrian. He's our Psyker." He smiled politely. Adrian looked sullen.

Rhianna had a look of concern on her face. Ophelia was lost in a book she produced from her bag. It was a copy of Puella Magi Modaka Magica.

"For brevity's sake," Ophelia said, "He doesn't have usual questions. Neil did a very good job explaining the basics."

"His main concern, it would seem," Adrian interjected, "is what he is doing here and why Neil is so quote-unquote 'freaked out' by what happened the other day. He is also concerned about how he can help us. And yes: I am reading your mind. The word you are now thinking of is banana."

"To be fair, this isn't even the weirdest thing to happen to me lately." Dex said, taking a drink of water. "I would say that pretty much covers it." There was silence for a moment. No one said anything. Dex heard the ticking of the clock as the silence, though only lasting for a few moments, seemed to stretch into eons.

"Okay so if someone can explain what the Hell is going on, that would be awesome at this point." Neil couldn't take it anymore. The silence was maddening to them. Someone needed to say something. More than that, someone needed to give an explanation. Being attacked by a random group of Grafters was one thing. Having your best friend exhibit signs of all Gifts simultaneously was another thing all together.

"Technically," Jules responded, "he's a Healer. And that is what he will be listed as. If he wants to be a part of The Order, of course. In actuality, he's a Conduit. And yes, Ophelia, before you say you haven't seen that, rest assured I have. After all," he said with a wry smile, "it takes one to know one."

"And you blindly release this information?" Adrian said. He was exasperated. "There are things going on that threaten to topple this Order that dates back to the first Apostles and now you are so suddenly free and giving with all of our information, little prince?" To say that Adrian was upset was a bit of an understatement. His voice and his body language suggested not standard anger. Dex could feel that, beneath his frustration was worry. There was something worrying him. Suddenly, Adrian's eyes narrowed and focused on Dex. "You would do well to learn quickly to control your telepathy."

"I mean, you admitted to reading my mind and I didn't consent. I don't even know how to control this stuff. So maybe ease up a little bit, okay?" It was simple: Dex had to give as good as he got. This wasn't about dominance. It was about establishing his right and merit to be here. "I'm assuming you four run the show. Like, you're the chapter heads or something. Which I'm guessing is why this whole thing was secret and hush hush. A person off the street shouldn't just waltz in and get a job offer from the top brass. Which means there's a lot not everyone knows. Which means that, whatever a Conduit is, you want it kept under wraps so I become a wildcard and catch people off guard." More silence.

"I think Ophelia is right. This just might work," Rhianna said, casting a glance and smile at Ophelia.

"Simply put, a Conduit is someone who's over all gift is to literally be a way to expel more positive energy into the world. Their body becomes flooded with positive energy. As a side effect to all of this, they have access to all four Gifts. One is more powerful than others, and that is their base Gift. Conduits are meant to help safeguard the world and come into power when they are needed." Jules spoke calmly and with authority. There was no reason to assume that he was wrong. Neil leaned over to Dex.

"Dude. You're, like, the chosen one or something."

"Awesome. I have more responsibility."

"No, you don't," Jules suddenly said. "You have a choice. I'm assuming that Neil explained how you could get out of all of this?" Dex nodded. He looked over at Neil. They were wearing a Spiderman t-shirt. He wasn't sure if it was done on purpose. Maybe it was a happy coincidence. Dex laughed to himself. He wished it was that easy. He wished he could simply write things off like that. The more he saw- the more he learned about how the world really was, however, he began to believe that coincidences were not so much coincidences. It almost seemed, at times, that there was some kind of grand Rube Goldberg machine that we called the universe. Each thing that happened caused something else to happen to some kind of ultimate end.

"With great power, there must also come great responsibility," Dex said under his breath. It was one of the most misquoted lines in comic book history. People assumed that the line that Stan Lee wrote in Amazing Fantasy #15 was "with great power comes great responsibility." This was one of the things that Dex would argue about at length with people. He argued that when the "must" is taken out of the line, then it loses the imperative nature of the line. For Dex, the original line doesn't give wiggle room. If you have been given an amount of power, you must then have the same amount of responsibility. It gives weight to the whole thing. It forces a person to understand the true weight of their power.

"Just tell me the problem and tell me the plan to deal with it," Dex said. He was resolute in this. In truth, while he understood that he did have a choice, he also understood that in reality, there was no real choice. Something deep inside of him wouldn't allow himself to turn from this. Be the change you want to see in the world, his mother would tell him. This was his chance to do just that.

"We have a problem with a possible traitor," Adrian said. Dex was surprised that Adrian was so freely giving information now. This could only mean one thing: something Dex had done or said had convinced Adrian that he could help. At the very least, it showed him that he was a dependable person. Whatever the case may be, Dex felt that he had earned the approval of Adrian even though he knew that Adrian would never confirm this. "Too many things have gone wrong. Even with a host of prophets, there are things that are missing. All signs point to someone internally making a mess."

"So, you can't trust... what are they called... some of the field agents?" Dex asked.

"We don't know how far it goes," Rhianna replied, "but we need someone we can trust to keep an eye out. This is where you and Neil come in."

"Am I finally getting a team?" Neil asked hopefully.

"Yes, but not yet. That is part of the problem. We can't say much more than that, but this is something that we are working on." Adrian said this but shifted uncomfortably. Dex had the feeling that there was even more that he wasn't saying for some reason.

"Right," Dex said. "I'm the new guy who can crack the case. Cool, cool, cool. Just one problem: I don't know what I'm doing. I can't control any of this."

"Well, that's why you need to get a good night's sleep. Your training starts tomorrow," Jules said with a smile. Dex was concerned. He couldn't read Jules' body language. He wasn't sure exactly what his smile meant, but he knew it would be difficult.

Chapter Three

Just like that, Neil and Dex left. There was little else to say other than Dex's training was to start tomorrow. He had no idea where he was starting. He had no idea when he was starting. For all he knew, he could be picked up in the middle of the night like he was rushing some fraternity. He could be black bagged and stuffed into a van. He didn't know. He didn't want to ask Neil. They had stayed quiet on the walk back to the car. Jude was there, and while curious about the meeting, they knew they had to stay quiet. To be thrown into all of this so suddenly was overwhelming. He was being brought on board almost as an agent of chaos. He was being expected to find a dangerous individual with no other information while learning and trying to gain control of his Gift. This wasn't how it was supposed to work out. In every story he had read, there was always some kind of training to happen before everything got flipped upside down.

They got to the car with barely a word spoken to them. Dex simply took off. He took off in a sprint, his sword hanging by his side. Despite Neil's objections, he kept going. He wasn't even sure where he wanted to go. He just knew he had to go. There was a storm of emotions inside of him. He was scared. He was angry. Above all else he was angry. If his parents were still here, they would know what to do. How dare they? How dare they leave him with this mess. Surely, they had known, right? They could have prepared him in some way. But no: they had to selfishly die in a freak accident. He knew his mother would tell him that it would all work out in the end. His father was a bit more pragmatic. Take a hammer and piece of wood. Get some nails. Get that frustration out. So that is what he was going to do.

He knew the area well enough. There was a forest nearby. At this time of day no one would be there. He heard the car behind him. Of course

Neil would get in the car and follow him. He wasn't trying to overtake him which he could have easily done. Instead, he was following him. Neil knew Dex had to get it out of his system. He made it to the forest, his legs and lungs burning with the feeling of exhaustion. "Physician, heal thyself," he said sarcastically to himself. Then he felt better. Of course. Of course that was going to happen! He couldn't even be sarcastic in this new world he found himself in.

He found the biggest tree he could. He drew Ruach and assumed an offensive stance. This was all a joke, he thought. No guidance. Everything was a mess. Secrets and lies. He drew the blade over his head. He heard the familiar sound of rushing wind. Ruach lit up, burning with a bright yellow glow. He screamed. It was not out of rage or fear. He screamed out of sadness. He screamed at the world, broken hearted by its true nature. As he brought the blade down, there was a rush of wind. The light from Ruach spread to the top of the old pine tree. The tree was split down the middle. He stood there, panting from the use of his power, tears streaming down his face. He calmly put his sword away. He turned and saw Neil. There was a mighty crack and the tree fell in two pieces. Dex simply nodded and wiped his eyes.

"Yeah," he said. "We can head home now." The two walked back to the car.

"I um… I just wanted to let you know that whole thing with the sword is pretty awesome. The way you can channel energy through it. It's, like, a really neat way to use that power."

"Thanks, I think," Dex replied. They got in the car and headed home. Neil's playlist must have been on shuffle because there was a different band playing now. *"And we'll all float on okay. And we'll all float on okay."* These words from the Modest Mouse song echoed through Dex's head. Things weren't necessarily the best right now. Life was kind of a chaotic mess. All Dex wanted was to be a normal man in the throes of his grief and loss slowly getting better over time. Apparently, that was too much to ask for. Oh no: we had to have this whole other level of issues for Dex to deal with.

On the other hand, if Dex was being honest with himself, shouldering this burden was possibly the best way to deal with his grief and loss. His father taught him of hard work. His mother taught him to be the change he wanted to see in this world. If this is the case, then it's possible that those lessons were going to help Dex. He reasoned that because of the lessons that his parents taught him, he was more than suited, at least emotionally, to handle this responsibility.

There was little conversation at home as well. Each needed to get ready for the night which they did. It wasn't that their friendship was broken or anything. Far from it: it was hard to go through the things they just went through and not be closer. No, this was a sort of professional curtesy. Neil knew that whatever was going to happen tomorrow, Dex would need his rest. Yes, he spent a few days sleeping already. However, that wasn't really his choice. He felt good. At least he felt good physically. He was working on feeling good emotionally. That may take some time and that was okay. No- Dex knew in his heart that Neil harbored no ill will towards him. He reasoned that if Neil was a problem, if by some chance he was the mole causing havoc in The Order, then it stood to reason that Jules and the rest wouldn't have divulged sensitive information in front of him.

Right?

A terrible thought occurred to Dex as he lay in bed. What if Neil was the issue? What if Neil was the one who he had to watch and ultimately deal with? The thought sickened him. He went back and forth thinking about "the greater good" yet try as he might, he couldn't get to a place where he felt that he could bring him to justice. No. He knew Neil. There was no way, in Dex's mind at least, that Neil was the culprit. On the other hand, how many anime and manga had he consumed where the childhood friend was the main antagonist? It's entirely possible based on the laws of a story. But this wasn't a story, he countered himself. This was real life. But he also kept this huge secret from you about The Order. Could they really be trusted? Yet on the other hand, Dex was sure that was for his benefit. At the end of it all, it boiled down to an issue of faith. What was that verse his mom always talked about? It was something about faith being the belief in the unseen or something. Did he really have the faith to believe that Neil was some malcontent? No. If there was one thing Dex believed in- had actual faith in- in was Neil. He knew that Neil would never betray him. He had faith in that.

Eventually, Dex found himself asleep. It was a nice and peaceful sleep, all things considered. Oh, sure there were dreams, but Dex knew that by the morning he wouldn't even remember them. Besides, real life had become more fascinating than dreams at this point. His dreams, like his life, were somewhat chaotic. It didn't matter as they all vanished with the coming of the morning.

Instead, Dex woke up rather early for him. It was about eight in the morning. He tried to go back to sleep. He begged God for just even five more minutes yet his prayers fell on deaf ears. Against his will, he got up and got ready for the day. He grabbed a shirt that had Edward Elric from Fullmetal Alchemist on it. He had always enjoyed that manga and anime as it was the first series he got serious about. To him, the character was best summed up in an exchange about his title of Fullmetal. He responded that it sounded heavy and he liked the weight of it. To Dex, this was important. If a person was to have a title, they should respond to the weight of said title. Today, with whatever what going to happen, he needed to be reminded of the weight of his newfound responsibility.

As he made his way to the kitchen for breakfast, he was shocked to see Ophelia sitting at his table eating some cereal and reading a copy of Neon Genesis Evangelion manga. She seemed blissfully unaware of Dex being downstairs or she simply didn't care. In truth, Ophelia was not as carefree as she appeared. Instead, the opposite was true. She cared quite a lot. She felt, however, that she was a head of the curve. Most people would assume that knowledge of the future would lead to a sort of nihilism. If everything is predetermined, then nothing really matters. The choices a person make don't matter because that would be all part of some greater cosmic plan. Ophelia realized early on, however, that the choices did matter because they were still made. She likened it to watching the movie Titanic over and over again. Yes, she knew what choices the characters would make. She knew what would happen. Yet in that moment, she knew the characters didn't. Their choices, while not mattering in the long term, mattered to them in the here and now. This gave her a lot of comfort.

"Neil went out for an early morning jog and then he has to do a shift at The Cathedral. I came in as he was leaving and he let me in. But you already knew that." She said all of this quietly while eating and reading. She was right. Dex had this odd sense of déjà vu once again. Did he dream this scenario? He wasn't sure, but he knew what happened next. Next, she would say, "Yes, that's how your Gift of prophecy works."

"Yes," she said right on que. "that's how your Gift of prophecy works."

"So you're the first stop on my training montage?" Dex asked as he poured himself a bowl of cereal.

"Yes. Because I'm the quickest and easiest," she replied. He sat down next to her.

"That's a great series. I didn't like The End of Evangelion movie, though."

"That's because despite the way you portray yourself, you're an optimist who longs for the happy ending."

"I would say that is a fair assessment," Dex said. "So; what pearls of wisdom do you have for me?"

"None," she replied honestly.

"You just wanted cereal, then?" he asked.

"No. I'm supposed to tell you to pretty much deal with it." She looked up at Dex. "The cereal is just a plus."

"So I can't control this prophecy thing?"

"Nope. And you aren't meant to. You're a Conduit whose main gift is healing. Your flashes of the future aren't strong. There is no way to control them. It's just meant to reassure you that you are on the right path and give you the proper nudge you need."

"That doesn't sound like fun," Dex replied truthfully taking a spoonful of cereal in his mouth.

"Prophesy in general isn't fun. It sucks. You get asked questions like why you didn't stop 9/11 or wars. What we see is what we are meant to see. Sometimes things fall through the cracks because they are supposed to. We never know the reason why. I don't think we are supposed to. We just go with it and do what we are meant to do." She picked up the bowl and drank the rest of her milk. Then she used her hoodie sleeve to wipe her mouth. She looked at Dex intently. Her large, brown eyes were warm and caring. "Everything that happens happens because it's supposed to happen. The same is true for what we see. We can try to force it, but we will always see what we are supposed to see for reasons we don't always understand."

"Not sure if that's super helpful, to be honest. So what: we're all just puppets on a string but you can see the strings?" Dex asked.

"More or less," she replied, "but that doesn't take away the fact that choices we make are our own. They matter to us because we still make them."

"I've got to be honest: this isn't exactly what I thought about when I thought about training."

"Oh no. This is the easiest one you have today because we just sit here and wax philosophical about the implications of seeing the future. Which we've done. You're going to headquarters now to learn from Rhianna. Then you'll meet with Adrian. Then finally you'll meet with Jules."

"Awesome," Dex said sarcastically. "I certainly hope they will be giving me lunch."

"Lunch will be provided," Ophelia assured him. "You'll get an Italian sub."

"Cool, cool, cool," Dex replied. He looked at her and smiled. "I'm assuming that're you're the most chill of The Four, right?" Dex remembered knew that The Four where essentially those that were in charge. One person with each Gift made a squad. The Four.

"I have never been called chill before. But I would agree with that assessment," she said with a half-smile.

"Well, I assume I had better be off. I trust you'll lock up?" Dex asked her.

"Yes. That won't be a problem."

"No boys in the house while I'm out," he said with a laugh.

"I'm just going to have a cup of coffee and leave. Don't worry about that," she replied.

"Yeah, no. I wasn't really worried. It was a joke," he said worried that he had offended her.

"I'm sorry. I didn't realize. Jokes are usually funny," she said with a wry smile.

"Alright," Dex said with a smile. "You got me. You win. Hopefully we will run in to each other again."

"Oh we will. This story is far from over and even I don't know how it ends yet," she said. Dex grabbed his keys and Ruach and headed out the door. What a day this was shaping up to be, he thought to himself. Coffee and talk about destiny versus human choice is always a great way to start the day. Why was it his life that went so off the rails? Assuming this was some kind of destiny, then why was it afforded to him? Why not someone else that would be better suited to it. Let's face it: Dex knew English literature, comics, anime, and how to use a sword. This did not, in his own mind, make him fit to be sorting out the problems of some secret organization. These things don't happen in real life. Perhaps, as he thought about Ophelia's words, that she was right. Perhaps everything really did happen for a reason and there was some kind of guiding handwriting out the story of Dex's life. If that was the case, then why couldn't this author have given him a happier story? Why did it have to be filled with trial after trial? He thought that, perhaps, the answer lies in character development. Anyone who has studied stories can tell you that problems the protagonist face are given to them so that they can grow as a character. If someone was writing out the story of his life, he then had to assume that whatever happened to him in the past and now happened because it would cause him to grow.

It was not the best answer, but it was the only one that he could come up with.

He started up his truck and decided to see what God or the universe was telling him. The best way to do that was, of course, to shuffle his playlist.

"Make my story! I'll make my existence a statement they won't forget. It's a big decision I have to live with. Through all the tears, I'm stronger than the rest. There will be a day when I'm looking back on my life. I will find a way so that I can say that I kept on going, passing every test." Fine, he thought to himself. Message received. He would take Lenny Code

Fiction's advice and Make My Story. He was glad he was listening to an English cover of the song by Johnathan Young so he could belt out the lyrics as he drove.

He pulled up to The Cathedral of Heroes. It was now about nine-thirty in the morning. He saw Neil through the window looking rather bored. He wasn't sure how or why Neil got stuck with the opening shift, but he knew that Neil didn't mind. Aside from a few people, the shop was almost always dead in the morning. As he opened the door, the familiar ding went off signaling to the shop that someone came in.

"Dex!" Neil said excitedly. "I trust you had a... a most enlightening breakfast."

"Oh yeah. Mornings are for contemplation and coffee anyway," he replied while looking at the new arrivals rack. "So, do you know where I am supposed to go?" he asked Neil.

"I mean, more or less? I know where I'm supposed to send you. I don't have, like, your itinerary or anything."

"Nothing like a trial by fire, huh?"

"I'm sure you'll be fine. I talked to Rhianna this morning. She said they were going to ease you into this whole thing. But I'm not sure what all that means." Neil shrugged their shoulders. "How bad can it be?"

"I should slap the mess out of you right now. You've watched enough movies to know never to say that. What is wrong with you?" Dex said with mock disgust.

"Okay, chosen one. Let's get you going. She's expecting you by ten." Neil led him to the back and produced the Skeleton Key. "You ready for this?" they asked Dex.

"Absolutely not so let's do this."

"That's the spirit!" Dex passed over the threshold into the familiar stairwell with the red steps. The door closed behind him. For a moment he turned to face it. What exactly was on the other side of this door? He reached his hand out to the doorknob slowly. He held it in his hand and hesitated.

"It's just a forest, isn't it?" Dex asked without turning around.

"Yes. In a world of fast travel, unless we are under attack here, it doesn't really matter where we are. The Council has a Skeleton Key they share. It's based out of the shop. The Four have their own. So we get where we need to go when we need to go there." Dex turned around and saw Rhianna. She was ready for training wearing a tank top and leggings. Her red hair was tied up into a tight dancer's bun. He noticed a small purple scar on her stomach that Dex assumed was part of something bigger. Truth be told, Dex was intimidated. This woman looked like she could utterly destroy him in a fight. "I trust you had a fine morning with Ophelia?" she asked pleasantly.

"Yeah. She's really chill. Didn't train so much, but I got a lot of information from her."

"Information is training. Don't ever forget that. Now follow me. We don't have as much time as I'd like to have." She turned and headed up the stairs. "First," she said walking and not turning around, "you are officially here for combat training and healer's orientation with Jules should anyone ask. Is that understood?"

"Okay, but you need to just go ahead and assume that I am going to tell Neil everything," Dex responded plainly.

"If we didn't want you to tell them, then we would have said so. They're a part of this."

"And what is this?" She hesitated for a moment, almost looking like she wanted to say more but couldn't.

"We don't exactly know. All we know is that something isn't right. We have identified key players that are supposed to help us unravel this mystery. And even then, information for you is on a need to know basis. The less you know, the safer you will be." She tried to hide it, but she rolled her eyes when she said that last part. She approached a door on her right and opened it. Stepping in, she said, "Second, you have to realize that everything else you will learn today is built upon the lesson we go over here. Jules will explain more later, but you have to get used to having positive energy under your control. It's crucial for the final phase of your training. Third," she said turning on the lights revealing a gym, "this type of training will happen once a week. Attendance is mandatory. And you will practice lessons on your own time as well. Understood." Now Dex was even more intimidated.

"Yeah. I get it. I'm a dog of the military now." he said jokingly. She turned to face him.

"Dex, I get that this is a strange situation. I get that humor is how you deal with stressful situations. You also have to realize that what we are doing is serious. We can have fun and joke, but I need to know that you know this is serious." Dex couldn't answer. He could just nod an affirmation, slightly embarrassed. "Okay," she said. "then let's get to it." She pressed a button on the wall and humanoid dummies popped up from the floor. She turned and faced Dex.

"At this point, we have to operate under a few assumptions. First, you have been channeling positive energy off of reactions to situations. Second, because it isn't your main Gift, let's assume that you need something to channel the energy into. So, let's test both at one time." She turned around and held a palm straight facing a dummy. "Focus the energy somewhere in your body. That's your centering point. It could be your hands or chest- wherever. Just pick a point and focus energy there. Then you make that energy go where you need it to go." Her palm lit up and a beam of energy came racing out of it towards a dummy. Its head was blown clean off. "Now you," she said simply.

Wonderful, Dex thought to himself. Trial by fire indeed. He took a deep breath and closed his eyes. Where would his centering point be? Think it through logically. There were two places that it should be: the head or the heart. If it was the head, that would make sense. However, if this power was reflective of himself, then he had to assume that the heart would be a better place. While it doesn't store emotions, the heart was always thought to be the center of the person because of its importance. It came to symbolize love. If he wanted his Gift to be fueled by love, then how did he fill it up? He thought about what he would do with power. He thought about those he knew that he loved and how this power would help him to keep them safe. Finally, he could help make the world a better place. It's not that he wanted to. He would rather have been at home eating junk food and watching Netflix. The problem was he had this Gift now. Now he finally had resources available to him to help out and fix the world. He thought about his parents and how proud they would be of him. He thought about Neil knowing he needed a teammate. He couldn't let them down.

His chest began to feel warm. It was as if he drank a sudden cup of hot coffee that centered in his chest. Right. Now stay there, he thought. He opened his eyes, still thinking of his loved ones. So far so good. He raised a hand. Just like Goku, he thought. He traced the warmth in his mind from his chest to his hand. Good. Now, go out of the hand and, like, shoot towards that dummy. He saw himself in his mind's eye. A beam of energy blasting forth through his hand puncturing a training dummy. He waited. And waited. And waited.

Nothing. There was no blast. There was just Dex standing there with a warm hand. He began to get frustrated. Dude come on, he thought. Not in front of the laser woman...

He held it for a few more seconds and dropped his arm. He was obviously upset.

"Dex," Rhianna said sympathetically, "this happens all the time. This is normal. It's always hard the first time and this was designed to make you fail to prove a point. Try it again holding your sword." Dex rubbed his eyes and then drew his blade. "Focus just like the last time. Instead of trying to discharge the energy, try to gather it in the blade."

He went back to that place in his mind. He gathered his emotions and placed them squarely in his chest. Once the warmth was there, he tried to move it to his hands. That seemed easy enough. He took a deep breath. He imagined what it would be like for warmth to travel up the blade in general. There would be a contact spot where the energy would be transferred. That would start to be the hottest. It would then logically disperse throughout the blade. This is what he was trying to accomplish. He opened his eyes. He was shocked to find out that it worked. He stood there for a moment, admiring the blade. It glowed. It actually glowed. This time he had done it on purpose. Rhianna was smiling and clapping her hands.

"Well done, Dex Machina. Well done. I am very proud of you."

"So what now?" he asked, his voice filled with wonder.

"Hit a dummy to kill it. I'm testing another theory," she replied.

He sliced clean through a dummy. Even at the blade's sharpest, he shouldn't have been able to do that. Dex suppose that the energy that encased the blade made it more powerful.

"What now?" Dex asked.

"Channel the energy through your sword." Dex did as he was told. "Now, hit me with the sword."

"Nope," Dex said as he put the sword away. "Not going to happen."

"Yes, it is," she said.

"I'm not super comfortable doing that to a person," Dex countered. "Okay. Then defend yourself." She raised a fist and blasted him. Dex flew backwards a few feet. It felt like getting punched in the chest. "That was a light one. Each one I land from here on out will be stronger." She raised her fists in a boxing stance. With a left jab, she hit with another blast. It was stronger and this one landed on his face. Dex held his sword in a defensive stance. A right hook was coming and another blast along with it. He channeled the positive energy through his sword and slashed at the blast. He was able to deflect it, but just barely.

Rhianna decided to change tactics. If he could now deflect her blasts, she would have to get close and personal. She fired a shot off to Dex's right side. And he lunged to deflect it, she stepped in closer and landed an energy filled punch with her left hand to his stomach. He doubled over a bit. Left jab, right jab: over and over again she was throwing punches to him. Dex had no choice. He would have to block her fists with his blade or be pummeled. As she came around with a right hook, Dex brought Ruach up in a diagonal pattern. His blade connected with her fist, but it didn't go through it. She suddenly stood up and rolled her head around in a circle and shook her hit hand.

"Okay. We're good. Thank you."

"You want to tell me what the hell that all was about?!" Dex asked with a sense rage in his voice.

"As a reflex, you are using your channeling to blunt your attacks.

You're turning a slashing weapon into a bludgeoning weapon. Why?" She was very interested in why he would be doing this even as a reflex.

"I just... I don't want to kill anyone. I um..." he felt slightly embarrassed saying it. He sighed. "I promised my parents when they bought me a sword I would only ever kill as a last resort." Rhianna's look softened.

"Dex, that's a very mature stance. You don't have to be embarrassed about that. It takes a lot of courage to have convictions like that. And we learned you can control it. You've got a lot of work to do, but you're not off to a bad start." She looked at her watch. "Well, that's all the time I get this week. I'd say practice at home. Experiment with more and less energy. See if you can change the color or something. See what happens. Sound good?" This woman, Dex thought, was a teacher through and through. She could easily be teaching some kind of high school or college class.

"Yeah," he said. "I'll work on it. Where to now?"

"Three doors down on the right from this one. Adrian is waiting there for you." Dex nodded and headed out the door. After the door was closed, Jules came out from another room.

"He's got more talent and control than he realizes, but he doesn't know how to use it," Rhianna said. "By the way: think you can look at my hand. I felt several cracks when he hit it." Jules came closer and placed his hand on her hand.

"That was very risky," he said, healing her hand with a soft glow. "Even if he has some control and even if he can pull the punches with that sword, it was still dangerous. Less lethal doesn't mean nonlethal."

"Oh, I knew it would hurt," she said flexing her healed hand. "but you gave me a job to do. So I was going to do it." She looked sad for a moment. "If I can't tell him everything, then I might as well take a few shots to help save his life."

"It's too dangerous for him to know too much too soon. We've talked about this. It would destroy him or possibly corrupt him or worse. It has to be this way: at least for now."

"And when he does find out? What happens then? Has Ophelia seen that far? Have you?" she asked pointedly.

"Neither of us have and we are the only ones with prophecy Gifts monitoring him right now. When he finds out, he will have a choice to make and if we've done everything right, then we don't have anything to worry about."

"You're placing an awful lot of faith in that young man," Rhianna said. The teacher in her believed in him, but she also didn't want to put him in a bad situation.

"I have faith in him. I have to," Jules replied solemnly.

Dex made his way to the third door on the right. He knocked gently. Adrian was the one that worried Dex the most. It wasn't that he was scared of him per say. He just seemed so cold and distant. Dex understood that in a secret organization, people would have secrets. Adrian radiated secrets like neon signs in the comic shop.

"Come in," a terse voice said. Taking a deep breath, Dex entered the room. It appeared to be a smaller study than where he was last night. This looked more like an office than anything else. There was a large mahogany desk with an imposing leather chair behind it. In front of it was a less comfortable looking chair. Adrian sat in his chair scribbling noted in a small red leather-bound book. He finished what he was writing and placed the ribbon on his page. Opening a drawer, he stashed it inside. "Have a seat." It wasn't an offer: it was an order.

Dex sat in the chair. It was as uncomfortable as it looked. Adrian just stared at him, measuring him. He was reading everything he could about Dex without going into his mind. Dex swallowed. His leg began to bounce. He could do nothing to hide his anxiousness and both he and Adrian knew it.

"This is what it is like to hear a voice in your head," Adrian's mouth remained closed but he heard his voice. It had to have been in his head. "You can't communicate this way unless I give the permission. Psykers are used to link squads together during missions. They are also masters of reading the mind like I showed you last night. We have the ability to make people see what we want them to see." A small pink elephant now stood on Adrian's desk. Dex could hear it trumpet. He could smell the hay it had just eaten. "What you see and hear and feel and taste: all of that is dependent on what I want you to experience. Some of us know how to control the mind and therefore the body." Dex's right arm shot straight up in the air. He looked at it and looked at Adrian who was smiling. Try as he might, he could not lower his arm. He struggled as best he could, but it was to no avail. Finally, he regained control of his arm and lowered it swiftly, hitting the arm of the chair he sat in.

"I can't do that. There's no way I can do that," Dex said slightly irritated. "So what? Why do that? Why tell me all of that? You just want to flex your might or something?"

"You need to understand the reality of what is out there. Psykers may not be as brash and in your face as garish blasts of light, but they are formidable."

"This is supposed to be training though. If I can't do that stuff then what's the point?"

"Why haven't you read me yet, Dex Machina?" Dex was taken back by the question. He hadn't realized that was his Gift. He looked at Adrian. Studying his body language, he noticed that Adrian was leaning back slightly in his chair with his arms folded across himself. This suggested that he was subconsciously trying to create separation between the two of them. His arms suggested that he was protecting himself. His face was different from last night. There wasn't concern, but smugness. That's what he could see. However, he wasn't getting any emotion off of Adrian. Dex deduced two things. First, his Gift of being a Psyker must be tied to being able to feel a person's emotions. He was an Empath. Second, Adrian must have been actively stopping Dex from using his ability. He couldn't control it yet so it must not be rather strong.

"Because you won't allow it," Dex finally said. "It's not strong, which means it's easily deflected and detected. Which is probably why you look so smug. But because I'm a Conduit, you don't know if it would suddenly be more powerful if I try which is suggested by your separation and protective body language." Now it was Dex's turn to smirk a bit. Don't be intimidated, he thought to himself. Stand your ground.

"Reading body language is easy. Reading the mind undetected while protecting your own is different. So, I want you to try. Let's begin." Dex felt Adrian rooting mind. It was not painful. It was more like when he had his wisdom teeth extracted. It felt very awkward- almost like it should hurt but didn't. "Ah. A man of literature," Adrian said. "No wonder you do subtext well. Let's go deeper, shall we?" Dex's mind turned to his parents. No, he thought. No; he didn't need to see this. Get out, he said in his mind. Do something. Think of something else. He shifted his thoughts to a monkey toy clanging cymbals. It was challenging. Adrian narrowed his eyes and redoubled his efforts. Dex's thoughts went back to his parents. It began a mental game of tug of war.

I have to try something else, Dex thought. Focus. Think about it in the same way as Channeling. Focus on his emotions. Start with his body language. He didn't look smug. He looked almost angry. But why? Why was he angry? Think it through. The Order essentially needs Dex for some reason. Adrian has to train him. Naturally, he wants Dex to be as strong as possible. But this almost seemed like something else. Maybe, Dex thought, Adrian had a vested interest in his strength. That was all that it took- just one small kink in his armor. Dex felt it.

"Why are you so concerned?" he asked Adrian. Dex's head began to hurt as Adrian redoubled his efforts to stave off a mental attack. Dex knew he wasn't as strong as Adrian, so he had to use any advantage possible. "No. Tell me: do you think I'm not strong enough? Do you think I can't help? I'm not going to give up," Dex said through gritted teeth, the pain starting to overwhelm him. "You have a vested interest in this, don't you?" The more Dex spoke, the more the battle intensified. "If you're so concerned that I'm not strong enough, then there's a reason you want me strong. So, who is it I'm supposed to protect, Adrian?" A look of shock overtook Adrian's face. Dex wondered if he had taken things too far. Adrian's face contorted into one of frustrated anger. Dex had dared to get too close to Adrian. He did not like people assuming that they could get that close to him. Adrian felt as though he needed to protect people not from himself, but from his past. There were things that he had done that didn't need to be discussed. His past was just that- the past. If people were to get close to him, then there would be no doubt that they would gain a better understanding his past and that would complicate matters.

Reflex took over Adrian. The only thing Dex could do now was give into the blackness of unconsciousness.

Chapter Four

Dex awoke to a very concerned Jules standing over him. He was standing next to a less than ambivalent Adrian standing next to him. The good news was that his head no longer hurt. The bad news is he had no idea what had happened to him.

"I have been told," Adrian said coolly, "that I am to apologize. Therefore, I am sorry." He turned around and went back to sit at his desk. Dex's eyes scanned the room. This offered only a slight explanation of how he ended up on the floor. He stood up and brushed himself off. He actually felt really good. It was almost like he had a full night's sleep. Adrian looked at Jules. "He was only unconscious for a few moments. And I am confident that a valuable lesson about the powers of the mind was learned."

"That's not the point," Jules said exasperated. "At some point we all have to work together and trust one another."

"Yes. I agree. At some point, your majesty, that will need to happen, but it is unlikely to happen today as this young man literally just started training." Adrian shrugged his shoulders. Jules let out a small sigh.

"You're right," Dex finally said. "There's a good chance I was just being an ass. I'll keep learning and working. Eventually, I'll win you over with my charm and talent. I'm sure of it."

"Your empathy is tied to your ability to read a person's body language. When you find yourself doing that, remind yourself to temper it. Skirt around the edges of the mind. We will work on mental fortitude as we move forward." He pulled out his small notebook and wrote some things down. He looked back up and Dex. "Good work today, Dex. He's all yours now, Jules." Adrian then went back to writing in his notebook.

"Let's go, Dex. We have a schedule to keep." He gently touched Dex's shoulder and ushered him towards the door. They left quietly, without a word. They started walking down the hall. Dex didn't want the silence. He wanted some kind of explanation.

"So, that was weird," he finally said to Jules.

"He wants you strong for what may come next. Adrian is very passionate about The Order. All of The Four are. In some way or another, The Order helped us. For some, it saved us." Jules pulled out a Skeleton Key from his pocket.

"So, is this the back story montage, then?" Dex asked sarcastically.

"Each person has a right to their own story. That includes when they tell it. Now come on. Let's go have lunch." Jules opened the door to the smell of a deli and walked through it. Dex wasn't sure where they were exactly. Literally, they could have been anywhere- anywhere in the world. Dex was hoping for a deli in New York as he had never been there. The experience would have been fun for him. Instead, however, he realized they were at Ralph's Kitchen which was a block from the comic bookstore. "Lunch break and then down to business. We have a job to do to help you learn to heal others." They walked out from the storage room into the main dining area. Jules waved and flashed a smile to Big Ralph, the owner and proprietor of Ralph's Kitchen.

"Ay, Jules! Good ta see ya! Your booth is over there. Your other order will be ready in a bit. Can I get you guys something to eat?"

"How about two Italian subs? Does that work for you, Dex?" Jules asked.

"Yeah that's fine. What do I owe you?"

"It's already taken care of," Jules said. "It's part of a larger order." He sat down in the booth and Dex joined him.

"Well, so far, this is probably my favorite training of the day," Dex said. The waiter brought them each a glass of water.

"No this isn't the training. This is lunch. Training comes after. Then you have combat analysis."

"I'm sorry, what?" Dex inquired swallowing his water.

"Oh, that's not too major. We just want to see where you are at in combat."

"Yeah, but shouldn't the Prophets essentially tell you where people go?"

"Certainly, sometimes, but not always," Jules said. "Didn't Ophelia tell you? They see what they are meant to see."

"She did mention that, but it seems to me that this would be crucial information."

"We don't always get to pick what information is crucial to us. Look at yourself: if left to your own devices and not scooped up by us, you may have run from your power or even been Corrupted. Yet it was part of some greater plan that we met. And we met because you know Neil. And Neil met us because of Rhianna. There's always something bigger going on. Every so often, we catch a small glimpse of it." Jules smiled kindly.

"So then where exactly does being a Conduit fit into all of this?" Jules laughed.

"It's not so bad. You get used to it. A new Conduit is birthed when they are needed. Sometimes they work for the positive side, other times they work for the negative side."

"So, I could still break bad? Is that what you're saying?" Dex asked. The thought worried him. He had an understanding that human beings and power did not always work well together. It was a tenuous relationship they had because power is a very corrupting force in humanity. To compound that with literal powers, then, could potentially spell even more of a problem.

"Dex, there is always a chance. There's a chance I could be Corrupted. It's unlikely, but the reality is that it is never certain for anyone. The good news, however, is that it's a not a final destination. People have a unique capacity for change. My advice would be not to worry too much about it. You'll have to worry more about killing me in combat." He took a drink of his water.

"Wait, what?" Dex replied.

"Yeah, it's totally like a Highlander situation. 'There can be only one' and all of that." Big Ralph brought the sandwiches and sat them down.

"The other stuff will be ready whenever you are, Jules."

"Ralph, you're a literal life saver. Thank you." Dex was still sitting there, dumbfounded. Jules turned to look at him, as Dex sat there concerned with all the color drained from his face. "Dex. That was a joke." Dex blinked a few times and couldn't help but laugh. This was absurd. The stakes were the world being plunged into darkness or not and here this man was, dressed like a bum and making jokes about the whole thing. Dex looked at Jules. He had these kind, brown eyes with a hint of sadness. He wasn't old, per say, but he looked like he had seen a thing or two. His hair and beard were long and at first looked unkept. However, there also appeared to be a method to craziness of his hair. It almost reminded Dex of the ocean: chaotic but with a purpose. "Excuse me for a moment," he said. He closed his eyes and bowed his head in a silent prayer before his meal. A few moments later he lifted his eyes and began to eat.

"None of this makes sense," Dex said, taking a bite of his sandwich.

"What do you mean?"

"This. All of this." Jules nodded.

"There certainly is a certain amount of absurdity to it all. So just ask."

"Ask what?" Dex inquired. Jules shrugged.

"Anything. You're right: we've thrown you to the wolves. We've just told you to go with it. It's not fair to you." Jules shrugged and took another bite of his sandwich. "So ask anything."

"Har far can my healing power go?" It was a question that Dex had wondered. The more time passed, the more he realized just how badly hurt Neil was. He had to understand his limits in regard to healing.

"You can bring a deceased person back to life, but you shouldn't."

"Why not?" Jules sighed.

"Because it's one of the fastest ways to become Corrupted. Resurrections do happen, but they are always rare. They are confirmed by at least three unconnected Prophets and that is always done a head of time. It's not like someone dies and suddenly they have to call people. No: people who resurrect others know well in advance what they will have to do." Dex was curious.

"So why does it lead to being Corrupted?"

"Being Corrupted means you've been misusing your Gift for a prolonged period. God ultimately decides the lifespan of things. So resurrecting people willy-nilly goes against a plan. It says that you know more than God. It's about pride. Not good pride but a dark and powerful pride."

"So no Zombies. Got it." Dex joked.

"Actually, most Corrupted Healers do make zombies. However, the more talented ones make Dolls. They encase a bone in a wooden statue and control the statue's movements. The human body has two-hundred and thirteen bones. So an adult skeleton can make quite an army."

"Dolls, Zombies, Grafters: any other entries in the Monster Manual I need to be aware of?" Dex was more than a little nervous.

"Well, there are Vampires and Werewolves. I mean, where do you think the old stores come from? Vampires are Corrupted that use their Gifts so selfishly, they are transformed into avatars of greed. They literally have to take the life of others because they think and feel only for themselves. Werewolves are similar, but their vice is rage. They give into their rage that it consumes them and shapes their bodies. Silver is ineffective in both cases. You can actually heal a person of Vampirism. I'll give you some stuff to read on it."

Dex just sat there, chewing on his bite for an extra-long time. He really had just been joking again, but it once more backfired. He was in over his head. He knew his face looked disgusted. He looked at Jules. He had a look of almost sorrow on his face. Go slowly, Dex told himself. Read his body language and try to subtly check his emotions. Jules' eyes looked sad. It wasn't that he was sad about anything terrible. No, Dex realized: it wasn't sadness. It was guilt. He felt guilt. He fully understood what he was asking Dex to do. He had no choice- no other solution because of some grand master plan than to involve Dex. He felt bad about that. Dex could feel it. As soon as he did, he switched it off. This way he could practice his empathy since he had to be ready for... something.

"Dex, I am sorry. I am so very sorry. Isn't the truth, no matter how horrible- no matter what it costs- isn't that better than a pretty lie?"

"What is truth?" Dex responded, quoting Pontius Pilot.

"The truth is that you can change the world. Which is what we are going to do with your healing training." They finished their meal and headed to the counter. Awaiting them where two large cardboard boxes filled with subs and bottles of water. "Grab one," Jules instructed Dex. They took their boxes and headed to the door.

"So where are these going?" Dex asked.

"Under The Bridge," Jules responded. Dex understood now. The Bridge was a place near the college campus that had a large homeless population. They were only about three blocks away with no car in sight. "Walking builds character. Plus, my augmented Gift of healing provides an aura of healing. So, this is kind of like a cheat code for endurance training. Though you will feel it tomorrow."

"What does giving food to the homeless have to do with healing?" Dex asked.

"Everything. Healers aren't just there for the body. They tend to be the emotional support of their team. They are the optimistic ray of sunshine in a dreary situation."

"Buddy, you've got the wrong guy then," Dex replied with a laugh.

"No I don't. See, my Psyker gift allows me to see a hidden truth about someone. And you, Dex Machina, for all your dreariness and sarcasm, are a hopeful optimist."

"Don't you mean hopeless optimist?"

"No: I don't." Jules said with a smile. "Think about it: what does the homeless population not have? Access to healthcare. While we feed them, we heal them."

"Guerilla healthcare for all: I like it."

"These people, for whatever reason, have been pushed to the fringes of society. Even if it doesn't make a difference in the long term, it makes a difference to them now. That's what we do: make a difference now. They need help. And if a person needs help and you can help, then you have a moral obligation to help. With great power, there must also come great responsibility." Dex stopped walking for moment. He said it right. He got it right. He sped up to keep up with Jules. As they approached The Bridge, Jules said, "Let's get to work."

Under The Bridge was a small town populated by tattered and old tents. Old and broken shopping carts we filled with what anyone else would have considered garbage. Some were being used over barrels as makeshift grills. An older woman in a brown worn coat saw them first.

"Hey everyone! Saint Jules is here!" she said with a large smile. Jules smiled back. With a laugh.

"You know I don't need a name like that. Jules is fine." He looked at Dex and whispered quickly and quietly, "Heal her. Try to heal her from a distance. She's been having trouble with her foot again. Focus there and try to heal her at a distance." Dex looked back with confusion, but he already knew what Jules was going to say as a wave of déjà vu washed over him. "I saw it in a dream. Do it."

He focused on his chest, the seat of his power. He raised two fingers from the handle of the box he was holding and looked at the woman's feet. Just... I don't know. Just get better. Heal. He felt it, then: the warmth. It was the same warmth from when he healed the child's knee. He felt it exit his fingers and could see a short of shimmer in the air. It was as if a bit of reality was bubbling around itself. The wave went to the woman's foot and suddenly, the pronounced limp was no more.

"Well done, Dex. Healing at a distance is very uncommon. This is your augmented healing Gift." Healing at a distance. It was interesting. The last two times Dex healed someone, he had paid his hands on them. With this revelation, he now understood that he can help people and not be near them. Obviously, in a combat situation, this would be quite useful.

The people began to form a line in front of them. One by one, they came and were handed a sandwich and a bottle of water. Jules, with his healing aura, was already healing people. For Dex, he decided that the simplest way would be to touch hands with the person that he was serving. One by one, the people thanked them for the food. One by one, these people were healed. Dex didn't know what he was healing them from. It could have been sores, disease- it could have been anything. He kept going. He felt like he was getting tired. He wasn't too sure how much longer he could keep it up, but he knew he had to. He had the power to help these people. He could do something for them, so he was going to.

There were all kinds of people there under The Bridge. Some were old, some were young. There were all different races. The one thing that

Dex knew was that these were people. It seemed an odd assessment to make, but Dex felt it was important. Too often, people were looked down upon because of a number of reasons. For these people, because they were homeless, they were easily forgotten unless someone wanted to make themselves feel better. They were a prop to coax the brain into producing some happy chemicals when people applauded them for their selfless giving. But these people weren't that. They were people- real living and breathing people. Dex wondered to himself how often Jules did this. Obviously, the people knew him. They had even gifted him the nickname of Saint Jules. In order to build that relationship, it would have taken time. Yet Dex never heard a story of the man in the conical hat and poncho helping the community under The Bridge in the local news. It wasn't because this was some secret mission for The Order. No, this was just helping for the sake of helping. This was a good deed for the sake of being a good force in the world.

The last person in line was the same kindly old lady that had announced Jules' arrival.

"Did everyone get food?" she asked Dex.

"Yeah. I'm pretty sure."

"Well that's good."

"Here. This is my last one." Dex handed her the sandwich and drink.

"Oh no. That's okay. You have it. You did all this work."

"No, no, no, no, no," Dex protested. "I ate earlier. I'm good."

"Well, thank you," she said taking the items. "I'm Cindy."

"Dex," he replied shaking her hand and making sure she was healed.

"You're a good Healer," she said with her mouth full of food. Dex was taken back for a moment, but it made sense. Not everyone with The Sight was in The Order.

"Was it that obvious?" he asked with a chuckle.

"Well you have a sword and you're hanging out with Jules. Plus, you pointed to me and my foot felt better. I'm not stupid, you know."

"It's my first day on the job," Dex admitted sheepishly.

"How do you like it so far?" Dex shrugged.

"I mean, it's not so bad. I like being able to help people." She laughed.

"Me too, Dex! Me too! That's why I'm here. Jules can't help all the time, so I fill in the gaps in between visits."

"Wait, you're a Healer?" Dex was confused.

"Yep. Darn good one, too, but not at a distance like you."

"Then why are you here? Couldn't you parlay that skill into... something else? Work for The Order?"

"They have Healers. They have Healers much younger than me. What: should I go be a doctor? No: I'm right where God wants me to be."

"God wants you to be poor and homeless?" Dex asked. The idea seemed odd to him. If this woman could help people, if this woman was a part of God's master plan, then why would God allow her to be poor?

"Dex, what do you know about fishing?" she asked.

"I used to fish all the time with my dad."

"And how many times did you cast your hook on the land to catch a fish?" Dex was confused.

"Huh?"

"Did you ever place your hook and worm on dry land expecting to catch a fish?"

"What? No. The fish were in the water."

"Exactly!" she exclaimed with a smile. "Exactly! You had to go to where the fish were. If I want to help people, I have to go to the places that have people that need help, right? Look at your shirt. Some cartoon hero I assume, right? You telling me that guy never went to places he didn't necessarily want to go for the greater good? Honey, I'm fine. Don't you worry about me. If I'm doing what I'm supposed to be doing, it's all good." She smiled. She seemed to be happy. Her smile looked authentic. He felt her emotions. It wasn't just that she was happy: she was content. It wasn't that she had needs. She was just happy and content to be doing what she was doing where she was doing it. She was at peace: a peace which, to Dex, defied logic and understanding.

"Well," she said taking a hold of his hand once more, "take care. And don't be a stranger. It's always good to see a friendly face around here. And relax- there's a plan and a reason. Just take care of your loved ones and yourself." She smiled and she was off. Jules walked back over to Dex.

"Well, I think that's all the sandwiches. Shall we go?" Dex nodded and followed Jules. After they left The Bridge, Dex finally asked Jules the question he had been waiting to ask.

"You knew about Cindy, didn't you?"

"Oh of course: she's a peach."

"No, I mean, you know she's a Healer, right?"

"Yes of course."

"Then why is she there?" Jules looked at Dex.

"You already asked her that question. Why would you ask me?"

"Because it's not right." Jules stopped walking.

"According to whom? You? Are you sure you want that responsibility?"

"I am just saying that..." Jules interrupted Dex.

"Let me stop you there. Whatever you are thinking, whatever you may say, it's not going to change the fact that she's there because she wants to be there. She is called to be there. I get there once a month. My main job is to provide them with food and some healthcare. Sometimes local churches drop off items or food, but not as often as they need. Cindy is there 24/7. She's caring for their physical, mental, and emotional needs. Could she be somewhere else? Yes: she could. Does she want to be? No: she doesn't. She is where she is supposed to be. It may not make sense to you, but eventually everything works out how it is supposed to." He turned and walked towards a construction site with a trailer in the foreground. He pulled out the Skeleton Key as they approached the trailer door. "Terrible things happen daily. We can't change those things. The things we are meant to change- that's our fate or destiny or whatever you call it. And we do the best we can with the hands we are dealt."

"And you're okay with that answer?" Jules shrugged.

"It's the only answer that makes sense. It's all I got because I have faith." He opened the door and stepped through into the stared corridor once again. "Now come on: we have more training." They walked up the stairs back to a large gymnasium. This one was lined with different weapons. Dex could see halberds, staves, and a whole host of different weapons over the walls. There was a person standing in the middle of the room. She stood in workout clothes with her hands taped up. She had short blonde hair slicked back and a nose piercing. She was well toned with what Dex would consider a six-pack. Instantly, Dex felt inferior. Sure, he was in okay shape, but this woman would utterly destroy him in one on one combat.

"Dex, this is Mary. She sits on The Council with Jude. The Council will oversee your field team and send you on missions."

"Hey. How's it's going?" Dex said rather kindly.

"Fine," she replied curtly. "I'm here because Jules asked me to test your combat skills. By the looks of that sword there you're what: some kind of mall ninja?" She raised an eyebrow when she said that. "That internet BS won't fly when you have someone actively trying to kill you." Dex was angry. How dare she make assumptions about him? Who was she that she thought she could come in here and just call him out like that?

"Mary is our Battle Master. She is responsible for assessing the combat readiness of all new recruits. She's a Healer like you and incredibly skilled at many forms of hand to hand combat." Dex could feel Jules' emotions. It was a sort of giddiness. Jules was anticipating what was about to happen like someone about to see a live boxing match.

"Is that your weapon?" she asked. "Do you actually know how to use that thing?"

"Why don't you come find out?" Dex asked. He was getting hot. He could feel energy bubbling up inside of him. Hold it together, he told himself. No need to lose control.

"Oh honey: I'd love nothing more than to beat your ass for real," she said sarcastically. "Sadly, I have rules to follow. Go find a practice blade."

"Why?" Dex asked in a mocking tone. "You scared I might hurt you?"

"Only if I let you."

"Then you don't have anything to fear. I know how to pull my punches." Mary laughed. She looked at Jules.

"So what do I do with this? This boy has a death wish. You trust him to not let me kill him?" she asked.

"I'll allow it. I'm curious," Jules said. Mary shrugged.

"Well okay then," she said. She looked at Dex assessing him for a moment. Who was this punk, she thought to herself? She thought he had an air of superiority. Was that it? No: it had to be something else. This kid either had an axe to grind or a burning desire to prove himself. Mary disliked that. She couldn't stand people who thought for some reason or another that they were better than others. What did this kid have that she didn't have? Sure: he has some training, but does that mean he was better than her? Mary was set to prove him wrong. She walked over to the wall after studying him and decided on a katana as well.

"I figured that I could at least show you how to use that thing," she said with a cocky smile. Before Dex could respond, Jules shouted.

"Begin!"

Mary took off in a sprint straight towards him. Damn she's fast, Dex thought to himself. She raised the blade to her left side. Obviously, Dex thought, she was going to attack on the left side. Dex unsheathed Ruach with the sound of a rushing wind. He was ready. Block the first attack, he thought. She raised her blade up, readying a might blow. Dex was there to parry it. He smirked to himself. Yet Mary smirked as well. Dex looked confused. He didn't notice her right leg moving. It hit Dex right in the head. His world went black for a second and then he regained his composure. She was on the attack again. He parried the next blow and jumped back this time. Not this time, he thought. This woman was serious. He realized that he would have to go on the offensive if he was going to make any headway in the battle.

Now it was his turn to run. He ran straight to her but didn't raise his blade. He didn't want to announce his attack as she did. She ran straight to him as well. At the last possible second, she dropped to her knees and swung her sword behind her. Dex realized that she was going for his legs. He had only moments to react. Suddenly, as if by some deep-seated instinct, his entire body felt warm. It was the same warming feeling when he channeled energy earlier. Dex didn't know what happened, only that he did a front flip out of nowhere to avoid the slash at his shins.

He landed behind her. He brought his blade up high and started to bring it down towards her. She looked up and blocked it. Mary used her knees as a springboard and jumped do her feet pushing Dex's blade up high. Her left leg extended behind her, kicking Dex square in the stomach. It hurt, but Dex quickly healed himself.

"Are you going to actually hit me or not?" She asked with a cold smile. Dex was getting madder. His body felt warmer. It wasn't just in his chest: it was his whole body. It was as if positive energy was started to flood his entire being. That was Dex realized what was happening. He wasn't just a Healer: he was a Conduit. His entire being was being flooded with positive energy. His muscles burned- not with pain or weariness, but with potential energy. He could use this, he thought. If he gave himself to this power, he would easily overpower her. There was still some part of Dex, however, that knew he couldn't do that. He understood that. If he suddenly got much stronger, it would be suspect. No: he reasoned that he would have to keep this power under wraps. After all, that was the plan. No one outside of a select few could actually know about what Dex could do.

While this was very easy to say and reason out, it was more difficult to accomplish. The power inside of Dex yearned to be set free. It was as if his body was begging him to be used to its fullest potential. But Dex knew that wasn't the right answer. An internal struggle began inside of Dex. Not only was he fighting against Mary, who was very skilled, but he had to now fight against himself. Mary could tell that something was off. Something shifted. She wasn't sure what it was, but something had just happened. Dex seemed to be struggling now. That made no sense to her. He was good. It was obvious that he had some training. So then what changed? She decided to test him. While locked together in a battle pose, she headbutted him. Stars filled her eyes as well as his. Each healed themselves and shook it off, though a bit of blood came out of Dex's nose.

"Enough of this," she spat. "Stop it. Whatever you're doing, stop it now. What: just because I'm a girl you're holding back?"

"No!" Dex protested. It would be so much easier to just tell her the truth. He wasn't holding back because of sexism. The truth was he was afraid of what he could really do if he let it all go. He knew there was power inside of him. He could feel it. The problem was he just didn't know how much. He decided that the best course of action was a simple half-truth. "I promised I wouldn't kill unless I had to. I don't want to hurt you."

Mary looked Dex, studying him for a moment. She was trying to figure him out. He obviously had talent. She knew he could do well but holding back wasn't the way to do that. One last gamble, she thought to herself. One last chance to see what he was made of. She charged again, aiming the point of her blade straight at him. In training, it was important to train as if you may have to kill your opponent. This was why training weapons and gear was so important. But they were past that now.

Dex watched as she ran towards him. She's trying to literally kill me, he thought to himself. Her face was covered with determination. Her eyes were a blaze, but what with what? It wasn't rage or hatred. It wasn't even anger. No, Dex decided. It was a type of concern mixed with anger. He felt her concern for him. She wasn't angry that he had skill. She was concerned that for some reason he was still holding back. Fine, Dex decided. Just a bit. Let just a bit out. This time, he would control it. He willed the energy to build inside of him. He felt the warmth all over his body. His eyesight became sharper. His breathing slowed.

He took off straight towards her. Right downward slash: her blow was easily blocked. She brought her blade up, but with incredible speed Dex was able to once again block that blow as well. Each time she swung, Dex was already there blocking him. Mary knew she couldn't make any headway. Dex knew this as well. He was overcome with déjà vu and he knew what was about to happen. He knew she would do one more strike and move to punch him in the face. He blocked the sword slash and looked at her right fist. It came towards his face. He could have easily blocked it. It wouldn't have been hard at all. He knew it was coming and he could have easily literally disarmed her.

Instead, he allowed it to hit him square in the face. It didn't even hurt as the energy flowing inside of him was constantly healing him at this point. Mary stood up and put her sword away. She looked almost disgusted.

"Why?" she asked. "Why did you do that?"

"Do what?" he asked, returning the energy to him and returning Ruach to its sheath.

"You gave up. Why?"

"I didn't," Dex protested. "you punched me in the face- nothing I could do about that." Mary looked at him.

"You're good enough to not get yourself killed. You held back almost the entire fight. You fought defensively. You barely showed any offense at all. In this line of work, sometimes you have to get your hands dirty. You better come to grips with that now. You won't get killed, but you're going to get a team member killed one day." With that, she turned and walked away. "Keep an eye on this one, Jules. Something's not right with him yet."

"It's his first day," Jules offered. Mary shook her head.

"That's not what I meant, but I'm pretty sure you already knew that." She turned to look at Dex. "I'll see you next week. You better bring you're 'A' game next time." With that, she exited the gym. After she left, Dex turned to Jules.

"So this is your master plan is it?"

"What do you mean?" Jules asked.

"Don't give me that," Dex spat out. "You tout all this 'master plan' crap and you pull something like that? You put in me a no-win situation. You knew- you knew that I couldn't control all of this... whatever it is."

"You did remarkably well," Jules countered. "For your first real battle understanding your abilities..."

"But I don't understand them!" Dex interrupted. "I have barley a vague grasp at best as to how this crap works. All I know is I have to work extra hard in battle to control this." Dex's breath was heavy. He was angry. None of this seemed fair or even right to him. There was a heavy silence in the room. Jules understood Dex's frustration. Dex didn't understand anything. He didn't understand the role he specifically had to play and for now. It had to be that way. Finally, after a bit, Jules decided to address Dex.

"I had thought that this would be the best way to show you. I thought that showing you the need to hold back in real time would be a valuable lesson. If I have erred in this, I truly am sorry. As it stands, we only have one more training exercise. And this one isn't weekly." Jules removed his poncho and folded it with care. He walked over to the side of the room and placed it gently on the floor. He removed his hat and placed it on top of his poncho on the floor. He was now wearing a simple white karate gi.

"So go for it," Jules said standing in the middle of the room. "Pull out your sword and go all out against me."

"No," Dex said. "You don't have a weapon. It wouldn't be fair."

"I've been a Conduit for a while now. Trust me: it will be fine." Jules took a battle-ready stance and his fists began to glow. "If you want to know what you're capable of, then now is the time. I can promise you this: when you unleash your full power, you'll understand better."

Dex wasn't sure what to do. It seemed odd and dangerous. However, this was his life now. Normality was gone forever. He pulled his blade out and swung it at Jules, igniting it with positive energy. Jules calmly placed a hand up to block it. Okay then, Dex thought. Let's do this. Their battle was long, lasting for well over an hour. All inhibitions were let go. Each attacked the other with a wealth of power. Dex found the whole experience to be rather transforming. He got it. He understood. He didn't just understand what he was capable of, but he understood the responsibly he had. He understood the weight of it all.

After the battle, while they were cleaning up the rubble, Jules suddenly embraced Dex.

"I am so proud of you."

"Why? I didn't even do anything."

"You're wrong. You changed. Remember: I can see your truth. You get it. You're starting the understand the weight of everything now."

"Then tell me why all the secrets."

"Sometimes we have to do things blindly. We have to walk in faith not knowing where our feet will land. I'm asking you to have some faith-at least have some faith in me. Please." His eyes were begging with Dex. He really believes in all of this, doesn't he? In the depths of his soul, Dex realized that Jules is a firm believer in what he is doing. If he was being honest with himself, it worried Dex. He wasn't sure if Jules's faith in him was misplaced or not, but he knew that such conviction was can be a dangerous tool.

The evening ended with a host of leather-bound books given to Dex to read at his leisure. The books were written by Conduits of The Order past and contained a breath of knowledge. One, in particular, was one the subject of vampires and how a Conduit had the ability to cure them of their state. Jules was kind enough to use the Skeleton Key to take Dex straight to his house. He reminded Dex that this training would be once a week and Dex obliged. They said their good nights, and Dex entered the house.

Neil was sitting on the couch watching an episode of My Hero Academia. When they noticed that Dex walked in, they paused the tv on a smiling image of the pro-hero All Might.

"Well look at you, Mr. Marathon man," Neil quipped. "And how was your day?"

"It went as well as can be expected," Dex answered getting a water bottle from the fridge. He walked over to the couch to join them.

"So that's all I get?"

"Well, I mean, how do I know I can even trust you?" Dex replied sarcastically. Neil punched him in the arm.

"Words can hurt, Dex."

"Yeah it was just a joke. Anyway, I mean, it was fine. Pretty intense all things considered. Gotta do all this once a week for a while."

"Yeesh," Neil said with a grimace. "That's rough, buddy."

"Not so bad," Dex replied with a shrug. "It will all be worth it in the end, I suppose." Neil got excited suddenly.

"Dude! They are totally going to put us on a team together. We'll have missions to go on. We'll get a Psyker and a Prophet. It's going to be so awesome." Neil took a drink of his tea. "So what's your code name going to be?"

"Dude, I'm not giving myself a code name."

"That's no fun!" Neil pouted. "I mean, if we're going to be superheroes, we may at least as well have code names." Dex looked over at Neil.

"You already picked one out, didn't you?" A little embarrassed, Neil responded,

"Maybe..."

"So what is it?" Neil rubbed the back of their neck.

"It's... um... so I was thinking maybe along the lines of Superstar. Because, you know, the whole bright light thing." Dex wanted to laugh, but he imagined Neil would be hurt if he laughed at them.

"I mean I think that's a good name," Dex said sympathetically. "It fits you." Neil smiled.

"You would just go by your full name," Neil said. "I mean, it already sounds pretty cool. So that can be you." Dex laughed. He suddenly started to feel sore. He hadn't been feeling it but now he realized that Jules wasn't near him. The healing aura wasn't around him, so he was starting to feel the effects of the day.

"Yeah, that's not a bad idea. So listen: I'm gonna head upstairs for a bit. Kinda feeling tired."

"What do you want for dinner?" Neil asked.

"I don't know. Just make whatever. I need a nap or something. I'm, like, exhausted."

"Understandable. I'll see you in a bit."

Dex trekked upstairs, his head full of the day's events. He had run a marathon of training and was no closer to any answers about anything. He only knew he had to keep moving forward. For whatever reason, this was his life now. He had to keep moving forward. He laid down on his bed, simply drained. He plugged his phone in and pressed shuffle on his playlist. The Flaming Lips began to sing him to sleep. *"'Cause she knows that it's demanding to defeat those evil machines. I know she can beat them. Oh Yoshimi. They don't believe me. But you won't let those robots eat me. Yoshimi: they don't believe me. But you won't let those robots beat me."*

Chapter Five

Several weeks had gone by and April gave way to May. Dex's week began to fall into a sort of rhythm. Thursdays were his all-day training sessions. He began to work at The Cathedral of Heroes three days a week excluding Thursdays, obviously. He worked Wednesdays, Saturdays, and Sundays in the evening. He thought he was rather blessed to be able to work with Neil as much as he did. Wednesdays were the most chaotic as that was when the new comics came out.

All in all, working at the shop provided a sense of normalcy that Dex longed for. In his spare time, when he wasn't training on his own, he still managed to tutor English for students. It became something that he did less and less, though. Eventually, he was certain that he would have to give it up all together. Perhaps this was for the best, he reasoned. His life had seemed to be consumed by this brave new world he found himself in. Never in his wildest imagination did he ever think something like this would happen.

Often times, Dex wondered what his parents would think of all of this. How would they have reacted? Then again, if his parents were still around, would any of this ever happened? This thought kept him up at night sometimes. After all, if his parents never died, then he would have never been at the cemetery that day. On the other hand, it seemed plausible that he still would have had his powers. He wasn't gifted powers by some terrible accident and his parents' deaths, while tragic, didn't force him to adopt this lifestyle. More likely than not, it was something that he was born with. It was either that, or he was specifically chosen for these powers. He had been reading the books Jules gave him and while they were a breath of knowledge, they didn't exactly provide any answers to this question. Eventually, he reasoned, all of this power would have come out in some form. Dex just wished his parents were. There with him guiding them in person instead of via memories and lessons.

As a part of his training, he made sure to still make time to visit with Ophelia. It wasn't so much that he made time per say, but she would just show up at his house. Like clockwork. Always at the same time on Friday mornings. It got to the point where he would wake up early to make sure the door was unlocked. She would walk in quietly, almost always reading a different manga or comic and make herself at home. Sometimes they shared breakfast. Other times they watched some tv and simply chatted. One day, Dex decided to ask her a question. He had spent the night before making breakfast muffins. He was up before she got there, readying for their time together. She opened the door and walked straight to the table.

"Blueberry, please," she said as she sat down. Of course, she already knew about the muffins. Nothing hardly suppressed her. She pulled a copy of Books of Doom written by Ed Brubaker and penciled by Pablo Raimondi. He handed her a muffin, which she gladly accepted.

"That's an amazing series," he told her as he went to get some coffee.

"Yes, it is. It very well might be my favorite story about Dr. Doom. He's a very complex character."

"Triumph and Torment is pretty good too," Dex said grabbing a muffin and a coffee as well. Dex looked at Ophelia sitting there, quite comfortable. She looked incredibly relaxed. Dex felt that from her as well. She was calm and content, like most days she came to visit. Suddenly, her emotion changed. There was a slight twitch on her face as she furrowed her brow ever so slowly.

"No, I don't have new pearls of wisdom for you."

"Didn't ask if you did," Dex countered quickly.

"No, but I know what you want to ask, so just ask it." Her voice suggested a hint of... not anger but indignity.

"You already know the question. Why should I even ask it?"

"Because you're supposed to."

"Suppose I don't, though. What then?"

"But you're going to. That's not even an option at this point," she replied. "Because if you don't ask now, you know you'll never get another chance to ask." Damn, Dex thought. She was right. Be it fate or something else, Dex knew this was his chance to ask. He had to do it.

"You haven't taught me anything more than when you first came here. Sure; we have fun and talk and all that, but you don't have to come here. So why do you keep coming?" Ophelia sighed.

"I had thought that at this point, it would be obvious by now. Perhaps I gave you too much credit."

"Look Ophelia, I'm touched and honored that you have a crush on me, but..."

"Excuse me?" she countered quickly. "You think I have a crush on you? I am six years older than you. I'm not a cougar."

"Well, yeah... I mean... you don't? Like have a crush on me?" She placed her book down and held her cup with two hands, enjoying the warmth. After taking a sip, she said,

"Please don't flatter yourself. Though you are not bad to look at, that's not why I come here every week. Truth be told, I am not really one for romance in general. I like companionship. And I enjoy your companionship. But no, I don't want to have some kind of romantic entanglement with you." She took another drink. "You really don't get it, do you?" she asked.

"I feel as if I am missing a few things," Dex admitted, his face reddening. Ophelia smiled a half smile. This was why she came. She wasn't looking for a romantic relationship. She never really saw anyone romantically. No, she liked spending time with Dex because he simply saw her as a person.

"Imagine being in a different world than everyone else, but it has been like that since birth. It's a world where sounds are a bit louder, but only to you. It's a world where things that are supposed to feel soft feel harder than normal to you. And you're in this world since birth. And no one understands until later when the doctors explain to your parents what it all means. Then imagine that world shifts even further. You gain the Sight and suddenly, what was once just chaotic is even more chaotic and loud. And then, you find you can see the future. But, like, in a really strong way. So you get recruited by Jules because he's the first person in a long time to just accept you as you are with no conditions. He doesn't mind that you read all the time in an effort to keep outside stimuli down. He doesn't care if you wear hoodies even in the middle of summer or that you tug your hair when you get nervous. And then, you meet this guy who reminds you of Jules. And you try, for once, to make friends even though it is so much harder for you to do so." Tears welled up in her big brown eyes. She instinctively wiped her eye with her long sleeve, moving her glasses with ease. "So that's why, Dex Machina. No, I'm not in love with you. I just like being around you because you're either really kind and accept me in general or are too stupid to know that I'm on the spectrum. I had assumed that by now it was obvious." She opened her book back up and began reading, yet instinctively began tugging on one of her long braids softly.

Well, there it is, Dex thought. He sighed.

"Ophelia, can I be honest with you?"

"I would hope so after I just bared my soul to you," she replied still reading and tugging her hair.

"So, it was totally the second one, but now that I know... I just want you to know that nothing has changed. Other than I know now. And I didn't mean to offend you or anything. It's just... for the longest time it's just been Neil and I, ya know? And it's nice to know that you aren't working. It's nice to know that we can actually be friends now." He smiled at her. She looked up at him.

"I'm not really a hugger but I know in situations like this it is customary to hug. So please just act as though we hugged, okay?" Dex raised his mug in a toast.

"How about just a toast?"

"Yes," she said softly with a smile. "that will work." They lightly clinked their mugs.

"Honestly," Dex said, "I assumed you and Rhianna were already BFF's."

"No. We are co-workers. She is the definition of the opposite of myself."

"Exactly. Same way Neil is the opposite of myself. I just figured hey-opposites attract."

"I... I wouldn't know where to even begin a friendly relationship with her," she admitted.

"I mean, maybe start with a phone call? Like, 'Hey: want to grab a cup of coffee or something? We can just go to Dex's and steal his.' Not too hard, right?" Ophelia thought for a moment.

"I thought the goal was to make friends. How is that even a possibility with crappy coffee?" She kept her head down towards her book but looked up at Dex.

"I think you'll be fine. Seriously. You're a cool person. Just be yourself."

"Thank you, Dex Machina," she said. Though her face didn't show it, Dex could tell the conversation meant a lot with her.

In truth, Dex had been growing closer with each member of The Four. Well, except for Adrian, but that was its own headache. It wasn't that Adrian was a bad person or anything. Far from it: he was a great person and everything a teacher should be. No, it was, instead that he kept everyone except for Jules at a distance for some reason.

One of the best moments in Dex's training came when he was early for an appointment with Rhianna. Neil was there getting some target practice in.

"Hey," he asked Neil. "Mind if I watch?"

"Dude, I don't know if I can perform with you watching. I'm shy," Neil joked.

"We both know that's a lie," Dex laughed. "No, seriously. I'm supposed to be, like, learning more and more and stuff. So watching you work is probably going to teach me something."

"I mean, It's pretty standard stuff. I see the dummy. I blast the dummy. A new dummy pops up."

"Okay, then how about we have some fun." Dex had a mischievous grin on his face.

"Aw beans... you know the last time I saw that face I wound up dressed like the tooth fairy screaming at a dentist's window 'GIMME YA SMILE BONES!'"

"Okay first, that was hilarious. Second, the tutu is optional this time."

"But it's still on the table?" they asked. "Because if it's not on the table, I'm not sure I want in."

"Dude!" Dex pleaded. "Just listen, okay? So you know I'm a Conduit, right?"

"Yeah..." Neil said cautiously.

"And you know how I showed you the whole glowey/sparkly thing to super charge my body?"

"Yeah..." Neil answered again.

"Okay, so I have this idea that, like, if I focus positive energy around my body while charged up in some way, it will act like armor." Neil thought for a moment.

"Okay, so that is, like, not an unreasonable assumption to be honest."

"Right?" Dex said. "But we haven't been in combat yet for real because they still won't give us our team for some reason. And I can't do it against Mary because the whole secret thing." Realization came across Neil's face.

"Oh, I hate where this is going..." they said with a slight fear in their voice.

"Oh, I *love* where this is going," Dex countered with slight joy in his voice.

"Just to be clear, you're about to ask me to shoot at you, right?"

"Oooooh..." Dex said grinning from ear to ear. "That's a bingo..."

"This is... this is the dumbest idea that you have ever had. And I am so totally here for this." Dex pointed to Neil, smiling.

"Yes! That's my friend! Okay so I'm thinking..." Dex didn't get a chance to finish the sentence, because Neil had grown overzealous and had blasted Dex prematurely. He went flying backward about three feet after the blast rocketed his midsection. He slammed into a dummy and fell.

"Holy crap! Holy crap!" Neil said, panic in their voice. "Dex I am so sorry. I totally misread the situation. Are you okay?"

"Dude!" Dex yelled. "I didn't even have time to power up!"

"What do you have to do some Sailor Moon sort of thing? I didn't know! And you're just gonna pause midbattle and be all, 'Yes good gentle Vampire. Please do not attack me as I become a magical being.' Because I'm pretty sure that isn't going to happen." Dex shook the stars from his eyes and healed himself quickly. He stood back up.

"No; it's fine. I get that. Just, like, give me a moment, okay?" Dex didn't even close his eyes at this point. He had been practicing with flooding his body with positive energy since his first training with Jules. By his estimation, about ten percent of his true power was undetectable. He didn't have to worry about putting off an aura with that amount. "Right," he said with a deep breath. "Hit me." Neil hesitated.

"Like, now?"

"Yes, please."

"Okay so, like, how hard?"

"I don't know, dude! Just like, start with a punch like blast. Like last time."

"Where do you want it?"

"Surprise me!" Dex said with a goofy grin. Neil shrugged and blasted him again. He slid about six inches back but didn't fall.

"Holy crap," Neil exclaimed. It worked!

"Hell yeah it worked!" Dex said. "Do it again! Crank that blast up, though. Let's see how this works." What happened next was a series of shots to Dex from Neil in various degrees of intensity. Finally, Neil blasted Dex hard enough to not only knock him over, but to send him scooting towards the door on his back. It was at that precise moment that both Rhianna and Ophelia walked in the door, holding coffee cups. The two bent over to look at Dex who landed at their feet.

"So," Rhianna said, with her teacher voice, "who wants to tell me what's going on here?"

"Full disclosure: I knew what they were here but not what they were doing. I had assumed they were talking or training, but not like this." Ophelia said quietly.

"So how much did you see?" Dex asked, still lying on his back, attempting to act casual.

"Well, when I opened the door, I saw Neil winding back like he was about to anime blast you into oblivion. Then I saw you take the hit, fall and slide." Dex nodded.

"Yeah, I mean, that pretty much brings us up to date."

"You can get up now," she told Dex.

"Yes, ma'am," he said hurriedly getting to his feet. Rhianna sighed.

"I need you two to be more careful, okay? I don't mind you practicing like this, but it needs to be done in a proper environment, okay?" Neil looked down, embarrassed. Dex looked down too. There was no need to try to read her emotions at this point. She wasn't mad: she was just disappointed. Rhianna sighed. She rolled up her blue shirt a bit. "See this?" One night, I was hanging out with this girl I was interested in. She was trying to be all hardcore playing with a gun. She shot me. Not only that, but we were on a balcony. I fell off and landed on the fence. That coward ran off. She left me there to die because we had both been drinking. Jules was walking by. He moved me and saved me. All of this was before I learned what I could do. But my life could have been over very quickly because I was too busy screwing around. I was young and having fun, but it wasn't safe fun. Please. I am begging you. Just come to me first and we can work all this out, okay? If you want Neil to shoot you, I am totally okay with that. But we need to do it safely, okay?" Neil and Dex nodded.

"Since you two want to train together, go ahead and give me fifty laps. Then we can do some other training," she said as her and Ophelia went over to a table with a few chairs in the corner.

"Fifty?" Neil asked. "That's... I mean that's kind of a lot."

"Yeah. And you need to train the body so hop to it. We're finishing our coffee. And Neil could use the cardio." They sat down with their drinks. Neil looked at Dex and shrugged. They started doing their laps.

As this became more and more normal, Dex also had to balance out an actual "normal" life as well. Part of that was working in the shop. Saturdays were his favorite days to work because in the evening, there was a group that came in to play Dungeons and Dragons. They were a well-knit group with a skilled Dungeon Master. It was always important for Dex to try to listen in to what they were doing. Not only was the story fascinating about a traveling carnival, but it also showed how a diverse team could work together. There was a Tortle, a Tiefling, a Gnome, a Half Elf, and a Loxodon. Each character was unique and brought things to the group. The Loxodon bard inspired the half elf rouge to sneak very well and dispatch four sleeping guards. The Tiefling would use her wits to cast spells in a very effective manner. The Gnome and the Tortle were the tanks, responsible for doing the heavy lifting. Not only that, but if Dex was being honest, it was just fun to listen to.

Dex was enthralled with it all not just because the game itself was fun, but it gave him a chance to learn more about outside the box thinking. Their solutions to problems that they came up with were less than orthodox. It wasn't just a "raid the dungeon and get loot" solution. They worked out how to solve problems in unique ways. For example, Dex couldn't wait to see how the forged artifact gambit would pay off. He reasoned that this too was a part of his training. After all, sometimes you had to take risks. Sometimes the stupid plan that shouldn't work actually did work. He realized that he could easily take these lessons and apply them to when he finally was a part of his own team.

That, however, was problematic in and of itself. Dex and Neil, for all their training and dedication, didn't get assigned a team. They had met with The Council several times, but their answer remained the same-they were working on it. Recruitment was down and they had to find and identify the right people that would mesh well together to form an effective unit.

"Look guys," Jude said sympathetically, "I totally get it. I know you want to get out there and get to work but look at it from our perspective. Let's say that we find a Psyker. Then they have to go through a battery of tests to check out their abilities. Then they have to actually work well with you. Psykers in general link the team together for mental communications. And you don't want just anyone in your head. It's risky. We are working on it."

The Council consisted of four people as well. Jude was the most sympathetic to their plight. Mary, however, was not.

"Plus, after working with you both in combat, I'm not unconvinced you two won't get the team killed anyway. Dex you, specifically, are too cocky while simultaneously refusing to take this seriously." She looked at him in a cold gaze.

"I am working hard. And I can beat you in a fight," he countered.

"Then why don't you? You keep holding back and it's obnoxious."

"I told you. I don't want to hurt you."

"We literally fight with swords! You think some Werewolf or Grafter is going to take it easy on you? You lack a killer instinct and that's dangerous."

"Oh no it's there: I just don't get off on needlessly planning to kill when we can help people." Mary's face became red with anger.

"Some people are beyond saving," she said through gritted teeth.

"And when that comes up, I will deal with it appropriately," Dex said. "But to go in guns a blazing planning on scorching the earth is not my style."

"I think," Tonya interjected, "that we are missing the point. The point is that we really are trying here. There's just a lot of... complications. And we are working it out. Please just trust us." Tonya was the calm, cool center of The Council. As their Channeler, she was pragmatic and realistic, yet handled situations with care and compassion. She was, in Dex and Neil's opinions, the balance between Mary and Jude. Neil spoke up.

"What about it, Paul? Have you seen any leads as to our team will be?" Paul, who was their Prophet, was listening intently as usual while simultaneously a mile away from the conversation. Dex felt urgency emanating from him, but the feeling of déjà vu washed over him and he knew Paul's response.

"I've been looking. I mean, I've been actively looking. I'm trying to guide my visions, but for some reason, there's nothing there. It's... confusing." Dex knew that Paul just told a lie. While it was no doubt confusing, he was also concerned about this fact. That concern worried

Dex. He reasoned out that there was some force out there that was actively trying to obscure Dex and Neil getting a team.

It was then that Neil suddenly blinked rapidly and shot a quick side glance to Dex. Had they had a Psyker with them, they would have enhanced any mental protections that they have. Dex felt it too: a slight pressure in his head. Adrian had decided that it was not only Dex that needed to up his mental defenses, but Neil as well. They trained with Adrian and each other to train their brains to signal to them when someone was rooting around in there. Dex was sure it was Jude. Instantly, they changed their thoughts. Give them something that they expect. Do not think about anything else- no thoughts about a traitor or Dex being a Conduit. Just focus on feeling bad and left out that you don't have a team.

It wasn't as if Jude was being rude. In fact, this was standard procedure. Adrian had taught them that Psykers routinely checked on people's minds to make sure they were okay. Should there be any hint of corruption or anything, they could help guide the people. It was a sort of failsafe in The Council that ensured the teams were functioning as they should be. Jude sighed, looking concerned. He knew that they were trying to hide something, but he didn't know what and that bothered him.

"I'm just trying to protect you. Honestly."

Dex and Neil left the room and headed back to the shop. Once outside, Dex looked at Neil.

"You buy any of that?"

"Not one bit," Neil said. "it doesn't make sense. The Order has offices all over the world. It shouldn't be that hard for someone to be identified as our Prophet or Psyker. Someone is stopping us from getting our team."

"But why?" Dex asked. "What could be gained from doing that?" Neil shrugged.

"It's highly possibly that whoever is doing this isn't even located in this branch. They could be halfway around the world doing it."

"Well then, I guess that settles it," Dex said grimly. "At some point, we may have to go rogue."

"But not, like, in a bad way," Neil interjected. "No: it'll be more, like, a buddy cop movie. Like this whole, 'take your bag and your rules and shove it' and then we go save the world."

"Oh, totally," Dex said. He looked at his watch. "Come on: we gotta head to Big Ralph's Deli. Jules is busy and can't deliver the sandwiches today. So I said you'd help me."

"Next time you volunteer me for outreach, ask first. I had to reschedule a hair appointment." Dex tilted his head and gave Neil a look as if to ask if they were kidding him. Neil quickly countered with, "Not that it's bad. And I rescheduled it for later. Don't give me that look. I hate that look. It was half a joke."

"Jokes are supposed to be funny," Dex countered as they walked.

They made it to Big Ralph's and ate a delightful lunch. After the meeting with The Council, it was nice to have a bit of normalcy. Yet Dex thought that perhaps he had been looking at things differently. Perhaps this was, in a sense, the new normal. Over and over again there had been one phrase that was repeated to him: just go with it. Perhaps this dichotomy that Dex was feeling was a false dichotomy.

"Okay, so how do you manage all of this," Dex asked Neil suddenly.

"I mean it's not that big of a sub so I take it one bite at a time."

"No. Dude, I mean, like, how do you manage living in this world?"

"I mean it's not that big of a world so I take it one bite at a time."

"Dammnit, Neil," Dex said slightly exasperated.

"No, seriously," Neil said. "I mean, I've been at this for a few months prior to you joining. And it was like my world expanded in a huge way. It became massive. The only way I could deal with it was to take it one step at a time. Control what I could control and just roll with everything else. Eventually, it became... I don't know: normal? It at least became manageable." Neil shrugged. "I mean, at least that's my hot take." They took a bite of their sandwich. Dex thought for a moment. Perhaps they were right. Perhaps Dex needed to just slow down and do what he needed to do when he needed to do it. Don't worry about tomorrow because today has enough troubles of its own.

After their meal, they gathered up the boxes of supplies and hopped in Neil's car. Dex took over music duties and shuffled his playlist. His brow furrowed as the song started. *"Like an angel with cruel and merciless intent. Go forth young boy and you'll become a legend."* It was an English cover of Cruel Angel's Thesis by an artist named AmaLee. To be honest, Dex didn't know what to make of this message. It worried him slightly, but he pushed it out of his mind. He had a job to do today so that was what he was going to focus on.

They had parked under The Bridge and got out. After retrieving the boxes, they started to make their way towards the tent city. Dex was suddenly overcome with a strong sense of panic. He looked at Neil, who was fine, albeit a tad hot. No: there was a strong emotion of panic coming from somewhere. Déjà vu came and left Dex with a feeling dread. He took off running with the box as he knew he had to. Neil was confused but followed behind him.

When they got to the tent city, some people were moving out of the way. They were moving and hiding from something. Dex sat his box down and looked at Neil. Their face went white.

"Earworm demon," Neil explained. "It latches on to someone and wrecks their mind."

"Yeah I read some about them. Can you shoot it?" Dex asked. Neil reluctantly shook their head.

"Not if it's still attached to a person. The sudden psychic connection being severed could really hurt them." They looked at the scene once more. There was a man in the middle of a crowd ranting and raving. Cindy was next to him trying to talk him down. Dex understood it wasn't going to work. Around his neck, like some sickening, pulsating boa was a large pink and red worm. What Dex assumed was the head was attached to the man's right ear. He had a gun in his hand.

"They don't care!" he screamed, as tears streamed down his face. "No one cares! God doesn't care! We are the forgotten and the lost!"

"Dale, you know that's not true: people do care about us!" Cindy protested.

"Lies! We are here! No one else!" Cindy looked over to Dex and Neil.

"Look! We have guests! And they care, right? You both care about us." She looked at them, her eyes pleading.

"Yeah we care. Let's just put the gun down and talk," Neil said gently. They started to move towards the man, but he raised his gun at them.

"Don't you move! Don't you dare come any closer! You all don't give a damn about us here! Using us to feel good about yourselves." Cindy moved closer.

"Dale, that's not true. They really do care. I know these two. They really care about us." The worm around him pulsated and glowed a dull red.

"Liar!" he screamed as he swung his arm towards Cindy. Neil moved quickly, their hand brought to shoot the gun from Dale's hand, but it was too late. There was a flash and a bang. Cindy fell over, spun around by the shot hitting her body. Dex took off reaching his arm out to Cindy, starting to heal her. Dale swung the gun around and pointed it at Neil, who raised his hands, the glowing starting to subside. They didn't want to hurt this man. They wanted to help him.

Dex made it over to Cindy, who began to stir. The bullet began to push itself out of the wound on her shoulder, but she was still bleeding.

"Are you okay?" He asked her, still healing her.

"I just got shot, but I'm alright. I can heal this now. You stopped it from going through me. Forget about me: just help Dale!" He looked down as Cindy touched her shoulder. The hole was already starting to close. He stood up and faced Dale, who swung his arms frantically between Dex and Neil who inched towards each other.

"Hey. Dale, was it? It's okay. Keep the gun pointed at me," Dex said putting up his invisible armor. "It's all going to be fine. We just want to help you. Neil. Stand behind me, please." Dex wasn't sure how his skill would work against a bullet, but he knew he had a better chance of not getting hurt. Neil slid behind him, arms still up.

"We gotta get that thing off of him," Neil told Dex quietly.

"How?"

"I don't know, man. If we force it, it's gonna hurt him. We have to convince him somehow not to listen to the thing."

"You here to just make yourself feel better, huh? Slumming it with us scumbags then off to your homes and jobs and all that crap, huh?" He started looking for a next target. Dex started to walk towards him.

"Hey! Keep it on me," Dex said. "Point that thing at me and we can help you. You want help, don't you?" The worm began to pulsate and glow once more.

"I'm sick of this! I'm sick of living like this!"

"I get it," Dex tried.

"Like hell you do!" Dale shouted. Okay. This wasn't working, Dex thought to himself. Time for something else. Dex looked at the man. He was scared, his wide eyes filled with fear and tears. He had been talking about being forgotten, not being seen. What was the demon telling him? What was it saying to him? Suddenly, Dex remembered a time his mother was busy with housework while his father was working. All he wanted to do was play, but Neil couldn't come over and his mother was busy. He found one of his dad's screw drivers and started carving stars into the bannister. He had gotten in trouble for that, but the plan worked. She stopped what she was doing and was paying attention to him. Dex felt it then. This man was overcome with sadness. All he wanted in the world was for someone to actually know him- to see and to hear him.

"Follow my lead," Dex told Neil. With his arms still up, he inched closer. "Dale," he said to the man, "my name is Dex. This is my friend Neil. We've been friends since we were kids."

"Hi Dale," Neil said with a nervous smile. "It's nice to meet you. Why don't you tell us more about yourself?" Dale looked confused.

"What's the point? So you can share this story and look like heroes?"

"No," Dex replied, shaking his head. "We just want to get to know you." Neil understood now. Make a connection with him.

"Yeah," Neil added. "Like, okay: I was kicked out of my house at eighteen. I moved in with Dex and his parents then. Been living with him ever since." Dale's eyes leaked tears as the worm began to activate.

"You live with his parents? You actually have a family?"

"Not exactly," Dex said. Damnit, he thought. Did he really have to go this far? He guessed he really wasn't left with much of an option at this point. "My... um... my parents died a few years back. Neil is the only real family I have." It's not that it hurt Dex to talk about. He just didn't want to. There was, however, an affect it had on Dale. The gun dropped slightly even though the worm was still glowing.

"You lost people..." he said quietly. Dex and Neil nodded. "I lost people, too," he said.

"Can I ask what happened?" Neil said.

"Two tours in Afghanistan. Squad got hit by a roadside bomb. Lost most of them then. When we got back, the rest didn't want anything to do with me. They wanted to move on and not think about it. It was all I could think about..." Dale lowered the gun further as Dex and Neil crept closer. "Ya know, when you're over there, it's all 'support the troops' and all that crap. But when you get back? What do you get? You get forgotten. You get a VA that takes too long. You get treated like a monster just because you wanted to help. Support the troops my ass," he said bitterly.

"It hurts to lose people," Dex offered, "and it hurts to be forgotten. All you want to do is be seen. And I see you. Neil sees you. Cindy sees you. Dale, you're a valid person." Dex could feel the confusion and confliction inside of Dale. He wanted to feel what Dex was saying, but he felt too far gone and forgotten. Dex placed his hand Dale's shoulder. It was the first sympathetic touch he had felt in a long time. He startled him: not because it was a shocking touch, but because it was sympathetic. It almost felt warm to Dale. However, he was conflicted. He didn't realize his confliction was due to the earworm demon working so hard to destroy him. It was working overtime now since there was a glimmer of hope in Dale. There was no recourse left for the demon.

"I'm so sorry," Dale said sniffling and crying. "I am so very sorry..." He placed the gun underneath his chin.

"No!" Dex shouted. There was a flash. There was a surge of power in Dex. He moved with incredible speed. Dex placed his hand on the muzzle. The blast hurt his hand, but it didn't pierce skin. Dale was wide eyed in amazement. Dex moved his hand and shook it as if it just got struck.

"Why?" he asked quietly.

"I told you cared about you," Dex responded, checking out his hand.

A quick heal took the pain away but other than it being sore, he was fine. That was all it took for the demon to detach Dale. It slowly unraveled from his neck and fell to the ground, slithering away. Neil looked at it.

"Ope! That one's for me." They calmly shot the demon with a large blast, turning it to ash to be blown away. "Right. Now, everyone else okay? We good? Because we have a bunch of sandwiches here." Cindy came over and hugged Dale.

"You stupid, stupid, man..." she cried as she hugged him tight. "We have to stick together. We are here for each other, you got that?" She looked at Dex. "This one is just like Jules. I promise you can trust him." Dale wiped his nose on his already dirty coat.

"Yeah, well, let's go. I know the way to the police station but I'd rather ride if that's okay." He started heading off towards the car.

"Why would we go there?" Dex asked confused.

"Because of the gun and all that," he said.

"How about I take the gun and get rid of it? And you can have a sandwich. And I'll see about getting some more supports for you. Would that work?" Dex asked. He looked at Cindy. "It that okay with you?" She nodded.

The rest of the time under The Bridge was uneventful. Dex pulled double duty and made sure everyone was physically healthy. Everyone was fed and they were all doing well. Dex and Neil said their goodbyes and headed back to the car. Dex had already called in a favor from a student he tutored who was working for a social work degree. She agreed to stop by under The Bridge and talk to Dale about what supports not only he needed but for the community as well.

They reached the and sat down, finally breathing for a moment because of all the excitement.

"It is **criminal**," Neil said, raising their voice for emphasis, "that we don't have a team. We handled that so good, bro."

"It wasn't even, like, a real mission."

"Yeah but we made a difference. We actually did some good. And no one got hurt. Do you realize how easy it is for that situation to have gone sideways? We didn't have a Psyker. And we handled it by ourselves. I see this as an absolute win!" Dex had to agree. It was a good feeling. It was a win. And he could see how they would be great in the field.

By the time the end of July rolled around, Dex had a better understanding of his powers as a Conduit. He was now, more than ever, itching for a team. Yet still, much to his frustration, there was no team given to them. This would have been all well and good, but sadly it was at this point that the dreams began.

Chapter Six

The dreams began innocently enough. After all, who hasn't dreamed of a beautiful woman before? After the first one, Dex barely thought about it at all. Dex was more confused by the fact that he remembered it vividly as most of his dreams were forgotten to the dreaming upon waking. No: this dream was different. It seemed so... real to Dex. It wasn't something that was out of the ordinary. Instead, it was just a very fast and quick conversation. Yet, for some reason it stuck with Dex. It bothered him simply because he remembered it. He had flashes of dreams that he may have remembered before. After all, how often does one lead the Justice League? But this was different. It seemed to not even be a dream.

When he awoke after the first dream, he remembered it all very clearly. There was a woman on a cruise ship. She wore a red dress and had jet black hair in a bob style haircut. And her eyes. Those ice blue eyes...

"Dex?" she asked. "Dex Machina?" Her ice blue eyes seemed to pierce his soul and almost freeze them.

"Um... yeah?" he responded rather confused. She smiled.

"Good. I found you. That will make this easier."

"Make what easier?" Dex asked.

"This whole thing. But this is all I get for now. First contact is too dangerous to keep up long due to physic energy of emotions going off making it easier to track. But we will talk again, okay?" Dex couldn't do anything else other than nod an affirmative. Then his alarm went off. He didn't notice it at first and it was folded into his dream. He heard it in the midst of his dream while he watched the woman with the black hair walk away. *"With your feet on the air and your head on the ground. Try this trick and spin it: yeah. Your head will collapse, but there's nothing in it. Yeah. And you'll ask yourself..."*

His eyes snapped open to Black Francis of The Pixies *singing "Where is my mind? Where is my mind?"* He rubbed the sleep from his eyes sighed, still not being able to make heads or tails of what just happened. She looked nice in more than one way, Dex thought. How long had it been since he had an honest date? It had to be almost a year by now. That had to be all it was. For some reason, his subconscious was creating a woman looking for him. Obviously, this just meant that he should get back out there and date.

Dex laughed at the absurdity of that thought. Good lord. I'm seeking direction from dreams like I'm some TV doctor quack. It was a dream and nothing more. Period. End of discussion.

A week later, Dex had all but forgotten about the woman in the red dress. After all, there were a dozen more important things to worry about. He was glad that his friend had kept her word and had gotten some support for Dale and the others under The Bridge. Alice, his friend, had set up intern hours for her class to interview and identify supports and services the people needed. There was real headway being made here and Dex, as well as Jules and Cindy, were overjoyed.

"We should go and celebrate," she told him over the phone.

"Yeah we should. We can gather up the class and just go have some fun." Had they been together in person, the Dex would have noticed her blushing.

"Um, actually I was thinking more just you and I like, we could go get some drinks or something."

"Yeah, you're probably right. It would be hard to get everyone together." Unbeknownst to Dex, it was at this point Neil's head slid around into the door frame, an interested look on their face. Alice and Dex made a plan to meet at Cocoa's House which was a high-end bar that specialized in drinks and chocolate fondue. Neil was grinning ear to ear. Dex looked at them with a quizzical look on their face.

"Someone has a date..." they said in a sing song voice.

"It's not a date. It's just two people getting together for drinks." There was silence. Neil looked at Dex. They raised their eyebrows at Dex. He sat there for a moment, the gears in his brain working it all out. Realization settled on Dex like an atomic bomb.

"Oh..." he whispered.

"Yep," replied Neil smiling.

"I didn't sign up for a date!"

"Oh, but you just did!"

"Crap," Dex finally said. He looked at Neil with pleading in his eyes. "I am not looking for romantic companionship!"

"Not my problem!" Neil said throwing their arms in the air. "This is very literally a you problem, not a Neil problem." Neil backed away to their room.

"Traitor!" Dex yelled after them. He sighed. Well, he supposed that he had a date in a week now.

Later that night, he decided it was time for bed and he laid down. His head was still swimming. He wasn't sure where dating really fell into this world he found himself in. Suppose, he thought, he did enter into a relationship with someone who was Blind and didn't have the Sight. He would then have to lead a double life full of secrets, right? Or his partner's mind would fill in the blanks as best it could. On the other hand, if his partner had the Sight, then that would also present difficulties. It would be logical to assume that either way, they would be in danger. He wasn't really sure what to do with all of this.

Eventually, he fell asleep though his head was still running in circles. Normally, this wouldn't have been an issue, but he found himself back on the cruise ship with the woman in the red dress.

"You have a date?" she asked laughing.

"I mean I feel like it's just two friends going out for a drink. I don't view it as a date." She shook her head.

"It doesn't matter what you view it as. It matters what she views it as."

"Okay," Dex said, "but I don't even know who you are."

"Crap," she said. "I wasted time. Okay, look- all you have to know right now is that you have to find me."

"Delightful!" he yelled. "I don't know who you are and now I have a mission? Can you give me some help?" She sighed and looked sad.

"Yeah, but not right now. Just know that you have to find me."

He woke up.

Dex could have chalked up the first dream to some strange subconscious message, but this one was different. This time, however, couldn't be a coincidence. Could it? He decided to consult with Neil about this.

"Bro I literally have no clue what you're talking about. I go pew-pew with laser hands. I have no idea about mind stuff. Anything in those books Jules gave you?" This breakfast conversation was not very helpful so far. Dex shook his head.

"Sadly, they haven't been helpful in that regard. However, I did find that the only way to heal a Vampire is if you're a Conduit. So I got that going for me, which is nice."

"You should ask Adrian," Neil suggested.

"Let's call that Plan Z," Dex replied with a look of concern on his face. Neil shrugged.

"I mean, ask Jude?"

"Nope. Can't do that."

"Why not?" Neil asked.

"Because this seems really weird and I am unsure if it should be public knowledge..."

"Oh," Neil said quietly. They hadn't even thought about that issue. It was possibility. "If that's the case, then literally the only help you can get on this is from The Four. Specifically, Adrian." It was at this point Ophelia walked through the door.

"Hello Dex. Hello Neil." She walked into the kitchen and started pouring herself a bowl of cereal. She looked at them. "Yes: I know the conversation. That's part of the reason I'm here. The other part is because I like your cereal selection and coffee."

"I'll make you a cup," Dex said.

"So is this, like, what you two do?" Neil asked.

"Pretty much," Dex and Ophelia said together. Neil made an acknowledging face and nodded. They looked at Ophelia. "So, do you have any insights for our boy, here?" She pulled out a trade paperback collection of Fantastic Four comics.

"This collection begins at Fantastic Four issue number five-hundred and seventy. It's the official start of Johnathan Hickman's run on

Fantastic Four in which Reed Richards seeks to solve everything." She opened the book and began reading it. "Do you know I selected this book for the start of my reading today?" Dex shrugged. "Neither do I. But I knew I was supposed to be reading it today." Neil sighed.

"Not helpful," they said finally.

"No," Dex interjected. "It's extremely helpful. It was the start of a new creative team that reshaped and redefined the Fantastic Four as a series." He looked at Neil. "It was the beginning." Neil thought on this for a moment.

"I'm sorry: I'm not super used to all of this. Can someone please explain this to me?"

"Essentially," Dex explained to Neil, "this is an omen of a beginning. A beginning of what we don't know. But this is the start of something. This is, specifically, a start of trying to solve things. But it could also mean I'll mess up, but that I will keep trying. You kind of have to, like, read between the lines with this and make some assumptions."

"Very rarely do I pick something to read for fun. Coincidence isn't a world I live in," Ophelia said, reading and spooning some cereal into her mouth.

"Okay, but still I don't see how this is helpful. Like, it just signifies something beginning..." realization spread across Neil's face.

"There you go," Ophelia said quietly. Neil was giddy.

"This is it. This is the beginning of... whatever it is we have to do, isn't it?" Dex nodded solemnly.

"Time to get to work, Superstar," Ophelia said taking a sip of her coffee. Neil looked wide-eyed at Dex.

"Dude! What's the point of a secret code name if it isn't a secret?"

"Dex didn't tell me. I saw you say it a while back and was waiting for the right time to use it."

"The point," Dex interjected, "is that this is big news. Whoever this woman is, we have to find her. And she has been less than helpful in that regard."

"Obviously," Neil replied. "This is, like, top level secret stuff here."

"But," replied Dex, "we still don't know if she's the problem or not. So we have to tread carefully. I mean, why not just call or text or something?"

"Because that's too easily monitored, duh. She obviously thought this was the best way to get in touch with you. Which means she's a Psyker," Neil answered. Ophelia looked up and said,

"Honestly, you don't have to be a Prophet to figure out the next move here." Dex closed his eyes and drew in a big breath. He let it out slowly. He knew what he had to do.

"Fine," he said begrudgingly. "I'll go talk to Adrian. Either of you two coming?"

"Dude, I'm a Channeler. Plus it's your dreams- not mine." Neil put his hands up in protest.

"No," Ophelia said quietly. "I want to finish my coffee and eat my cereal."

"I mean, I can wait?" Dex said rather desperately.

"No. This way I can get to know Neil more."

"Ugh!" Dex said in protest. "Fine. You cowards. I'll be back later." He made his way to the door. Once the truck roared out of the driveway, Ophelia looked at Neil.

"Have a seat," she said reading.

"Oh fun! Is this, like a free tarot card reading or something?"

"No," she replied sternly. "This is a very serious conversation."

"So no fun, then?" they asked innocently.

"Fun can be had later. But right now, I need to ask what you know about Hickman's run on Fantastic Four." Neil ran their hand through their hair.

"Not a whole lot to be honest. I know Dex loved it. I know it led to The Future Foundation."

"Why did it lead to that?" Ophelia asked.

"Because Hickman killed off Johnny Storm for a while..." their voice trailed off. "Look, I'm not as patient as Dex. You have to speak clearly to me." Ophelia sighed.

"It could be nothing. It could be that I'm over analyzing things here, which happens from time to time. The fact that this run ends in death and you mentioned tarot cards is rather ominous to me."

"Aw, beans..." Neil replied sadly. "So, who is it? Who is going to die? Because there's, like, a lot I haven't done. I never got to see Venice..." Neil was trying their best to deflect this with humor. Ophelia shook her head.

"The death card doesn't work like that. It just means an end of some kind and self-reflection. It doesn't usually mean regular death."

"Cool. We're in the clear," Neil said relived. Ophelia shook her head again.

"No. Because an ending could be death. Truth be told, something is hindering certain psychic and prophetic powers right now. We're flying sort of blind at this point."

"That's not super helpful or encouraging," Neil admitted sadly.

"I hear that a lot. But it's true. Whatever is going to happen is going to happen. And I know Dex. He can kind of roll with the punches. He's working on it. But he takes loss to heart and it nearly destroys him." She put her book down and locked eyes with Neil. It was uncomfortable for her, but she had to do it. She started tugging on one of her braids. "Whatever happens next, he's going to need you. You're his rock."

"Awesome. No pressure there. I mean, yes, of course I'll be there for him. It will be fine. We can get through this. We've gotten though other crap before."

"I'm glad to hear it," she said reassured.

"So what now? What do we do now? Do we, like, paint each other's nails or something?" Neil asked. She shrugged.

"To be honest your nails need a touch up. And by the looks of them I wouldn't trust you to do mine." Neil laughed.

"Dex said you had a sense of humor. I didn't believe him, but here we are."

"As it so happens, Rhianna wanted to have a spa day. And she wanted me to ask you to come along. And you're going to say yes."

"What if I say no?" Neil asked.

"You won't. It's a free spa day and the chance to get to know your mentor outside of a learning environment. You've been dying for a chance like this." Neil opened their mouth in protest but said nothing.

"I.. I... I'll go get my keys," they said through gritted teeth.

While Neil and Ophelia got to know one another, Dex headed off to the comic store. He wasn't really in the mood for any music. He had too much to think about. He couldn't shake the feeling that there was more to this than he realized. He was also concerned that he wasn't being told everything. Plus, now he had a kind-of sort-of date thing to deal with. To add to everything else, he had to go to talk to Adrian which would be... difficult. While he was sure he had proven to Adrian that he was more than capable, he had a hard time connecting to him.

Dex, as a person, enjoyed connections with people. The connections he forged with people helped make him feel more complete. At the very least, they allowed him to throw more of himself into his work or training. It was easy to train with Jules. It was even easy to train with Rhianna. Adrian was different. He always kept Dex at an arm's distance. The idea of going to him with this issue worried him because he feared Adrian would view it as some sort of weakness and he was certain that Adrian disliked weakness. But before he could do even that or worry about that, he had to get there. Which means he would have to deal with whoever had the Skeleton Key. Maybe deal with them was not the best way to put it. It made it seem to Dex that he already couldn't trust anyone. And while, yes, he had to be careful as to who he trusted, to go in with the mentality that he couldn't trust anyone had to be more harmful than helpful, right?

On the other hand, he did have an urgent message that had to be delivered bit by bit and in secret. That would make someone assume that it was a secret that could be found out. Which meant that someone was monitoring communications- even psychic ones. If that was the case, it was safe to assume that some prudence would be needed about who knew what and what could be said around certain people. This lead him right back to not exactly trusting people, which he didn't like. However, he also decided that he needed to err on the side of caution and at least be a little careful.

When Dex got there, he noticed that it was a rather slow day. Only a few regulars were in the shop, and he. Saw Tonya and Jude behind the counter talking about who had to work tomorrow as it was new comic day. They looked up and saw Dex. Instantly, his head began to hurt showing that Jude was scanning him. His mind switched to thinking questions about when he was getting his field team assignment and how unfair it was. Jude sighed. Tonya said,

"Just can't get enough of this place, huh?"

"It's the smell. The aesthetic of how the shop smells is what does it for me. Plus, I want to get some more training in." Jude laughed.

"Mary isn't here. She can't kick your butt right now- it's her day off."

"Good thing I just want to hit the gym, then. Need to bulk up to prove I'm deserving of a team I guess."

"Oh, come on, Dex: it's not like that. We told you and Neil we need to keep you both safe. We have to find the right fit."

"Dude, just... just don't, okay? Don't give me the speech right now. I thought this was an organization that helped people. I didn't think I was signing up for some kind of bureaucracy crap, okay?"

"Dex, it's not like that," Jude protested. "There are rules in place for a reason."

"And those rules are holding not only myself but Neil back. I'm used to being treated like crap. But Neil? They've been here longer than I have and the fact that they aren't on a team is criminal. So here I am: a Healer. We only need two more members. And you're going to tell me that there is no one in the world that we can work with?"

"Dex, there is a system at work to help keep field teams as safe as possible. And I promise you: keeping you and Neil safe is my top priority. We are on it."

"Oh yeah. We are so safe sitting on our couch binging anime. We're just bored because we could be doing more," Dex countered.

"Look: it is what it is. I'm sorry."

"How about I take you over to the gym?" Tonya offered. She was desperate to cut the tension down in some way. This seemed to be the logical solution. She had to separate the two. She understood both sides of the argument here. The only logical solution to keep the peace was to keep them apart for now and let them cool down. Dex nodded.

"Yeah. I've got work to do." He didn't like being so standoffish. It kind of went against how he really was, but that was okay in a sense. He just wanted to help and this seemed like the best possible way. It just wasn't the way he wanted to be. He wanted to be authentic. He wanted to help people come together, not push others away. It did help that, in some way, he was upset about not having a team. However, given the current situation, he was sure that he had to be careful about who to trust. That included members of any team he was on.

Dex followed Tonya off towards the back. When they got to the back, she looked at Dex for a moment.

"For what it's worth, I agree with you. I know I can't really say more, but I agree with you, okay? I need you to know that." Dex didn't know what to say. He simply nodded and said,

"Thank you." He stepped through the door. Dex wasn't even sure if Adrian was there. He was hoping that he was. He realized that now that he probably should have phoned ahead. But honestly: what else could he even be doing? This guy probably lived for his job, so he had to be there.

He got to Adrian's door and knocked.

"Come in, Dex," he heard Adrian say inside. Of course, Adrian knew he was trying to come in. He frickin' knew everything. He took a deep breath and went in. Adrian was at his desk scribbling in his notebook. "To what do I owe the pleasure of this visit."

"I... um.... I need your help. Or advice. Or both." Adrian raised an eyebrow at this news.

"Well, the situation must be truly horrific if you've come to me for advice. Or help. Or both."

"It's a Psyker thing. I think I've been contacted in a dream twice by the same woman. Given... everything I don't know what to do with this. Or about it." Dex looked at Adrian. He looked as if he didn't really care about what Dex was saying. Adrian's time was much too valuable to be interrupted in this way. Dex decided on a risky gambit. He knew Adrian was a prideful man. He enjoyed being the one in control. He decided to give Adrian some control. "I remember these dreams, which is weird. I like, never remember my dreams. But these? I remember them. So, I'll show you. Dig in my mind and I'll show you the dreams. Please." He looked at Adrian like he was looking at his last hope.

Adrian studied Dex for a moment. He wasn't be brash or confrontational. This was a different Dex he was looking at. This was a Dex who understood his limitations. This was a humble Dex here out of need.

"Show me," he finally said. So Dex opened his mind to the dreams. Afterwards, Adrian was quiet for a moment. Dex thought for a moment that he looked like he had seen a ghost or something, but he wasn't sure and he dared not try to read Adrian's emotions. He pulled out his red leather notebook to consult and take some notes. Dex sat there waiting for him to say anything, his only comfort being the ticking of the clock. Finally, He closed his notebook with a snap and looked at Dex. "You need to find her."

"Just that? That's all you're going to tell me?"

"That's all I can tell you right now, Dex Machina." Dex looked annoyed.

"I'm really getting sick and tired of this crap. You want me to do all this stuff but you people never give me the full run down."

"For once," Adrian replied with a hint of sadness in his voice, "I agree with you. It isn't right and I understand your frustrations and I..." he paused for a moment, looking for the right words to say. "I trust Jules and his judgement implicitly. The fact is if you know too much that information can fall into the wrong hands."

"I know when to keep my mouth shut," Dex snapped back getting angry.

"Mouth yes, mind no. And we have to assume the enemy will go to whatever lengths they can go to in order to destroy The Order."

"So get us a Psyker. You're, like, the top Psyker here and you can't find us one?"

"There are two types of weapons in a war: those that announce their presence and those that are too subtle to detect. You, regardless of your feelings on the matter, must be the second. Where any of The Four to directly intervene, it would cause those forces to be driven underground. Please understand what I am saying: the only thing you can do- the one thing you must do and make your top priority- is to find her." Adrian looked at Dex. "Please." Dex was taken aback by this. Adrian now, moved from his position of power to a position of asking. Dex didn't need read his emotions to understand the magnitude of this. While he still didn't understand why Adrian was actually showing human emotion and asking, he knew it was important to him. He knew Adrian was actually trusting Dex to do this. He had no choice but to find the woman.

"I'll find her: don't worry," Dex said. "Thank you." He got up to leave but Adrian began to speak.

"One more thing: she obviously is working hard to give you the information that you need. Don't belabor the point in your next conversation by discussing your love life." Dex's face got red with embarrassment.

"Got it," he said and quickly left the room. No sooner did he leave than Jules entered from a hidden side door.

"You realize, friend, that you are the only one allowed to use that door other than myself."

"Well," Jules said, "it makes it easier to eavesdrop on Dex."

"Good to know you don't actually trust him," Adrian said with a hint of bitterness. Jules shook his head.

"You misunderstand me. I'm just making sure it's all going according to plan."

"This plan is reckless. It could wind up costing people things and people they hold dear."

"It's necessary," Jules asserted. "It has to be this way." Adrian let his face show his disdain for the current situation. "Adrian, when I cured you of your vampirism- when you finally made the choice to get rid of your Rameses the Damned persona- I was told it was reckless. And it was. A Conduit healing a Vampire is dangerous. There is the chance of death for them if too much blood is drained from them. The previous Four said it was too dangerous but I knew- I knew- it needed to be done. I had that faith. And I have that faith again."

"Are you throwing that up to me, little prince? Because at least I'm not shirking off my royal duties." Jules shook his head defensively.

"You know I'm not. I would never do that just like you would never bring up my past to me. I'm just saying that I believe in something bigger than myself. I have faith. I'm asking you to have the same faith in me now as you did then." Adrian sighed. There was no one he trusted more than Jules. He knew that Jules wouldn't intentionally hurt him. That fact just really didn't help in the current situation.

"If anything happens…" Adrian began.

"It won't. I promise," Jules assured him.

Dex had too many things to figure out at this point. His head was spinning. While Adrian was helpful in a sense, he couldn't help but be annoyed. If he just had a team, all of this would be easier. As it stood, whatever he had to do, it was just him and Neil. While that normally wouldn't be a problem, in this case it was life or death. At least, it could be but Dex didn't know everything that was going on. He knew he'd have to rely on his skills at improvising, but even then, in an extreme case. Dex doubted himself, which was a feeling he hated.

As he got to the door, he was overcome with déjà vu and knew that Jude was coming through. This was useful as he didn't know until then how he was going to get back to the shop.

"Oh. Dex," Jude said. "You need to come through?"

"Yeah, thanks man," he replied.

"Listen," Jude said stopping Dex, "I know you think I'm being a hard-ass about the team thing, and I'm sorry. I really am. It's just…" he looked around. "Something isn't right here." Dex was shocked to hear this. He had to maintain his composure, though, so that he didn't let on anything.

"What do you mean?" Dex asked in a confused voice.

"It's just… things aren't going how they're supposed to, you know? And I'm doing my best, but it's hard. I just… I just want to help." Dex nodded.

"I get that. I really do. I suppose that everything happens when it's supposed to happen. Doesn't mean I have to like it."

"Right. And I know you just want to help. I know you do. But I also want to keep you safe. I owe it to you and everyone else."

"Heavy is the head that wears the crown," Dex said. "I get it: I just don't like it. Sometimes, you gotta do what you gotta do." Dex shrugged. Jude thought about that for a moment. He was right, Jude thought. Sometimes you gotta do what you gotta do.

"Thank you, Dex. I appreciate that."

He got home and found a note from Neil stating that they were going on a spa day. He decided to just lay down and relax on the couch watching some tv. It wasn't long before he was back on the boat with the woman in the red dress.

"Seriously," she said. "who sleeps in the middle of the day? I get, like, this feeling that you're in the dreaming and I can contact you, but at this hour?"

"No," Dex said shaking his head. "Not doing this. Give me details now. Adrian said to get to the point. So get to the point. Tell me where to meet you." She was taken aback by that revelation, yet she decided to comply.

"Yeah... um... okay. In two weeks. August 14th. A cruise leaves from Cape Canaveral. Be on it. I'll be there." Dex was woken up by Neil.

"Dex. Dex!" Neil said shaking him. "Look: they're blue." They held out their hands for Dex to look at look.

"Dude, what the hell?" Dex said sitting up. "I was talking to her. Like, seriously, dude." He looked around to see Ophelia and Rhianna standing there with Neil. All three of them were wide eyed and wondering what was going on. "Well fine," Dex said. "Story time." He filled everyone in on the information that he had gained and learned. Rhianna shook her head.

"Honestly I know about as much as you do at this point. I'm thinking Jules and Adrian aren't telling me everything, either. I'm not sure. Either that or what you've added to everything I know is privileged information." She shot a look over to Ophelia, who was on Dex's computer. "What do you think about all of this."

"Here's the cruise," she said quietly. "Tickets are on sale. You should probably go ahead and buy them. We can get you there with the Skeleton Key."

"You cannot be serious," Rhianna replied in a frustrated tone. "They can't go alone. They need at least a Psyker if not a Prophet advising them as well." Ophelia shook her head.

"That's not going to happen in time. You don't need to be a Prophetess to know that, Rhianna."

"Holy crap: It's happening. We're going rogue." Neil said. They couldn't hide their excitement. "Superstar and Dex Machina: Rogue Squad. Holy crap: I love it."

"No one is going rogue," Rhianna asserted. "In order to go on a mission, you need to be sent by The Council or The Four. And you also need a full team."

"Well, obviously," Neil replied like that was basic knowledge. "Hence the whole 'going rogue' thing. We don't have a team. But we have to go. This is what we've been waiting for."

"It's too dangerous," Rhianna protested. "Dex: tell me you agree with me?" But Dex wasn't on the couch. He was already entering information in on the computer to pay for the cruise.

"Ophelia!" Rhianna exclaimed. "Are you seriously allowing this?!"

"It's going to happen either way," Ophelia quietly protested. "There's not a lot I can do about it at this point. I might as well help." She shrugged. "It is what it is."

"That is a terrible way to look at things," Rhianna said in a defeated voice.

"But it's true. And your feelings aren't going to change that."

"Right," Dex said suddenly. "I booked us a royal suite because I know you're extra like that Neil. What's the vacation policy for The Order?" He looked at Rhianna as he asked that question.

"This is not happening!" Rhianna said in an aggravated voice.

"Oh no: this is happening," Dex said plainly.

"If you don't have a team, then you can just go. Just let The Council know. They literally can't stop you," Ophelia said.

"I can't believe you're actually condoning this," Rhianna said shaking her head.

"How can I condone something that's supposed to happen?" Ophelia asked.

"This is absolutely unsafe." Rhianna replied.

"Well tough!" Neil finally said. "I'm sorry, but look: the truth is we were told that we were supposed to do something. This random woman messaging Dex is the first real lead we have on this. This is a thing that is going to happen. Sorry." Neil didn't like being confrontational, but they believed in this. Dex simply shrugged his shoulders.

"It is what it is," he said.

"I don't have to like this," Rhianna said.

"You just have to trust us," Neil said. "And if you don't trust us, then you just need to trust Jules." Rhianna sighed.

"I hate this. I really do. I think it's putting you both in a terrible position."

"But you trust Jules," Dex said, "so that makes it okay."

"It doesn't make it okay. It just makes it a thing I have to deal with."

There were only two other hurdles that Dex had to get through in order to board the boat. The first was dealing with The Council. While they couldn't prove anything, the whole thing seemed ominous to them. Mary, especially, felt as if they were lying about something. There was, however, no proof for The Council to deny them a leave for a cruise. After all, officially it was just a vacation.

The second hurdle to cross was Dex's somewhat date. All in all, it was fine. It was very clear to Dex that Alice had romantic intentions. Dex was careful to never reciprocate those moves. He made it clear that, because he was just some dumb guy, it was two friends sharing a meal. It wasn't great for Dex. He felt terrible about the whole thing. However, he felt this was the best way to keep Alice safe. She was a great girl and Dex knew that she could find any partner she wanted. Dex was just confident that it wasn't with her. He was about to embark on a sort of mission that could not only kill him but could potentially alter the course of humanity as he knew it.

On the other hand, he could also just wind up getting himself and Neil killed. There were too many unknowns. He was running into this whole thing halfcocked and with delusions of grandeur. But either way, the only solution was to protect Alice who literally had nothing to do with it.

All of this would have been fine with Dex if not for some simple fact: the woman who contacted him stopped contacting him. He didn't even know if he was going to find someone who was alive or not. Only one thought kept him sane, knowing he was doing what he was supposed to be doing:

It is what it is.

Chapter Seven

Before Dex's alarm went off, the door to his room slammed open, scaring him and almost making him fall out of bed. Luckily, he sat up.

"Today's the day!" Neil shouted in a sing song voice.

"Neil: what the ever-loving Hell are you doing?!" Dex yelled. "I… I… what?"

"Dude!" Neil protested. "Today's the day of our vacation. Our super-secret not-technically-a-mission mission!" Dex looked at the clock and sighed. He rubbed the sleep off his face for a moment.

"Dude, I had, like, fifteen more minutes…" Dex whined.

"Oh, I'm so sorry. Shall I come back in a bit and redo this bit later?" Neil asked with mock concern.

"No. No: it's fine. Just, like, give me a few and I'll be down, okay? What time do we need to leave?"

"Well, because we've unlocked the fast travel skill, we've got, like, an hour before we have to leave and go through security and all that crap." Dex stared at Neil.

"You're already wearing a Hawaiian shirt?"

"Dude! I'm trying to blend in!" Neil replied defensively.

"Oh no yeah: I see that. The bright pink flowers and flamingos will totally achieve that."

"We're just two people on a vacation. That's the story," Neil explained.

"No, I get that," Dex explained, "but that shirt is very bright and you just woke me up."

"Look dude: just come downstairs. I already brought your luggage down and made breakfast. Grab Ruach and come eat." Neil turned and went downstairs. Dex sighed. He understood their excitement, but this was actually pretty serious. It had been two weeks since he last heard from the woman in the red dress. Though the whole situation was strange, he couldn't help but worry about what she was doing. Communication had been vague enough as it was and then, all of a sudden, it just stopped. He had made a promise to Adrian and he needed to fulfill that promise. There was something else going on here- something ominous in the air, but Dex didn't know what that might be.

After throwing on some clothes that were decidedly less flashy than Neil's, he grabbed his sword and went downstairs.

"Alright: what's for breakfast?" he yelled down as he descended. There was no answer. Odd, Dex thought to himself. Neil had been so excited not just a few minutes ago. For the. First time he could remember, he actually wished the sense of déjà vu would wash over him. Just let me know Neil is okay, he thought. He reached out to find Neil's feelings. There. Right there they are. But what they were feeling was not joy and excitement. It was anxiousness and worry. A thousand uninvited thoughts danced in his brain. Ten percent, he thought. Go ten percent power and draw your sword. He felt the energy spread throughout his body, giving his muscles a familiar burning sensation. He quietly drew his sword and snuck downstairs.

Back to the wall, he saw that the living room was empty. He slid around the corner, still feeling the anxiousness of Neil. He peaked into the kitchen. There they were. They sat at the table; their face looking paler than usual. They locked eyes with Dex.

"Dex Machina," a warm familiar voice said. "Glad you could join us." It was Jules. Dex breathed a sigh of relief and put his sword and energy away.

"Neil, you damn near gave me a heart attack. You're throwing off anxiousness like a high school freshman who just got put in the game on the varsity team."

"Yeah, well imagine my surprise to come back downstairs and find the literal head of The Order in our kitchen telling me he needs to talk with us before he sends us off on our merry way..." Neil replied. They shifted uncomfortably in their seat. It wasn't until this exact moment that Neil finally understood the magnitude of the whole situation. They weren't a full team. They lacked the full vision of a Prophet or the cohesion that a Psyker provided. Yet here they both were essentially being sent on a covert black book operation. Adding to what Ophelia said to them about a change coming only fueled the anxiety they felt in this moment.

"I told them to not to worry several times, but... well obviously that didn't work," Jules said in a somewhat helpful voice. Neil scoffed.

"Yeah that's like being told by a teacher not to worry about things. It instantly makes you worry," they explained. Jules sighed and looked at both Neil and Dex.

"How can I help, then?" he finally asked. Dex looked at Jules. He looked as if he was tired. No: not exactly tired. It was more of a sadness masquerading as tiredness. He had a feeling that if he had asked Jules if he was okay, then he would simply reply with the age-old lie of just being tired. Dex wasn't too sure about what to do with this information. There was a feeling of both sadness and tiredness coming from Jules. He had come himself to see them off which meant that this was much more important than they even knew.

"What can you tell us?" Dex asked.

"I can tell you anything. I can tell you everything. Doing so isn't wise at this point. There is too much interference. What I can tell you and not put you in danger is that there was a Psyker that was identified to be on your team."

"Great," Neil said. "Where are they?"

"Not on your team. There's a certain amount of paperwork that has to be completed in order for teams to be formed. The paperwork of this person has been lost numerous times."

"Good to know," Dex replied.

"No: this is terrible news," Neil interjected.

"It's good because it shows us that someone is actively trying to keep new teams from being formed. It's damn near proof positive of someone actively messing things up," Jules clarified. Dex sighed.

"And I assume that the forms were lost in such a way that it can't point to any one person or place?" he asked.

"Exactly," confirmed Jules.

"So then why didn't you guys override the whole thing?" Neil asked. "Like, just put the team together."

"Because it would have tipped our hand as we've already explained. And because we haven't officially found a Prophet for the team."

"So, what's the play here then?" Dex asked.

"Get to the bottom of your dreams. Find her," Jules said.

"That's all we get?" Neil asked.

"Dex, have you read those books I gave you?" Dex nodded.

"Yeah. They were pretty interesting."

"Good," Jules replied. "Now: I would very much like some coffee. Ophelia keeps saying how good it is."

"How is any of this helpful?" Neil asked in an exasperated voice.

"Good Lord," Dex said rolling his eyes and getting up to get a cup of coffee for Jules. "Subtext, Neil. No: we can't know anything. But by Jules coming here, it shows us that this trip in general is serious. It has the stink of a traitor all over it. He's telling us to get ready because some crap is about to go down. But he's not officially telling us anything." He handed Jules a cup of coffee and he took a sip.

"That is good coffee," Jules said. "It's right on the spot."

"I too would enjoy some coffee," Adrian said suddenly. Neil about jumped out of their skin.

"You have got to be kidding me," Neil said. Adrian looked at them.

"Ophelia says it's very good," he told them coolly.

"Adrian, I thought we agreed that I would be the one to send them off," Jules asked rather annoyed.

"I came for coffee. Goodness, Jules: didn't you hear what I just said?" He turned and faced Dex who was there with another cup of coffee. He handed it to Adrian. He reached out to take it from Dex and his hand touched Dex's for a moment. He looked Dex in the eyes. "Thank you, Dex Machina." Dex gave an understanding nod.

"No problem," he said. Adrian turned to Jules.

"That's all I wanted," he told Jules. He took a sip of the coffee. "Good Lord: this is bitter. Is there no cream or sugar here?"

"It's on the counter in a tin can," Ophelia said quietly.

"I'll get it," Rhianna said helpfully.

"Screw it! I'll just make a pot!" Neil threw their hands in the air and went to make a full pot of coffee. "Apparently it's a damn party in here..." Ophelia sat down and pulled out a copy of a manga titled Moonphase.

"We're just here to offer moral support," Ophelia said quietly.

"Oh no: this isn't ominous at all," Dex said sarcastically.

"Relax. There's nothing to worry about," Rhianna said. Ophelia replied,

"Jules already used that line."

"Well, damn," Rhianna said, taking a mug of coffee.

"Look," Dex finally said, "if there's something you all want me to know, just tell me. Don't give me the run around here."

"I guess we are all here collectively to make sure you two have everything you need. We all have a bit of a vested interest in this." Rhianna was always there with a kind and hopeful word.

"But you've all done that whole vague old janitor thing to pass knowledge. So if you want me to succeed, then tell me how."

"Lord you are slow," Ophelia said while reading. "We fully believe you two will succeed in whatever you need to do. We're here not out of duty, but because we actually like you two." She took a sip of her coffee. "Great with subtext my ass..." she muttered to herself. A hush fell over the room followed by several reddened faces. There was a flash. It was Neil holding their phone.

"This is adorable. I may use this for my Christmas cards this year."

"And there went the moment," Dex said taking a drink of his own coffee. He sat the mug down and sighed. "I'm very grateful for all the help and support you all have given us. I know I haven't always made it easy. I know for a fact that Neil has rarely made it easy as well." Neil shot Dex a glare but then quickly conceded the point. "But you all trust us. And we aren't going to let you down. We will get to the bottom of this. And we will be fine. And when we are done, I'll call you to come pick us up. It will be fine." Jules came over to embrace him.

"I have faith in you, Dex Machina." Jules looked at his watch. "By my count, it's about time we sent you both off. I'm assuming you're both packed?"

"Neil already brought the bags down," Ophelia said.

"Must be nice, seeing the future," Neil said slightly jealous.

"I noticed the bags by the door when I came in," she responded.

"Ah. Yes. That actually makes more sense I suppose."

Good-byes were given. The door to the outside became a door to a restroom in port where they could easily find the dock and check in. Once they were gone, Rhianna was the first to speak. Her brown eyes were glassed over with tears that were a mix of sadness and pride.

"Those two... they have no clue what they're in for..." Ophelia stood up and put her book away, walking over to Rhianna.

"None of us know what exactly is going on. That's the problem. When you don't know what's next, then you have to just let things happen and trust that's how it's supposed to happen."

"If any of them are hurt in this little experiment..." Adrian was interrupted by Jules.

"They'll be fine. The Prophet Gifts have been happening less and less due to some kind of interference. But I know they will be home safe and sound after this. Ophelia: what have you seen recently?"

"You were right Jules. It is him. He's ultimately the one behind everything. I just don't know what the endgame of this all is yet." Ophelia began tugging on one of her braids.

"We should have told them," Rhianna said sadly.

"We didn't have conformation on it all until now," Adrian said. "Until this moment, all we had were guesses. Now we at least have some sort of starting point. It's all starting now."

"No," Jules said with a hint of fear in his voice that chilled the others, "it started a while ago. This is only the beginning of the end of this one part."

Dex and Neil heard none of this. Neil was too focused on where it was they needed to be going. Dex was already on the lookout and had to be told several times by Neil to keep up.

"It's like I'm a mom dragging a toddler around here..." they complained.

"What if she's here?" Dex asked, still keeping a look out for her.

"You really think some woman in a red cocktail dress is suddenly going to show up in the port? She said find me on the boat. She's probably already there. We have to check in and get through security. That's the main goal right now." Security. That thought actually unnerved Dex. While he technically didn't have contraband on him, he did have Ruach with him. He had become so used to taking it with him anymore that it was second nature for him to have it. He didn't notice may weird looks or slide glances in general. When he was reading the books Jules gave him, there was an estimation that at least two million people in the whole world had the Sight. However, only about a million or so of those would actually activate it. Even fewer, he had learned, was blessed with a Gift. Dex understood that it was highly unlikely that he would run into many others on the cruise with the Sight. But that still left the question of how to get the sword past the metal detector and this anxiety built in Dex as they approached the security check point.

"Bags on the machine. Empty your pockets or everything in the bins provided, please." This man was absolutely uninterested in his job and it was clear by not only his demeanor but his speech tone. Neil went first and went through fine. Well of course they did, Dex thought. They aren't carrying a freshly cleaned and sharpened katana. Dex emptied his pockets and started to walk through the machine.

"Sir. I'm going to have to ask you to stop for a moment."

"Aw beans..." he heard Neil say, running their hand through their hair and then rubbing their neck.

"Something wrong?" Dex asked innocently.

"I need to check your cane," the man replied.

"My... cane?" Dex thought for a moment. Ruach. "Oh yes: my cane." He nervously handed the sword to the man.

"Sorry," he said, "but people try to sneak extra booze on these things all the time. I've seen more than a few cane flasks in my time." The man began expecting Ruach and Dex's heart just about stopped. "Go on through," he told Dex. He did. Well, it's been a good run with Ruach, he thought to himself. I'll miss that sword. The man looked up and down the sword. "Here you go. Thank you and enjoy your cruise," he said handing it back to Dex.

"No problem. I totally get it," he responded with a nervous laugh. Neil's shoulders were shaking with trying to hold in the laughter.

"That is bloody brilliant," Neil said laughing. "Seriously. It's all, 'Oh excuse me while I board a boat with a frickin' sword that you think is a cane'."

"That was so nerve wracking..." Dex said rubbing his eyes.

"Hey, look on the bright side: we did it. That's a good sign, right?"

"I mean, maybe? Like, I guess? I mean, a win's a win, right?"

"Exactly! Exactly! Take the win and soon we'll be sipping mojitos on the deck," Neil said with a smile.

"I absolutely hate mojitos," Dex said with a grimace.

"Then drink, like, I don't know straight whiskey? The point is we need to celebrate a win when we get it." They approached the concierge as Dex replied,

"And when we find her, we will celebrate." He turned to the woman behind the counter. "Hello. We have a reservation under Dex Machina." The woman looked at them for a moment.

"Why do you have a sword on your hip?" she asked him. Dex and Neil went pale.

"It's a cane," Dex said sheepishly.

"That's a sword. What is that, a katana? Is there, like, an anime convention on the boat I'm not aware of?"

"I got this," Neil said quietly to Dex. They placed an arm on the counter. "Young lady, I am sure an educated woman such as yourself is familiar with The Order. We are two high ranking officials on an official mission. So please: it's best not to ask questions and just check us in." They turned to Dex and gave him a look as if to say everything was fine.

"Okay, so where is the rest of your team if you're with The Order?" She asked coolly.

"Aw beans... Welp I tried. I'm out of ideas," Neil said with a shrug. Dex sighed.

"Look: we actually are with The Order. And we just need our room because we need to meet someone there. What Neil told you is, like, a half-truth. But we just need to get to our room. Please?"

"Are you two really with The Order?" she asked quietly. Dex and Neil looked at each other. They turned back to her and nodded. "Oh. Oh wow. Okay. This is, like, pretty big. Okay. So here's the deal I will totally check you in, but if there's any problems on the cruise, can you two help?" Neil flashed a cheesy grin at her.

"Ma'am, that's why we're here." She squealed with excitement.

"I knew it. I knew it! I knew The Order existed. Okay. Okay. Calm down, Sara. Hold on: let me check you two in." She turned to her computer and began to type furiously. "Okay. Here's your keycards. And if you need anything, don't hesitate to ask. Ask for Sara C, okay?"

"Thank you," Dex said humbly. "We really appreciate all your help."

"Don't worry- we'll keep you safe," Neil said with extreme niceness. They grabbed their bags and went off towards their rooms.

Their suite was situated on the front of the boat in one of the uppermost portions they could have rooms. Their nearest neighbor was well off down the hallway. They turned and looked off the railing, seeing a view of the port and smelling the salty air. Dex always loved the ocean. Perhaps, he pondered, it wasn't really the ocean he loved. Oh sure: he did enjoy the smell of the sea and the sound of the waves to be sure. Yet if he was being honest with himself, he had to realize that every time he was at the sea, he was there with his family. Perhaps it wasn't the ocean in general that he loved: perhaps he just loved the remembrance of being with family. The smell of the salt filled air reminded him of time spent fishing on a boat with his dad or building sandcastles with his mom. He sighed and turned to the door longing for simpler days.

The door, however, was already open. Neil had already walked in eying the massive room. They had access to a full kitchen, living room, and two separate bedrooms. Neil was on the balcony overlooking the ocean. They stood with their arms outstretched, smiling and facing the ocean.

"I'm the king of the world!" they cried. They turned and faced Dex. "I want you to draw me like one of your French girls, Jack." They both couldn't help but crack up at the joke. After a few minutes of laughing, Neil finally spoke wiping tears of joy from their eyes. "Right: well I can cross that off my bucket list now."

"It's good to laugh," Dex replied. "It's needed. If we don't laugh, we may cry from the weight of it all."

"Dude, it's going to be okay. I don't know how or anything like that, but I know if we work together, we can get through anything."

"Yeah I know," Dex replied with a smile. "It's just… I've been looking at the itinerary and trying to figure out where the best possible starting point is to find this woman." He pulled out a folded piece of paper from his back pocket. Neil came over to look.

"Okay," Neil said. "Looks like tonight is a big dance party and dinner."

"Lord help me: I hate club music," Dex said sadly.

"Yeah well I don't. And to be honest, almost everyone without kids will probably be there. It's the best starting point we have. Look: there is a nice buffet dinner before. And I love shrimp so I want to eat it now before they serve us the old, nasty shrimp. I'm not spending the cruise sick."

"Well, regardless of your shrimp needs, I think you're right. The best place to look is where the most people will be. And I think it's safe to assume that this party is the place to start. We only have three days to find her, so we have to move fast."

"I can totally go check out the spas and stuff," Neil offered. Dex gave a soft chuckle.

"Oh, you are a credit to The Order, you are. Such self-sacrifice."

"Look: I'd love to just lounge about in here until after the boat leaves so I can relax and get ready for tonight. But if we want to get serious and look, we have to make it to the main deck. There's going to be a bunch of people waving and cheering as we start to push off to sea. I saw it on YouTube."

"Right," Dex said rolling his eyes, "and you can totally trust people on the internet." Neil had a look of fake exaggerated shock on their face.

"Do you really think people would do that? Just go on the internet and lie?" Dex just laughed. He looked at Neil who actually looked authentically happy. Neil didn't have the best life growing up. While their parents were still living, they didn't contact them for personal reasons. Sometimes, that's not the way life works out, sadly. Neil was never officially adopted by Dex's parents, but they might as well have been. When they needed love and acceptance, Dex's parents where there for them. They welcomed Neil with open arms as one of their own since they first met them.

"Neil," Dex said suddenly. "You know, I've been thinking: if I have to be stuck in this situation of doing some black book ops shit for a clandestine organization that answers to no government and keeps the world from falling into chaos... well... I'm glad that I'm doing this thing with you." Neil laughed.

"Dude: I feel the same way. I'm entirely convinced that we can take on the world together. I love you, man." The two shared a hug.

"I love you, too," Dex said breaking the embrace. "Let's get up there and start walking around looking for the girl of my dreams."

"I'm sorry: what?" Neil said wide-eyed.

"We have to find the girl from my dreams," Dex said realizing his mistake. "That's what I said: girl from my dreams."

"Don't do that. Don't try to gaslight me," Neil said laughing. "I have, like, very good hearing. I know what you said."

"It was just a mistake. I misspoke."

"Paging Dr. Freud. Dr. Sigmond Freud, please take the call on line one," Neil said.

"Oh, stop that!" Dex said punching Neil in the arm. "You know what I meant."

"Oh, I know exactly what you meant," they replied with a knowing grin. "You can't take that back: I won't let you."

"Dude, we have a job to do..." Dex said deflecting the misspoken word. "Come on: don't do this. You totally know what I meant."

"Yeah I do," Neil said with a knowing grin. "Yeah I do." To be honest, Neil had been hoping that Dex's kind of/sort of date with Alice would have panned out. It was built up to be some big, huge point in Dex's life and the whole thing, they felt, was just glossed over and became unimportant. Neil knew that Dex was the kind of person who literally lived for other people. He would go out of his way to make sure other people were happy and taken care of. It was time, they thought, for Dex to have some happiness. Neil had flirted once before the idea in their mind about a different kind of relationship with Dex. The idea was somewhat fleeting and left Neil a little sad. They knew that wasn't what Dex wanted from them. Over time, Neil let go of those feelings and settled into a different role which they now cherish as their most important relationship with them. They just wanted to see Dex happy. Dex never had a sibling and neither did Neil. Over time, Neil grew to love Dex in different ways. Neil loved Dex. Dex loved Neil. What they had transcended romantic relationships. It was a pure love.

"Okay," Neil said. "Let's get to the main deck." It wasn't hard to find the main deck. All they had to do was follow the throngs of people going for their moment in the sun. It was still a bit of a big deal, Dex assumed, to go on a cruise. He doubted that it was as big a deal as it was to Dex and Neil, but that was beside the point. He had to be very careful. His Psyker power was based off of human emotion and the deck was a literal buffet of emotion. Even walking to the deck, Dex could feel the happiness and joy and fear emanating from the people. More than once, Dex had to make sure he wasn't inadvertently skimming people's emotions. He had to think back to his training with Adrian. Keep it all in check. Don't go throwing it around so willy-nilly.

Once they got to the deck, there was, as expected, throngs of people. They were all waving and having a good time. There was music playing, but it wasn't such bad club music. It was more just a random assortment of music. He recognized the song instantly as Pinch Me by the Barenaked Ladies. *"It's the perfect time of year somewhere far away from here. I feel fine enough I guess considering everything's a mess."* Lord, Dex thought. That's true. He should be rather happy. He should be thrilled to be on a cruise with his sibling, but he wasn't.

Dex understood the reality of the situation. This was only the beginning, he feared. This was it: This was what he had been training for. The fact of the matter was that there was something nefarious going on in an organization that helped define who he was as a person. He would never go so far as to say that The Order saved him, but he did feel as if it gave him a sense of purpose. Until he joined them, he had been simply drifting through life. Oh sure: everything was fine and dandy. He had food and money and his bills were being paid, but that was it. There was no... Dex guessed that pizzazz was the word. There was no passion in his life. The Order offered him that. It gave him a sense of purpose that he was truly grateful for. Yet he also couldn't help but be frustrated by how The Order was run. His mother always said that friends don't make secrets and secrets and secrets don't make friends.

"You see your dream girl?" Neil asked suddenly. Dex shook his head.

"No- not yet."

"Well, it's still early. There's no guarantee that she'd even be here right now. But this is the best place to start looking sadly."

"I know we will find her. I'm just... I don't know... worried? I mean it's been two weeks and there has been no contact. For all I know, she could be dead and this could all be some sort of trap."

"Well," Neil said hopefully, "if it is a trap, then the worst thing they could put into it is us two together. Because I'm sure we can turn it on them."

"How?" Dex asked. "How are you so sure that we're not in over our head? We don't have a Prophet or a Psyker. We have no help here." Neil placed a hand on Dex's shoulder.

"Because I believe in you," they said quietly. "I believe in you." That was all it took. That was all Dex needed to hear. Oh sure: it was nice to hear from The Four earlier in the morning, but they, as teachers, pretty much had to say those things. It was expected of them. But Neil? There was no real reason for Neil to have as much faith in Dex as they did. That gave Dex hope.

"We're going to do this," Dex said. "It's too important to fail. We are going to find her."

"Do you know why we have to find her?" Neil asked. This was a question that they had for a while but hadn't given voice to it until now.

Neil had some grave concerns. They weren't Dex. They didn't bend and change as easily as Dex did. Neil was a concrete person. That's why they loved math. Two plus two was always four. Nothing could change that. If Neil looked at the situation objectively, which they always did, then they saw a huge mess. They had little to no information. The Order wasn't as helpful as it should be and, in fact, it could very well be broken according to all the information that they did have on it. No: something wasn't right about all of this. The numbers didn't add up to Neil and that bothered them.

"At this point, it's because I made a promise to Adrian," Dex replied honestly.

"I mean... I hate to say it, but could the issue be Adrian? I mean, look objectively here: he's the strongest Psyker in The Order. He knows how to manipulate people. It's not out of the realm of possibility that he is the one causing all the problems and distress in The Order."

"Dude, Lord knows that man grates my nerves. But Jules trusts him. If I'm being honest, I trust Jules."

"So, you don't trust me?" Neil asked. Dex shook his head.

"I didn't say that. I trust you the most here. Jules has told me more than once that he trusts Adrian implicitly. Now, do I agree with you that he's hiding something? Absolutely. Do I think he'd betray The Order? No- I don't."

"He gives me the creeps," Neil said.

"Dude: you never had to let him root around in your brain before. It's so weird."

"Okay all you party people: this is it! We're pushing off now!" the DJ yelled and played an air siren noise. The boat began to move slowly. This was it- they were heading out to sea.

"Well I suppose that it's too late to protest now," Neil said as the boat kept moving. "I'm going to go get a mojito and see if this lady is near the bar. That sound good?"

"Totally," Dex said. "But keep your phone handy and connected to Wi-Fi. We need to stay as connected as we can, okay?" Neil nodded in agreement and went off, dancing as they went.

Dex wondered to himself what he was even doing here. Neil was right: we are in way over our heads. Nothing about this was normal. But you know what? He didn't really think he could keep using that excuse anymore. Sure, this was all strange and weird and dangerous, but it was also the life he had been living for a while now. If that was the case, then why even worry about? Since that day at the cemetery months ago, his life was different. Yet is was still his life. Not once in the months preceding that day did things happen that were anywhere near normal, but it was a consistent strangeness. Dex reasoned that continuing to point out the strangeness of it all to him wasn't helping. This was his new normal. He had no choice now but to adapt to it all.

He decided that the current best course of action was to head to the bar and find Neil. He might as well celebrate a bit and have some fun. He didn't make it but halfway to the bar before Neil showed up to meet him with some red drink in his hand.

"Arrgh, me matey! Here be a pirate punch for you," they said laughing. Dex laughed and accepted the drink.

"See anyone interesting?" Dex said taking a drink. Neil shook their head.

"Negative, Ghost Rider. But I was thinking there are obvious places that we can cross off the list already. Like, we don't have to check out the kid clubs or the teen hang outs."

"Right," Dex affirmed. "And she wasn't in a uniform. I think her dress was intentional. I think that's what we will find her in."

"Well just make sure to get the woman of your dream's number so you two can keep in touch," Neil said laughing.

"Oh, you've got to be kidding me! I just misspoke! That's it!"

"Sure Jan..." Neil said dismissively. "Anyway, if you're right, then this is a bust for us. But we got a good drink. Probably best for us to head back to the room and come up with a plan." Dex nodded.

"We make the plan. We stick to the plan," Dex began.

"The plan goes bad. Then we improvise. Just like always," Neil finished.

"Exactly," Dex said holding his drink out for a toast with Neil which they happily obliged.

They went back to their room and began getting ready for dinner. It was rather odd for Dex to be dressing up a bit on a cruise ship. He figured that he should just wear sandals and flip flops the whole time, but he also knew that his wardrobe had to be functional as well. To that end, he had packed a pair of dress slacks and a simple white shirt as well as a sports jacket. Neil however, always more fashionable of the two, decided to wear a matching suit outfit with a longer, flowing coat. They had a light blue bow tie to set the outfit off.

"Right," Dex said when they were all ready, "the plan. We go to dinner. We will probably have to make small talk with people. We hit the buffet at separate times to maximize the potential of seeing her. She will likely be wearing a red dress and have black hair in a bob cut."

"Right," Neil said, nodding in agreement. "When one of us finds her, we contact the other, meet up and come back here for a debriefing. Easy-peasy."

"Right," Dex said.

"Right," Neil replied.

"It's not going to be that easy, is it?" Dex asked.

"Plan for the plan to go haywire and you'll never be disappointed," Neil replied with a knowing nod and grin. Dex sighed. Neil ran their hand through their hair. "We can do this, right?"

"I think we can. I'm like, eighty percent sure we can. That's, like, a B so we should be pretty good here." They made their way to the dining hall and had an uneventful dinner. Though they looked for the woman, they couldn't find her. They did, however meet a lovely couple from Ohio who couldn't help but share pictures of their eight grandchildren with Dex and Neil. The food was... well it wasn't terrible but Dex was not sure that they should have advertised the beef as prime rib.

The next logical step was to scope out the dance party. The music wasn't necessarily too loud, but it wasn't what Dex would call good. Neil loved the playlist, but Dex was getting worried. Where was she? They only had a limited amount of time to find her. So where was she?

"Hey: I'm going to go get some fresh air," Dex told Neil.

"I'm going to go hit up the dance floor. For... you know... recon purposes..." Neil blushed. Dex gave them a quizzical look. They sighed. "Okay, look. There's a really cute woman over there at the bar. She looks rather lonely. So, I thought maybe she could use some cheering up and we could dance and I could look for your girl at the same time." Dex laughed.

"You do you, boo. You do you." Dex left to make his way to the deck outside the ball room. Fresh sea air and less noise was what he needed to clear his head. It was slightly unfortunate, however, that he didn't get a chance to clear his mind. As he approached the deck, staring out into the distance was a woman facing the infinite blackness of the night sea. She had a bob haircut and was wearing a red dress. She stood there, holding a cigarette in her fingers.

It was her.

Chapter Eight

Time slowed for Dex. This was it. She was a real, physical person standing in front of Dex. So what now? What is it that he was supposed to do? Should he just saunter up to her and say, "Hey- I dreamed about you?" Yes, Dex thought. That wouldn't be creepy at all. His palms began to sweat. Wonderful, he thought. Now I have this flare up I haven't had since high school. Wonderful. He continued to stand there in a bit of awe just looking at her- studying her. She seemed to exude a sort of cool confidence. This was a girl- no. This was a woman who knew who she was and was confident in that fact.

"It's rude to stare," she said without turning around. She stood still, almost like a statue, cigarette still burning in her hand. Odd, Dex thought. She hasn't taken a puff of that thing yet.

"I'm just wondering who you're avoiding," he said approaching the railing.

"I just wanted a smoke."

"Except you don't have a purse or anywhere to hold a pack or lighter."

"Maybe someone gave it to me," she offered, not looking at Dex. He placed his elbows on the rails.

"This isn't the smoking section of the ship," Dex replied.

"Maybe I'm bad and don't care about the rules," she offered.

"Maybe," Dex admitted, "but you haven't even taken a drag yet. And there's no smell coming from that thing." She sighed and waved her hand. The cigarette disappeared.

"I always forget about the smell," she admitted. "It's the Achilles Heel of that illusion."

"So you're either waiting for someone or avoiding someone," Dex offered. "Which is it?" She finally turned to face him. Her eyes were still the pools of blue ice water that Dex remembered. She made a face as if she was trying to remember him.

"Do I know you?" she asked.

"Not yet," Dex said.

"Who are you?" She asked. She seemed to know the face but couldn't quite place him with a name.

"I'm Dex- Dex Machina." A wave of relief washed over her. Finally, she thought. He's here. We've met and now... now the fun can begin.

"I'm Cassandra," she said with a knowing grin.

"Well, now that we know each other, what happens next?" Dex asked.

"Aw Hell..." she said with a frown on her face. "It's him."

"Him who?"

"Some barfly that has been trying to pick me up all night. I don't even remember his name. I think it's like, Chad or something?" A man approached him with two drinks in his hand and a drunk smile on his face.

"There's my girl," he said with slightly slurring speech. He turned and looked at Dex. "Okay. You can go, thank you."

"Look buddy: the lady isn't interested in you. And you're clearly drunk, so you should move along."

"Don't do that," Cassandra protested. "I'm not some dainty little thing that needs saving." She spoke to Dex directly into his mind after she said that. "Play along. I have a plan." Dex nodded in understanding.

"Oh, that is just typical SJW crap isn't it? A man tries to help a girl and suddenly he's a misogynist?"

"Hey: screw you, pal! I never asked for your help. What: you have some white knight fetish or something? Have to come save the dainty little girl? Is that it?"

"Good Lord!" Dex exclaimed in fake outrage. "Men can't just be nice without some alterative motive? Is that what you think?"

"Well clearly you think you need to prove you're some big, strong man!" she exclaimed.

"Look, I'm going to go..." the other man said and started backing away slowly.

"Oh, now look what you've done!" Cassandra yelled. "You made

Chad upset and he's leaving. Feel like a big, tough man now? That's what gets you feeling good, huh?"

"Look buddy: this chick is clearly crazy, so you may just want to save yourself the headache, okay?" The man turned and walked away at this point.

"Typical He-Man bull crap: calling a woman they can't control crazy!" She looked until he was out of earshot. "Oh, thank God," she said with a sigh of relief. "He just was not taking the hint."

"Right," Dex replied. "So, what now?"

"Why don't we head back to my room?" she said out loud with a smile. Dex's face got red. "Not like that: we need to talk," she told him in his mind.

"Let me let my friend know what's up," He said with a cocky smile playing along. "Yo. Found her. Meet at the rail by the main entrance. Now." He pressed send and a few minutes later, Neil came to them looking a bit sad.

"Well I struck out," they said. "I asked this cute girl wanted to dance and she ran the other way. I'm not you, Dex. I'm not used to that reaction."

"Ha," Dex replied sarcastically. "Anyway, this is Cassandra and I figured we could all go hang out together."

"Just be cool and go with it," she said to Neil in their mind. They nodded.

"Cool, cool, cool," they responded. "Let's go."

"I'm linking us up: hope you both don't mind," Cassandra said telepathically.

"Wait," Neil protested in both their minds. "Isn't that just for teams? Like, isn't it dangerous?"

"It's already done," she replied. "I mean, who did you think you two are supposed to be partnered with?"

"Wait: you're our Psyker?" Dex asked.

"Not now," she responded. "There may be people listening."

"We are literally talking with our brains," Neil interjected.

"Yeah. Now shut up because there's a bunch of crap going on. They are monitoring it all," she replied. They finally, after a few minutes of walking, made it to her door.

"Wait," Neil said out loud. "Something's not right here."

"What do you mean?" Cassandra asked.

"There's negative energy in there..." Neil said. Dex had a puzzled look on his face. This must be a Channeler thing, he decided.

"What's the play?" He asked Neil.

"Just get ready for anything," Neil responded. Ten percent, Dex thought. Power up now, ask questions later. He went powered up and placed his hand on his sword. Cassandra produced her card and opened the door slowly. The room was an absolute wreck. Tables were over-turned. The bed sheet was stripped off. Someone had come in here and wrecked everything.

"No signs of life," Neil said telepathically. "No one here but us girls..." Dex relaxed a bit and powered down.

"This was a message," Cassandra said. "They know I'm here."

"Then get your stuff gathered up. You can stay with us. We have more than enough room," Dex said.

"I'm not staying with almost total strangers," she replied.

"Typically, teams live together anyway. So we might as well start now. Plus, you said you were supposed to be our Psyker anyway, so it shouldn't be an issue." Neil said. "That is if you're telling the truth."

"You see this room and you think I'm lying?" Cassandra asked. Dex looked at her. She had a look on her face that showed she was hurt. Dex could feel the indignity radiating off of her. She had been through a terrible ordeal these past two weeks. She was constantly on the move and looking over her shoulder the entire time. Dex could feel the hurt she felt at the suggestion that she couldn't be trusted.

"She's telling the truth, Neil," Dex said. Neil nodded. Cassandra was a bit confused, but there were other things she had to deal with now.

"Watch the door," she said. "Let me gather up my things." She only took a few minutes and her things were gathered up in a few bags. "No talking," she said. "I'll follow you guys to your room. Then we can talk." Neil and Dex nodded in affirmation. This whole thing was troubling to

Dex. He decided to power up a bit in case even the walk to his room turned sideways. He was on high alert: looking at every possible person as if they could attack at any minute. He didn't know what else to do. This was the start of what he needed to do. She obviously had information that was important, so he had to protect her. Not that she needed protection. It was clear that Cassandra was very skilled in her Psyker abilities. No: the whole point of this was just to get their team together. Someone didn't want that to happen. If that was the case, which Dex thought it was, then the most important thing was them simply finding each other.

Cassandra was slightly confused. Why? Why did it have to be this way? Adrian had kept telling her to trust the plan, but their communications were few and far in between. Someone could be listening, she was told. She was only told what she needed to know, which she hated. How could she solve a problem with little to no data on the situation? But Adrian would just say that he trusts Jules. She got that. She understood better than anyone why that would be the case. But it didn't help her. All she needed was a guiding hand- someone to just take her and help her get to where she needed to be. She knew she wasn't going to get that. She never got that. It wasn't that she was bitter over it. She was used to it. It was a callous that grew over time to teach her that she couldn't rely on others: only herself. Her resilience, while important, still didn't help the fact that she felt she needed guidance- especially from Adrian.

Once they made it to Dex and Neil's room, the three breathed a collective sigh of relief. They locked and deadbolted the door. Neil ran over to make sure the balcony sliding doors were firmly shut and locked.

"I'll get us some drinks," Neil offered helpfully.

"Wow," Cassandra said. "You two don't go anywhere simply, huh?"

"It seemed like a good idea at the time," Dex said sheepishly. "Let's have a seat." Cassandra sat her bags down and walked over to the couch. Neil brought a pitcher of ice water and three glasses already filled.

"Thank you," she said to Neil taking a glass. She took a long drink, steadying herself. "I have been waiting for this moment for quite some time. Now that it's here... it's... it's so real now, you know?"

"How long have you been waiting for us?" Neil asked.

"Since April. Adrian actually graced me with his physical presence to tell me that Jules knew who other members of my team would be."

"Did that include a Prophet?" Dex asked.

"I don't know that. All I knew was that my team was going to have someone named Dex and someone named Neil. Six months later, I heard through the grapevine that someone named Neil joined as a Channeler. Then I just had to wait for Dex. That's when I was blacklisted from getting any information on recruitment information." She took another drink of her water.

"So does that mean you're the one who alerted The Four to a possible traitor?" Dex asked. Cassandra nodded.

"It's not just me. I have a contact in your home office who has been thinking the same things. They just don't have the same connections that I do. But we keep in touch anonymously. They're the reason that I knew you finally joined The Order when you did."

"But you don't know who that person is, right?" Neil asked. Cassandra shook her head no.

"We only talked anonymously online. And then after I found you, there was suddenly even more psychic interference. I talked to Adrian about it, and he said the problem isn't just with Psykers- it's with Prophets too. There is some kind of massive interference in general. So I couldn't contact you because I didn't know who was causing it or who could be hearing. But then again, when Jules plans something, it happens. Plus, this whole thing was backed up by Ophelia," she said.

"They knew the whole damn time and didn't tell us," Neil said bitterly. "Like, how much easier would all of this have been if they just set it up?"

"That could have made things worse," Cassandra said simply. "They don't know who the traitor is so the best chance to find them and ferret them out was this option."

"So, the whole time, this big master plan was just to get us together? Why? We don't even have a Prophet," Neil did their best to hide their frustration and anger, but they felt it so strongly that Dex couldn't help but feel it too. If he was being honest, Dex was feeling the exact same way.

"Easy there, big shoots," Dex said confusing Cassandra. "One thing at a time." He looked at Cassandra. "So why the cruise? Why did we have to vaguely meet you here?"

"I went to Adrian again for advice which was a mistake. He said he couldn't help me, so, you know just more of the usual from him. So I asked Ophelia what she thought. She suggested the cruise and even helped me find one that would be the best fit." The revelation hit Dex like a large explosion.

"Wait," Neil said confused. "Didn't Ophelia..."

"Yeah. She's the one who directed me to this cruise as well." There was silence in the room. They all decided to take a drink and let this discussion sit for a moment. There was the gentle, muted sound of the sea filling the room. All of this: everything up to this point had been meticulously planned out by The Four. To be honest, they shouldn't have been as surprised as they were. Dex and Neil were told explicitly that they were not being told everything. Cassandra, while a member longer and having her own special connections, was also purposefully left out. Neil ran their hand through their hair and then rubbed their neck.

"Okay. So as I see it, there are two logical options here. First, we can't trust them because they're using us in some dark, nefarious scheme. Second, we can't trust them because they are using us to save the world. Either way, the message is pretty clear: we're on our own here."

"We can still trust them," Dex and Cassandra said at the same time.

"Well. That certainly was odd," Neil said looking away and taking a drink. Dex and Cassandra had said the same thing for the same reasons, but only Dex knew that. They had both felt inside the minds of The Four and knew they were doing things for noble reasons. While they knew that, they also knew that Neil was absolutely right: they were all on their own.

"Welp," Neil said standing up, "water isn't going to cut it now. I'll go get the wine." They left to get a bottle.

"White if you have it, please," Cassandra called after them. She turned and faced Dex. "He's got the right idea."

"They," Dex said.

"I'm sorry. I didn't know," she replied.

"No problem," Dex said, "but why not red wine?" Cassandra shrugged.

"I just prefer white. That's all."

"I'm not sure if this relationship will work then," Dex said with mock concern.

"Scotch or whisky?" Cassandra asked.

"Whisky if I have a choice. Straight. Two fingers," Dex responded.

"Same. So I think we can move past the wine issue, don't you?"

"I'd say that's fair," Dex said with a laugh. She's quick and good with sarcasm, Dex thought. This might actually work. Cassandra looked at Dex. Why was he like this? Did he think everything was a joke? No: he knew this was all serious. This humor was something else. Maybe, she thought, he was one of those who tried to use humor to defuse tense situations. Those types of people were either fun to be around or very irritating. She wanted to assume it was the latter with Dex, but something about him made her think more of the former.

Neil came back with three glasses and the wine. They poured a glass for each person.

"Did he already whine about your choice of white over red?" Neil asked, filling her glass.

"Yes, but we struck peace over whisky."

"Horrible burning liquid of death," Neil said grimacing and pouring Dex a glass.

"Neil has a more... well they call it a 'sophisticated pallet," Dex explained as Neil filled themself a glass.

"Pardon me for being extra," Neil said sitting down. "Well then: shall we toast? To new beginnings?" Dex and Cassandra nodded. The three clinked glasses gently.

"L'chaim," Dex said and took a drink.

"So here we are- just the three of us. All together because of some guiding force. So what now?" There was a collective sigh from them all after Cassandra's words. What now? That was the million-dollar question. Where do we go from here?

"We need to fill out the team," Dex said. "Obviously, the teams are set up as four person squads for a reason. While we will be okay given the circumstances, we still need a Prophet to help us." Every fiber in his being was urging him to spill it all to Casandra. He desperately wanted to explain how he was a Conduit and explain all of his Gifts, but he couldn't. At least not yet. It wasn't that he didn't trust this woman, it was that he was concerned. There were several things about the situation that just didn't sit right with Dex. He could, in all actuality, forgive The Four for guiding them in the way that they had. After all, it made sense from a certain strategic standpoint. However, there was a certain amount of all of this that made Dex feel like they had been tossed to the wolves. He had no idea what was going to happen on this cruise. Because of that, he felt like he had to play it somewhat safe for the time being. Cassandra shook her head.

"I'm not sure that's the top priority right now. I mean, we are literally on day one of a three-day cruise and my room was trashed. They left traces of negative energy to send a message. Whoever is doing all of this wanted to send a message that they know I'm here. And they know you both are here most likely. This was a message clear and simple. I think we need to focus on survival at this point." Cassandra was trying to be practical. She understood the gravity of their situation. They were stuck on this boat for at least two more days. Sure, she could phone Adrian for help, but that presented its own complications that she didn't want to deal with. She had to do this on her own for a number of reasons. So, for her, the logical first step would be survival. They had to make it off this cruise safely to get to the next logical step.

"Honestly," Neil said, "we should just go rogue. I mean, we were all kind of entrusted because we are the remainder of an equation, right? If that's the case, it's kind of safe to assume that we can just go about our days doing what we need to do for the greater good, right? Like, we are the wild card here meant to tip the balance. So, whatever we do, we are doing the right thing." Neil was trying to be practical, but they couldn't help but feel that this was the best solution. After all, they knew that they and Dex were supposed to tip the equation. They were supposed to be the wildcard here. So why not live into that? Why not just act with impunity as they were essentially told they needed to do? To Neil, it seemed to be the best solution to all of this.

"I think," Dex finally said, "that we will need to do all three at the same time."

"What do you mean?" Cassandra asked.

"Well, obviously Neil is right. We aren't supposed to be together. Yet we are. We need to do what we need to do in that regard. Not necessarily going rogue but doing what we need to do. If we are some part of a plan, then the plan might be for us to just do what we need to do. Yet Casandra raises a good point. Our immediately goal is just to survive for the time being. Like, we know people know we are here and we are at a disadvantage because we don't know who they are, but they know who we are. We need to move to a defensive position. Yet, I'm also right because along the way, we really need to finish out our team. If we can have a full team, then we can be good to go for whatever we need to do." Dex took a drink of his wine. Too fruity, he thought. It had notes of grapes and flowers. It wasn't as bitter or shocking as he would like, but it would do for the time being.

"So, what: we're all right here?" Cassandra asked?

"Exactly," Neil replied with a smile. "That's what makes us such a great team already."

"Our immediate goal," Dex clarified, "is to get off this boat. We have to take all of this sone step at a time. We get off this boat, we find a Prophet, and then we do whatever we have to do." That exclamation landed with a sort of thud in the room. Not only did all three of them feel it, but they knew that it was true. They had to survive.

"So just to clarify," Neil said taking a huge gulp of wine, "we're stuck here for another two days with someone who knows we are here and wants to stop us. But we have no idea who they are or why they want to stop us. Is that a pretty accurate summation?"

"Yeah: I think that about sums it up," said Cassandra.

"Delicious," Neil replied rolling their eyes.

"Well, obviously Cassandra can have my room."

"Don't do that, Dex. I'm fine on the couch," she protested.

"Honestly, I'm not being some ultraistic hero here. I'm a light sleeper, so if someone were to break in, I'd hear them better on the couch. And I can scream really loud."

"Lord, please don't scream," Cassandra said. "I've linked us up. Like, all you have to do is think about us both and you can send a telepathic message to us. Please don't wake me up with screams," she pleaded.

"Well excuse me," Dex said. "I'm pretty new to all of this so I'm not well practiced or versed with all this fancy-schmancy telepathy stuff."

"Oh, it's crazy useful," Neil interjected. "Like, even if we are separated, then depending upon how strong the Psyker is, we can still get messages to one another."

"I'm pretty sure I can handle the range of the boat," Cassandra said coolly.

"Good to know," Neil said with a nod.

"I think that it's getting late and our best is to get some sleep because no one knows what tomorrow will bring." Dex was right, of course, but he felt bad after he said it. He could have sugar coated it, of course, but what good would that have done? No: better to confront the bitter truth of things right now than later. After all, they needed to be somewhat realistic about their current situation.

"You are such a party pooper," Neil said with a sigh. "Fine. I'll go to bed DAD!" they finished their drink and headed off to their room, leaving Cassandra and Dex alone.

"You sure you're okay on the couch?" She asked suddenly. "I don't want to take over here..." she looked down when she said that. Honestly, she really didn't want to be a problem for Dex and Neil. She didn't know the specifics, but she knew that they all needed to be together. However, that didn't mean that she wanted to impose.

"Honestly? It's not a problem. My mom and dad always taught me to be extra nice to guests, so it's really fine."

"Where are they now?" she asked innocently. Dex paused. Well crap, he thought to himself. I guess we are having this conversation now.

"They... um... they passed away five years ago. Car crash."

"Oh," Cassandra replied, her face getting slightly pinkish. "I'm sorry... I didn't..."

"No, no, no: it's fine. I mean, we have to get to know one another anyway, right? So this is pretty much an okay conversation. That's why the teams live together- so they can work as a very cohesive unit. Besides: you didn't know." Dex could feel his own face reddening. "I mean, parents are parent, right? Besides: we're grown adults now so we can do what we want to. I mean, within reason, of course."

"Right," she agreed. "We are adults. And the past informs our future, but we aren't bound to it." She took a long drink of her wine. The conversation, while not terrible, was still a little awkward. Lord knows she didn't want him to pry too much into her own past.

"So, this has been a weird day," Dex finally said after a moment of silence.

"It's been a weird few weeks," Cassandra corrected him.

"Months," Dex countered.

"Life," Cassandra finally said. They both laughed. It did seem to both of them that life did have a funny way of.... well they would both say screwing them over. Yet each of them, for all the tragedies and slings and arrows they suffered, knew that these events shaped them and made them a stronger person. Could they really complain about that? Yes: yes they could. Would they want things changed? It seemed to Cassandra and Dex, who thought about this before, that it wasn't that they would want to change things. They each found they couldn't. If they changed things, then they wouldn't be the people that they were today. If they were being honest with themselves, they liked who they were as people. To change the past to make it easier would mean to change themselves in fundamental ways they didn't want to. No: better to suffer the slings and arrows of outrageous fortune and be happy with who they were than try to bemoan the past they couldn't change.

"Okay: real talk," Dex finally said. "What do you think is going on here?"

"What do you mean?" Cassandra asked.

"I mean, all of this is a little too... I don't know... convenient?"

"Fate has a funny way of doing that," she said with a knowing look.

"Lord: not you too," he said shaking his head.

"Honestly, you may be one of the most thick-skulled people I have ever met. You've been with The Order for at least a few months now, right? And you can't see some guiding force at work in literally everything?"

"Oh, I can see Jules and them at work," Dex admitted, "but do you really subscribe to some grand plan? I mean, doesn't that take human agency completely out of the picture?"

"But the choices still matter to me. What I do in my life is my own decision. No one person controls me. But would God control me? Absolutely."

"Doesn't sound like a very nice God," Dex admitted. "Like, God doesn't trust us enough to make our own decisions?"

"No. I believe those decisions matter because we still make them." She shrugged and sighed. "I mean, if I look at this world, then I have to see how crazy and messy it all it. So the idea of some benevolent force guiding everything... I don't know. I find it comforting."

"Some people would say that's a weak way to look at the world," Dex interjected.

"And I would tell them that their opinion is noted, but of no consequence to me," she said proudly.

"I mean, I've talked with Ophelia about the nature of fate before, but it just seems so weird to me."

"Why would you have talked to Ophelia about that?" Cassandra asked.

"I mean, we've hung out and just talked before."

"But why? Typically, The Four only associate with those that they need to train." Dex froze for a moment, but he didn't let his emotions show. He realized that he very well could have just over shared some information that he shouldn't have. She still had no clue about who he really was. Skim her emotion, he thought. Read her. She had an inquisitive look on her face: a look that said she wanted to know more. Based on her surface level emotions, he could tell that he had piqued her curiosity. So now he had no choice but to pull it back some.

"It was a special orientation. Since we are some black ops squad, they made Neil and I get to know each of the Four." He instantly thought of a monkey clanging two cymbals together: his go to defensive image should someone read his thought. Her face contorted and he got a small headache, a sign that she was trying to read his mind. He couldn't fault her for that. After all, if the situations were reversed, he would be doing the same. She really didn't have a reason to trust him other than fate or the workings of The Four. She sighed.

"Look: I can see that you've gotten some training from Adrian. That much is clear." The jig is up, he thought. "But," she continued, "we are going to have to trust one another. This isn't a game. This is life or death." Dex nodded.

"And there will be plenty of time for explanations later," he said, "but right now, as you said, we need to focus on what is in front of us. I promise you this: if you shoot straight with me later, I'll shoot straight with you." He didn't bother with trying to block her at this point. What he was saying was true. She nodded in agreement.

"Well, on that note, as it is late, I will take my leave and head off to bed."

"I'll let you know if there's any trouble," he told her. She nodded and went off to his room to sleep. Not a but a minute later did Neil come out of their room and sit on the couch.

"You're sweet on her," they said with a smug grin.

"So, I'm going to need you to shut the hell up," Dex countered.

"Girl: please," Neil retorted. "You could cut the tension with a knife."

"That's not why we are here," Dex reminded them.

"Okay, and I get that, but if I'm wrong call me a liar." Neil sat there with a smug look on their face. They knew Dex too well. They knew that Dex could not honestly say that he wasn't attracted to her. However, what Neil failed to take into consideration was the fact that, in spite of Dex's feelings, he still knew they had a job to do.

"The most important thing we have to do right now," Dex said, "is get off this boat safely. Everything else will fall into place later. But right now, we just need to survive. I felt the negative energy, too in her room It was that strong." Neil was taken aback by this.

"So, that's not something you should be able to do," they said softly.

"Oh: I am very aware of that. So if I could feel it, then it's safe to assume that there is something very nefarious afoot."

"Apparently," Neil said. They were quiet for a moment and then finally said, "We're in it deep, aren't we?

"We are in it deeper that I thought possible," Dex replied. It was true. Sure: Dex knew they could expect some really heavy situations. He never, in his wildest imagination, thought it would be like this. They were literally out to sea stuck on a boat for three days with some force that wanted to do them harm. The thought terrified Dex. Sure: he and Neil were itching for a real mission, but they didn't have a full team. Yes, they technically had a Psyler now, but they were still missing a Prophet. Dex's Gift of prophecy only worked so well. It wasn't like they could rely on it in substitution of a full prophet.

"It is what it is," Neil said with a shrug.

"It is what it is," Dex agreed.

"Right. Well, need my beauty sleep. So I guess this is all a problem for tomorrow Neil," they said.

"Agreed. Good night, Neil," Dex replied. Once they had left the room, Dex got up and made sure all the doors were locked. He studied the front door for a moment. How should he set up a sort of alarm system? Yet at the same time, would it even be worth it? If someone really wanted to come into the room, they could easily barge in. Plus, being on a boat made it difficult as well. After all, most of the furniture was firmly affixed to the floor. He walked back over and grabbed the wine bottle. He poured the rest of the time down the drain, needing only the bottle. Sending some positive energy into it, the bottle cracked easily into rather large pieces. He carefully placed those pieces under the doormat reasoning that someone stepping on them would crack the glass and alert him.

He laid down on the couch with Ruach at his side.

"Hell and damnation..." he said quietly to himself. It wasn't that everything was too weird. Dex prided himself on being able to roll with the punches. The problem was that it's all becoming real to Dex now. It became very apparent that Jules and the rest have been pulling strings from the shadows. While he understood the need for that, it was also annoying because he felt like he was still no closer to understanding what was going on. Furthermore, they were now thrown into all of this with an absolute stranger. While Dex trusted her as much as he could, he still didn't know her. It was just chaos after chaos.

Little did Dex know that Cassandra was having her own sort of existential crisis about the whole situation in her new bedroom. She lay in bed furious and hurt by Adrian, which if she was being honest with herself, was pretty much par for the course. While she trusted Neil and Dex as much as she could, given the circumstances, she couldn't help but feel like there was something that Dex wasn't telling her. He wasn't showing all of his cards and that frustrated her. Teams had to be chosen carefully and built upon as much trust as possible. To Cassandra, all of this seemed too hastily thrown together. If there was any one of The Four she trusted implicitly, it was Ophelia. And yet, the revelation of her guiding hand forcing these three people together didn't sit right with her. She quietly scanned Dex and Neil to see what they were doing. Neil was already asleep. Dex noticed immediately and spoke to her telepathically.

"Hey. You need something?" he asked kindly.

"I was just making sure you all were okay," she replied lying down in her bed.

"I'm pretty good, considering everything. I'm pretty sure Neil is already asleep."

"Oh yeah," she confirmed. "They're already out."

"Dude could sleep through a tornado," Dex replied laughing. It was quiet for a moment. Cassandra was not a fan of uncomfortable silences.

"Hey Cassandra?" Dex finally said.

"Yeah? What's up?" she asked.

"I just..." just say it, Dex thought to himself. "I'm going to be a good teammate, okay? Like, I promise I won't let you down." Wow that was weak, they both thought to themselves privately.

"I know," she replied quietly. She turned on her side and stared out the window to the blackness of the night sea. The old sailors of the past assumed that there were monsters under the chaotic waters because they couldn't see what was in the oceans. She couldn't help but agree with that thought now. "It's going to be fine. I get that this is a...well it's a less than ideal situation to form a team."

"Well the good news is Neil and I know each other and we are both super nice and once this is over..." Dex paused. He had to choose his next words carefully. "once this is all over, I promise we will actually get to know one another, okay? I believe in this team." Cassandra was confused. This just added more proof to her that he was hiding something from her. Yet at this current point in time, she had no choice but to just go with it all.

"I know," she replied. "I know. Now let's get some sleep so we can relax some for the time being."

"Good night, Cassandra," Dex said.

"Cass," she replied.

"Huh?"

"My friends: they...they call me Cass. If you want to call me Cass you can."

"Thank you, Cass," he replied. Until this moment, Cassandra didn't know it was possible for a person to mentally blush.

"Goodnight, Dex." Eventually, sleep found them both. All in all, they had to at least be grateful to be on this cruise. The calm sounds of the wave and the gentle rocking of the boat calmed their minds and the fell into a deep, dreamless sleep.

Finally, Dex awoke to a pounding on the door.

"Dex? Dex Machina? It's Sara. Can you please open up?" He jumped up, grabbing his sword and powering up about five percent of the way. the floor mat crunched under his feet as he got to the door. Looking through the peep hole, he saw a pale and crying Sara.

"Guys: wake up," he told Neil and Cassandra telepathically. "We have an issue here." He opened the door and looked at her.

"I um... I don't know what's going on here but you said if I needed help, I should ask so... please help..." Cassandra and Neil came to the door, looking at Sara. However, they were now all three transfixed on dead body in a pool blood a few feet to the left of their door.

"Aw beans," Neil said quietly.

Chapter Nine

"So, I'll be the first to admit: I didn't have murder mystery on my cruise ship bingo card, but here we are.," Dex said. Sara was radiating fear and anxiety. Dex was sure Casandra could feel it as well.

"Why don't you come inside and calm down," Neil suggested. "Let's take this one step at a time."

"No one else is in the area," Cassandra said to Dex and Neil telepathically. "Do you sense any negative energy, Neil?"

"Nope. This was a good old-fashioned murder," they said. "We need to try to get security footage."

"Sara, what exactly happened?" Dex asked aloud. She sat down shaking. Cassandra handed her a glass of water.

"I... I just wanted to see if you guys needed anything, you know? Like, we have people here from The Order and I knew you guys would help with stuff. So, I wanted to be a good employee and low-key give great service. And when I turned the corner, I saw someone laying there. And I approached thinking it was just some drunk. But they weren't just some drunk. It's some dead guy... and the blood..."

"Hey: it's okay," Cassandra said. "We're going to take care of things. Just relax." The room was flooded with a sense of calm and Sara visibly relaxed. "I calmed her emotions down some," Cassandra said telepathically.

"Her heart is racing and her breathing is insanely fast," Dex noted. "Good call, Cass."

"Wait," Neil interjected suddenly. "Are we doing nicknames now?"

"Calm down, Superstar," Cassandra said, looking at Neil. "We have bigger things to deal with."

"I can't believe you told her," Neil said wide eyed.

"First of all, he didn't," Cassandra said. "I read it in your mind on accident while you were sleeping. Second: we literally have a dead body to deal with, so that takes priority."

"We're going to go start investigating," Dex told Sara aloud. "You sit here and relax. Let us handle it. Come on you guys." He got up and started walking towards the door. "We need to check this body out," Dex said to them aloud. They all three went outside and stood near the body but didn't want to go too near it. Neil wasn't there when Dex identified the bodies of his parents. They waited outside. Cassandra and Dex had both been around death before, but her experiences were less cordial than Dex's.

"I think we need gloves, so I'm going to go look for some and check in on Sara." With that, Neil went back inside.

"They've never seen a murder victim before. Neither of us have if I'm being honest. I'm just... I don't know. Maybe I have a stronger stomach," Dex explained.

"First time is always shocking, but you got to rip that Band-Aid off at some point," she replied. "Let's see what we can find out." Neil brought them a pair of gloves and looked at the body.

"Okay. So before I go back in, can I recommend checking the temperature? Like, see if they are hard and cold. And expect ship authorities to come soon because they literally have a morgue on board and Sara alerted her supervisor." With that, Neil went back inside.

"They're really good with people," Dex said, "so they're doing good work in there. He can try to get more information."

"Well she wasn't lying," Cassandra said. "I read her mind. No signs of psychic tampering."

"Oh for sure," Dex said. "I picked up on that, too."

"What do you mean?" Cassandra asked.

"I mean, I didn't feel like she was lying. She has no reason to lie. It felt like she was telling the truth." Cassandra looked at Dex. She wanted to push the issue, but they were standing next to a literal dead body. Time was of the essence. The longer they took to examine the body, the more time it would harder it would be to find evidence. Turning to look at the body, Cassandra was shocked that she recognized him.

"Aw crap..." she said.

"What's wrong?" Dex asked.

"Look at that body. Recognize him?" Dex stared for a moment. He even tried squinting. Suddenly his eyes went wide with realization.

"Oh..." he said quietly.

"Yep," Cassandra said sadly. "It's that guy trying to pick me up last night. Which, if anyone was watching us, puts us both as suspects. At the very least it gives us motive."

"Yet clearly we didn't do this," Dex said.

"Right."

"Who the Hell are you people?" a gruff voice behind them said. They turned and faced a short, squat man. He wore a Hawaiian shirt and khakis and a very annoyed look on his face.

"Neil," Dex called telepathically, "We're going to need your people skills out here."

"Tell them you're undercover FBI," Neil responded. "Cassandra: can you make that believable with badges and stuff?"

"Yeah," she said as Neil showed up.

"Dex! Cassandra! Aren't you finished with the initial investigation yet? Washington will have my ass if we don't get that in soon!"

"We were going to start, but then this guy..." Dex was soon interrupted by that guy.

"Hey! I'm the one that's in charge of the security on this boat! Not you!"

"What's your name, sir?" Cassandra asked innocently.

"Why don't you call me Sergeant Mark," the man said.

"Private security for the cruise, I imagine?" she asked.

"Yeah!" he yelled defensively. "And now I got a bunch of paperwork to fill out because..."

"Let me stop you there," Cassandra said. "You see that person there?" she said as she pointed to Neil. "Captain, please show this man your credentials."

"Just flash your wallet like a badge," she said in their minds. Neil did as they were instructed.

"I'm pretty sure Captain at the FBI and head of the Special Crimes Unit trumps your paycheck," they said flashing their wallet. "My task force has been tracking this guy for months and you want to come in here and just blow that investigation? I got the guys in Washington breathing down my neck for more information and now he's suddenly dead! If you think I'm letting you have first crack at this body before my team looks it over, you got another thing coming there, buddy." Neil then stood there triumphantly with their hands on their hips wearing an expression daring him to say something. Cassandra prodded his mind to understand the consequences of what would happen if they went against the FBI. The man's face went white.

"Look, can... can you just have the girl who found him let me know when you guys are done? I'll... um... I'll go get some coffee till you guys are done. I am so sorry for the interruption." Neil stepped over and shook the man's hand.

"You're a good man, Sergeant Mark. Your country thanks you. Truly you are an American patriot." With that, the man blushed and left. After he was gone, Neil gave a sigh of relief. "I totally didn't think that was going to work," they admitted.

"Honestly? That was some of your best work yet," Dex said.

"I'm impressed," Cassandra said. "So yeah: you can call me Cass too if you want."

"Hooray! I'm useful and a friend!" Neil squealed. They looked down at the body and had a quizzical look on their face. "Wait: something is wrong here. Give me those gloves," they gave Neil a pair of gloves and they put them on.

"Didn't think you'd get into this," Dex admitted.

"Girl, please," Neil said dismissively. "I was better at anatomy than you. I just had to get over the shock is all." Neil bent down and touched the blood on the ground. They looked at Dex and Cassandra. "There is something wrong with the blood," they said. "That blood shouldn't be that see through." They rubbed the blood together on their fingers, making an odd face and pulling their fingers a part. They shoved the fingers in Dex and Cassandra's faces who instinctively backed away.

"Look! It's not that sticky. It should be stickier."

"That's some great science there," Dex replied.

"No: they're right," Cassandra interjected. "Look at their neck. She put on a glove and moved the man's head slightly. He had a rather large, jagged wound on the right side of his neck. "Whatever killed him had to pierce the jugular vein if it made a whole that huge. There only looks like there is a lot of blood, but there should be a lot more. There are no drag marks, so he was killed right here, but this on the ground? It's not the eight to twelve pints it should be." Neil smelled their fingers.

"It smells like blood, so it wasn't cleaned. So why is there less blood in the pool around him than should be and why is it not like regular blood?" Cassandra placed her fingers inside the wound.

"It's cold," she said. She touched his forehead with the back of her other hand. "Too cold to match the temperature of the rest of his body." Neil shook their head.

"It doesn't make sense," they said. "It's like this is some kind of perfect murder." Perfect murder. The words resounded in Dex's head triggering a memory from a creative writing class in college.

"Perfect murder," he whispered.

"What's up?" Cassandra asked.

"I took a class on creative writing," Dex explained. "We had to do a murder mystery but we had to try to make it so that the killer committed the perfect murder. Like, one girl had her killer put cyanide in a CPAP sleep breathing machine. She switched out all the tubes after and burned almond scented candles in the room to mask the smell. But me? I had two people go on a skiing trip. Waiting for the right time, my killer tripped the other under a cliff overhang. They got hurt, but them they stabbed them in the chest with a knife. But then he went and found a large icicle and stabbed them in the same with it so it looked like an accident." Dex looked at Neil and Cassandra. "He got killed by an icicle."

"That would explain the watered-down blood," Neil said with an acknowledging look. "So we're dealing with a Grafter. Someone with an ice demon arm?" Cassandra shook her head.

"That would make it look like there is more blood. The icicle would have to be fairly large to make this hole. I'll admit to it melting and sloshing around on the sea at night. But there still is a large lack of blood here."

"Aw beans," Neil said running their hair through their hair. "That's why they used an icicle. They were trying to make it look like there was still a lot of blood." Neil squatted down by the body and stuck a few fingers into the wound. "You two owe me a manicure after this." They rooted around and found the jugular vein still intact. Neil placed it in between their thumb and index finger. They squeezed. Two small red drops welled up about two inches apart. Neil sighed and put his ungloved hand on their forehead. They were quiet, looking out to the sea.

"We have a Vampire," they finally said quietly. "We have a damn Vampire on a boat out at sea pretty much on an all you can eat buffet for them." There was a pause. The reality of the situation was finally sinking in on them.

"About three thousand people," Cassandra said. Three thousand people on this cruise ship. And we have to find the vampire."

"But why kill this person like this?" Dex asked. "It seems to me that if I was going to be a Vampire on a cruise ship, then I'd drain them and toss the body overboard. No fuss: no muss."

"It's because this is a message," Cassandra explained. "They weren't feeding because they were hungry. They wanted us to know that there is a Vampire on the ship. It's the same reason my room got tossed. They are trying to intimidate us. They want us to make mistakes out of fear because we are being hunted."

"Then why not toss our room as well?" Neil asked.

"Because they didn't know you were on here," Cassandra offered.

"Nobody outside of The Four, as far as we know, knew we were coming. So we're missing something here. Someone somehow got tipped off to us being here," Neil said.

"I assumed The Council or something would send you with a team," Cassandra said. Dex shook his head.

"They don't know about this mission. We made the decision to keep it on the down low. They just assumed Neil and I went on a cruise. No indication at all that we are on a secret mission. They may have suspected something more, but they did not at all know what we were doing."

"Someone had to put two and two together then," Cassandra said. "I mean, this is the guy that you and I spoke to early last night. So, at that point they understood we were connected."

"Then it's not Sara," Neil said. "Because she knew we were in The Order when we got on the boat."

"Can we assume that this is someone who was at the dinner party last night? Someone saw us all walk off together. They tracked down our room here and left us this morning gift." To Dex, this made the most sense. Neil and Cassandra nodded.

"I think we need to go check in on Sara," Cassandra finally said. "We need to send her off and deal with any and all questions that may come from this."

"Well, let's get to it," Dex said. The three walked back into the room to see Sara sitting on the couch eating an apple.

"I hope you don't mind," she said. "I was a little hungry."

"No, it's cool," Dex replied.

"Sara," Cassandra said. Then she paused. She wasn't sure how to start this conversation. She knew they needed Sara as an ally, but did she really want to terrify her? Sadly, Cassandra felt there was little to no choice. She sat down next to Sara. "Based on our investigation, we think there is a Vampire here on the boat." Her eyes went wide with fear.

"We have to tell the captain," she said. "We have to turn the boat around and get to safety." Cassandra shook her head.

"It's not that simple," she replied. "If we do that, we risk tipping them off and them going further underground. And we need this lead. We will find them."

"So, what do you need me to do?" Sara asked.

"We need you to be ready to help in whatever way possible. Right now, we have no leads. We're going out tonight to the dance party again and try to flush them out."

"Can you, like, I don't know: scan for their evil vibes?" Sara asked. Neil shook their head.

"They already tossed Cass's room. I felt negative energy there, but unless they are actively using their Gift, it's not on display. That was done for the purpose of telling her that they knew she was here."

"And the Vampire doesn't want to be found, but they want us to know they are on the ship," Dex added. "My guess is that we are all going to look for each other. Finding them won't be hard: it's what will come after that could be a problem."

"But," Cassandra added, "we aren't giving up. And I want you to know that we are going to do everything we can to protect the people on this boat. Do you trust us?" Dex looked at Cassandra. It was clear that this wasn't her first time working on something like this. She was a natural born leader. Truth be told, Dex was sort of jealous of how she was handling the situation. She worked with empathy and kindness yet showed toughness. It wasn't an arrogant kind of toughness. It was this dependable, durable quality. Sara thought on Casandra's words for a moment and slowly nodded her head in agreement.

"Yeah. Yeah: I trust you." She grabbed a notebook and scribbled down her number. "This is my cell phone. I'll have it on all the time. Let me know how I can help."

"Thank you," Cassandra said taking the paper. They said their good-byes and she left to go get the inspector to start the investigation. After she left it was quiet for a few moments. Each of them- Dex, Cassandra, and Neil- were awash with many emotions. The one emotion they felt the most at this point was anger. They were, in fact, unjustifiably in a position they would rather not be in. Even more than that was the fact that they were put there by their mentors. To say that they were upset and angry with them all was a bit of an understatement.

"I need you two to understand," Cassandra finally said, breaking the silence, "that this is par for the course being in The Order. I'm not talking about the whole secrecy thing. I'm talking about death. For us, it's not some far off concept. It's a reality. It will always be a reality for what we do. If either of you aren't okay with seeing a lot of freshly dead bodies, then let me know and we can end this partnership now." Neil and Dex looked at each other. While having brushes with death and fighting, this was the first real time they were confronted with the notion that innocent people will die. But this? This man died because they were here. Dex couldn't help but realize that. Would this man still be alive if they never came on the ship? But then, he reasoned, they wouldn't have met Cassandra. They wouldn't have a team. Someone would be further along in their goals. No. Dex realized a sad and simple truth- it had to happen this way.

Neil sighed and rubbed their neck. Sure: they had been around dead animals in classes and such, but this was just slightly different, they thought. They knew in the pit of their stomach that this wouldn't be the last time they saw a dead body.

"It is what it is," Neil said, staring out into the ocean.

"It is what it is," Dex agreed. Cassandra nodded.

"Good. Now let's work on a plan."

The plan was both elegantly simple and incredibly stupid and dangerous at the same time. One of the things Dex learned from watching and listening to the players in The Cathedral of Heroes was that in Dungeons and Dragons, it's usually not a good idea to split the party. However, they were faced with locating a needle in a haystack. Ergo, they felt as if they had no choice but to split up. The only saving grace that they had was that they would still be linked up to each other's minds. Cassandra was a powerful Psyker and could keep them all connected with no problem. They also had the advantage of them not being an official team. They concluded that, while they met, the invisible enemy couldn't not assume they would share the link with one another. Cassandra and Neil, both being more adapt at looking comfortable in a party scene, would go to the dance albeit far away from one another. Dex, meanwhile, would note the comings and goings of the attendants and be on the lookout for anyone suspicious.

"Stick to the plan," Neil said.

"Watch the plan fail miserably," Dex replied.

"Improvise like we should have done all along," Cassandra said.

"Oh, I do like her," Neil said.

"A fine addition to our collection," Dex responded. Cassandra sighed.

"You two will be the death of me,"

"Hey!" Neil interjected. "You still need to move into our Fortress of Solitude."

"I'm not sharing a room with either of you," Cassandra said.

"We have, like, two spare rooms. It's perfect," Neil said reassuringly. Dex replied,

"I feel like I'm not getting a say in this."

"Don't be a baby. I'm a good roommate," Cassandra said.

"You can hide the waifu pillow," Neil said in a false secrete tone.

"What? No! I don't..." Dex protested. Cassandra put her hands up defensively.

"Hey man: I don't judge." She laughed. It felt right for her. It felt good. To be honest, they all knew what was going on. There was no way not to. But this? Laughing with new friends? It helped and she was grateful for that. Cassandra didn't have the easiest time in The Order. She felt as if she constantly had to prove herself and be the leader in everything. She became a skilled combatant with a staff and honed her psychic abilities to rival Adrian's. To actually be a part of a team that felt like family to her was something she was thankful for.

The rest of the day was a blur with planning and answering a few questions from the people investigating the crime. Neil was especially useful in this endeavor and Dex and Cassandra were able to avoid suspicion fairly easily with some telepathic nudging. Sara was able to do some work and provide pictures of the dance area. With that, they were able create a sort of floor plan and take note of entrances and exits. They decided that it would be better for them to stay in during the day. Let the enemy think they were hiding scared. After all, it was unlikely that they would do anything in the middle of the day with everyone walking about.

"We need to think about what to wear tonight," Neil said suddenly.

"That doesn't seem that important," Dex confessed.

"No. I think Neil is right," Cassandra rebutted. "After all, we are going to want to draw some amount of attention to ourselves. And we will want to be easily seen by each other." Dex was kind of speechless at this thought.

"I swear to you both there is no way in hell I am wearing a glowstick."

"We don't even have those," Cassandra said confused. Neil shielded their eyes and looked away blushing. "Oh," Cassandra said surprised.

"I mean, I was thinking it would be fun and there would be parties..." Neil said defensively.

"No: that will actually work for us," Cassandra said. "It's a good idea. We have to blend in." Neil smiled a bit at this and perked up a bit.

In the end, Cassandra decided on wearing her red dress again as it was the flashiest thing she brought with her. Dex reluctantly wore a bright Hawaiian shirt and some khaki slacks. Neil, however, went all out. They wore a fun bright pink crop top with skinny jeans and worked very hard on their makeup.

Before they left for dinner, Neil asked,

"So at what point do we phone in for back up?"

"We don't," Cassandra asked curtly. She needed to do this without help from the higherups. "I'm sure The Four would be too busy and The Council can't be trusted at this point." She looked at them both. "We're still on our own here."

"They better have fresh shrimp then," Neil said crossing their arms and pouting.

"If one of us goes down for real, then we call for help." Dex turned and looked away after he said it. "We have to be pragmatic here. I'm all doing this on our own, but we have to be realistic as well."

"So, you don't think we can do this?" Cassandra asked sadly. Dex shook his head.

"I never said that. I'm going to fight with just about everything I have here. And if I go down, then you call for help. And I expect the same from you two. We all don't need to die."

"I'm not dying here," Cassandra replied. "So, I'm good. Don't worry about me."

"I'm pretty sure I still have a list of things to do and dying on a boat isn't one of them," Neil said with a shrug.

"And I know I'm not going to die. Good. It's settled. No dying." The problem Dex had with this was that he didn't know if he should go all out for all of this. He had never been in a real situation other than with the earworm demon. And even then, he didn't go all out. Yet he knew in the very depths of his soul that to save Cass or Neil he would gladly use every ounce of his power to do so. So he had to play it all by ear.

"Almost time to go," Neil said looking at their watch. We need some pump-up music."

"Shuffle, please," Dex said looking out the window. "You know the rules."

"Rules?" Cassandra asked.

"Dex believes in the power of music to speak to us," Neil said sarcastically.

"Prove me wrong, and I'll stop," he replied. Neil pulled out their phone and hit shuffle. The piano tones started softly, yet they echoed throughout the room.

"When there's nowhere else to run, is there room for one more son?" Brandon Flower's voice filled the space with both hope and sadness as was always the case when Dex heard "All These Things That I've Done." This song always held special meaning for Dex, so he was glad it started playing. There was always a longing in the song for the singer to be seen-to be known in the midst of a changing world. Dex felt that tonight.

"I've got soul but I'm not a solider." Over and over again, the words grew to a crescendo dancing around their minds. Dex never was much of a fighter. Sure he knew how to fight, but he avoided it at all costs. Neil was similar minded as well, though they often defused the situation with humor. Cassandra knew she could fight and fight well, but she was still always hesitant to do so. Yet here the three reluctant soldiers stood preparing to do battle. Dex stood up after the song was over.

"Alright. Let's get to work." Dex checked the strap on his sword one last time. Cassandra closed her purse and jumped and did some air punches to loosen up. Once the three got to the dining area, they split up and sat at different tables placed around the room. Dinner was fun, they all supposed. The shrimp sadly already started to turn, but the meal was more than adequate.

"I'm not picking up any negative energy. But then again, I didn't think they were dumb enough to use it here," Neil said telepathically.

"Everything seems to normal," Dex remarked.

"Of course it does," Cassandra said. "They don't want to make too public of a scene. We need to be looking for people watching us."

"Only one that I've noticed is Sara," Dex replied. "She's been keeping a far eye on us."

"Well lucky for you you're not wearing a dress. I lost count of the horny old men staring at my chest."

"You should totally plant a scary image in their head the next time someone does that," Neil offered.

"That's not a terrible idea," Cassandra admitted.

"If we're being hunted as well, then the best bet to get one of us would be at the dance party. I think that's where we will need to be on our toes," Dex said changing the subject back to more pressing matters.

"Agreed," Cassandra affirmed. "Let's proceed with phase two then."

Phase two of the plan consisted of them all waiting around awkwardly while the tables and chairs were moved from the mail hall floor.

"I'm going back to the room," Dex said. "I want to check it out and make sure we can still reach one another." The others agreed that it was a good ideal and soon Dex was alone back in his room. There was no negative energy. The room was fine, as he expected it would be. "Can you all still hear me?"

"That's a Texas-sized 10-4," Neil replied.

"Yeah. You're good," Cassandra said.

"Okay. Good. Doing a once over of the room and then I'll be back."

"The party starts in about five minutes," Cassandra reminded him.

"Don't worry I'll be there. Wouldn't miss it world." He took some time to stroll about the room and stare at the setting sun over the ocean. This is your life now, Dex, he said to himself. This is what you've been waiting for, right? A chance to make a difference. It didn't matter to Dex in this moment that he felt betrayed by The Four. What mattered to him was that he was here now. He was the one who was here. He was the boots on the ground working hard to make a difference. And to Dex, in this moment, that was enough.

He locked the door and headed out back to the party.

"I'm on my way," he told the others. "All's clear on this front."

"Sounds good. We will keep in touch," Cassandra said.

"You sure you don't want to switch me jobs?" Neil asked.

"Hard no," Dex said quickly. He did not want to have to listen to blaring club music all night long. And, as Dex discovered, it wouldn't be too long until said music started. By the time he got back to the hall, the music was already pumping and people were coming and going.

"Alright, everyone. This is it. This is our best shot to find them," Cassandra said. "I'll be scanning people for signs of Vampire thirst. Neil is looking for any forms of negative energy and we will see if someone tries to capture us."

"I love being bait," Neil said. "It makes me feel special."

"Please," Dex retorted. "Statistically speaking, I'm more likely to get picked up then either of you. I'm out here with little to no witnesses."

"You'll be fine. The plan is to drive whomever to you anyway, so that will save us some trouble." Cassandra was right, of course. They couldn't risk too many potential witnesses or casualties. The goal here was to stem the loss of life.

Neil and Cassandra, while working hard and looking for a potential Vampire, at least were having some fun. It was, while a terrifying thought of Vampire hunting, the most normal each of them felt in a long time. Yes, they took their responsibility seriously. That didn't mean, however, that they couldn't go and have some fun. Dex on the other hand, was enjoying the peace and quiet. The motion of the ship coupled the gentle sound of wave relaxed Dex. Yet they couldn't help but feel uneasy. It's too perfect, he thought. I'm too relaxed. This is too nice. Something is wrong here. His vigil had revealed nothing out of the ordinary other than a disturbing amount of people who apparently couldn't hold their liquor. Dex was starting to think the whole thing was going to wind up being a bust. No one outside of a stray few people who asked him for a light or a cigarette approached him.

"Any of you two find any leads?" Dex asked Cassandra and Neil.

"Not yet," Cassandra replied.

"No, but that girl I met the other night wanted to dance now so I got that going for me, which is nice."

"Good for you, Neil," Cassandra said. "Just be sure to respect her boundaries."

"This girl has no boundaries," Neil admitted. "She is super handsy. Like, a total one-eighty from last night."

"But she ran off when you approached her last night?" Dex asked.

"Yeah. But she's like... I mean I think she wants me to go to her room or something."

"Does she smell like booze?" Cassandra asked. There was no answer. Dex stood up placed his hand on Ruach.

"Neil? Does she smell drunk?" Dex asked with urgency.

"Damn, ya'll. Sorry. Morgan put her tongue down my throat and it was hard to concentrate. But I can confidently say that she doesn't smell or taste like booze."

"Offer up your room," Cassandra said.

"Wait, are we doing the honey pot scam?" Neil asked.

"No," Cassandra replied with a sigh. "Something doesn't seem right. Take her out by the exit Dex is at and I'll meet you all there. Dex: meet me right by the entrance. I'll scan her as you all pass by." Dex moved into position and soon Cassandra joined him.

"Okay," Neil said, "Morgan and I are almost at the door. Get ready." Cassandra looked at Dex and spoke out loud.

"Try to relax and just go with this, okay?"

"Huh?" Dex asked, but it was too late. She grabbed Dex and pulled her face right next to her face as if they were going to kiss. They didn't. She whispered in a hushed voice,

"I don't want them to notice us. Just hold this position for a few moments, okay?" Dex blushed and gave a short nod.

"Where do I put my hands?" he asked.

"I don't know. Haven't you ever kissed someone before?"

"Well yeah, but you know... boundaries..."

"You are adorable," she laughed. "Place them on my hips. It's fine." Dex did so and looked into her eyes. Those eyes. Those ice blue eyes that were both so fierce and comforting at the same time. Dex lost himself in those eyes for a moment.

"At the door," Neil announced in their heads.

"Scanning," Cassandra said.

"Where are you guys?" Neil asked.

"We're hiding. Just head to the room and we'll follow you," Dex said.

"She's hungry," Cassandra said grimly.

"Well I know she was at the dinner," Neil said. "She told me she was displeased with the shrimp as well."

"Then it ain't shrimp she wants now," Dex said. "I think we just found our Vampire."

"Aw, beans," Neil replied. "Of course- she wasn't really into me."

"Don't count your chickens before they're hatched," Dex said. He and Cassandra broke their embrace, each one blushing slightly.

"We should probably follow Neil," Cassandra said in a hurried tone.

"Absolutely," Dex concurred. Don't think about it, Dex thought to himself. Focus on the mission at hand.

"Hey guys?" Neil said suddenly. "Morgan's, like, really adamant to get to the room so we are running now. So, I mean, if you think she's a vampire could you all, like, I don't know, hurry up some?" Dex and Cassandra shared a glance and picked up the pace.

"Wow! She's a great kisser and all, but very aggressive." Dex and Cassandra were now in a full sprint.

"Vampire!" Neil said. "Confirmed Vampire!" Dex powered up to ten percent and opened the door. There was Neil, their hands glowing and ready, and the woman named Morgan in a bit of a defensive stance with fangs barred.

Chapter Ten

A Vampire was standing before them. Never in Dex's wildest dreams did he think that his life was going to turn out like this. Oh sure: he thought he understood Vampires. He had seen movies and read Vampire romance novels to impress a girl, but this was real to him now. Of course, he shouldn't have been surprised. He had seen first had the reality of the world. He had seen and fought a demon. He had seen and fought Grafters. Those, however, made somewhat sense to him. He had never even seriously thought about them even being real. To him, the demons at the very least could have always existed. After learning about Gifts and those with the Sight but no Gifts, it then made sense that, if demons were real, then people would try to obtain their power. Vampires, however, were nothing more to him than Gary Oldman or some good-looking young man. They always could not exist. And yet now, in the world he now inhabited, they did indeed exist and everything he had heard about them was a fairytale.

"Well come on, then," the Vampire named Morgan said. "Take me out if you're brave enough." Something seemed off. Dex, of course, had already drawn Ruach. He was sitting at about ten percent of his power which was undetectable. Neil was ready for a fight, and Cassandra had assumed a hand to hand stance. All of that being said, other than her being a Vampire, there was something off about Morgan. Dex noted that she was wide eyed and frantic looking. Was this because she knew she was done for? She had to know that she couldn't escape. Yet it is probable, he reasoned, that she targeted Neil possibly for their interaction last night. Yet now, she seemed sure that the three would fight her.

Then there was the issue of her emotions. There was hunger, as to be expected, but there was something else. There seemed to be a sense of sadness to her. Perhaps that was her fear. After all, the hunger she was feeling was an insane amount, which didn't make any sense. If she had fed, even some late last night or early this morning, she should not be this hungry.

"Cass," Dex said telepathically, "something is wrong here. We need a reading on her."

"Should I start blasting?" Neil asked.

"No," Cass replied. "Dex is right. Something is wrong. She's starving." Neil scoffed.

"I mean, she is a Vampire."

"No," Dex replied. "If she fed last night or this morning, even some, she shouldn't be this hungry." Dex slowly put his sword away and powered down. "I'm going to try something," he said. Morgan looked at him confused. "Guys, lower your guard. I think she needs our help."

"If she comes after any of us, I'm going to drop her like a sack of potatoes," Cassandra said.

"And that's fine, but I think she's not the Vampire we are looking for." Dex said. He stood upright and placed his hands up in front of him. Out loud, he said, "Look, we know something is wrong here. And we want to help you." Morgan looked at them. Something had changed. She had known and understood that the vampire who called himself Sextus had said there were three agents of The Order on the ship. She had used her gift of Prophecy to learn that this exact moment- the standoff- would occur with these people. So why, then, didn't they just attack outright? They should have fought and killed her on sight, she thought. Yet this man was seemingly giving up. And there was the woman who followed his lead. And then there was that sweet idiot, Neil.

"Don't," she said softly. "I'm a killer. I killed someone last night. And I'll do it again."

"I think we both know that's not exactly true," Cassandra said, tapping her head. "I'm a Psyker."

"Morgan, please. Don't do this." Neil was pleading with her. They really didn't want to hurt this woman. "We can help you." Tears welled up in her eyes. She shook her head.

"Please," she said softly. "I don't want to kill anyone. Please, just kill me. Please." Dex, Neil, and Cassandra looked at each other. "I don't know how much longer I can control this... this urge. Please. Just end it for me."

"Morgan, was it? My name is Dex. You know Neil. And she," he said point to Cassandra, "is Cassandra. Now, I'm fairly sure we can help each other. I just... just please trust me, okay? We can help each other. And if we can't, then I promise that we will take care of you, okay?"

"Dex, no!" Neil said telepathically. "We can't kill her! Please."

"She's a Vampire. There's no easy way back from that," Cassandra said.

"I have to save her," Dex said firmly. "I have to. And I can. Please trust me." Neil nodded but Cassandra was confused. Once again, there were things that were not adding up to her. Her time in The Order proved to her that a cure for vampirism was possible, but there was no way a newbie like Dex could know what that was. You would have had to be a very skilled Healer like Jules to pull something like that off. Perhaps that was Dex's plan. Perhaps he wanted to take her to Jules for a healing.

"If this goes south," Cassandra warned, "I'm shutting this down. All I need is an intact brain to extract information."

"Dex won't let it come to that, right?" Neil was obviously worried. It was possible, Dex thought, that he had formed some kind attachment or bond with Morgan.

"Let's sit down," Dex said aloud, "and start from the beginning, okay?" Dex slowly walked over to the table, his hands raised, and sat down. Neil and Cassandra followed. "I promise you- regardless of what you've been told, there is a cure. And I will make sure you get it." Morgan looked hesitant. It would have been easier, she thought, to force them into a fight. The Psyker was the problem. She didn't want to get put to sleep and still be this way. She never was very stealthy which would have been the easiest way to pick them off. Then there was Neil whom she really didn't want to hurt. But this Dex character promised that there was a cure. Sextus never mentioned a cure, but then again why would he. She understood from the start that he was just using her as a new Vampire for something. Slowly, she retracted her fangs and stood up straight. She sat down at the table.

"No one ever mentioned a cure," she said as she sat down, the hunger still gnawing at her, running a hand through her long, brown hair.

"So you're not working alone, then?" Cassandra asked. Slowly, Morgan shook her head no.

"I'm a new Vampire. I just turned a few days ago. I um..." she looked down as if she was remembering a painful memory. "I wanted to be an actress." Her hazel eyes welled with tears and she brushed some of her long chestnut hair out of her face. "And, well, that's a stupid little kid's dream. And I was running out of money, so I thought why not use my Gift of Prophecy to just get a few scratch-off tickets. And it worked. And it kept working. Then I figured, why even work then? So, I started hitting casinos and winning big on machines. I knew when ones would pay out. I would force people off of them. And um..." she sighed. "I guess I got greedy. And no one told me what would happen." Neil ran and grabbed a box of tissues and gave it to her. "Thank you," she said softly.

"But why are you here? Did someone make you come here?" Cassandra asked. Morgan nodded again.

"He goes by Sextus. Apparently, all the vampires think it's cool to rename themselves something terrifying. It's supposed to honor some guy named Ramses the Damned who was... I don't know some big famous evil guy that died?" Dex noticed Cassandra wince at that name of Ramses the Damned. "They wanted to call me Morgan le Fay. I didn't want to be that: I just wanted to be Morgan. I fought and clawed for so long to be Morgan and... they just wanted to make me change, too."

"Then what?" Neil asked. "This guy finds you after you turned and then what?"

"He promised to help me. Wanted to teach me to be a proper Vampire and take the world. Wanted me to be his queen of the dead." She looked at them with a hint of fear in her eyes, her voice wavering a bit. "He's a necromancer." The revelation landed with the thud of a dead body in the room.

"Where is he now?" Dex asked.

"He's hiding someone on the ship," she said quietly. A hint of fear spread into the room as the three of them realized the situation. They had gotten to the wrong Vampire.

"Did he kill that guy?" Neil asked. Morgan nodded yes.

"He said he wanted to teach me how to feed. He said right outside this room was the perfect spot. When I didn't finish him off, he pulled an icicle from a black bag and stabbed him. There was still so much blood..." she shook her head, trying to get rid of the memory. "I ran. If I didn't run, I was going to lap it up like the dog I am."

"You're not a dog," Cassandra said sympathetically. "You're a person. And a good person at that." Morgan laughed and shook her head.

"Obviously I'm shit if I'm stuck as a Vampire. And I can't even do that right."

"You aren't stuck and I'm going to cure you. Everyone deserves a second chance." Dex said. "But we need to know what Sextus's plan is." Cassandra shot Dex a confused look that he didn't notice.

"The plan was I pick you off one by one. And then he uses his Dolls to take over the ship. Then him and his vampires have a floating base."

"Great," Cassandra said sarcastically. "Dolls."

"So what's the plan?" Neil asked. Cassandra went to speak, but Dex was filled with an odd sense of déjà vu and cut her off.

"We cure her and then we deal with Sextus."

"You can't," Cassandra protested.

"Oh no: I can. And I will," Dex asserted.

"How do you even know how to do that?" she asked.

"Read it in a book," he replied.

"So, you've never even done it?" she replied incredulously.

"I've got the basic theory down." Cassandra shook her head.

"Theory and practice are two different things," she said with a hint of worry and anger in her voice. Dex turned to look at Cassandra.

"When those Dolls attack, there's going to be causalities. There's going to be blood. Morgan is starving as it is and the last thing we want on our conscience is her giving into her hunger. This is the best plan." He looked at Cassandra with hopeful eyes. "Believe in me. Please." This was, to Cassandra, the stupidest plan she had ever heard of. Yet Dex's eyes gave her some unknown form of confidence.

"What's the plan?" Neil asked again, slowly holding Morgan's hand out of sympathy. They really did feel for her. They understood what it was like to lose yourself to an identity that was thrust upon them and Neil would move heaven and earth to make sure no one had to feel that way ever again.

"Cassandra goes and calls Sara. She's going to need to alert to captain that they need to hightail it back to the dock. Tell them, I don't know-pirates or something are going to attack. I heal Morgan, then the four of us go and find Sextus. Hopefully we can get him in time. If not, then we fight."

"Why are you doing all this for me?" Morgan finally asked. It didn't make sense to her. Why would these strangers care what happens to her? Sure, she knew Neil was nice and kind and sweet, but these other two didn't know her at all. Cassandra turned and looked at Dex. She then turned to Morgan and said,

"Because it's the right thing to do," Cassandra said. Dex nodded and she headed off to call Sara. Dex turned to Neil.

"Find me some orange juice or oranges or some kind of sugary fruit. Get them ready for me." Neil went to the kitchen and Dex stood up and sat next to Morgan.

"There's not a lot of time and you aren't going to like the cure, but this is our best shot." He placed his left forearm on the table. "You're going to need to drink my blood." She shook her head no.

"I can't do that. I'm not a monster."

"This is the only way," Dex insisted sadly. "I can make my blood heal you."

"I didn't know Healers could do that," she replied confused. Dex hesitated. Something inside of him was telling him to trust her, but now was not the time for that.

"It's complicated, but this is the only way. I read about it, so it should work." Her fangs popped out instinctively, the hunger welling inside of her again.

"What if I take too much?" she asked in a worried tone. Dex gave a nervous chuckle.

"Well, don't. When the fangs fall out, we'll know we are done. It might hurt as you'll be growing replacement teeth."

"How do you know all this?" Morgan asked slightly amazed. Dex shrugged.

"I told you. I read it in a book." By his estimation, he would need no more than about fifteen percent of his power to flow through his veins. While this didn't show any physical changes, Dex felt the world around him slow and his skin getting warm. He looked at Morgan and said, "Let's begin." She looked at Dex. His face was one of utter calm. It was as if he had the situation completely under control. She looked at his upturned wrist lying there on the table. She tenderly grabbed his hand. It's warm, she thought to herself. It could have been to her that it was warmer than it should have been, but the she knew in the pit of her stomach that the warmth came from the blood with in. She licked her lips as if she was staring at the most delicious dessert in the world. Morgan looked up at Dex as she slowly brought his wrist to her mouth. Dex nodded reassuringly.

Up until this point, Dex had given blood exactly twice in his life-once when he was sixteen just so that he could say he did it, and once more two years back in memory of his parents. It wasn't as if it was a terrible experience. He remembered that there was a pinch and a bit of burning. Then he sat and had to pump a rubber ball for a little bit. When the needle came out, it burned once again. It was just an experience. He expected that this experience was going to be like that. To some extent, it was. There was a sharp pinching feeling. Yet there was also the warmth of her lips on his skin.

This was no kiss, however. This was something else. Tears streamed down Morgan's face as she knew what it was that she was doing. She was actively taking the life force of someone. She was taking their blood. It should have repulsed her, the warm copper tasting liquid filling her mouth and filling her stomach. Yet she couldn't stop. It filled her. It made her fell whole. Yet someone, in the back of her mind, she understood that it was a false sense of fulfillment. No matter how good it made her feel during the action, she knew that feeling would fade. She had never tried hard drugs, but she had enough of an understanding to know that this was how it began- this feeling of being whole. It was easy to see how people could become addicted to this life. For her, she focused on this as a one-time thing- a means to an end and nothing else.

Dex had improvised in situations before, but not to this degree. Of course, he knew all about the theory behind this. The super charged blood cells in his blood stream would be transferred to her. They would essentially seek out and destroy the negative energy in her own blood causing the transformation as a white blood cell seeks and destroys viruses and bacteria. However, this was compounded by the fact that she was near starving. Her body literally needed the blood of others to survive. She had not once given into those urges, so the negative energy has starting to attack her body causing hunger pains. In short, Dex had no real way of knowing how much blood she would need to cure her. There were ten units of blood in the human body. Typically, they take one unit of blood during a blood drive and even that can make someone dizzy. Dex was reasonably sure this would take much more than one unit. Typically, the process for giving blood takes about a half of an hour. However, Dex could also feel the blood leaving his body with each suck. So it could be less than that.

About five minutes into the ordeal, Morgan began to scream in a gargled, muffled mess, Dex's blood spilling out over both of them.

"Don't stop now," Dex said feeling lightheaded. "Keep going until the fangs pop out." She was crying tears of pain at this point. Cassandra came back at this point and started to walk towards them. Dex shook his head and Neil stepped in front of her.

"We're almost done, I think," Dex said slurring his words a bit.

"You're killing him!" Cassandra cried.

"Please, I'm tougher than I look and the lady said she'd give me a cookie and juice after this," he replied in a haze. Just then Morgan's head shot up, screaming in pain and spraying blood everywhere. She looked terrified at what had occurred. Dex sit in the chair, slightly slumped over. She grabbed his wrist and dug out two fangs from his wrist.

"Get a first-aid kit! Hurry!" she screamed. Neil came running with the kit and began bandaging his wrist tightly.

"Hey, buddy. I already stopped the bleeding. I'm a Healer," Dex said. It was true the bleeding had stopped. Morgan looked around at the mess. She opened her hand and found the teeth. The reality of what just happened sank in. She rushed to the bathroom to vomit and Cassandra followed her.

Neil grabbed Dex's head and sat it up. It seemed that Dex just wanted to flop around.

"Hey there, buddy. Buy me dinner first," Dex said with a slurred and soft chuckle.

"You're so incredibly stupid. You know that, right?"

"Did it work?" he asked. Neil laughed and cried a bit.

"You crazy asshole. Yes. It worked." Dex nodded.

"Good," he said. "I need some orange juice." Neil poured him a glass and shook their head.

"This isn't going to help much," they admitted.

"It will help fine. Get me some fruit or cookies, please."

"We have no idea how much blood you actually lost."

"I'd say about four units," Dex admitted. He took a drink of the tangy juice and it cooled his dry mouth though he didn't like orange juice.

"Rough estimation?" Neil asked.

"That's about what it takes to do that according to what I've read. Could have been more given that the poor lady was starving." He looked at Neil. "I didn't want to worry anyone."

"You need medical attention and blood transfusion of your own," Neil said. Dex shook his head.

"I'll be fine in a bit. My body heals itself and if I keep a low level of power coursing through my body, it will help."

"Why did you risk it for her?" Neil asked. Dex shrugged and sat his empty glass down. He grabbed a cookie and took a bite.

"It was the right thing to do," he said. "Plus, I'm, like, eighty percent sure you have a crush on her." He took another bite. "This is a very good cookie." Neil blushed.

"She's just nice, okay? And she needs our help. That's all."

"Yeah, keep telling yourself that," Dex said with a laugh.

"Can you fight?" Neil asked.

"Oh yeah," he replied.

"Good. Because now we need to find Sextus and take him down."

While that conversation was happening, Cassandra found Morgan in the bathroom vomiting. Cassandra pulled Morgan's hair back and held it and she remembered faintly her days in college. After a few minutes, she was done. Morgan stood there sobbing; her mouth still covered with the sticky blood. Cassandra grabbed her and hugged her.

"It's okay," she said quietly in her ear. "It's over now." After a moment, the embrace ended.

"I'm sorry," Morgan said. "This is just... I mean I don't get it."

"I think everything happens for a reason and this is just a part of all of this."

"Why are you guys helping me?" It was a fair question and one Cassandra wondered as well. Of course, there was the obvious reason: Dex. Dex said he could help and she believed in him. Yet at any point, it would have been easy to disable Morgan and deal with the bigger threat. Instead, she went along with a dangerous and reckless plan. Was this because of Dex? Perhaps it was something else. Perhaps, for the first time in a long time, Cassandra felt like she was actually making a difference in the world.

"It was the right thing to do," she simply said. "Plus, you gave us a lot of useful information."

"I'm just... I don't know... I'm not used to people being super nice to me."

"No, I get that," Cassandra said. "But we have to stick together if we are going to get through this. Can you fight?" Morgan laughed.

"Sort of. I grew up with four older brothers, so I guess sort of? I had to learn to defend myself because my brothers... they always used to bully me for being me. I mean, I can at least see where an attack is coming from, I guess."

"Wait," Cassandra said suddenly. "Your Prophecy is still working?" Morgan looked confused.

"Yeah. I mean, why wouldn't it be?" Pieces started to fall in place for Cassandra. It was as if for the first time in a long time, she was standing in a spot where she could see how the cogs of her life were starting to fall in place.

"I'm going to go get you a fresh outfit. Why don't you relax and get a shower? Then we can figure things out, okay?"

"Thank you," Morgan said. "That would be nice." She went to her room and grabbed a pair of sweats and a t-shirt. It was the best she could offer under the circumstances. She then decided to check on Dex and Neil in person. By the time she got there, Dex was standing unsteadily washing off his hands.

"How's the patient?" She asked Neil.

"You want the truth or a lie that will make you feel better?" Cassandra responded with a look as if to say just tell it to me straight. Neil sighed. "He's okay, but he's not great."

"What do you mean?" Neil sighed.

"He's loopy, weakened, and ready for a fight."

"College frat boy mode: got it," she said with an eye roll.

"I hope you're ready to go beast mode, because in a fight it's just us two until his body heals."

"Maybe not," Cassandra said with a glimmer of hope. "Morgan's Gift of Prophecy is still working properly."

"Wait, what?" Neil replied disbelievingly. Cassandra nodded.

"Yep. She can access it whenever she wants. Which means that the short in Prophecy is only effecting members of The Order."

"Because someone is only blocking them," Neil said with realization. Cassandra thought for a moment. Typically, she liked to do things by the book. However, this was nothing if not an extenuating circumstance. She remembered a joke a pastor once told her in her childhood. A young child wanted a bike but couldn't afford one. So, knowing that Jesus forgives sins, they decided to steal a bike and simply ask for forgiveness later.

The joke was funny and obviously not what one should do, but a truth emerged in her mind: it's easier to ask for forgiveness than permission.

"We need to link her up with us," Cassandra finally said. "She can help guide us to where we need to go." Neil nodded.

"Let's go tell Dex," they said. As they walked over to Dex who was now sitting back in his chair, he looked at them and said,

"Just link her up already. It's the right call and we don't have all day." Neil sighed and Cassandra was confused.

"How did you know what I was going to suggest?" She asked. Dex smiled and laughed.

"There are more things in heaven and on earth, Horatio, than are ever dreamt of in your philosophy."

"He's right, though," Neil said, nervous that Dex's cavalier attitude would give himself up as a Conduit too soon. "What's Morgan doing right now?"

"Cleaning up a bit," Cassandra replied. "I gave her some fresh clothes. She's doing fine. I'll go talk to her." Neil went to speak, but decided it was better for Cassandra to talk to her. They felt like they already knew her pretty well and, despite just wanting to talk to her again, he understood this was a better solution. They simply nodded in agreement. Before she left, Cassandra turned to Dex, looked him dead in the eye and said, "Get thee to a nunnery." After she left, Dex looked at Neil and said,

"Oh, I do like her."

"Yeah... you're not super subtle with it..."

"Huh?" Dex asked.

"Nothing," Neil said quickly. "She's going to go check on Morgan and link her with us. That should give you some more self-healing time. Then we can work out a plan."

"We'll be fine," Dex said dismissively.

"How do you know that?" Neil asked. Dex shrugged.

"Because I believe in us."

"You seem pretty out of it," Neil said. Dex straightened up and walked a straight line without wobbling.

"Dude, it's mostly an act. If I keep my power level humming at about five percent, I'm perfectly fine. That's how I'm healing myself. I just need to not turn it up too much or I may run out of juice before I'm totally healed. I don't want people to know I'm fine. We need the element of surprise."

"Well that certainly was surprising to me," Neil admitted. For the first time in a while, a glimmer of hope appeared to Neil. Perhaps they could pull this off.

Morgan was getting out of the shower when she heard a knock on the door.

"Hey. It's Cassandra. You doing alright?"

"Yeah. Give me a moment and I'll be out," she said. She took the clothes and started to get dressed. Thankfully shirt was a hoodie and the pants were just leggings. While she found legging to be rather annoying and awkward to wear at times, there were certain things a girl just had to get used to and this was one of them. After she was dressed, she looked in the mirror. What in the world did you do now? How could you go and get mixed up in all of this? Your mother had such high hopes for you and now you're an ex-Vampire helping some secret religious-like militant group. She thought back to how she got here. Like most small-town kids, you either get out or you live there forever. She had chosen former, realizing that if she was to be herself, she had to leave. It just didn't go according to plan. Being in a family of five kids wasn't easy. You're always struggling to be seen- to be heard and noticed. Yet for her entire childhood, she had to not be seen. She hid because if the reaction from her family told her anything, it told her that she wasn't going to accepted. She knew she wanted to be an actress. To be able to be in those fancy clothes and to try on different personalities was like a dream come true to her. Perhaps that was her greatest regret. Not the moving out and living a life that would eventually lead her to become a vampire and place her where she was now. No: it was the fact that she had no one in her life actually saw her or noticed her. They saw only what they wanted- what they expected. But that wasn't her, and she realized that her "family" really didn't love her for her. She looked at the mirror and sighed. By her estimation, everyone was about in their mid-twenties like she was.

But they had their crap together. They knew the world and how it really was. And they cared for her. They didn't have to, but they moved heaven and earth to help her. Perhaps that was what she was really longing for. Perhaps it wasn't fame or money, but just to be important to someone for once in her life. She just wanted to feel like she belonged.

She opened the door and Cassandra was there waiting.

"You doing okay?" She asked. Morgan nodded.

"Yeah," she said softly. "I think I'm going to be okay. Is... what was it... Dex? Is he okay?"

"He will be. He's a Healer so he can self-heal, but it will take some time."

"He didn't have to do that... I could have stayed here until we got to help." Cassandra sighed.

"Look, if you ever tell him I said this, I will deny it, okay? But he was right. You had no business being stuck as a Vampire. He was right. It was the right play."

"So what now?" Morgan asked with a hint of fear in her voice.

"Now we find Sextus and stop him. And you're going to help us with that."

"I'm not a great fighter," she said. "I took self defense lessons, but it was out of necessity."

"Maybe not, but the rest of The Order is scrambling to figure out why the Gifts of the Prophets aren't working. And yours are working fine. You can help keep us alive."

"You want me to join The Order?" Morgan asked with disbelief in her voice.

"Yes," Cassandra said, "but not officially. Our team doesn't have a Prophet. And that can mean the difference between life and death. I think you should join us."

"Wouldn't that, like, need clearance from higher ups?" she asked confused.

"Normally, yes. However, we are sort of running black ops as it is, so we kind of can do what we need to and want to. And everyone agrees you'd be great with us."

"But you all just met me..." she said reservedly.

"Girl, they literally met me a day ago and we all just... clicked. And I know you and Neil clicked," she said with a laugh causing Morgan to blush. "And I know you can hang with Dex. And I like you just fine." Cassandra smiled. Morgan looked at her. She wasn't lying as far as she could tell. She didn't have many options at this point, but she felt... almost called to this place. It wasn't accident that lead her here. She was here for a reason. So, she would take her chance and run with it.

"I'm in," she said with a half-smile. "What do I need to do?"

"We need to come up with a plan to stop Sextus. I'd rather be proactive than reactionary. Any information you can give would be super helpful."

"I don't know much I'm afraid," Morgan replied. "I know he's here, but he never told me where. I'm assuming that the Dolls are stored on the lower levels, but I haven't seen them."

"It's a start," Cassandra replied kindly. "Let's go talk to Dex and Neil and we will figure out our next steps from there." They rejoined Neil and Dex in the living room. "We know the Dolls have to be hidden somewhere below in the storage decks. If we can find them, we might be able to destroy them before they are used."

"Quick question: how do we do that?" Dex asked.

"Destroy the head. The bone controlling it could be anywhere, but there are wires and such in the head. It works just like a regular zombie: take out the head," Neil replied.

"Always double tap!" Dex said loudly and obnoxiously.

"Furthermore," Cassandra said in an attempt to interrupt Dex's ramblings, "Morgan's Gift of Prophecy is still working perfectly. I think she can tell us when and where Sextus is."

"Are you okay with that, Morgan?" Neil asked. "Because we don't want you to be uncomfortable or anything."

"No, no, no: it's fine. I want to help. And... I mean... you guys helped me and it's the least I can do."

"You aren't obligated," Neil said. "I just want you to be okay."

"Neil, I appreciate that, but I want to do this. I want to feel a part of a team again." Morgan smiled lightly and placed her hand on Neil's hand. "It's okay," she said reassuringly.

"I explained to her about what it would mean to link her with us. And she's agreed to it. This is going to help us out tremendously." Cassandra closed her eyes for a moment and opened them. She spoke to them in their minds.

"Morgan? Can you hear me?" she asked. "If you can, just respond in the mind. Just think the words and we should be able to hear." There was silence for a moment, and then Morgan's voice filled their heads.

"Um... hello? Sorry. I've never done this before," she said.

"We read you loud and clear," Neil replied telepathically.

"Good," Cassandra said out loud. "Now if we get separated, which I think is a terrible idea, then we can stay in touch with everyone."

"Awesome. The easy part is done," Dex said. "So let's get to the hard part." Everyone nodded in agreement.

"Morgan, can you try to see when and where Sextus will show up? We need to get a drop on him." Morgan nodded and closed her eyes. It was quiet for a few moments. Suddenly, Morgan furrowed her brow. She looked confused. Tears started running down her cheeks.

"Guys, I'm sorry," she said wiping her eyes. "I am so, so sorry. We're too late. He's already woken up the Dolls. They will start their attack in ten minutes." They were all thinking the same thing. Was this it? Was it too late? Did we already lose? Dex stood up quickly- perhaps too quickly. His face showed confidence, but he wobbled a bit. That was unplanned, he thought. It shouldn't have made me that dizzy. I don't have enough time to fully heal myself, do I? He looked at everyone. Their faces matched expression: fear. Say something, he thought desperately. This is the part in the story where you make a rousing speech and get everyone hyped up. This is the moment that can define you.

"I must not fear," he said quietly taking a page from Frank Herbert, "for fear is the mind killer." He pulled out his phone and pressed shuffle on his music. The drums and the orchestra started. Smashing Pumpkin's song "Tonight, Tonight" filled the room. He kept his eyes on his phone, not wanting to make eye contact. *"And our lives are forever changed. We will never be the same. The more you change the less you feel."* Yes. This was it. This was the moment where they all changed. The song continued and he looked at his team. Realization spread across their faces. Whatever happened tonight, they would never be the same. A part of them all had just been lost forever and they didn't even notice it. This wasn't a terrible thing; it was just a thing. This was life. As the song ended, he made sure to lock eyes with the other three people.

"Believe in me as I believe in you. Tonight." He paused as the song ended. Putting his phone away, he placed a hand on Ruach.

"Let's go save some lives."

Chapter Eleven

"Let's go," Cassandra said taking charge. "Sara alerted the captain. They're returning to port now. We need to get below and find Sextus. Morgan: do you have any idea where he might be?" Morgan shook her head no.

"Something is blocking me from seeing where he is going to be. It's really weird. I can't see anything about him. It's like he's being shielded."

"Ophelia told me Prophets only see what they are meant to see, so don't worry too much about it," Dex said. Morgan looked confused.

"Who is Ophelia?" she asked.

"She's the head Prophetess," Dex answered. "She's super nice. You'll love her."

"We have five minutes to find him and take him out," Cassandra said tersely. "We need to move. Introductions can be done in person later. Start at the lower levels and work our way around: that's the plan."

"We need to split the party," Dex said. "We can cover more ground if we do."

"That is literally a terrible idea. We weren't split on separate levels before. This is something completely different and is terrible right now," Cassandra said, moving towards the door. The other three followed her lead.

"No, it doesn't always end in a TPK," Dex said defensively.

"What?" Morgan asked.

"Total party kill," Neil explained. "It's a Dungeons and Dragon's term. It means when the entire party is killed in combat or something."

"It doesn't always end that way. Yes, it's a gamble, but we are against the clock and we can cover more ground." Dex was somewhat confident of his abilities. The only hitch in the plan was Morgan. Could she fight? She would need to be with someone who could help keep her alive. That was narrowed down to Neil or Dex. Dex was a Healer and could fight. Neil would go above and beyond to protect her. That's not to say he thought that Cassandra couldn't fight. Far from it: he was confident that she could. He just didn't know what her fighting style was or how useful it would be. Plus, if he was being honest, he wanted to be with her. It was odd to him. Perhaps it was because he just met her and wanted to get to know her more. Perhaps he wanted her to spend more time with Neil. Whatever the reason, that was how he felt.

Dolls were odd creations. Instead of raising a zombie, some necromancers would take one body and use the bones to create an army of Dolls. Since Sextus could clearly do this, he was obviously a powerful necromancer. However, they didn't know if he himself could fight. If they could take him out, the dolls would become lifeless once again and the threat would be over. This is why the plan was to find him. Dex was sure splitting the party would yield the best results.

"We're stronger together," Cassandra said. "No way we are splitting up unless we have to." They reached an employee elevator. Cassandra, who had been told the code by Sara to use it, punched it in.

"But if time is a factor," Dex argued, "then we need to split up." Cassandra turned to him and faced him She seethed with anger at his recklessness.

"You may want to get yourself killed, but I have no intention of dying on this ship," she yelled. "We find him together and take him out." Neil looked at Morgan.

"I hate it when mom and dad are fighting," they said as a joke. In unison, Dex and Cassandra turned and looked at them.

"Stop that," the two said in unison. They then turned and stared at each other and started laughing. It was absurd. Neil and Morgan started laughing. They all found solace in the fact that, even in the seriousness of the moment, they could at least connect with each other. This was what a team was all about.

"He's likely to be storing the Dolls in an area without a lot of foot traffic. Some place where people don't go often."

"The morgue," Neil offered. "No one would go there unless they needed to. They only needed to store one body there. Plus, I mean, I don't want to type cast anyone but he is a necromancer so her could be staging things there. Probably not enough room for all of them, but he might be there."

"It's the best lead we have so far," Cassandra said as they entered the elevator. She pressed the button to take them to the floor the morgue was on. As fate would have it, she had happened to meet the captain at the dance party. The captain knew the ship inside and out and she sort of downloaded their information about the ship from their mind thinking it would come in handy later. As it turned out, it really did come in handy.

They got off the elevator and headed straight to the morgue. Cassandra punched in the code and the door opened. The coolness of the room and the hum of florescent lights greeted them all. Dex was immediately transported back to the last time he was in a morgue. He tried to shake the memory from his head and found himself unstable. Neil grabbed his arm and helped him up.

"I got you, buddy," they said sympathetically.

"Thanks, boo," Dex replied with a laugh. "I'm okay: really." He was not, though. He remembered. It's cold, he thought to himself again. The hum of the florescent lights filled his ears as he approached what he called the cabinet of the dead.

"There's not enough room in here for all the Dolls," Cassandra said. "There's about a dozen drawers. That still leaves close to two-hundred still unaccounted for."

"That's if there are any in here," Neil said.

BANG!

The noise startled everyone. Morgan gripped tight to Neil's arm. They raised their fists in a defensive stance and caused them to course with power.

BANG! BANG!

More noise. The doors of the cabinets were beginning to move. Cassandra pulled out a small metal cylinder. Holding it in her hand, she let go and caught it in a fluid motion as it transformed into a staff.

BANG! BANG! BANG!

Dex placed his hand on Ruach. He was confident in his abilities even without being powered up to ten percent. He was, however, worried that this would force him to expend extra energy.

"Stay back, Dex," Cassandra said.

"Like hell I will," he replied. Cassandra went to say something, but she was cut off by Morgan's scream. Doors started to pop open with adult sized wooden limbs climbing out. Where some of the hands were replaced with swords or clubs or axes. They scuttled out of the drawers, falling to the floor with a sound that reminded Dex of wooden blocks. They moved in slow and deliberate jerks, standing on unsteady feet as if for the first time. They had the appearance of adult sized wooden drawing mannequins. They wooden ball joints gave a creak with each movement, heralding the arrival of some unnatural abomination. Their faces were completely blank with no discernable features. That was the worst part of them to Dex. They showed no emotions. They were automatons created with dark energy with one expressed purpose: to kill.

A flash of light and one toppled over, Neil had blasted a head clean off.

"Head shot!" they exclaimed in a lower voice that sounded like a video game announcer. The Dolls looked at their fallen comrade and at the four. They moved with an eerie speed, ready to kill. The battle was intense. Neil was obviously doing the best of the four in terms of a kill count. Morgan ran to the door and grabbed the best thing she could find- a fire extinguisher. She swung it around wildly, knocking a few over in the process. Cassandra drove her staff into the neck joint of one of them. She jerked the staff down suddenly, lodging it in the joint of their neck. Doing a round house kick, she powered the staff to knock the Doll down, tumbling over a few with it and snapping the wooden joint, severing the head. Dex swung Ruach with as much strength as he could. Although his blade was incredibly sharp, he didn't have the strength to cut through the wood. Plan B, he thought to himself. He lunged straight at a Doll, sinking the blade into its head. Sending some positive energy into the blade he was able to short out the wires inside and destroy the monster.

After a few minutes, the battle was over. They all stood there, taking a moment to breathe.

"Something's wrong here," Neil said. "This doesn't make any sense."

"What do you mean?" Morgan asked.

"I don't mean to sound alarming, but these things didn't put up much of a fight." Cassandra counted the wooden bodies.

"Twelve. Assuming that Sextus used all the bones, then there are still two-hundred and one dolls out there." She looked at the others. "I've fought Dolls before. Neil's right: we should have been overwhelmed considering we sort of have two non-combatants with us."

"Hey! Dex interjected. "I took out a few."

"Dex, you could have taken them all out on your own if you were totally fine," Neil said softly. Dex went to say something, but he shut his mouth. The fact of the matter is that Neil was right. Even at ten percent, he would have been able to take them all down. Being in a weakened state did have an effect on him. Casandra stared at Dex through narrowed eyes. Assuming he was good with that katana which it appeared that he was, then Dex was on par with where he should be. Yet she had to admit to herself that being weakened meant that he should have been able to do more. But twelve Dolls single handedly? In her mind the math didn't add up. Morgan had a thought. Her face contorted into one of anger and disappointment. She yelled and threw the fire extinguisher. It clattered noisily on the pile of Dolls with an unhuman sound.

"We didn't stop him."

"It's a start," Cassandra offered. Morgan shook her head.

"It's not enough. You don't know him. He's dangerous." Déjà vu washed over Dex and on cue Cassandra's phone rang. It was Sara.

"Hello?" Cassandra answered. "Sara calm down. Slower. Where? What does the captain think? Yeah. Start getting people into the ballroom. Barricade the doors. We're on our way. Don't panic." She hung up her phone. Dex was already heading towards the door. "Where are you going?" she asked him. Dex gave her an incredulous look.

"The ballroom," he replied. "We have to help them fortify."

"We can't," Cassandra replied. "We have to find Sextus."

"Putting everyone in a bucket and asking them to wait patiently until the Dolls come is not safe," Dex argued. "They need more muscle than what they have." Suddenly Morgan went wide eyed with a look of terror. Dex felt déjà vu. She looked at him with a quizzical look on her face as if she was trying to understand something that she had no frame of reference for.

"We have to split the party," they both said at the same time. Morgan looked at Neil.

"You and I will go and help in the ballroom. Dex and Cassandra will find Sextus."

"I'm sorry," Cassandra said with a laugh. "Is everyone crazy but me?" Neil looked at everyone. Surely, they thought, there were strength in numbers. Yet he knew Dex could easily defeat Sextus and the Dolls. But Dex was weakened so that complicated matters. It boiled down to trust. Did he trust him? No, they realized. Neil didn't trust Dex, but they did have faith in him and to Neil, that was stronger.

"Don't do anything I wouldn't do," Neil said as they hugged Dex.

"Don't worry- I won't. I'll do something stupid but heroic," he responded, holding his best friend tight.

"They'll be fine," Morgan said reassuringly. "I've seen... something. I'm not sure, but we were all together. But we definitely not here and we were fine. I can't look too far out, but this flash just came to me. It will be fine," she said with a reassuring smile. Her eyes were sincere and Dex knew she was telling the truth. He looked at Cassandra. Her demeanor started to change. It softened up some. Perhaps she read Morgan's mind. Perhaps she simply started to have faith in Dex. Whatever it was, she was starting to believe. Neil grabbed Morgan's hand.

"Are you ready?" they asked. She nodded and the two of them were off. Cassandra turned and looked at Dex.

"You owe me a damn good explanation for all of this," she said.

"You'll get one," he promised, "but after we get off this boat."

"If we make it out alive," she said moving towards the door.

"We take the elevator up to the midlevel," he responded ignoring her.

"That's exactly what I'm talking about!" she yelled punching in the code to the elevator. "You act all nonchalant and spout off all this crap that doesn't make sense."

"And again, when we are done, I will explain. Not really the time and place for that right now," he said stepping into the elevator.

"And again," she replied frustrated, "if we live."

"Give me something to look forward to then," he said with a smirk pressing the floor button. "Incentivize me."

"You can't be serious," she asked with a legitimate laugh.

"Let me buy you dinner."

"Oh Lord: you are serious..." she replied shaking her head.

"You want answers and I want to give them to you. And I want dinner. Like a fancy dinner."

"You're asking me out on a date in the middle of all this." She couldn't believe it. The audacity of this man was staggering to her.

"Not a date," he clarified. "Just like last time with Alice- dinner and drinks. That's all."

"You really think this is the time and the place..."

"I think I don't know what's going to happen," he snapped at her interrupting her. "I don't know what is going to happen on this ship. I'm not a planner- I'm an improvisor and that doesn't always work. So no: I don't know how this is going to turn out even with what Morgan said so yes: I do want something to look forward to." He turned to face her. "You want the truth? I'm scared. I'm scared about what is going to happen and I literally just want one thing to look forward to." The doors closed and he folded his arms defensively in front of him. Cassandra felt mad at herself. She had been spending all her time trying to lead that she didn't think about how this could be affecting her teammates. She sighed and said,

"I want Italian food. And good Italian food. Don't cheap out and take me for unlimited breadsticks." She smiled a bit.

"Italian it is," he said with a half-smile.

"So we should have gotten the elevator code from you but we didn't so we're taking the stairs," Neil suddenly said in their minds. It was a misstep and a miscalculation on their part.

"We are okay!" Morgan said loudly. "Neil is a little winded and I think they need to add some cardio to their work out!"

"Morgan, hun," Neil said out loud to her. "You... you don't need to be loud, okay? Just think in a normal volume and they can hear you."

"Sorry," she told everyone telepathically. "First real time doing this."

"Let us know when you get there," Cassandra replied. They came to a large set of doors. Neil placed their hand on the handle, but Morgan grabbed it back.

"Wait," she said to him. "Dolls. Three of them coming down this hallway." Neil nodded.

"Watch this," they said with a proud tone. They placed two fingers along the edge of the door. Their hand lit up, but no energy seemed to go anywhere. They traced their fingers down the to floor, remaining contact. "Get down," they told Morgan. "I have to maintain contact, but I don't want them to see us." They both got down on their knees.

"What are you doing?" Morgan asked.

"I made a trip line out of positive energy," Neil responded. "Best part is they can't see it. They'll walk headfirst into it and..." Neil giggled slightly. "they'll lose their heads." Suddenly, they could hear the wooden clunking footsteps of dolls. A large sound akin to dressers falling over came shortly thereafter. Neil let go and their hand returned to normal. "Let's see our catch." They peered through the windows on the door and sure enough there were three freshly decapitated Dolls lying in front of the door. They pushed the door open, be careful not to make too much noise.

"How did you know that would work?" Morgan asked. Neil shrugged.

"I've been trying to practice with different Channeling abilities, namely shaping and recoloring things. I figured an invisible trip line would work."

"That's amazing," she said with wonder in her voice. "Honestly I don't know how you all do it."

"Well you're going to join us, right?" they asked headed down the hallway. "I mean, you don't have to and we could still hang out and stuff, but this would be more fun, I think. And I think that you'd be great with us."

"Pretty sure we already decided that, Superstar," she said with a laugh.

"Honestly, I should never have told you that," they replied with a grimace.

"No, no, no: it's cute. Really." If Neil and Morgan were being honest, they were actually having a rather great time. Yes, there was the threat of death by Doll at any moment, but at the same time, they felt as if they were just two people living. Like they were actually living a real authentic existence. This wasn't some cookie cutter life they were living. Instead, they were able to be authentic with each other.

"Tell me more about Dex," she asked. "What's his deal?" Neil laughed.

"Dex is Dex and will always be Dex."

"What's his role on the team?" she pressed. Neil shrugged.

"He's the Healer," they replied worried about where the conversation was going.

"Then how can he see the future?" she asked pointedly. Morgan had a little understanding of The Order and the systems found within. She understood the importance of team composition. What she didn't understand is how Dex was doing something that, by all accounts, they shouldn't be doing.

"I suppose if I say Dex is Dex again, that won't be enough to satisfy you," Neil said with a sigh.

"You would be guessing correctly," Morgan affirmed.

"Is this one of those things that I can totally promise you that I and or he will explain post leaving this ship?" Morgan considered their response.

"As soon as we leave this wretched ship, deal?" she asked.

"Deal," they replied, "but the ship isn't wretched. It's actually extremely well built. Plus, we got to meet you so, you know, silver linings and such." Morgan smiled. In the midst of all of this craziness and terror, at least she finally felt as though she belonged to something.

Suddenly, she stopped.

"We're almost to the ballroom. Five Dolls are approaching the main doors. Not everyone is in there."

"So we clear the Dolls and open a path for people."

"The trip line won't work," she said sadly. There's not going to be a good vantage point to set it up."

"Are they all together in one hallway?" Neil asked.

"Yeah," she replied.

"Right: time for something stupid and heroic. Which hallway?"

"Right side corridor." Neil held their right hand in front of them. And began gathering energy into a ball, holding their right wrist with their left hand. As they approached, the ball of energy turned blue and began to grow in size.

As they approached the rotunda area near one side of the ballroom, Neil leaned forward and threw their left arm behind themselves. They ran towards the five Dolls in a self-proclaimed ninja run. They screamed as they launched a massive ball of energy that filled the hallway, vaporizing the Dolls.

"Oh my gosh: that was amazing!" Morgan said. Neil came back panting.

"Yeah, but I gotta recharge now. I just need a few minutes and I'll be good."

"Dex! Casandra! We made it to the ballroom. We're going to help the build a barricade and keep a path open for people to come in," she announced telepathically.

"Good idea," Dex said. "I'm proud of you both. Stay safe and call for help if you need it." Dex and Cassandra had reached their location by this point. He was feeling marginally better at this point. However, at this point they saw about ten Dolls shambling towards them down a hallway.

"Aw beans..." Dex said. Cassandra looked up and gasped. She reached in her purse and brought out another cylinder out. She slid it on the end of her staff and a scythe blade unfolded itself.

"I got this," she said confidently. She broke off into a run and ran towards the Dolls. What happened next was nothing short of amazing. She dispatched the Dolls with ease, her blade severing joints and decapitating them.

"Impressive!" They heard in a loud, deep voice. They turned and faced a man dressed in a long black trench coat and no shirt. His head was bald with some sort of tribal tattoos covering his scalp. He clearly wasn't an indigenous person. The tattoos looked like he was trying to be edgy and cool and had no real connection to any sort of tribe. This man was an obvious poser. He smiled at them, showing his fangs. A large battle axe was laying on his shoulder.

"Most impressive," he said.

"Oh, okay," Dex said swaying a bit and his words slurring again. "You're that vampire guy Morgan told us about. Compass?" There was silence. Sextus looked confused.

"I'm sorry: what?" he asked.

"Yeah. Compass. Some ship tool name or something: I don't know."

"Did... did you mean sextant?" Cassandra asked.

"Yeah that!" Dex said with a smile. "Sextant!"

"Sextus," the man replied. "But I can see how that would be confusing to a man of limited cranial capacity."

"That's why I don't wear fitted hats," Dex said sadly. "I can never find a good fit. Shame on you for bringing that up."

"Dex: what the hell?" Cassandra asked in his mind.

"Trust me," he replied. "All part of the plan."

"You're losing it," she said.

"And I also did plays during high school."

"Wait, what?" she asked confused. "Neil. Morgan. How are you all doing? Because we found Sextus."

"Things could be better," Neil replied grimly. "The barricade has been built, but people are still in hiding. Those that aren't are trying to get in but..." Neil was silent.

"We've found at least a dozen bodies by now..." Morgan said solemnly.

"Damnit," Cassandra said aloud.

"Let me guess," Sextus taunted. "Your little plan not working well? How many have my Dolls killed already?"

"Not sure," Dex responded. "But we're working pretty well on taking them out."

"Twenty-five," he said with a dark grin. "I can feel every kill they make." He ran his hands down his neck as if he was enjoying the feeling of those kills. "They all screamed."

"Good Lord: what a walking cliché," Dex said with his eyes rolling. In a mocking tone, he said, "Oh look at me: I've killed twenty-five people. I'm wearing all black so you know I'm a villain. Please." He spoke with his regular voice. "The evil vampire chick from Twilight was a more interesting villain than you." He drew Ruach and pointed it at Sextus. In a serious, low growl, he said, "You're just a sub-boss in this dungeon." Cassandra stared at Dex. Why was he doing this? What was his endgame? Assuming he meant to tell her he was simply acting like he was in a weakened state, what could he possibly accomplish by making him mad. "It's because I'm mad," he said in her mind. "That's why. I'm not going to kill him, but I am going to hurt him. And we will get what we need from him." Cassandra was frightened. She wasn't frightened of the situation, but she was frightened of Dex. No, she had not known him very long, but he seemed to have changed. There was a shift in his whole demeanor. He went from some bumbling fool to some serious hardcore warrior and she couldn't figure out where this confidence came from. His sword suddenly dropped to the ground as he was holding it. Damnit, he thought to himself. This is bad.

Suddenly, the door surrounding them opened. Dozens of Dolls appeared in the doorways.

"It's a shame you all couldn't have just died. Morgan was even more useless than I originally thought." Cassandra pointed him. "You don't get to talk about her like that." Now it was Dex's turn to be afraid. She planted an end of her on the ground and vaulted into the air. Her body spun like a beautiful and deadly top taking out a number of Dolls in the process. Sextus smiled.

"I'm going to enjoy killing you," he said with a sneer. "Sadly, I have to make sure that one dies first," he said pointing at Dex. "Orders are orders and we would want to mess with 'the order,' now would we?" Something was wrong, Cassandra thought. His phrase: it didn't make any sense. Was he implying he was taking directions from The Order or was he saying he didn't want them involved? Or was he just suggesting that he shouldn't mess with the order of everything?

"It's fine," Dex said. "Just go help them. "I'll take care of him."

Cassandra was confused. What Dex talking about? It was then she got her answer.

"Guys,' Morgan said in their minds, "we need help. The Dolls are swarming the ballroom. There're still people trying to get in. We're going to be overwhelmed." Her voice was full of panic.

"I overestimated myself," Neil chimed in. "I tried to go big and flashy. Should have saved that move, I guess. I can still fight, but assistance would be much appreciated." Dex turned and faced Cassandra.

"Like I said. Go." He leaned against the wall for support. Cassandra didn't know what to do. She didn't think Dex could handle this on his own- at least not in his condition. If she left now, what was going to happen? He would maybe buy them a little bit of time, but inevitably, more people would wind up dead. Damnit, she thought to herself. I am in over my head. One chance, she thought. If I can put him to sleep, that could save the day. She focused in on Sextus rooting around in his mind to begin to shut him down. A Doll swung their bladed arm towards her, breaking her concentration. She barely was able to jump back in time.

"Admirable thought," he gloated, "but ultimately foolish. You attack my mind and my Dolls will attack you. Let's call it a bit of an insurance policy. I did my homework here." They were overpowered and not at all ready for this mission.

"I said go!" Dex snarled at her. "Go now or it will be too late." He turned to look at her again. "Believe in me as I believe in you," he said. She started to head off toward the ballroom. Before she was out of earshot, she said,

"Dex: don't die. You owe me a fancy dinner." Dex nodded and she was gone.

"Delightful," Sextus said. "Now we can finally get down to business."

"How about we just skip all the crap and monologuing and you tell me what it is you know about me."

"Direct and to the point. I respect that," Sextus said as they drew their axe off their shoulder.

"No point in drawing things out," Dex said and shrugged.

"No, there isn't." He raised his hand and pointed at Dex. Suddenly, all of the Dolls around them surged. They began to try pile on Dex, cutting and slashing his body. It happened in a flash, as if by instinct. Time slowed down. His body was encased in yellow energy visible to all. He merely drew his blade. A swath of positive energy emanated from it, destroying every Doll around him. He casually placed the blade back in its sheath and dropped back down to ten percent power. He began to breath heavily and slumped against the wall.

"It's a damn shame," Sextus said. "Man: I would have loved to fight you in your prime. But here we are. I guess dreams don't come true. I'll just settle for that sword. Seems like I can get people to charge it for me." He didn't see, Dex thought. He only saw the sword glowing. He just assumed that it holds a charge. He doesn't know what I can do yet.

"Who told you I was a good fighter?" Dex asked with a laugh. Get him talking. Give your body some time to heal itself. Going to about twenty percent power at this point was foolish. He needed to buy himself more time. "Come on, bro. Help me out here. So few people tell me nice things." Find something to use. Read him. What is his body language telling you?

Sextus stood there confidently. He placed his axe on the ground with one hand on it at all times. He was confident, yes, but still defensive. Why was he defensive?

"You knew I'd be like this, right?" he asked the Vampire.

"I had assumed," he replied casually. "My contact spoke highly of you, but said you have delusions of grandeur. You fed her, didn't you?" he smiled. "Tell me- did she enjoy it?" He didn't know, Dex thought. He didn't know that Morgan was healed.

"Not at first," Dex said playing along. "I didn't think she would take as much as she did, but here we are." Sextus smiled.

"The first time is always the best. That warm liquid filling your mouth. The knowledge that you are taking someone's life. And look at you now. This is your reward. You can barely hold a sword."

"And you're still being defensive," Dex said. "Look at you. Even after Cassandra left, you haven't quit holding that axe. If you really thought you had already won, you'd be doing a lot more gloating than you are." He looked Sextus in the eyes and smirked. "You're scared of me."

Rage. Rage. Rage. It was all Sextus felt at this point. How dare this insect say he was scared. There is a difference in being scared and being cautious. He was told not to underestimate him. But now? Now he was just pissed.

"Let's just make this simple," Dex said. "If you give up now, we can take you into custody. You'll be tried for your crimes by our justice system and, if found guilty, you can be imprisoned. Call off the Dolls now, and we can do this in a safe way. It's your only option at this point." Sextus laughed.

"Counteroffer: I kill you, I kill your little friends, and then I kill every person on this ship." He had confidence, Dex thought, but he couldn't help but notice a twinge of doubt in his voice.

"No," Dex said calmly. "I don't think you will." Sextus sighed. He wasn't going to make this easy, was he?

"That's a shame," he said lifting up his battle axe. "I had thought we could do this the easy way."

"I mean," Dex responded with a laugh, "this is going to be easy for me." Sextus approached him laughing and shaking his head.

"I'm almost sorry to kill you. But please know your blood will taste very sweet to me. Hard fought kills always are."

"And here it was because I thought I ate too much sugar." Sextus became mad.

"Is this a joke to you?"

"Far from it," Dex replied.

"Dex," he heard in his mind. "You still okay?" It was Neil.

"I'm fine," he responded. "You guys okay?"

"Getting there. We just need more time. Then we can get to you." Dex paused for a moment. It wasn't going to work. He couldn't stall him any longer. Neil and Cassandra and Morgan weren't going to reach him in time.

"I've got this," Dex said almost believing his confidence. "Cassandra?"

"Yeah?" she responded. He paused. What should he say to her?

"What are you going to order? At the restaurant." Sextus approached him slowly, dragging his axe along the ground and grinning the kind of insane grin that made people weep.

"Chicken parmigiana," she said with a hint of sadness. "You?"

"Probably lasagna." Cassandra laughed and sniffled. "Sounds good. I'm... I'm looking forward to it."

"Me too," he said sadly.

The axe came down swiftly. In one fluid motion, Dex unsheathed Ruach and blocked the two-handed blow single handedly. Dex was looking down, but he felt the disbelief radiating off of Sextus.

"How?" he asked in an amazed voice. Dex stood up straight, his right hand holding onto Ruach. He lifted his head slowly and saw a terrified Sextus. Dex was scowling- his eyes literally blazing with positive energy. Twenty-five percent was more power than he wanted to use, but he had to end this in one blow.

"How?!" Sextus screamed. Dex moved his right hand down by his side, disarming his opponent.

"Because I'm Dex Machina," he said calmly. Sextus didn't see the next blow. A raising diagonal slash from the right to the left sent him slamming into the back wall. His body was burned with the positive energy, leaving him with a mark on his chest. He was still alive- just hurt badly. Dex stepped towards him.

"I made a call," Cassandra said. "Reinforcements from The Order are coming. A whole lot of people are on their way to help." With each step, Dex could feel more and more energy leaving his body. He was going to pass out. At least that's all he hoped would happen.

"Good," Dex replied, his power level dropping to ten percent. "Sextus is down. He's alive. Have someone come get him."

"Why can't you bring him up?" Neil asked with fear in their voice. He was now at five percent power.

"I'm thinking I may need to take a nap for a bit." He was at two percent power. His vision was beginning to blur. The walls were moving.

"Dex, no! Stay awake!" Neil pleaded. He was now at one percent power.

"I'll be fine. I'm going to get the lasagna." It was then he slumped over.

"Dex? Dex?" he heard the other three calling out to him, but things were getting dark. He closed his eyes. He heard footsteps.

"No," Sextus said weakly. "No please. I did everything you asked. I can finish him off." The last thing Dex heard before he lost consciousness was the sound of metal sinking into bone and flesh.

Chapter Twelve

In the beginning, there was darkness. There was nothingness. There was no light that came, but only awareness. I am, he decided. I exist. This became the basis of his reconstitution. Once he was sure he existed, the next question to answer was who he was. Male. Twenty-five years old. A son. An orphan. A friend. Then came his name, slowly at first- a mere whisper. Dex. Dex Machina. That's me, he decided. This is who I am. Yet now he needed a body. In the darkness of wherever he was, he fashioned his body as he remembered. A head. Legs. Arms. But then something else happened- something he didn't intend. In the distance was a point of light. It was as if the darkness was pierced by something. Yet the light didn't grow. Instead it raced towards his body. It's warm, he thought. Suddenly there was another and another. Multiple points of light raced towards his body not engulfing him but filling him.

"Dex. Dex?" I know that voice.

"Dex wake up!" I know that voice as well. It was at this point he realized that he could move. But where to go? There was nothing around him. Well this is rather dull, he thought to himself. Where to go: that was the question.

"Dex... please..." that voice. He realized he knew where it was coming from. On some sort of instinct, he began to float towards the voices. Yes, he thought, as a point of light appeared. I'll go there.

There was beeping and he opened his eyes. He looked to the right and then the left. There was an IV and wires. Cassandra. Cassandra sat in a chair in a corner. She was asleep wrapped in a blanket.

"Cass?" he asked in a hoarse voice. She inhaled sharply at the sound of her name and blinked her eyes awake. She looked around. When she noticed that it was Dex talking to her, her eyes got wide with excitement.

"Dex!" she exclaimed. "You're finally awake!" she pulled out her phone. "Hold on- I told Neil I would text them when you woke up." She furiously taped a quick message and pressed send.

"Wait: what's going on?" Dex asked confused. "Are Neil and Morgan okay?" Cassandra nodded.

"Yeah," she said with a smile. "They're both fine."

"Thank God," Dex said relieved. The memories were coming back to him more clearly now. He remembered everything.

"What happened after I passed out? How long was I out for?" He asked desperately.

"The Council came with five other teams. They got rid of all of the Dolls. Only about fifty causalities..." her voice trailed off. She was upset by this. Her head turned down slightly. Dex was upset as well. They should have been able to do more.

"They found you passed out after you killed Sextus." Dex looked confused.

"I didn't kill anyone," he insisted. "I knocked him into a wall and passed out."

"His head was split down the middle with his own axe. His brain was completely destroyed. We can't use it for information now. A good Psyker can use an intact brain to play memories. But we can't do that now."

"There is no way I would have used his axe. And there's no way I would kill someone if I didn't have to!" he shouted. His heartrate was elevating. Machines beeped faster about him. Cassandra walked over to him and placed a hand on his arm.

"Hey. It's okay. Calm down. I know. And so does Neil and Morgan. And The Four know." Dex laid back a bit. Was he being set up? He remembered footsteps. He remembered Sextus begging. He went to speak but Cassandra interrupted him.

"I already scanned your memories," she told him. "Only Adrian and I were allowed. Unfortunately, for the time being, the official story has to be that you killed him." Dex looked saddened by this news. "It has to be this way for now," she said reassuringly. "We have to keep things quiet. Yes, we got a lead and an advantage with Morgan, but we aren't any closer to finding out who the traitor is."

The door to the hospital room swung open. Neil and Morgan rushed in. Neil ran to Dex and threw their arms around him.

"You big, stupid, son of a..." they trailed off crying. "A week!" They yelled. "You were in a coma for a week!" Had it really been that long, Dex thought to himself? It didn't seem that long. Neil let go and Morgan stepped next to them.

"Please don't do something like that again," she said quietly, her eyes filling with tears. "Please don't try to kill yourself for me."

"Spoiler alert:" he said with a smile, "I will always risk my life for my team." Dex sighed. "So what happened when I was brought here?"

"You were low on blood and needed a blood transfusion," a voice from the back said. It was The Council. Jude stepped forward smiling. "Apparently you have a rare blood type. But as fate would have it, Jules is a perfect match. He gave you his blood." Dex smiled, but he knew it was a lie. He knew he himself was the universal donor: type O negative. Something else must have been going on for Jules to use his blood.

"I must say, for not having a full team, you all did fairly well. It's impressive."

"Yeah," Mary said with a smirk. "You killed a guy." Dex wanted to protest. He desperately wanted to. But he knew that he couldn't. He was stuck and he didn't like it.

"You got to do what you got to do," he replied with a sad grin. Mary looked at him and gave a small laugh of disbelief.

"And look at that: you went out and got your own team in spite of what we've been saying." Morgan blushed and Cassandra looked angry.

"Yes," Jude interjected, "We will still need to approve the team composition which will also take time."

"No need," Cassandra said self-contentedly. She grabbed her bag and pulled out a piece of what looked like parchment. "The Four have already signed off on it." Mary stared in disbelief and snatched the paper out of her hand. Her jaw hit the floor.

"That can't be real," she said, her mouth agape.

"Oh but it is," Cassandra replied sweetly. "As you can clearly see, it even has Adrian's own seal on it. We're an official team." Jude was dumbfounded. How could this be?

"Then I will surely see you for training," Jude said. "As well as the other lady."

"I'm a transfer, so no: you won't," she responded with a smile.

"I'll be taking care of Morgan," a quiet voice said from the doorway. It was Ophelia. She was reading a reprinting of the very first Avengers story line. "Her's is a special case that requires my attention due to past trauma." She looked up at The Council. "This is per Jules."

"Well," Jude said with a smile. "I assume that there is nothing else to discuss then. We just wanted to check in on the patient. I think perhaps now we will take our leave and let you rest with your friends." They said their goodbyes and began to leave. Mary walked over to Dex and leaned into him. He could feel her hot breath on her ear.

"You're not fooling everyone. I hope to God you're ready for this." She turned and left without saying a word.

"Yes, Morgan. She is always like that," Ophelia said, still reading her book and having a seat. "Are you and Cassandra getting accustomed to your new housing?"

"Oh yes!" Morgan said sweetly. "Neil helped us get all moved in and settled. And Rhianna helped me get some new things since I didn't have anything and helped me with my perscriptions." She looked down slightly embarrassed.

"Morgan, it's okay. You're on a team and we look after our own."

"That's great!" Dex said with a smile. He was glad that they would be close. "Where did you guys move to?" There was silence. No one looked at Dex. "What is it?" he asked again.

"You already know where," Neil responded slightly embarrassed. "We talked about it before." Gears were turning in his head. Oh, he thought. OH!

"Oh," he said quietly. They moved into his house.

"It's not a problem, is it?" Morgan asked fearfully. She literally didn't have anything- especially not a house to live in. Rhianna had to go and get her a whole new wardrobe. She helped her find the right doctor so she could get her shots and stay on schedule. She was grateful for that, but also slightly embarrassed.

"What?" Dex asked confused. "No! It's awesome! I love it." There was a sigh of relief from Neil.

"We didn't want to spring it on you so soon, but... I'm glad you know," they said.

"Look alive, people," Ophelia said. "Here come the big three." On que, Rhianna, Jules, and Adrian entered the room. Adrian rushed over to Dex. He was... grateful. He seemed actually happy for once which made Dex nervous. He grabbed Dex's hand and shook it. Dex winced in pain as he squeezed the IV still in his hand.

"Thank you, Dex Machina." He said sincerely. "Thank you for helping my daughter." There was silence in the room. Cassandra's face reddened instantly and she darted her eyes around the room, desperate to not make eye contact with anyone. Time slowed to a crawl. No one spoke. The realization was still working its way in Dex's mind. His... daughter?

"Wait," Morgan said confused. "You're his daughter? And you're going on a date with Dex?" All eyes turned to Dex. Now his face got red. Neil started snickering. They tried to hold it in as best they could, but it led to full on laughing.

"I'm sorry," Adrian said with a laugh. "I'm a bit confused." He turned and faced Dex with eyes full of ice and fire somehow.

"Dinner," Dex squeaked out. "Get to know you dinner. To get to know each other. She wanted Italian. Not a date."

"Not a date," Cassandra said. "Strictly a business dinner." Adrian's left eye twitched.

"Well," he said with a strained smile, "I am glad to hear it. I am sure you two children will have fun."

"Damnit, Adrian," Cassandra yelled. "I'm not a child!"

"Cassandra, you can call me father or dad it wouldn't kill you..." he said meekly.

"Then act like a father," she said finally.

"I think," Rhianna interjected, "we need to stay on task here. We have a lot to discuss."

"Yes, well, perhaps we should do this in private," Adrian said. "We don't need... everyone involved." Dex shook his head no.

"Absolutely not," Dex said. "This is my team. Anything you want to say to me you can say to them."

"Dex," Adrian said softly, "we need to protect people who don't understand..."

"Hey Morgan and Cassandra: I'm a Conduit. Short definition means that I have a bit of everyone's powers. So is Jules." Dex looked at Adrian and smiled. "There. Now I think we are all caught up."

"I have several questions," Morgan finally said.

"And we will answer them," Jules interjected.

"Not until you answer ours," Neil said. Dex was somewhat shocked. Neil was rarely confrontational, so this was rather uncharacteristic for them. "We kind of collectively agreed on the ship that we are tired of being jerked around. We know this whole cruise thing was a set up. So spill it." They crossed their arms in front of them. "Please," they added. Jules sighed and turned to Dex.

"I trust you are feeling better, at least?" His eyes were warm, Dex noticed. His head was slightly tilted. He is leaning towards me, suggesting that he has a vested interest in myself.

"Tell me what happened. Why did you give me your blood?"

"For the same reason you gave Morgan yours- to heal you. I used my blood to replace yours and keep you healing yourself. In short, you needed to be recharged."

"Why the set up?" Dex was still bitter about them orchestrating all of this.

"Because we don't know who to trust. Even if we told you the plan," Jules said, "there was a chance that the information would fall into the wrong hands. And we needed the element of surprise."

"So leave breadcrumbs, is that it?" Neil asked. "We're just expected to put the pieces together and be your task force?"

"Neil, it's not like that," Rhianna said sympathetically. "We aren't one hundred percent sure what we are facing."

"You know a hell of a lot more than we do," they responded bitterly.

"What are we facing?" Dex asked.

"Someone in The Order is working with a very dangerous person," Jules said. "They are enlisting the aid of Vampires and others to further their plans. We don't know who is working with them."

"Who's the mastermind?" Dex pressed.

"We would rather not say," Jules said plainly. "Someone else could find out. Until we have more concrete answers, that's the best we can offer."

"Then I'm out," Dex said flatly. "I'm not risking the lives of people I care about on a rumor. I need to know what we are doing."

"You need to find the traitor. That is the mission," Adrian said.

"What do you all think?" Dex asked his team telepathically.

"Honestly, I have no idea what is going on. But I trust Ophelia," Morgan said.

"They're still hiding something," Cassandra said, "but we don't have a good play here. We either follow along or leave. Those are the only two options."

"Agreed," Neil said.

"I have an idea," Dex told them. He looked at Jules and said out loud, "Let's make a deal."

"I'm listening," Jules said. Dex took a deep breath.

"We trust you and let all this slide until we find the traitor and deal with them. After that, you all tell us everything." Dex sat up. He grabbed at his IV, removing the tape quickly. Slowly, he pulled it out, feeling the sting and healing himself as he came out. It hurt, but it was a necessary show, he thought. He needed to show how serious and strong he was. He looked Jules in the eye. He had a hint of sadness in them, as if there was some pain he didn't want to acknowledge. Everyone was quiet. He assumed that The Four were discussing their options. Adrian's brow furrowed a few times in a sort of soft anger. Rhianna sighed. Finally, Jules looked around at Dex's team.

"Those terms are acceptable," he said softly.

"Good," Dex said. "Then we will have another discussion in the future. This is far from over." The Four nodded in agreement. Jules stuck his hand out to Dex to shake on their covenant. Dex looked at his team who nodded in agreement. He shook Jules's hand.

"I think we need to let Dex get ready to leave," Rhianna said. "Let us know when you're ready and we will send you back to the comic shop." He nodded and three of them left. Ophelia sat there, still reading. Of course, she would catch up with them, but she wanted to wait until the others left. She peered over the top of her book.

"I assume you four are committed to this, right?" she asked. Dex's team nodded. "And no matter what happens, no matter what you might discover, you all will deal with it together, correct?" she put her book in her bag and began pulling on one of her braids.

"We just want the truth," Dex said. "And we want to help." Ophelia sighed and put her book in her bag. She began tugging lightly on one of her braids. She stood up and grabbed her bag. She looked at the team with a bit of sadness in her eyes.

"The truth is this is all a really crappy situation. So make the best of it. I'll be outside when you're ready to go home." She gave a short nod and left the room.

"Well hurry up and get dressed then," Neil said throwing some clothes at Dex. "We want to get home."

"Then y'all need to leave the room," Dex replied. "Because I'm not changing in front of everyone." Neil nodded.

"That's fair," they replied and they all left the room. Dex sighed. He began to get changed to go home. He looked in the mirror. For a moment, he almost didn't notice himself. It was as if everything he had been through recently had changed him. He noticed a bit more muscle definition and a few scars on his arms. Those must have been from the Dolls, he thought to himself. He looked over by the hospital bed. There was Ruach, shinning in the corner. I wonder what my parents would say about all of this, he thought. Perhaps they would be worried. Perhaps they would be proud. Perhaps, he thought, he shouldn't dwell on what ifs. They would only serve to distract him. He met up with his friends and they all went home. Going through the front door of the house, Neil explained room assignments.

"So, Cass is in your old room and we converted the guest room for Morgan. Everything has been cleaned. Oh!" he exclaimed and ran to the fridge. He brought back a large, multicolored circle. "This is our chore wheel. You're on it, but you get a free pass today." Neil smiled at Dex. "It's good to have home, buddy."

"It's good to be home," Dex admitted. "It's good to have you all here."

"I mean, Cass pretty much lived at the hospital," Neil admitted. Her face grew red. "I mean, she didn't leave your side. But she got her room all set up."

"I was acting as a leader on the ship," she said quickly. "I just wanted to make sure my Healer was okay. That's all."

"So what did I miss?" Dex said, his own face turning a little pink.

"Not too much. I began training with Ophelia. You were right: she is wonderful. And we moved in. That's pretty much it," Morgan said.

"We all got questioned by The Council," Cassandra added. "And it's safe to say that, if your story about Sextus is true, that we have narrowed down the traitor."

"I don't think the traitor is the real problem," Dex said. "Jules was careful with his words. He said he would tell us everything after we found the traitor. That means, even when we find them, that this won't be over." Everyone was silent. The news was less than great. Dex looked at his team- his friends. "But we will get to the bottom of it." They all nodded in agreement. He looked at his watch. "Right now, Cass and I need to get ready."

"I'm sorry, what?" she asked confused.

"We have to go get dinner," he responded.

"Seriously. Like, you're going to do this tonight? You just got out of the hospital." Dex shrugged.

"No time like the present. I texted a friend and already set everything up. And I'm a man of my word. But first, I owe you all an explanation of what a Conduit is." He took a deep breath and explained the scope of his powers. There were questions, which was to be expected. However, if they were to be a real team, they would have to know the truth as well as why the truth couldn't be readily told to everyone. If Dex's suspicions were right, then it was safe to assume that secrecy was more important than ever. Once all things were said and done, Dex stood up.

"Well," he said stretching, "time to go get ready." He looked at Cassandra. "I got us a table at Giorno's." Neil whistled. Giorno's was the premier Italian restaurant in the city. Reservations were incredibly hard to come by unless you booked months in advance.

"I will help you get ready," Neil said suddenly and loudly. They ran off to Dex's room with Dex looking confused and following them.

"Oh you can believe that I am coming with you," Morgan said, heading to Cassandra's room. "I am here for the gossip."

"There is no gossip," Cassandra said with a sigh. "He promised me an Italian dinner and he's repaying his debt. Strictly business."

"Strictly business," Dex told Neil from the shower a few rooms away. "That's it. Just two people having dinner. No romance."

"No romance at all," Cassandra said from the shower.

"Dude," Neil told Dex as he was stepping out of the shower. "You're joking, right?"

"No joke," he responded, taking the clothes Neil picked out. "Purely professional"

"Absolutely professional," Cassandra said, putting on some eye liner.

"You're a terrible liar," Neil told Dex. "You asked me to pick out your outfit." Neil had selected a simple shirt and tie.

"I just... I need something normal right now, ya know?" Cassandra told Morgan. "And this is normal. It's dinner. That's all." Morgan handed her a simple black dress.

"That's all," Dex told Neil.

After a time, they were both ready and headed to Dex's truck. What am I doing? They both had the same thought. It all seemed so... foreign. It seemed so rushed. Surely, it was just dinner, right? Surely, they were entitled to something normal once in a while. After all, as they both believed, it was just dinner.

The truck roared to life. It felt good for Dex to be driving. If he was being honest with himself, he was feeling better than he had in a long time. Perhaps it was the weeklong nap. Perhaps it was Jules' super charged blood. He just felt good. The radio automatically synced to Dex's phone. His playlist began on shuffled with pop punk drums and guitars. "*You and I should get away for a while,*" Mark Hoppus sang. *"I just want to be alone with your smile."* Cassandra's face reddened.

"They're a good band," she said suddenly.

"Oh for sure," Dex replied. "Still my favorite band to this day." Dex's face reddened. While he was fine with Cassandra knowing his love of Blink 182, he couldn't help but be a tad embarrassed that a love song was playing. Surely, he said to himself, this was just a coincidence. After that song was done, Dex breathed a sigh of relief assuming that this would be the end of the musical interlude. Then a familiar yet different rift began. You have got to be kidding me, Dex thought as Quietdrive's version of "Time After Time" began.

"If you're lost you can look and you will find me time after. If you fall, I will catch you, I'll be waiting time after time."

"Dude!" Cassandra exclaimed.

"It's on shuffle!" Dex protested. "I literally have no control over what plays!"

"No I get that," she said with a laugh, "but you seriously couldn't use Cyndi Lauper's version? It's classic. What is wrong with you?"

"What's wrong with cover songs?" Dex asked confused.

"Nothing, but you can't say that Cyndi Lauper's version isn't better. I mean, at least go for a classic." She shook her head smiling. Awesome, Dex thought. A bullet dodged. At least until it was dodged until the next song began. Oh no, Dex said. Please. Not this song. A throwback to the simpler days of pop punk music began.

"Oh Dakota: I know our love is new. I barely know ya. I'm falling over you. It's the way you do the things you do that makes me fall in love with you. Dakota: are you in love with me, too?" Dex sighed and looked down, shifting a tad uncomfortably in his seat. Cassandra noticed this. She smiled and laughed to herself, tucking some hair behind her ear. It was hard for her to relax- to have fun. It wasn't that she didn't like him- far from it. She was attracted to him as she could tell he was attracted to her. It was strange, she thought, to be feeling this way about someone. Yet

she reasoned out that this was how relationships start. She didn't want to profess her love to him or anything, but she did want to spend more time with him. The problem was one of timing, she thought. Perhaps if they just got to know one another, then something could develop. Dex certainly hoped that and she did as well. Truth be told, this evening was going better than she had anticipated already. It was just fun. She couldn't describe it in any other way. What she understood about life was that it was hard. It wasn't always fun or nice. Her father, Adrian, left her mother and her for almost ten years. It wasn't until she turned eighteen and her mother was on her deathbed that he finally came back into their lives. She had moved on with her father, but she had never forgotten what he did or why he left. Since, she reasoned, that he didn't act like a father, she was then under no obligation to call him father or anything. This was such a welcome diversion for her.

"Well at least you know I like good music," Dex said, pulling into a parking spot.

"What I know is you disrespected Cyndi Lauper." Dex opened his mouth to defend himself again but was cut off. "Relax. I'm just joking. You don't actually need to be serious tonight."

"I am very serious about all my business meetings, Cassandra." Dex was stoic in his response and Cassandra felt a tad bit hurt by this for some reason. He looked at her with a steely gaze. "Now it's my turn to tell you to relax," he said breaking character and smiling. She laughed and punched his arm.

"Ow!" he said rubbing his arm. "You know I literally just got out of the hospital, right? I apparently had a small case of coma. And now you're punching me?"

"Don't play the sympathy card," she said opening her door. "This whole operation was your idea." Dex shrugged and got out of the truck following her in the restaurant. Giorno's was both high end and authentic Italian food. It was beloved as a great restaurant by all people. As they approached the front desk, Dex smiled and raised his hand. The man behind the podium smiled and waved them forward.

"Right this way," he said, grabbing two menus. They were seated at a small table for two near the newly renovated dance floor. There was some soft music playing and a few couples dancing, but they paid them no mind. The water came and gave them a glass of water. Cassandra ordered a glass of Pinot Grigio. Dex chuckled to himself and followed suit. After the waiter left, Cassandra asked Dex,

"I thought you weren't a fan of white wines?"

"I'm not," he laughed, "but you seem to have an aversion to red wine, so I figured I'd get a white." Cassandra's face reddened. She looked down, slightly embarrassed. She's fiddling with her napkin and doing everything she can to avoid eye contact, he said to himself. I've embarrassed her. "I'm sorry," he said, feeling badly. "I didn't mean..." she cut him off with a loud sigh.

"Look," she said suddenly as if she regained her composer. "If this is our getting to know each other montage, then I might as well rip this band-aid off." She looked at Dex with a bit of sadness in her eyes. Why was she looking sad? Dex pondered this but she was practically radiating a sense of sadness and grief.

"Red wine reminds me of blood. It's not a taste thing. I just... I can't drink it."

"I didn't know you didn't like blood," Dex said looking away. "You handled yourself well on the ship with the dead body."

"And I stayed away when you were healing Morgan because..." she hesitated and closed her eyes regaining her composure. "Because my father left my mother because he became a Vampire." The gears were turning in Dex's mind and he worked out this equation. If her father was a Vampire and Adrian was her father, then that meant...

"That's a bingo," she said softly, raising her eyebrows for a moment, looking away and taking a sip of her wine while Dex wore a look of understanding. "Dear old dad was a Vampire. He wasn't just a Vampire. He was the Vampire. He was Ramses the Damned." Dex couldn't hide the look of shock on his face no matter how hard he tried. Ramses the Damned had a long history of terrible things that he did. He was the penultimate Vampire- a modern day Dracula, both vicious and cruel. "Obviously he got better, but only after my mother died. It was then he decided that family was important or something." She looked Dex in the eye. "Yes, it's a sore subject. Yes, I'm still bitter as Hell about it. No, I don't like to talk about it." She rested her hand on her chin and looked away. "Well, at least you know all my skeletons now."

"It must have been Jules," Dex said out loud. "Only a Conduit can heal a vampire. That's who gave me the book that said vampires could be cured." Realization spread across his face as he finally understood. "Which is why he asked me if I read the books before we left." She shook her head.

"Secrets and secrets and more secrets," she said sadly.

"Both my parents are dead," Dex said to try to ease the tension. It did not help. Cassandra looked sad again.

"Yeah," she said. "I know. Neil filled me in." The waiter came to take their order. It was a welcomed reprieve from the conversation. Dex had ordered the lasagna and she, as promised, ordered the chicken parmigiana.

"Neil's a good person. It's not just my story to tell- it's theirs as well."

"You two are like bro... siblings. It's adorable to watch," she said with a chuckle. Dex stared at his salad, which the water had brought when they got their order. He poked an onion for a moment.

"I wouldn't have gotten through it without Neil." He gave a sort of laughing snort out of his nose. "For so long it had just been the two of us. And then this happened with The Order and everything spiraled out of control." He looked at Cassandra, her ice blue eyes captivated by his words. "But I think, in some ways, it was worth it. Because..." Dex searched for the words he wanted to say. "I don't know. This all feels right. I can't explain it. The more I try to exert control in my life, the less control I find I have. But I kind of don't care. Maybe instead of pulling my strings, I need to start pulling some strings. Or I just need to shut up and enjoy this moment with you." He poked his salad some more. "And even now it's just because of The Order. It's ironic." She nodded in a small agreement.

"But it's a good thing," she said with a smile, placing her hand on

Dex's. Dex smiled back at her. Almost as if she realized what she was doing, she quickly pulled her hand away.

Their meal was good. The conversation was better. They had talked of their past, their likes and dislikes- all of the things one would speak about. They spoke of the future, what their next steps as a group would be. Dex explained how his powers operated. Cassandra was a natural leader. She needed to know what her team would be able to do. A soft series of alternating notes began playing. They started to get to know one another, which was good. Dex was beginning to forge more connections with people. He was starting to open up more. Neil would be proud, he thought to himself.

"I love this song," she confessed to Dex. She looked at him and smiled. "Get up. We're going to dance." Dex hadn't danced with a woman in years. "Look," she said, "one of the best ways to really get to know someone is to fight them. We aren't doing that, so let's dance. Same concept." He stood up and they walked to the floor as Chasing Cars by Snow Patrol kept playing. Dex swallowed hard and placed his hands on her hips. The dress she wore was soft and gentle. She placed her hands around the back of his neck.

"Oh please," she said with a laugh. "We were closer than this on the ship. Remember?" How could Dex have forgotten?

"No, I remember, but this is different," he replied sheepishly. He was getting lost in the song, in her eyes.

"We don't need anything or anyone," the singer crooned.

"How is it different?" She asked curiously with a sort of smile on her lips. A trap. He had fallen into a trap. He looked into her eyes.

"You're breathing has increased," he said. "Your face is a little flushed and your pupils are dilated slightly," he said. "Either you recently did some drugs, or..." say it, he imagined Neil's voice saying in his head. "Or you're attracted to me." She blushed and laughed.

"Too damn, perceptive," she said shaking her head. "You're one to talk. You barely knew what to do with dancing. Do I make you nervous, Dex Machina?" Deflection, she thought to herself. It was her only tactic. Dex felt his face redden.

"If I lay here. If I just lay here. Would you lie with me and just forget the world?"

"I don't know what to do," Dex said. "This is the first time I've felt... not even normal. Just good- you know? Like, I'm actually just living. With everything else, it's just... nice."

"I don't quite know how to say how I feel. Those three words are said too much. They're not enough."

"Dex," she said, staring at him. There was silence for a bit, as they dance, simply looking at one another. They were assessing the situation, how they feel and the ramifications of everything. Was this wise? Did it make sense? Nothing else in their life made sense, so why would this? It is what it is.

"All that I am. All that I ever was is here in your perfect eyes. They're all I can see."

"Cass," he replied getting lost in her eyes.

"We just met," she said softly.

"I don't know where. I'm confused about how as well. Just know that these things will never change for us at all."

"Yeah. Yeah I know. I don't want to lose this moment- this feeling. It feels... it feels right somehow." he replied.

"Yeah," she said. "Yeah it does. Let's not ruin it by rushing anything, okay?" Dex nodded in response.

"If I lay here. If I just lay here. Would you lie with me and just forget the world?" They held each other tight. It was a promise. Both Dex and Cassandra would tell you that sometimes in life, there are moments where one seems to find a universal truth. The veil is lifted and they can see things clearly. For both of them, in this moment, they were each other's universal truth. They were the other side of a coin they didn't fully understand. The only logical conclusion was to nurture this connection however it presented itself. Whatever would happen was going to happen and for them, that would be enough.

After the dance, they left the restaurant a lot more comfortable than when they first arrived. Their collective body language was one of comfort and mutual respect and attraction. Dex thought on all of this and decided that it was good. Everything was fine until they got in the car. Hitting shuffle on his play list created a result that Dex was not ready for. Suddenly, Matt Skiba's voice filled the truck.

"Tragedy. Erase my memory. Now all I see is this black rain."

"Oh nice," Cassandra said smiling. "Too many people discount Blink's Skiba era stuff."

"Yeah," Dex said with a fake smile. Of course, the song was good to Dex. It was Blink 182. But the lyrics disturbed him. He had just had the best night he had in a while. Yet as the song continued, he continued to have to hide his fears about the future from Cassandra.

"I went and searched for some answers but all I found were monsters. They're under my bed- haunting this tie that's been severed, this tie that's been severed." A song that Dex normally loved sent a chill of apprehension through his body. Best not to dwell on it, Dex thought. This can be a problem for Tomorrow Dex at the earliest. Tonight was still a good night. He did his best to push his worry from his mind.

Arriving home was slightly no better. They entered the door giggling and laughing and found Morgan holding a bag of frozen peas on Neil's face. Dex and Cassandra reacted with worry.

"Geez dude," Dex said rushing over to check on Neil. "I hope the other person looks worse than you."

"Oh, they do!" Neil yelled with a mix of pain and righteous fury. "No one is going to get away with that!"

"Geez, hold still," Dex said healing his black eye. "There. That better?"

"Yes. Thank you," Neil replied raising their eyebrows and checking for pain.

"So, what happened?" Cassandra asked Morgan. Morgan sighed. She didn't really want to relive the events of the evening, but she knew that she had to. Sadly, she was almost used to it all.

"It's my fault," she said remorsefully. "I told them not to worry about it. It happens all the time and I just ignore it. You get used to small minded smooth brains." While it was true, that didn't mean it didn't still hurt.

"No one talks to people I care about that way," Neil yelled in defiance. "That's why I blasted him into a damn wall."

"Who said what?" Cassandra asked growing concerned. Morgan sighed.

"We decided to go to Big Ralph's for some pizza because you two shouldn't have all the fun." She looked down, embarrassed by the situation. "Neil went to the restroom and I was still at the table. Some guys came by and tried to pick me up. When I rejected them, they said I was a fake and fraud. You know- everything my bio family told me. Like, because I rejected them, there had to be something 'wrong' with me. So, Neil comes back and asks what's wrong and I said nothing, excusing myself to go to the restroom to try to calm down. One of them yelled to make sure I used the men's room and that's how the fight started." Tears welled up in her big hazel eyes.

"I mean," Neil said, "can you blame me? They swung first but I sure as hell ended it." Cassandra nodded.

"No. You were right. That's uncalled for." She looked at Morgan. "Morgan, you're a beautiful woman and those jerks couldn't handle you anyway. Narrow minded bigots need put in their place. Plus, you have Neil." Neil blushed and feigned embarrassment.

"Oh stop," they said bashfully waving Cassandra away. "but do go on."

"Why should she have to use the men's room? Was the ladies' room broken or something?" Dex asked. He was genuinely lost in the conversation. The other three stared at him.

"Oh honey," Neil said sympathetically. "Really?" Morgan sighed and laughed. He's sweet, she thought.

"Let's just say that the reason my family doesn't talk to me anymore is because I wanted to be an *actress* and not an *actor.*" Dex thought on this for a moment.

"Yeah," Dex realizing what she was saying. "I mean I get that, but it's still stupid. Like, you're Morgan. That's who you are. Period. And Neil was right to blast them. And I'll go toe to toe with anyone who says otherwise and that includes any famous British authors." Dex looked at Morgan. "No one messes with my family." Tears welled up in her eyes. "We aren't a team," Dex continued. "We're a family. And whatever happens from this point forward, we are there for each other. Deal?" the others nodded in agreement.

The rest of the evening was nice. Dex thought about it. It was an evening filled with laughter and love. It was an evening with family. Dex saw the evening and decided that it was good. This would be the last good day they would have for a while as the world promptly began to fall apart the next day.

Chapter Thirteen

The day started off like any other. The sun filtered into Dex's room, waking him from a deep sleep. He smiled to himself, thinking of last night. He reveled in the memories of the evening. Not just the dinner with Cassandra, but the rest of the evening with Morgan and Neil. This was his new family and he decided that it was good.

His alarm started to go off, playing a random song. Soft guitar strumming began though it increased with intensity. *"You and I in a little toy shop buy a bag of balloons with the money we've got. Set them free at the break of dawn till one by one, they are gone. Back at base bugs in the software flash the message 'something's out there!' Floating in the summer sky ninety-nine red balloons go by."*

Dex couldn't help but laugh. Cassandra would, most likely, give him crap for not having the Nena version. He couldn't help it. To him, the Goldfinger version was better. He laughed again as he got dressed for the day, letting the song play and nodding his head to the rock beat. *"Ninety-nine decision street. Ninety-nine ministers meet to worry, worry, super scurry. Call out the troops now in a hurry. This is what we've waited for. This is it, boys, this is war. The president is on the line as ninety-nine red balloons go by."* To say that Dex, who was usually so concerned with random songs, found himself distracted that morning was an understatement. His mind was preoccupied with being happy.

He made his way downstairs and saw that the chore wheel was in full effect. Neil was working on food while Morgan was working on dishes and laughing. Cassandra was tidying up a bit in the living room.

"You're awake now and out of a coma so your chore wheel duty starts today," Neil yelled to Dex while pointing a spatula at him. "You're on laundry duty today, so don't be weird about it." They finished plating the food and took it to the table. "Okay everyone," they shouted. "Breakfast is served." Everyone gathered around the table and sat down. It was like a family meal- something none of them had been blessed with in quite some time.

"So, what does everyone have going on today?" Neil asked. Dex shrugged.

"Nothing. I'm still technically off work. Maybe I'll work on my anime watch list."

"After you do the laundry," Cassandra added. Dex nodded.

"Yes, obviously," he replied. Cassandra laughed.

"Well, I know I have no plans," she added.

"Same," Morgan added. "I trained with Ophelia yesterday. "So, I'm free and clear today." Everyone looked at Neil. He swallowed his eggs.

"What?" they asked. "This is my regular day off. It's been that way for a hot minute." Morgan grinned.

"We have nothing to do today," she said with a smile. "Let's go have fun."

"What do you suggest?" Cassandra asked. Morgan thought for a moment.

"I'm not sure. I mean, movie marathon? Mini golf? Monopoly tournament?"

"Absolutely not," Neil yelled suddenly. "I still have nightmares..." Dex laughed.

"Neil is terrible at Monopoly. They always end up crying, even if they are winning."

"It's a mean game that extols capitalist virtues. If people shared their wealth, then the game would be nicer."

"That's not how it works comrade," Cassandra said with a laugh.

"Well that's how it should work," they replied defensively.

"How about we get our chores done and then we can go out for lunch. Something easy. Like going to Ralph's Kitchen?" Neil laughed out loud.

"Cassandra domesticated you already." They turned and looked at her. "You go, girl."

"Morgan," Cassandra replied sipping her coffee, "reign your partner in, please." Morgan and Neil blushed and looked down. They simply didn't know how to respond to this statement. Neil and Morgan shot each other a small glance, smiling a bit and blushing.

"I'm not wrong," Dex said, drinking his coffee. He paused for a moment. It seemed a little extra bitter this morning. Was this a new brand? Because it wasn't the new coffee he recently bought. He was saving that. "We might as well have a full-on fun lunch, right?" The rest of them thought about it. They nodded in agreement.

"Right," Neil said. "So, we go get our stuff done and then go have a fun lunch. Let's see where the day sends us." After breakfast, everyone went off to work on their assigned task. Dex was lucky: there were long breaks in the laundry being done. Everyone had their own hamper, so that made things easier. All he had to do was wash and dry a load, fold it, and place the basket in the correct room. It was made simpler with the fact that Neil, who was always very organized, had labeled everyone's hampers. At one point, he found Morgan sitting on the couch watching an anime called Future Diary. Dex sat down next to her.

"Spoiler alert: messing with time is a crazy thing to do," he told her.

"I've seen it before," she laughed. "I just... I don't know. I felt the urge to re-watch it."

"Ophelia would probably say that this is no accident," Dex replied.

"After spending time with her, I would probably agree with her," she replied truthfully.

"So, what's the lesson we learn here?" he asked. Morgan shrugged.

"Maybe that that the more we try to plan and control the future we find that we can't. Or maybe that those who try to change the past wind up screwing up. Maybe we have to use the past to shape the future." Morgan and Dex were quiet for a few moments. Finally, Dex spoke.

"So, how are you? I mean, we haven't had much time to talk to one another." Morgan was quiet for a moment. How was she? She thought on the events that had happened to her recently. She was healed from being a Vampire. She started learning how to properly user her power and Ophelia was personally teaching her combat, which was strange given Ophelia's gentle demeanor. She had to deal with the same prejudices she faced on a daily basis simply because of who she was. How was she? Truth be told, even with the chaos that had been going on, she felt good for the first time in a long time. She felt as if she actually belonged to something for once in her life. She felt whole and complete. She had started to put the past behind her which she was used to doing. Being a trans woman had its own issues, but she had become callous to what people could throw at her. Instead, with these people, she didn't have to hide who she was. She could just be who she was. Truth be told, she felt complete for the first time in a long time. She looked at Dex who had a slightly concerned look on his face.

"I'm actually better than I've been in a long time." She smiled slightly.

"I'm not, like, trying to be weird or anything," Dex said. He rubbed his neck. "I don't know. I guess I just want to make sure everyone is okay. Healer nature, I guess."

"No, I get that," she said sympathetically. "Cass is literally like the sister I always wanted. And Neil..." she smiled slightly. "Neil is Neil."

"Yeah, well I've known them for a very long time. And I'm super protective of them." Morgan laughed.

"You're adorable," she said smiling.

"I mean, I'm going to give them the same speech about you, so don't worry. Minus the whole known for a long-time thing. I mean, you drank my blood, so we're close now right? Is that how that works?" She gave him a weird look. "Look, I like my jokes like I like my coffee..."

"Dark, bitter, and strong enough to keep the existential dread at bay," she finished. "Yeah. Neil mentioned that." They both laughed.

"If you need anything, just let me know, okay?" She nodded and smiled, feeling even more at home.

Chores were done and now it was time for lunch. They had decided on taking Neil's car. Dex and Cassandra piled into the back seat while Neil and Morgan were discussing something. She looked as if she was pleading with Neil. They looked at the car and then back to Morgan. They sighed and handed Morgan the keys.

"Wait, what?" Cassandra asked confused.

"Well clearly they're letting Morgan drive," Dex said as if it was plain to see because it was. Morgan squealed and got in the driver's seat while Neil road shotgun. They made the symbol of the cross across themselves.

"Thank you, Neil," She said excitedly, starting the car. "I need to practice so I can get my license."

"Wait, what?" Dex asked with a look of concern on his face. With that, the car jerked to life and peeled out of the driveway as Neil began reciting The Lord's Prayer. Thankfully, Morgan was still rather skilled and the drive wasn't that long. They arrived in one piece at Ralph's Kitchen.

They entered with a wave to Big Ralph who was behind the counter.

"Just seat yerselves!" he said while shaping some dough into a crust. They sat and ordered some drinks and ordered a large pizza to split. Dex looked at his friends laughing and having a good time. He was happy. He could tell that everyone else was happy. It was good.

It was then, at this point, Ophelia burst into the deli. She looked around, almost frantically, tugging harder than normal on one of her braids. It was Morgan who saw her first, a look of concern spreading across her face. Dex noticed and eventually saw what was causing her distress.

"Ophelia?" he asked anxiously. The others looked.

"Something's wrong..." Morgan said quietly. Finally, Ophelia saw where they were sitting and started coming over. "She should have known where we were. She always knows." Dex decided that Morgan was correct with her assessment.

"Something's wrong," Ophelia said hurriedly looking around as if to see that the coast was clear. "I can't contact the other three."

"Where were they going?" Cassandra asked.

"There was some new mission they said they had to handle. Someone created a new type of zombie seen by everyone. You didn't need The Sight to see them and they illicit a fear like effect in people. But they haven't responded to messages and I'm getting worried..." A sad sense of déjà vu washed over Dex.

"And Mary has been brought up on treason charges, hasn't she?" There was a collective gasp at the table as Ophelia nodded.

"The other members of The Council brought forth evidence against her. Since others aren't here, they assumed original jurisdiction and charged her with treason. She demanded a trial by combat." She began tugging her braid more, her other hand stimming in the air. "They named you as their champion. I came to bring you to them." Dex shook his head. This was wrong. This was all wrong.

"Wait: what's going on?" Morgan asked.

"Mary is going to fight Dex to prove her innocence. Jules and the others are missing." Cassandra answered.

"This is a little too convenient," Neil said.

"I agree," Cassandra said, "but I think Dex has to go along with it." His head snapped towards her.

"I'm not going to kill her," Dex said. "I'm not going to be a hitman for a fascist take over."

"Dex, you don't have to kill her. You just have to win. And we can see what she knows. I mean, this has to be a setup, right?" Dex thought for a moment. As it stood, there were only two possibilities. Either she was, in fact, the traitor or she wasn't. That was it. Dex scoured his brain looking for some sign either way. Yes, she was always mean and nasty, but could she really betray The Order? Something Jules told him long ago hummed through his mind. There was always a chance anyone with a Gift could become Corrupted. But he also knew Mary. She was a tactical genius. If he even went to ten-percent power, he could easily defeat her. Part of Dex thought she knew that. But he was selected by The Council, which mean they thought he could win. Unless the play was to have her kill Dex in combat.

"Too many variables," Neil said telepathically. "You started thinking out-loud. But in this equation, there are too many variables. You can't account for everything."

"What if I say no?" Dex asked aloud.

"You can't," Cassandra said darkly. "You'd be dismissed from The Order for not following orders."

"Nothing like being a dog of the military," Neil said dryly. Dex wiped his mouth and threw his napkin on the table.

"Well then. Let's get to it."

They arrived at the headquarters of The Order. Only Dex and Ophelia were allowed in the sparing room. The Council stood on one side with Mary in the middle, already holding a longsword.

"The Council has charged Mary with treason and conspiring with enemies to bring about the destruction of The Order," Jude said with a hint of sadness in his voice. "She has asserted her right to a trial by combat. The Council hereby calls Dex Machina as its champion. The battle is over by submission, incapacitation, or death."

"Dex just do you best," Ophelia whispered to him. He nodded curtly. There was no need to respond. He stepped forward and drew his weapon as The Council and Ophelia withdrew.

It happened in an instant. Before he knew it, Mary was attacking him. He raised Ruach to block the vertical attack.

"This was the only way," she said quietly to Dex before backing up and flourishing her sword around her. Dex lunged with an easily avoidable attack. She stepped to the left and said, "I had to tell you the truth." She kicked him in the back and he fell to his knees. Another kick and he was on his stomach. He rolled over to his back, but Mary was already on him. He placed his left hand on the flat of his blade stopping Mary's own sword mere inches from his face.

"What is the truth?" he asked as he summered some power to shove her off of him. It created enough of a gap that he could stand to his feet. Mary lunged again as Dex parried the blow.

"You'll find the truth behind The Truth," she said. Why? Why wouldn't she just tell him what she knew? It was as if she couldn't because people were listening in. So logically that meant that someone on The Council was the traitor. Unless of course she actually was the traitor. It made no sense. Dex weighed his options quickly. He could throw the match and Mary would be free. If he didn't, he would have to fight to knock her out, which he could do. There was a flash of metal and a sickening sound of flesh opening. She sliced his left arm. Blood ran down his arm to his hand has he instinctively healed himself.

And just like that, with a gunshot, it was over. Mary fell backwards, a fine red mist about her head acting almost like a soft pillow, following her to the ground for her eternal rest. There was silence after the bang- the kind of silence in which a universe would have been created. Dex looked in horror at Mary's dead body. Ophelia was crying. The Council had already left.

"No," Dex said crying. "No. I can still save her. She's not gone."

"Dex," Ophelia said in an almost whisper, "she's already gone. You know that." Dex shook his head no, his tears splattering on the ground. Of course he knew she was gone. He could feel her energy leave her body. The smell of sulfur and blood filled his nose. It would be quite some time before that smell would leave him. The image of this, however, would remain with him always. He put Ruach away and wiped his eyes with his left hand, smearing some blood across his face.

"Where is The Council?" he asked in a low voice. He felt his power rising and for the first time in a long time, he didn't want to stop it.

"I don't know," Ophelia said. "They just left."

"Go get me the coordinates of where the other three left to. I'm going to Mary's study." He stormed off, his body burning with anger and energy. The rest of his team was startled by the slamming of the door open.

"Dex! What happened?" Cassandra asked in a scared voice.

"Mary is dead. She was murdered during our fight," he said not looking at anyone, wearing a scowl on his face. "The Council is missing and I'm going to her study for answers." He shot a glance to Morgan.

"Morgan: if you can, see if you can figure out where we end up."

"I've been trying," she said with a hint of worry in her voice, "but... I don't know. There's some interference. I've never experienced anything like this. All I know is that you will find the three, but that's it."

"Cass and Neil: prepare for war," Dex said. Neil had never seen Dex like this. Sure- they had seen Dex angry, but never like this. Dex's body shimmered on and off with a golden aura.

"Dex," Cassandra said, "I can't reach my dad telepathically," Dex stopped at Mary's study door and looked at Cass. She never called her dad anything other than Adrian yet now, in the midst of uncertainty, she was a woman who wanted to know if her father was okay. "Do you think he's okay?" she asked. Dex looked, for the first time at his team. They were all terrified. Say something, he thought to himself. Say anything. The Healer does more than heal the body. They care for their team in general.

"We'll find him. And we will make sure he's okay." He looked at everyone. "We'll find them all. Ophelia is getting us coordinates. Mary left us clues. We can do this. Cass, start working on a plan to storm a stronghold." He kicked in Mary's door with a determined thump. Splinters were everywhere. He had been here before, but never under the circumstances.

"What are we looking for?" Neil asked.

"The truth," Dex answered. Neil laughed.

"What is truth?" they asked. That was the question- what is truth? Dex knew that they were looking for the truth behind The Truth, but he had no idea what that even meant. The team spread out around the room, looking for anything that could help.

"This is a waste of time," Cassandra said. "If we need to move, we need to move now."

"We need more information on what we are facing," Neil said. "I'm not rushing plunging into a battle unprepared."

"Time is a factor," Cassandra quipped back at him, "and this is a wild goose chase."

"Why did she name her clock John?" Morgan asked confused. Dex looked at the clock on the wall. It was a standard wall clock with two googly-eyes affixed to it. Beneath it was a name tag that stated the clock's name was John. Dex had seen the clock before, but this was a recent addition to it.

"It's a clue," Dex said. "All that is new in here." Cassandra scoffed.

"Doesn't help us find the truth." Dex stared at the clock, transfixed by it. Something was wrong with it.

"It's broken," Neil said suddenly. "Like, there's no ticking with it." Dex looked at his watch. The time was wrong by more than a few hours. It read 2:06 pm.

"So John is saying 2:06," Morgan said. "What does that mean?" Dex shook his head. It didn't make any sense.

"Wait," Cassandra said suddenly. "PM wouldn't be two in military time. It would be fourteen in military time. I mean, why else would it say PM on it?"

"So John is really saying fourteen-six?" Morgan asked.

"Oh!" Neil said suddenly. "I know that one! My parents were super religious right. Learned that one at Bible camp. First time I kissed a boy, actually," they said with a giggle. "It's the whole 'I am the way, the truth, and the light' line. You know- in the Bible." Dex stared at Neil and back to the clock. John 14:6. That's the truth. Cassandra was a head of him, already taking the clock down and looking for something.

"There's nothing there," she said frustrated. They all looked around the room.

"What about the crucifix?" Morgan asked. On the wall facing the door was a large wooden crucifix of Jesus.

"The truth behind The Truth," Dex whispered. He carefully took it off the wall and examined it carefully. He noticed that there was something off with the back. The woodgrain didn't match up. He grabbed a letter opener from her desk and found a hidden compartment containing a flash drive.

"Turn on her computer," Dex said. Neil moved the mouse and the computer sprang to life. He slid the drive into the USB port and a folder opened with movie file. Dex clicked the file and Mary's face filled the screen.

"She knew," Dex said despondently. "She knew she was going to die." He pressed play.

"If you're watching this," Mary said with a sigh, "then that means that I've either been found out and you shouldn't be watching this, or I'm dead. If I had to fight Dex one last time, I at least hope I made him bleed a little." Dex laughed. Even from beyond the grave, she still wanted to give him shit. "If Dex is watching this, I really hope you're ready for this. I'm assuming that I'll get popped with treason charges. I've been talking with a vampire who wants out of that life. He's been feeding me information on what's going on. The reason the Psykers and the Prophets powers are going haywire is because there's this machine. I don't know what powers it, but it amplifies the user's Gifts by, like a billion. That much psychic interference also messes with prophecy. I don't know what it does, but it's not good. It can't be. So, find it and destroy it. Please. I'm literally staking my life on this hope." She wiped a tear from her eye. Her face shifted in the video and she became serious, her eyes will with hurt and betrayal. "If you're watching this, Jude, I hope you rot in Hell for what you've done to The Order." The video ended with silence.

Jude. Whatever was going on, Jude was at the center of it.

"He's the traitor," Neil said. "This whole damn time." They punched the wall with a glowing fist leaving a large hole.

"We'll get him," Dex said gravely. "We'll stop him."

"We need to find Ophelia. We need to know where to go," Cassandra said. As if on que, Ophelia came into the room visibly shaking. "The Council," she said. "They're dead. They're all dead." She fell to her knees crying. "I didn't know," she wept. "I couldn't see it happen. I found them in the hallway coming back here."

"Everyone but Jude," Dex replied. Ophelia nodded. "He's the traitor." Suddenly, Cassandra grabbed her head in pain. Dex had a headache as well. He shook his head, trying to heal himself which helped at least numb the pain. He then grabbed Cassandra gently, holding her head in his hands, helping her as well.

"Thank you," she said, nervously. "Must be a huge spike in psychic power causing some feedback." She turned to Ophelia. "Are you ready to send us?" she asked. Ophelia stood up and collected herself. Cassandra looked at Morgan.

"Are you okay with staying with Ophelia?" she asked.

"Morgan, I need you to stay safe," Neil said taking her hands. Tears welled up in her eyes. "I know," she said. "Yeah: I know. I've already seen this part for some reason." Neil gently kissed her hands.

"I'll be back," Neil said. "I promise." Morgan shook her head in agreement. She grabbed them by the shoulders and kissed them.

"You damn well better be," she said, tears streaming down her face. They all looked at Ophelia and nodded.

"I don't know what you're going to find there," Ophelia said solemnly.

"We'll find the three and we'll stop Jude," Dex replied. Ophelia nodded.

"Theme song time?" Neil asked, their phone at the ready. To their surprise, Dex shook his head no.

"No. Let's just go and save the world." Ophelia produced her Skeleton Key and opened the door to a dark forest. The three of them stepped through and heard the door close behind them. Cassandra pulled out her phone and called Morgan.

"Hey," she said. "We're here. Let us know if something comes up."

"Something is already up," Morgan told her. "There's reports of zombie outbreaks worldwide. The rest of The Order is in a tizzy trying to contain it, but these aren't normal zombies."

"Alright. Let us know if anything else comes up." She hung up the phone.

"Whatever Jude is planning, it's happening now. So let's move." She took off in a jog following a somewhat warn path. Eventually, after a few minutes, they approached a large gothic castle.

"Oh, what an ass," Neil said disgusted. "Of course he would pick this as a base. That guy is a walking cliché- I swear."

"That's not the problem," Cassandra said. "I'm picking up a lot of people in our way."

"What are we looking at?" Dex asked.

"It's not good. It's a regular who's who of villains. We've got a few Vampires, a Werewolf, some Grafters and some Corrupted."

"Do we have the element of surprise? What's the play here?" Dex asked her.

"I think if I get close enough to the Werewolf, I can knock them out. That needs to be the priority. I'd say you both need to cover me. Neil handles suppressive fire. And you need to get in there to find Jude. Let's take out the big guns here and Neil and I play clean up and back you up."

"Should we really split the party?" Dex asked with a laugh.

"Don't hold back and we should be fine," Cassandra said. She had an understanding of what she was saying, but she had never seen Dex unleash his full power. In truth, he didn't want to do that. Instead, he always wanted to play it safe and keep that as an ace in the hole. Dex nodded and understood he would have to go beyond.

"Let me go in first. You follow and head to the hairy one. They won't be able to resist a fight with what I'll show them." Neil and Cassandra nodded in agreement. Dex figured that Cassandra was right about one thing: this was no time to play it super quiet. His job was to attract a fight. He closed his eyes, thinking of his new family. When he opened them again, all Neil and Cassandra could see were brightly glowing orbs instead of his blue eyes. His body shone with positive energy. He nodded at them and took off in a sprint- faster than they had ever seen him move before. He approached the front of the castle and saw the crowd assembled, waiting patiently to kill any interlopers. Say something cool, he thought. This is totally you chance to say something cool.

"Hey fuzz ball! Come get it!"

"Nice," he heard Neil say in his head. While not very cool, it did work. He saw a huge monstrous beast covered in course brown fur. It turned it's dog like head to Dex and let out a strangely human howl. Running on all fours, it sought to meet Dex in battle, its claws tearing into the earth to propel it towards fresh meat. Dex drew Ruach, shimmering with energy. Bringing the tip of the sword to his right side, he managed to catch the beast by the jaw. The blade sunk partly into it's flesh and Dex heard a dog like yelp. He dug his heels into the ground and used the beast's own momentum to throw him high into the air, directed towards Neil and Cassandra. She ran towards the monster who skidded towards her. Placing her hands on its shaggy head, she closed her eyes, placing it into a deep sleep.

Neil pointed his hands towards the ground and fired blasts, propelling himself high into the air. He seemed to transform into some kind of an automatic weapon, firing blasts at a stunned crowd. Cassandra already had her staff out, ready for action.

"Go!" she yelled at Dex in his head. "Find Jude!" He looked back and nodded at her. Dragging the tip of his blade in the ground, he brought it upwards, sending a blast of positive energy through the air. It knocked over those that were in his way. He moved with lightning speed, entering the gap and gaining access to the castle door. He was confident in his team handling the rest of the enemies.

He found himself entering large wooden doors, leading to an entrance way in the old castle. He remembered he needed to find a machine, the three, and Jude. He was confident they would all be together, but where would he begin looking? He was struck by something Neil said. Jude is a walking cliché. Of course, he thought, triumphantly. He'd be in the throne room. But where exactly was that? Damn. This would be so much easier if he could use his gift of Prophecy regularly. He tried to think back to classes he had taken over the years. Where would the throne room be? Surely, he thought, it would be near the center of the castle. That was the only thing that made sense.

"Dex?" Neil asked. "You still okay, buddy?"

"I'm good," he responded. "Ya'll okay?"

"We're doing fine," Cassandra answered, "but The Order is struggling. These zombies seem to keep coming. And they are able to turn others into zombies."

"Aw, beans," Neil replied. "That's going to be problematic."

"Just find the machine and shut it down," Cassandra said. "we'll join you as soon as we can."

"That's a Texas sized ten-four," Dex replied. He assumed that the throne room would be towards the center of the lower level he was on. It's a shame, Dex thought to himself. Normally he would have loved to be in the position he found himself in. He was in an old, dilapidated castle filled with all sorts of cool and creepy things. If only I had the time to properly explore, he thought.

Heading towards the center of the castle, he approached two huge wooden doors. Something felt off. His head began to hurt a little more. He sniffed his nose as he thought it was running. It wasn't running- it was bleeding. Whatever was going on was happening behind these doors, he thought to himself. He gently opened the door. He was not ready for what he saw on the other side, as he peered into the room. In the elevated place where the throne would be was a wall of monitors. They seemed to be fixed on large cities. They showed battles with what he assumed was members of The Order and his hordes of zombies. To the left stood what he assumed was the machine. In three large tubes filled with a green tinted liquid, he saw Jules, Rhianna, and Adrian floating with some kind of breathing masks on their face. It gave a low, ominous hum and cackled with some kind of energy. That, Dex decided was not the weirdest part of the scene. Instead, that pleasure belonged to Jude, who appeared to have some sort of metal backpack on. He was... dancing? A sort of upbeat and jaunty tune by The Aquabats was playing as he danced to the rhythm. *"Chemical bomb, chemical bomb. Eyes melt, skin explodes, everybody's dead. It won't be long; it won't be long. People gonna run around losing their heads. A river of blood, who's gonna live? The earth is tired of humankind and I think this world is gonna wash up in Hell."*

Suddenly, he stopped moving, yet he continued to let the song play. Jude turned to face Dex.

"Well this is a surprise," genuinely stunned. "I thought you'd be out there fighting my zombies."

"You killed Mary," Dex said bitterly. "Why?" Jude shrugged.

"You said it yourself- sometimes you got to do what you got to do. I realized you were right, and I decided to step my game up."

"So is this the part where you explain your master plan?" Dex asked. Jude rubbed his chin.

"I mean, I suppose I could. Your team will be dead soon anyway."

"You grossly underestimate them," Dex said. Jude shook his head sadly.

"Honestly, I was trying to protect you. I didn't want you to have a team. I like you, Dex Machina. I never wanted to kill you."

"Then don't," he replied. "Just stop this all."

"Oh no," Jude said, with a mad glint in his eye. "See, that's the whole problem- people don't go far enough. I mean, look at what we can do, Dex. We shape human history on a daily basis. You ever stop to think why?"

"Usually I'm thinking about anime," Dex replied, moving closer and closer to Jude. Jude shook his head.

"We were chosen by God. We are a royal priesthood, Dex. We are the ones that will shape this world. Our very existence proves there is a higher power." He gave a short sad laugh. "And what does the world do? It keeps on spinning, only calling on God when it needs something. It's rude. It's obnoxious!" the longer he talked, the madder Jude was getting. Dex could feel the anger and hatred radiating off of him.

"I don't know man," Dex said. "Have them read the Bible? Like, shouldn't that work?" Jude shook his head.

"They've had the Bible for years and still ignore God. I started thinking: when do people need God? When they're in trouble. So, I'll give the world trouble. In order to send them to God, I'll send them to Hell first. Then they'll see," he smiled a maddening smile. "They'll all see."

"Scare people into Heaven- is that the plan?" Dex shook his head. "Sounds like a crap plan to me. Pretty sure that Jesus guy was all about loving your neighbor and helping others."

"This is helping!" Jude shouted defensively. "They don't know what they need, but they will. And then the world will be united." Dex motioned with his head towards the machine trapping the three.

"I'm assuming that rig over there has something to do with it?"

"Oh yes!" Jude said happily. "That machine augments my abilities to create constructs of pure thought. That's what my zombies are: they're a mental virus. It can augment anyone plugged into it. It uses the energy of a Channler to power me. The Psyker is needed to connect me to them. And the Healer keeps the others from burning out. It's almost like a perpetual motion machine." He pointed to his back. "And it's wireless!"

"Okay, cool," Dex replied. "So I just need to stop that machine to stop you." Suddenly, four long spider-like limbs sprouted from the metal backpack.

"Please. You didn't think it was going to be that easy, did you?" Dex laughed.

"You know, for a second there, I kind of did." A spider leg moved with insane speed, causing Dex to roll to dodge.

"The legs are full of human brains," Jude said. "That way, I can control them. Only took a few dozen or so." Another attack, pierced Dex's shoulder. Jude flung him into a wall.

"So your brave new world is built on a foundation of the dead?"

"Oh Dex," Jude laughed, moving like a monstrous spider towards him, "you got to do what you got to do, right?" the limbs moved with a terrifying speed, piercing Dex repeatedly and repeatedly. All Dex could do was take the blows, healing himself as he went along.

"And you don't even see how this is, like, a little messed up? Dex asked, spitting out some blood. Jude shrugged.

"You can't make an omelet without cracking a few eggs." Dex. Managed to blindly attack one of the legs, severing it. Jude reeled back, but somehow, he was able to cause it to regrow. "You can't win," he said sadly. "So either get onboard or die."

"Counteroffer," Dex said. "You surrender and free Jules and them. Then spend the rest of your life in a cell." Jude's face grew red with anger. Suddenly, all four spider legs pierced Dex's stomach. Damn, he thought to himself. I'm going to die here, aren't I?

"You are not worthy of God's love." He withdrew his weapons, and Dex lay on the ground bleeding out. He couldn't heal himself fast enough, even at twenty-five percent power to keep himself from dying. He could feel his current power level dropping. Damn. I'm going to die. Maybe it's for the best, he thought. This world was a mess. Maybe, just maybe, it did need some help. Maybe it did need someone to bust it into submission. Maybe it was for the best.

Suddenly, Dex thought of his mother and father. His mother was always a free spirit. His father said that he always needed to work hard to help people. Would this brave new world allow for that? Would the subjugation of people really help humanity? He reached out a hand and touched his own blood leaking out of his body. His parents wouldn't want to live in that kind of a world. If they wouldn't want it, Dex decided that he wouldn't want it.

Fifty percent, he thought to himself.

His blood began to move back into his body as he was lifted off of the ground. Dex was cocooned in a dazzling, white light. He couldn't see Jude's face, but it was one of bewilderment and terror. Suddenly, the cocoon shattered. There, in the air, was Dex Machina. He had grown a pair of overpowering white wings like that of a dove. He was there, flying in the air, staring at Jude. Jude's spider legs skittered up a wall, making him at eye level with Dex.

"What the Hell are you?" he asked.

"I'm Dex Machina," he replied.

"Well, Dex Machina, I will never stop. Ever. I will keep going. I will show this world how much it needs God. Throw me in prison- I'll get out and rebuild. I can fix this world."

"So no surrender?" Dex asked, cocking his head quizzically to the right.

"Never," Jude spat back at him.

It happened in an instant. At once, Dex was going to draw his sword. The room was filled with the sound of a rushing wind. Dex was behind Jude. Putting Ruach back in its sheath. When it clicked into place, Jude fell apart in two pieces to the ground. It was over.

Dex landed on the ground and returned to normal. He felt sick to his stomach. You damn fool, he thought to himself. Damn you for making me do that.

"Dex," Cassandra interrupted suddenly. "We're done out here. Morgan said the other zombies just vanished. Did you find them?"

"I did," he replied. "And Jude is dead." There was silence.

"Dex I'm so sorry, Cassandra said.

"It is what it is," he replied.

"It is what it is," Neil echoed.

"I'm going to check on the three and maybe they can take us home." Dex walked over to that machine. This damn thing, he thought angrily. Drawing Ruach once more, he shattered the glass carefully, freeing the three. They fell to the floor. Dex removed their face masks and they were breathing fine on their own. Just then, there was a loud buzzing sound, like an intercom coming on.

"Thank you for killing Jude," the voice said. "He was beginning to bother me, but I got what I needed, so he wasn't useful anymore. The machine performed better than even I anticipated." Dex looked around. There seemed to be some speakers placed somewhere.

"Um, yes. Hello. And who is there?" Dex asked.

"I'm Niall," the male sounding voice said in a cold, emotionless voice.

"Don't worry. We'll talk soon. Until then, you should probably ask Jules about me. And maybe about your parents." Rage filled Dex. Did Jules know something about his parents? Why did this Niall know? "I'll be seeing you." There was another long buzz and the line went dead. Dex heard gasping. The three had woken up and began to scramble to their feet.

"Dex," Jules said coughing. "Thank you. We were ambushed and overpowered." Jules. Dex could only see red when he looked at him. He was so damn tired of being misled. He was sick of being used. He was just sick of it all. He walked over to Jules and punched him square in the jaw.

Chapter Fourteen

There are moments that happen in our lives that do two things simultaneously. First, they forever alter the path one is traveling. These moments are massive changes and upheavals. They tend to forever alter everyone involved. Second, they force a person to wonder about the exact nature of time itself as time either seems to slow down or stop all together. This moment was that for Dex, Jules, Adrian, and Rhianna. Jules stood there, wide eyed, staring at the floor, his head in the direction that Dex had punched him. Rhianna covered her mouth and Adrian just kept looking at the both of them.

Dex stood there, still in the position of finishing his punch. His mouth was open- a snarl on his face. His breathing was labored and fast, matching the beating of his own heart which was much too rapid.

"Dex what are you..." Rhianna started to say.

"Stop. Now," Dex commanded.

"No," Adrian said taking a step towards Dex. "You need to stop."

"Or what?" He said looking at Adrian. "You'll bleed me dry?" Adrian went pale with a look of shock on his face. Jules remained frozen. Dex looked at the three, disgusted by the lies and untruths. Damnit. He desperately wanted to say something, but nothing was coming out. There were no words for what Dex was feeling. The closest thing he could come to was disgust. He was disgusted with The Order.

"How long?" Dex said, grabbing Jules by the shoulders. "How long have you known something about my parents?" Jules brought his hands up, causing Dex to let go. He straightened up and shook his head free of cobwebs.

"The whole time," he said plainly. "I knew them before you were born." Another punch came from Dex, connecting with Jules. Adrian moved to stop him, but Jules looked at him and said, "No." There was another punch. And another. Jules stood there, taking each blow as an act of absolution, healing himself only minorly after each hit. Eventually, Dex was tired. He slumped onto Jules who held him as he cried. For a moment, it was fine. That was until Dex realized what was going on.

"Don't touch me!" he shouted, shoving Jules back. It was at this point Neil and Cassandra came into the room. Neil and Cassandra surveyed the room, seeing Jude and the broken machine.

"Dex?" Cassandra asked. "You okay?" He wiped the tears from his eyes and looked at her.

"No, man. I'm pretty far from okay." He turned and looked at Jules. "Take me home. Now. Not to headquarters. My home. Now." Jules nodded and walked towards the door. He strode towards the door intently. He walked through the door and slammed it shut, feeling safe inside his house. Carefully, he went to the bathroom, catching a glance of himself in the mirror. Blood. There was blood on him. The messed-up part was he wasn't sure if it was his, Jude's, or Mary's. He got in the shower, not waiting for it to warm up trying his best to cleanse himself from the horrors of the day. He could clean his body, but he could never forget what he saw or what he heard or what he had to do.

After his shower, he went into his room. He tossed Ruach on the bed and fell down next to it. He was done. He didn't want to do this anymore. All the secrets and lies where too much for him. On instinct, he charged his phone, hitting shuffle on his play list after putting his phone on do not disturb. He decided that God was kind to him for once, playing a song matching his mood by My Chemical Romance. He listened to the words, feeling them in his soul. *"What's the worst that I could say since I'm better if I stay? So long, and good night."*

Back at the castle, Neil and Cassandra were both speechless.

"Dad?" Cassandra asked. "What happened?" Adrian snapped to attention. It was a bittersweet moment for him.

"You told him," he said sadly. "Why?"

"Dad," she began, "you're always saying your team needs to know everything about you. And I want that with my team, so I spoke to Dex..."

"Wait, what?" Neil asked confused.

"It doesn't matter now," Adrian said sadly. "What matters is this portion is over. Now we can move on to the next part." He looked at Cassandra and said, "At least, I hope we can move on from here." She understood what he was really saying and nodded in agreement.

"Why did Dex leave?" Neil asked. "What's going on?" Rhianna looked around at Jules and Neil. Jules hadn't spoken since Dex left. She sighed.

"Chickens are coming home to roost," she said simply. "Everything that's been done in the dark is coming to light. And now we have to deal with it all. I think," she said diplomatically, "we should plan to meet tomorrow. Everyone- including Dex. Ophelia is taking Morgan home. We will have some teams tear down the machine and study it. Right now, we need rest and you both do as well." Neil shook his head no.

"Honestly, you guys haven't been truthful with us for a while and I'm pretty sick of it. This crap better be good."

"I agree with you, Neil," Rhianna said. "And it's time for the whole truth to come out. And that will be tomorrow."

"Fine," Neil spat bitterly. Cassandra moved towards Adrian. She placed a hand on his shoulder, startling him. Once he saw it was Cassandra, his tension eased some.

"Hey. Dad," she said softly. "It's going to be okay. We'll talk tomorrow, alright?" She hugged him. It had been many years since his daughter had hugged him. The tears of happiness came easily to him though they had not come in many years. Neil and Cassandra departed to their home, joining Morgan.

"Another fine mess we're in," Rhianna said. She looked at Adrian who was still crying. "At least some progress was made." Jules shook his head dejectedly.

"It had to happen this way," he said quietly. "Still after all this time, he doesn't understand that it had to happen this way."

"Why?" Rhianna asked. "Why did it have to be this way? You know what Niall is capable of. And now he's finally out of hiding with this... machine. Why didn't we just tell them? We could have been more proactive."

"We aren't God," Jules said sternly. "Everything happens for a reason."

"And what reason is this is happening?" She asked angrily.

"Dex Machina will either save the world or end it," Jules said.

"You can't be serious," Adrian said. Jules nodded darkly.

"There is a date that the Prophets can't see past. One week from now."

"That shouldn't be a problem now that the machine is gone, right?" Adrian asked.

"We'll have to see," Jules replied. "But I have a feeling it won't matter. They see what they are meant to see."

"So what now?" Rhianna asked in an anxious voice. "We just wait for the end of the world?"

"We do what we always do. We have faith that there really is a plan in spite of us messing it all up," Jules replied solemnly. "We are not the masters of our destines no matter how hard we try."

The first thing Cassandra did when she got home was head to Dex's room. The door was locked and she could hear a song playing in his room. *"I can't get out of my bed. Think there's magnets in my mattress-might as well just be a casket for all I care. Oh no, now here we go again. The bad thoughts are creeping in. The bad thoughts are creeping in."* She hesitated. Every fiber in her being was telling her to knock on the door. Kick the damn thing down, she thought.

"Dex?" she asked in a loud voice. "Can we talk?" The music stopped.

"Not right now, please," he said. "Just tell Neil that The Order is connected to my parents and I'm attempting to climb out of The Big Sad. I'll be down later. Thank you." The music started back up again. *"Some days I wish I was dead. Think I'm broke and I can't fix it. It's an intangible sickness but it's there. Oh no now here we go again. The bad thoughts are creeping in. The bad thoughts are creeping in."* Cassandra nodded and said in a soft voice,

"Okay. See you later, Dex." She went downstairs to find a fuming Neil and a slightly terrified Morgan. They were holding on to the one constant they had in that moment- each other. Cassandra sat down on the opposite couch with a flop and sighed. Neil and Morgan looked over to her.

"Well," they asked grimly, "how's our boy." Cassandra shook her head.

"He said to tell you that The Order is connected to his parents and he's climbing out of The Big Sad." Neil sat up quickly alarmed.

"I'm sorry, what?" they asked. Morgan looked concerned.

"What's wrong, Neil?" They shook their head and put their hands on their face.

"No. No. No," they said over and over again. "This is bad. This is really bad." They looked up at Cassandra. "You're sure that's what he said? Like, those were his exact words?" Cassandra nodded, a knot forming in her stomach.

"Yeah. I'm positive." Neil sighed and flopped backwards.

"Aw, beans..." they said, rubbing the back of their neck.

"What's The Big Sad?" Cassandra pressed. Neil sighed.

"So, you know how Dex will sometimes say he couldn't have gotten over his parent's death without me? Like, this isn't bragging, but he's right. It got really, really dark after they died." Cassandra and Morgan shared a concerned glance towards one another. "Like, he didn't want to leave his room for weeks. He cried every day. I mean, he's brilliant- he could have done anything he wanted to. He wanted to be a teacher but damn near flunked out of college missing classes. Finally, he settled for a degree in English just because it was easy to finish. He called that time The Big Sad."

"So how did he get out of it?" Morgan asked.

"It took time. It took a lot of time. I basically just had to wait and care for him. Eventually, little by little, he got over it. Kind of. I mean, he still hasn't fully moved on from it."

"I don't think there's a lot of time here," Morgan said with a hint of fear in her voice. "I think we have, like, a week tops."

"What makes you say that?" the knot in Cassandra's stomach grew tighter.

"I can't see anything past a week from today..." the room was quiet.

"Wonderful," Neil said, running their hand through their hair. "We're officially on the clock to the end now."

"It could be something else," Cassandra offered hopefully. Morgan shook her head.

"No. Ophelia and I had been talking about this. I know she's concerned as well. And without Dex, we're down a teammate."

"Who said I'm out?" a voice came from the stairs. Dex entered the room with a smile on his face and sat down next to Cassandra.

"So what did I miss?" he asked cheerfully. Cassandra looked at him confused.

"Neil was telling us about The Big Sad," she said hesitantly. "Dex, it's okay if you're not fine. We're here for you." Dex laughed.

"No, no, no. Really. I'm fine. It was just shocking is all. I listened to some sad songs and I'm fine now." Dex smiled again. Cassandra looked at Neil who shook their head slowly. It was obvious that Neil didn't believe him. Morgan bit her lip and looked away. It appeared that she had something she wanted to say.

"Babe," Neil asked her, taking her hand, "what's wrong?" She shook her head.

"Dex, I can't see the future past next week. But I'm still seeing somethings. Ophelia says we always see what we need to see." She shook her head again, as if she was trying to remove an image from her head. "I see you a few days from now covered in blood and crying." Dex sat back and sighed. Cassandra took his hand.

"Well that's a bummer," he said after a few moments.

"Dex, you clearly aren't fine," Morgan said angrily. "Damnit. Stop it! Just stop it!" She stood up and pointed at him. "You're so full of crap- you know that? I mean really. You're all, 'oh we're a family' and all that crap but you don't mean it. If you did, you'd let us help you." Tears flowed freely from her eyes. "I have four brothers I will never see again. You do you know what it's like to lose your whole family? Because I do. And here I thought I found a new one and you're just sitting there not letting us be your family! Well what's the damn point then, Dex? Huh? You tell me what's the point because I sure as Hell don't get it." She sat back down next to Neil, crying. No one had ever seen Morgan get like this before.

Cassandra squeezed his hand that she was holding. She looked him in the eye. He was no longer smiling. His eyes filled with tears, but he was doing everything in his power to keep them inside. He was failing miserably.

"We care about you, Dex." She gently wiped a tear from his face. "I care about you." Dex shook his head and looked down.

"Please," he said quietly. "Don't." She shook her head no.

"I can't, Dex. You know that."

"Why can't you people just let me be for a while?" he asked quietly. "Why do I have to be the strong one yet again? Just man up, huh? Just go for a walk and get some fresh air- that'll cure you, right?" He wiped his eyes with the back of his hand. "Just let me stay here, please. I'm just..." he sighed, searching for the words. "I'm just damn tired of it all." He looked at everyone in the room. Some were crying. Some were sad. Even now, in the midst of his anger and frustration and sadness, he still had to feel the sadness of others. I can't just have one moment, huh? I can't just wallow in my sadness. No- I have to still feel and handle the pain of others. If Dex was thinking clearly, he would have realized that he can control his Gifts. Yet now, he couldn't. He didn't have the strength.

"Let's take it slowly," Neil said, their eyes ablaze with kindness and love. "What's got you so rattled, my dude?" Dex shook his head, trying to clear his thoughts and eyes.

"There was a voice," he said staring at the ground not wanting to look at anyone, "he called himself Niall. Said we'd talk soon. He um..." Dex took a deep breath and continued, "he said that I should talk to Jules about him. And about my parents." Neil closed their eyes as if they were looking away from something terrible. "So I asked Jules if he knew my parents." Dex gave a scoffing laugh. "He's known them since before I was born. Never mentioned it once. Not one time." He shook his head dejectedly. "The whole damn time. A set up. Just another damn brick in the wall to him."

"They want to talk to us all tomorrow," Cassandra said quietly.

"Of course they do," Dex said. "Because it's on their time." Dex grew angry. "He could have saved them." Dex was quiet and shook his head. An eerie hush fell over the room. "I know he could have. He showed me how powerful Conduits are."

"Dex," Cassandra said, "is that what happened with Jude?" He looked at her, confused.

"What do you mean?" he asked. Cassandra hesitated. She understood that Dex may not want to relive the whole affair. He had witnessed Mary's death firsthand and had been forced to take the life of Jude. She was certain that if they were going to help him through this, they needed all the answers.

"I think that, because we're linked up, we felt some of your power. You didn't give us a boost or anything, but..." she searched for the words, unfamiliar with this situation. "It was like you changed or something. Neil? Morgan? Did you all feel it?" Both of them shook their heads. Dex nodded.

"Yeah. That's the thing. I can control how much positive energy goes throughout my body. When I fought Jude, I was at fifty percent and my body... it physically changed me." He looked at them all wearing slightly troubled faces. "I knew it would happen. I knew because Jules showed me what happens when I fully let go." He shifted his gaze to the floor. "I know what I am able to do and I have to keep it in check all the time. If I don't, then someone could get hurt." His face began to contort with anger and regret. "And he can do the same. And he didn't help my parents." He sighed and leaned back on the couch. "That's why I'm so mad."

"You won't get answers you like tomorrow," Morgan said softly, "but some answers are better than no answers."

"I'm sure it will be some kind of 'it is what it is' crap like always. Well I'm sick of that. I'm sick of all this pain and hurt. I'm sick of being betrayed."

"You are, like, almost a step below Mother Teresa," Neil said. "You're a damn good person. And I'm here for you."

"So how do you want to handle this?" Cassandra asked. "Seriously. It's your call. If we go, we go together. If we don't, then we don't go together." She wrinkled her nose. "Damnit. That's hard to say rather well, but you know what I mean."

"You talk pretty one day," Neil said with faux sympathy.

Dex looked around. All eyes were on him, waiting to see what he would say. It was as if they expected him to speak something profound. No, he thought. Not profound but rather honest. But then again, what was the truth? Dex needed to think things through rationally but his anger was making that difficult. After all, this was at least a perceived betrayal if not a real one. This was leaning him to say forget it. This is a brake up. So long and good night. Yet on the other hand, Dex was also concerned with the greater good. He understood that his mother always told him to be the change in he wanted to see in the world. His thoughts shifted to his father almost by instinct. Work hard for those you care about. What's the worst thing I could say since I'm better if I stay?

"I don't have a choice," he began sadly.

"No, you do," Cassandra replied trying to be helpful. Morgan shook her head. Her eyes were filled with sadness and remorse.

"He's right, though," she said softly. Neil sighed.

"Well there it is," they said. Dex shook his head in grave acknowledgement.

"There it is." They decided that they had enough for the day. It would be best if they rested up. Cassandra went to make arrangements for the meeting while Morgan went off to bed. Neil stayed downstairs with Dex a bit longer.

"You're not fine," Neil stated as a fact.

"I'm not disputing that fact," Dex replied. Neil sighed and sat next to Dex.

"Do you remember when you offered to let me move in with you and your parents?" they asked him. Dex nodded.

"Yeah. You were in a crap situation and got kicked out. I couldn't let you live like that." Neil nodded.

"Yes. You did everything in your power to help me out of a bad situation." They looked at Dex, placing a hand on his shoulder. "And I'll do the same for you." Dex hugged them close.

"Thank you," he said quietly. "I appreciate that." Dex left the warmth of the hug and headed to the darkness of his room for rest. He lay in bed for a while, trying to have his brain think of anything else. It was going a mile a minute.

"Dex?" It was Cassandra in his head. "I'm sorry, I... I just wanted to check on you." He sighed.

"Do you want the truth or a comforting lie?" he asked her.

"I would prefer the truth, no matter how terrible it may be," she said with concern in her voice.

"I'm not fine," he said truthfully. He paused for a moment. Not wanting to alarm Cassandra, he added, "but I will be. Eventually. I think my parents deserve answers. I think we all deserve answers."

"Well I played dirty," Cassandra said with a slight laugh. "I hope you don't mind, but I gave us home field advantage. It shifts the dynamic. We aren't going to them, but they are coming to us. It gives us some power. And they agreed."

"Well I hope we have enough coffee," Dex said dryly.

"We do. We all know you love your coffee, so we made sure we have a lot." There was silence as she sought words to say. There was nothing she could say. She had no pearls of wisdom to help Dex feel better. She only had the truth. She hoped the truth would set him free.

"This really sucks," she finally said.

"Yes," Dex replied. "It really does."

"I don't suppose it helps any to tell you that I'm here for you."

"Oh, I know you all are here for me. And I appreciate that."

"No, Dex," she said with emphasis. "*I'm* here for you. Okay? I need you to know that. I am here for you."

"Thank you," he said, his voice cracking some even telepathically. "You know, my parents would have loved you."

"When all this is over, I'd love to hear about them."

"Sounds good," Dex replied.

"Good night, Dex."

"Good night, Cass." He rolled over to his side, looking out the window in his room. It was a clear night- his favorite kind of night. Yet he knew his friends were right- he needed to rest. He grabbed his phone and pressed shuffle. The simple guitar chords started, already lulling him to sleep as Billie Joel Armstrong began singing. *"Summer has come to past. The innocent can never last. Wake me up when September ends."*

It's unfortunate, Dex thought as the song played. No matter how many times he tried to move past it, he wasn't over losing his parents. Rather, maybe he was close, but with the idea that Jules could have saved them, he felt as though he was back in the past now. Perhaps he should let the sleep take him, he thought. It would be easier than thinking about this. *"As my memory rests, it never forgets what it lost. Wake me up when September ends."*

Dex awoke first the next morning. His understanding, from Cassandra, was that The Four would be there early in the morning. Thinking that was the case and remembering that his mother always said to prepare for guests, he decided to make breakfast. He did not, however, want to put a lot of effort into everything, and therefore simply put a few cans of cinnamon rolls in the oven. It was, as Dex thought, the literal least that he could do and still be cordial.

Afterwards, he brewed what would be his first of many cups of coffee for the morning. He sat at the table with a sigh, holding the warm mug in his hands, taking in the warmth and the aroma. He closed his eyes and took a sip. Dark, bitter- just like the world. Morgan come down first, already for the day just like Dex.

"Good morning," she said, grabbing a mug and a cup of coffee.

"It is morning, yes," he replied. "The adjective is yet to be determined."

"I wish I could tell you how it all turns out," she said sadly.

"Your Gift acting up, too now?" he asked. She nodded an affirmation.

"I can't seek things out, but I can get random flashes."

"Maybe because knowing the future is a tough gig," Dex offered.

"Maybe," she replied, "but maybe not. Maybe the lesson here is to live in the now. Maybe there is a tension The Order has been missing for a while. Like, move into the future informed by the past."

"Even if the past is bad?" Dex asked.

"Especially if the past is bad. I mean, look at Neil and myself. Statistically, we should probably be dead because of no support in our childhood. But we aren't- we're alive. We are informed by our past, but we aren't bound by it." She took a long sip of her coffee, filled with cream and sugar.

"I see Ophelia is rubbing off on you," Dex said with a smirk. Morgan shrugged.

"Maybe. But maybe, for once I'm also happy to be in a good situation and I will fight to keep it. Because I know what losing a family is like. And I don't want to do that again." She smiled. "I've decided to fight for the future. It's not because I'm forced to. It's because it's my choice."

"Some would say that your choice is predetermined," Dex countered.

"Maybe, but maybe that doesn't matter because in this moment, even if the choice was made long ago, it's still my choice that I make in the here and now. And even if someone else made it for me, I would have made the same choice." She finished her coffee and stood up. "Our lives and choices, even if preordained, matter to us. If they didn't, then nothing matters and that's not the world I want to live in." She left the kitchen, presumably to go get Neil, who could sleep through the end of the world, up for the meeting. Choice, destiny- Morgan's words rattled around Dex's head. He had realized that if he was going to continue down this path, he would have to make his peace with control in his life in some way.

It stayed quiet in the house for another thirty minutes or so. There was little say as they were all preparing for the arrival of their guests. There was the usual frantic cleaning and tidying up. Cassandra especially seemed to be working hard, making sure the house was in as near to immaculate condition as she could.

The Four came without warning at the appropriate time. It was not unexpected, but the use of The Skeleton allowed for unannounced travel. Neil and Cassandra greeted them cordially while Dex, on his third cup of coffee already, sat at the table silently with Morgan. She gently touched his shoulder.

"It's going to be okay," she said quietly.

"Have you seen that," Dex asked, "or is this hopeful optimism." She shook her head.

"I have faith in you," she said quickly as they approached the table.

"Please," Dex said, taking command of the situation early to establish a sort of dominance, "have a seat. We have coffee and cinnamon rolls.

Help yourselves." The mood was tense, but The Four began to get some things ready. After everyone was seated, there was quiet. It was the quiet that comes after the bomb, when you survey the damage and see that the world will need to be rebuilt. No one spoke or made eye contact. Finally, Jules sat his mug down and began.

"The story begins in a small country, many years ago. The king of the country decided to unite the country, there needed to be a state-run religion. His youngest son, Prince Vega, began to lead a squad of inquisitors to seek out and destroy all other faith systems. The older Prince, Vincent, was opposed to this idea." He looks like he is in pain telling this story, Dex thought. His eyes, normally so full of hope, seemed clouded by the pain of the past. He continued his story. "The older prince, one night, decided that strong arming people into the hands of a supposed loving God through torture was morally wrong. He left, determined to start over again simply going around the earth, helping when he could." His eyes grew watery. "The kingdom, like all kingdoms built upon bloodshed and violence, was toppled and the royal family killed. The older prince, heartbroken, came to America determined to making things right. He changed his name to Jules and joined The Order." Well, there it was. Jules' biggest secret. There was a collective from the younger generation.

"What's the point of telling us this now?" Dex asked.

"In order to know where we are going, we have to know where we have all been. The only people in The Order who know that story are all in this room. And I would appreciate it if we could keep it this way."

"I suppose," Dex replied coolly, "that after you traveled here at some point you saved Rhianna, healed Adrian, and met Ophelia. Right? So we can skip those parts."

"Dex," Adrian said suddenly, "please. We are trying our best to be open and honest here."

"Try harder," he said. "Get to the part where I was personally betrayed."

"I'm trying to," Jules said calmly, "but we have to get to Niall first. He grew up in the country I left behind. When the monarchy toppled, he fled to America and found me. He's a Conduit as well."

"So what does this have to do with Dex?" Neil said. They shot Dex a look and nodded.

"He attempted to join The Order with a plan. He wanted to create a machine to power himself up enough to save the entire world at once."

"Not a terrible idea," Dex admitted.

"His plan was to send a positive energy wave over the earth killing everyone without Gifts," Rhianna added. "It was morally repugnant and wrong."

"Again, what does this have to do with me?" Dex was beginning to get impatient. Cassandra placed a reassuring hand on Dex's hand.

"He needed three other Conduits for his machine to work the way he wanted it to work. That's why he approached me. Conduits have the natural tendency to find one another. He reasoned that I knew where others were and wanted my help finding them." He looked at Dex with sadness in his eyes. "So naturally, he wanted to know where your parents were." Dex looked away, closing his eyes and biting his lip. His parents were Conduits as well. Of course, they were. Nothing else in his life made sense, so why should his parents' lives be any different?

"So they were Conduits. That's how you knew them."

"I knew them because I fought them when they were Corrupted," Jules said plainly. Dex laughed.

"You're full of shit," he said dismissively.

"Dex," Ophelia said, "you're smarter than this. You're holding all the cards here. There's no reason to keep anything from you now." She looked in her bag, producing the same copy of The Books of Doom as she had read the first time she came to his house. Dex chewed his bottom lip for a moment.

"So what? You saved them and had them join your army?" Dex was getting madder and madder. His skin was feeling hotter by the second and he had to work to keep his power level down. Jules shook his head.

"No. They came to me in peace. They wanted to get out of that life when your mother became pregnant with you. I merely showed them how to refocus on Positive Energy and not Negative Energy. They didn't want to fight anymore and left all of that behind them. They were out of The Order before Niall got there, but he had head of them when he joined."

"Dude," Neil said in Dex's head, "I knew your parents were awesome, but this means they were heroes."

"It just means they grew up, which people do," Dex replied emotionlessly.

"Niall wanted them for his machine, thinking that people who have experience with both sides of energy would make him even stronger. I should have stopped him right then and there, but I..." Jules trailed off for a moment and shook his head. "I thought I could teach him. I thought I could save him. It turns out that you can't save everyone."

"So he goes into hiding," Dex added, "and only makes an appearance after my parents' death. So he must have found some new Conduits, right? Or what- he wants me?" Morgan gasped suddenly, her eyes being pools of tears.

"No," she whispered, looking at Ophelia. Ophelia nodded solemnly.

"What is it?" Dex asked, no longer caring about his power level. "What did you see?"

"She saw me telling you that Niall found your parents. They refused him outright, which made him mad. He killed them." The table began to vibrate as Dex's power kept climbing. He shut his eyes, trying to control it, to keep it in check with his temper. No, he thought to himself- not this time. He let his power go to fifty percent. The wings exploded out of his back. His eyes snapped open, tears streaming down his face with a scowl on his face. The table was cleared in an instant with the release of energy. Everyone but Jules was pushed backwards.

"Where is he?" Dex asked Jules.

"We don't know," he replied, unphased by the transformation. "We believe that within a week, he will unveil his master plan concerning the machine. We believe that he intends to destroy the world."

"How?" Dex asked, his voice a powerful growl.

"We don't know. We only know he has learned to walk a fine line using both Positive and Negative Energy. He believes in nothing but his goal of destruction."

"Dex," it was Cassandra, her short black hair flying around her face. Neil and Morgan stood up with her. They all surrounded Dex, enveloping him in their arms. Neil was crying.

"We got you, buddy," they said to him. They held him in spite of the energy flowing off of him. They held him in spite of the rage he was feeling. They held him because they loved him. Dex closed his eyes, still crying. Slowly, his power level decreased until he was back to normal.

"You better?" Neil asked him.

"I will find Niall and I will deal with him." His voice was as cold as the grave.

"We'll help," Cassandra said. She looked over at The Four, who regained their seated positions. "Tell us what we have to do," she told them.

"We know the plan and we know the timeline. However, we believe that the machine is creating fluxes in Prophecy," Adrian said. "It could be activated in a week. It could be activated sooner. We don't know. We know that when it is activated, we will know and we will have very little time to react." He reached into his black coat and produced a Skeleton Key. He placed it on the table and slid it towards Dex's team.

"We trust you," Rhianna said. "I'm sorry that we didn't show it to you before. We have complete faith in you. No more secrets. No more half-truths. We need you."

"Dex," Jules said softly. "There is not a day that goes by that I don't mourn the loss of your parents. I failed you. It will always be my greatest failure."

"Jules," he said softly. What did he want to say? Did he want to blame him? Certainly, he could and he would be right to do so, yet he knew it would accomplish nothing. He looked at Jules. He wasn't sitting there like the proud, stoic warrior he had come to know and respect. No- he was a sad broken man filled with regret. "Jules you did the best you could. We know only in part and we prophesy only in part. But now? Now we know. And we can make things right."

"Thank you, Dex Machina," he replied, a single tear running down his cheek.

"We will be in touch," Rhianna said. "If we find out anything, we'll pass it along to you. No more secrets." The Four left shortly after. There was a sigh of relief in the house after they left.

"Well thank God that's over," Neil said. "Now, let's get down to business."

"No," Cassandra said. "First we have to make sure Dex is okay." She turned to him. "How are you?"

"That's a good question," he answered truthfully. "I suppose since I am feeling like I want to kill someone, not too great. However, I do believe that we will stop him."

"We'll stop him. Together," Neil told him. "I promise." Suddenly, there was the sound of drums, followed shortly by guitar. The three of them looked over to Morgan, holding her phone.

"I'm sorry," she said blushing. "I just thought it was appropriate." Dex recognized the song immediately. He couldn't help but smile as he recognized the song. He realized in that moment that he was going to be okay. Everything was going to be okay.

"Another day and you've had your fill of sinking with the life held in your hands are shaking cold. These hands are meant to hold. Speak to me. When all you've got to keep is strong move along, move along like I know you do. And even when your hope is gone, move along, move along just to make it through. Move along."

"You know," Dex said wiping a tear from his eye, "I really do love you guys."

"Is this where we do another group hug?" Neil asked. "I just want to make sure I get it right."

"Morgan," Cassandra said, "control your partner, please." Everyone laughed.

The rest of the day was a simple, run of the mill day. They watched tv and cleaned and had a fine day. Later, in the safety of his room, Dex was able to look back on the events of the morning. In truth, he was furious- not at Jules, but at Niall. The most painful moment in his life, the loss of his parent, was because of him. He wanted to power. Dex decided that he would show him power. As he lay down for bed, he pressed shuffle on his music. Drums of war filled his ears.

"First things first I'ma say all the words inside my head. I'm fired up and tired of the way that things have been." He was done. This was a chapter in his life that closed, he decided. He was done being bound by the pain of the past. Instead, he decided, dwelling on his pain. Instead, he would use it to fuel him, no matter how dark things got.

"Seeing the lesson through the... pain. You made a, you made me a believer. Believer."

Chapter Fifteen

The day began with all of the opportunities and possibilities that Dex needed. Perhaps, he thought, this was going to be a brand-new day for real. Everything started out in a normal manner. Neil and Morgan had both been called into The Cathedral of Heroes since they had recently lost a number of staff. Neil, as someone with a lot of seniority, was called on to be the acting manager for the time being. The Four were going along and working on finding a completely new Council to help out with this particular jurisdiction. Unfortunately, the Four also needed to deal with the issue of Niall. All in all, this left Dex and Cassandra home by themselves.

"So what do you have going on today?" she asked him. Dex shrugged.

"Nothing, and I hate it." Cassandra laughed.

"What's so bad about relaxing? I mean, you've had a rough time as of late."

"We've had a rough time," he corrected her. "This isn't just about me- it's about us." Cassandra twisted her face in thought for a moment.

"I get that, but it seems a little like deflection to me." Dex sighed. Why was it that, when a person going through an upheaval and they said they were fine but they were obviously lying that people didn't believe them?

"I get what you're saying, but I think that we also need to be willing to do this stuff together. This affects all of us- not just me. We aren't going to get through this unless it's together."

"Then let's get together," she said suddenly. Her eyes widened as she realized what she was implying. "I mean," she added quickly, "let's go get lunch or something. You know, something normal to decompress." Dex went to speak but stopped for a moment. He already sort of had plans for the day. Nothing was set in stone, but he felt as if he had somethings that needed to be done.

"I have an idea of what I would like to do," he said, looking down a bit. He flicked his gaze upwards, looking at her. Her face was kind and filled with concern. He wanted her companionship more than either of them realized. Dex blushed and looked down. "It would be... nice if you would join me." He looked at her and realized she was smiling. "I'm trying," he said softly, "I really am. There are just some things I need to do. And it would be nice to have some help." She nodded with a small smile.

"Can we get lunch afterwards?" she asked.

"Absolutely. Just don't expect Giorno's again. I can only work my magic so many times," he said with a laugh. Cassandra smiled.

"Sounds good," she said. "It's a date." With that, she left to get ready. Dex decided that he too should get ready, though he was pained with a sense of guilt. Here he was, determined to make things right and now he had a date? I mean, it's not like he didn't want to have a date, he just felt guilty about the whole thing. Why should he be having even a brief moment of serotonin inducing fun when he had work to do? He shook the thoughts from his head, grabbing his Doctor Doom t-shirt, and heading to his truck.

"Hey," he said, coming down the steps and attaching Ruach to his hip. "So, do you know, like, how to drive and stuff? Like, do you have a license?" Cassandra gave him a strange look.

"Dude. I know how to drive. I'm just waiting on my new license to come in the mail."

"Well I was just asking because Neil let Morgan drive his car."

"She hasn't driven in years," she replied with a laugh. Dex blushed and looked away.

"I mean, my truck isn't a car. It... it drives differently. Because it's a truck." He looked at her, his face reddening and wearing an agitated face. "I just didn't know if you needed to know how to drive it. My... my dad's old truck handles differently than a car is all. And in an emergency, you may need to drive it in a pinch. That's all." He folded his arms in front of himself, protecting himself from the situation.

Oh, Cassandra thought to herself. This wasn't about driving. It's about sharing something important with me. She looked down feeling slightly embarrassed. She understood what he was really trying to do.

"I mean I haven't driven a truck in years. But I'm still probably a better driver than you," she said raising an eyebrow and her lips in a smirk.

"Yeah, okay," Dex said with a laugh. "Keep telling yourself that. Even Neil hesitates driving that thing." Cassandra shrugged. She paused for a moment.

"Wait: didn't we just get a Skeleton Key? Do we even need to drive?"

"I want to use the shop to get to where we need to go. Plus I want to make sure Neil and Morgan are okay in the shop. I mean, I may be suffering a case of melancholy, but I still care about them."

"Good point," Cassandra replied. "I've seen both of their rooms. They may need some help maintaining order." Dex tossed Cassandra his keys and they headed to the truck. Climbing into the passenger side was strange and disorienting for Dex. Neil almost never drove his truck, so the only time he ever really remembered riding in the truck was with his dad. Cassandra took a ponytail holder off her wrist. Placing it in her mouth, she gathered up her hair from the sides into a sort of top knot on the top of her head. Buckling up, she said, "I hate my hair being in my eyes when I drive."

"I mean, vision is usually a good thing," he replied, also fastening his seatbelt. She adjusted the seat and started the vehicle. Then she sat and waited. Looking over to Dex, she said,

"Well? Go on. Do your whole shuffle thing." Dex looked at Cassandra, who sat there with anticipation all over her face.

"No," he said quietly. Cassandra looked puzzled.

"No?" she asked. "Why not."

"Because I don't want to. I'm kind of sick of focusing on the future."

"Maybe it's not about the future," she mused. "Maybe it's just a message you need to hear. Did you ever think of that?" He went to speak but couldn't.

"That's a fair point," he replied honestly, "so let's do it this way: you use yours."

"What?" she asked with a laugh. "Are you serious?" Dex shook his head in affirmation.

"I'm very serious. Because it's not just about me. It's about the team." He looked at her with a half-smile. "It's about us." Cassandra felt her face redden. "Besides," he said with a dismissive wave, giving Cassandra a reprieve, "you know my music by now. And since we won't be fighting," he added, using her own logic against her, "this is a great way to see what you're like." He raised an eyebrow and smiled a daring smile. "Unless, of course, you're too scared to do it." Cassandra narrowed her gaze.

"Is that a challenge?" she asked in a disbelieving voice. Dex shrugged.

"I mean, unless you're not up for it," he said, holding the aux cord.

"Give me that," she said laughing, snatching the cord from his hand and muttering, "challenge me, will you..." She plugged her phone in and pressed shuffle. "*I'm sorry but I'm just thinking of the right words to say. I know they don't sound the way I plan them to be. But if you wait around a while, I'll make you fall for me. I promise. I promise you I will...*" Instantly, both of their faces turned red and they looked away from one another.

"The level of hypocrisy is astounding," Dex said quickly.

"What are you talking about?" she asked, confused.

"You gave me crap for preferring a cover of Cyndi Lauper's song over the original and here you are doing the same thing with When in Rome."

"The New Found Glory version is amazing!" she pleaded defensively. "It's... it's not..." she paused for a moment. "No, you're right this is the exact same thing and I'm sorry."

"Good," Dex said, a triumphant smile on his face. "Thank you." She began to drive off as the song continued. *"And when you're in doubt, and when you're in danger, take a look all around, and I'll be there."*

They arrived at The Cathedral of Heroes to find the place surprisingly intact. Perhaps since it was Tuesday, the day before new comics arrived, they were not rather busy.

"Okay. So this is The Red Hood. He's Jason Todd. He died in the Death in the Family arc. But he's back now because... because comics."

"So he's famous for being the Robin that died?" Morgan asked Neil.

"Essentially yes," Neil explained. "It was a powerful death that affected

Batman for many years. And then when he came back, it affected him in a different way." They turned their hard towards the door. "Well look who's up and at them."

"Got some reading to do," Dex told Neil.

"Well I hope it's more productive than the crash course that I'm getting," Morgan said dryly, raising her eyebrows for a moment.

"Babe, you can't work in a comic store and not know the basics," they told her.

"Dex, please help. This is sort of... I don't want to say boring, but that's the only word I can think of."

"Just wait till they get to their love and adoration for Kyle Raynor," Dex said in a warning tone.

"Oh we will get there!" Neil said loudly. "Trust me. Greatest damn Green Lantern in my humble opinion." They paused for a moment. "Wait. What are you reading today?"

"Good question," Cassandra said. "So far, all I know I'm here to help."

"We're going to go ask Jules for personal records," Dex finally explained. The other three looked at him.

"What?" Neil said. "What makes you think he has personal records?"

"Because my father does," Cassandra noted. "He's always scribbling in his little journal thing."

"Exactly," Dex said. "It's safe to assume that if one of them does it, the others might as well. It doesn't hurt to ask. And worst-case scenario, they will verbally tell us what I want to know."

"You think he'll be honest with everything? Even if it looks bad?" Morgan asked. The thought occurred to Dex that this may be the case. This is why he was secretly hoping for a written record of events in lieu of a verbal one.

"Jules told me he was going to be honest with me from now on. As of right now, I have no reason not to trust him. At least until he gives me a reason not to trust him."

"I mean, that's fairly logical, right?" Morgan looked at Cassandra for reassurance. She merely shrugged in response.

"I mean, maybe? This whole situation is like nothing I've ever seen before."

"If we're going with logic," Neil interjected, "then we should just, like, logically make the changes we want. Like, put ourselves in positions of power to make The Order better in the future. Right?" The thought for a moment. On the one hand, that certainly made sense. It fell in line with what his mother had always told him. Yet on the other hand, he couldn't help but still have sour thoughts and feelings about The Order as a whole. He knew that, no matter how he looked at it, leaving The Order was still an option. That, or something else altogether. He felt as if the organization as a whole had betrayed him. Based on that, he would have to make some decisions. Dex and Cassandra walked towards the back, confident that Neil and Morgan had everything under control. They, however couldn't help but feel a twinge of pity for Morgan and her history lessons.

"You ready for this?" Cassandra asked him, producing the team's skeleton key.

"Absolutely not, so let's do this." She gently opened the door, revealing to them the old, familiar staircase. The faint sent of moist, stone walls filled their noses. They walked up the steps, the sound of their steps reverberating off the walls. Before they got to Jules' office, they passed Rhianna's door. She was leaving with Ophelia and the pair were laughing. They stopped and looked at Cassandra and Dex.

"Oh," Rhianna exclaimed. "Wow! It's so great to see you both here." She embraced them both with a warm, motherly hug. "Are you guys okay? Do you need something?"

"We need to talk to Jules," Dex said plainly. "I still have some questions that I need to have answered." Rhianna had a look of worry on her face. Dex could feel her concern and care for him.

"He's talking to Adrian, but you two can go on in," Ophelia said quietly. "He's probably expecting you anyway." Dex sighed.

"Yeah, of course he probably is," he admitted. What was he hoping for, Cassandra wondered? It's Jules. Of course he was expecting Dex to come talk to him. No, she thought. That wasn't it. He was hoping Dex would come talk to him. It wasn't that Jules was expecting Dex. Cassandra reasoned that he was just hoping Dex would come talk to him.

"Dex," Rhianna said and then stopped. There were many things she wanted to say. She wanted to tell Dex how unfair it all was. She wanted him to know that she trusted him. She wanted him to know he was stronger than he realized. Dex sensed much of this from her.

"Thank you," he said quietly.

"We're supposed to go," Ophelia said quietly. "I've grown fond of our coffee time." She looked at Dex. "The past is over. The future isn't unless you want it to be." She looked at Cassandra. "Don't hurt this one. I like him." She went and walked away, saying, "I don't mean romantically. He's just a nice person who I have grown fond of. Don't get a big head, Dex Machina." After they left, Cassandra asked,

"Is she always like that?"

"Pretty much- yeah." Dex said with a smile. He would really miss Ophelia if he left The Order. He would miss Rhianna as well, he realized. He would miss everyone. They walked past the gym, still haunted with memories. Mary died there, but by now there was no trace of that. By now, it had been cleaned and scrubbed. There was no trace that Mary died there, much like now there was no trace of the former Council even at the comic shop. The thought unnerved Dex. They were soldiers in a war- nothing more. They existed to fight in a war that was, by all accounts, predetermined. Perhaps, Dex thought, that was what really bothered him. On the whole, he was fine with a lack of control in his life. After all, he could improvise out of most situations. No- what bothered him was the fact that if this was predetermined, then why did there have to be so much pain and suffering? How was it possible the tragedy of his parents' murder played a part in the not just the grand scheme of things, but it was for the greater good.

Murder. It was the first time since the revelation that he had used the term in regard to his parents. The thought stung Dex more than he realized. See, when it was an accident, that could just be described as something that happened by chance. It was a fluke. Even if it was a part of some grand plan, then it was far removed for human hands or interference. It would have been terrible and acceptable as something from God's play book. This isn't to say that Dex would have been okay with it. After all, this was the assumption he had been operating under since the event happened. Now, however, there was another person involved- Niall. This means that there was an agent involved. This means there were human hands directly responsible for the premeditated death of his parents. Dex found this fact to be inexcusable.

"Hey," Cassandra said, a concerned look on her face. "You still good?" Dex nodded which Cassandra rightly interpreted as a half-truth.

"I'll be fine after I get my revenge." Cassandra stopped walking, several feet from Jules' door.

"Whoa there," she said placing a hand on Dex's arm. "Revenge?"

"Yeah," Dex replied nonchalantly. "Revenge." Cassandra grew more concerned.

"Dex, you need to be careful here. I'm all for justice here and we will stop him, but revenge? Isn't that too far?"

"Cassandra, if you could take revenge on the thing that killed your mom, you would, right?" Her eyes widened in shock. "I'm human. I'm prone to human emotions. I would kindly ask that you let me experience them."

"I'm not talking about letting this slide. I'm talking about the motive here. Like I said, we'll get him. But how we get him is important. We have to do this right."

"Beware that, when fighting monsters, you yourself do not become a monster," Dex said grimly.

"And when you gaze long into the abyss, the abyss gazes into you," she finished. Dex took her hand and held it for a moment. It's warm, he thought. She's actually here taking care of me. No matter how mad or depressed I get, she's here. Dex hadn't felt this closeness to someone since Neil. Perhaps the shell around his heart was beginning to break after suddenly being rebuilt. He rubbed her hand with his thumb.

"Thank you," he said softly. She took his hand, interlocking her fingers with his.

"Together?" she asked.

"Together," he replied. Dex took a deep breath and went to knock on the door.

"Come in," he heard Adrian say, his hand mere inches from the door.

"Figures," Dex muttered to himself, opening the door. Jules was seated at his desk, looking strangely tired, which Dex had never seen before. When they walked in the room, his eyes seemed to lift with his sprits.

"Dex," he said smiling. "I... um..."

"Relax Jules," he said, looking away. "It's fine. Seriously."

"What brings you two in today?" Adrian asked curiously. Dex paused. He had to do it.

"Adrian, I was an ass the other day. I crossed a line and I shouldn't have." He looked Adrian in the eye. "You don't have to accept my apology, but I am sorry. I shouldn't hold a person's past against him. And I really am sorry. I will be better in the future." Adrian was shocked, but not as shocked as Cassandra.

"And this..." Adrian said slowly, "is why you came here today?"

"We did not talk about this. Like, at all. So this was news to me," Cassandra said.

"It's not why we came here," Dex admitted, "but I'm glad we ran into you. Because I was wrong. And I needed to try to make it right." Adrian nodded.

"Thank you, Dex Machina," he said softly, extending a hand. Dex took it and shook it.

"So why did you two come down today?" Jules asked.

"I was hoping you were as meticulous as Adrian," Dex said. "I've noticed him constantly scribbling in little journals. I assume he's documenting important things he sees or experiences. I was hoping you did the same, and I could get more information about my parents'..." Dex swallowed hard. "My parents' murder. It might help us find Niall and stop him." Jules nodded in acknowledgement.

"I was thinking the same thing, actually." He smiled at Dex. "Great minds think alike, I suppose." He opened a drawer and produced a stack of leatherbound journals. "These are, what I assume to be, the most relevant. I have marked out the beginnings. It covers a breath of history about Niall and your parents." He paused, looking pained. "I was trying to see..." his eyes teared up. "I was trying to see where I made a mistake. I... I never saw their deaths. I didn't know. But I was thinking maybe I did miss something. But I didn't." He looked at Dex. "I guess that makes it worse. I failed. I should have known better." Dex sighed. He felt Jules' pain, the burden of his feeling responsible for their murder. But he wasn't responsible. No, ultimately, that was Niall's fault.

"A wise man once told me that we only see and can control what we are meant to see and know." He shrugged at Jules. "It is what it is, I guess."

"I do like this one," Adrian told Cassandra. "Possibly the best one you've brought home yet. He holds Jules accountable with his own words." Cassandra blushed instantly.

"I... I didn't bring him home... we aren't..." but she trailed off.

"Thank you," Jules said suddenly, saving Cassandra. "I appreciate your words." He looked at Adrian and then Cassandra and Dex. "Adrian, shall we leave these two here so that they can study and see what they can find?"

"Yes. We can work elsewhere." Jules and got up and began to leave. Adrian walked past Dex and whispered,

"If you hurt my daughter in any way, shape, or form, I will shut down your motor functions trapping you in your body. Is that understood?" Dex gulped.

"Yessir," he squeaked out. With that, Adrian followed Jules out of the room.

"What did he say?" Cassandra asked after they left. "What did he tell you?"

"Oh, you know," Dex said in a stressed-out voice. "Just the usual paternal threat." Cassandra facepalmed herself.

"You have got to be kidding me," she said shaking her head. "That is classic Adrian."

"Oh come on," Dex countered. "I mean, it's the typical dad thing. He's just looking out for you."

"It's embarrassing," she said. "I mean we aren't... like..." she trailed off.

"Right," Dex added quickly. "Getting to know each other. Slow and steady."

"Right," she added. There was an awkward pause. They looked at each other, alone in a dimly lit room. They looked away, reaching for Jules' journals, touching hands. They laughed nervously.

"Ladies first," Dex said.

"Don't do that," Cassandra said. "Please. I am totally fine with letting you go first with a pick."

"No, no, no," Dex said defensively. "It's not, like, macho stuff. My mom would be mad if I didn't let you go first. That's all." This was, in fact, not all, but Dex didn't want to tell her that his dad always told him to let the pretty girl go first. There was too much tension in the room as it was. Each of them selected a journal and began to read.

The day was filled with emotional highs and lows. They had learned nothing terribly new from pouring into the journals. Everything that Jules had said had been confirmed. Dex had not properly anticipated the love and respect Jules had for his parents.

"I don't get it," Dex said during the reading. "I mean, they were bitter enemies. My mother was an expert Channeler. My father was a tremendous Psyker. So why did he go out of his way to help them?" Cassandra shrugged.

"It seems to be his M.O. I mean, my dad was the same way. But he went out of his way to help him too."

"And he wasn't pregnant like my mom was," Dex added. "So why? He literally stood to gain nothing from this. So why? And it wasn't like he mentioned that he saw something or a Prophet told him."

"Maybe it was simply to help," Cassandra offered. "I mean, he kind of seems like the kind of guy who would want to help a person just to help them." Dex sighed.

"He really didn't know," he said sadly.

"What do you mean?" she asked.

"Jules knew my parents. He set them up so they would be safe. He had no idea until after their murder that they were in danger or who did it." He shrugged. "It really wasn't his fault."

"I suppose that is good news?" she asked.

"I mean, I guess?"

"Hey look here," She scooted over closer to Dex and showed her the page she was on. "According to this, Niall was experimenting with his machine. They found and dismantled one after your parent's death. Says here he was attempting to use his Conduit blood charged as a self-replicating power source for the machine. Niall's results were promising, but they didn't yield the power that he needed."

"When my parents told him no, he must have switched tactics. That machine..." Dex thought back to the night he fought Jude. "It made Jude so powerful and that was with one Conduit. I can't imagine what it would do to a Conduit powered by three more." He shook his head in an attempt to force the thought out.

"As far as we know, he doesn't have enough Conduits. So, we need to keep an eye on you and Jules. It's either that, or he has figured out a way to use his blood to get his machine to work. That would be able to run it and give him time to get Conduits for use." She looked at her watch. "Hey. Let's go get lunch." Dex agreed.

"Yeah. I think we have what we came here for. I'm..." he searched for the words. "I guess I'm oddly okay with the outcome. If that makes sense."

"It does," she assured him. "So," Cassandra looked down. "Do you want to ask Neil and Morgan if they want to come or...?" she tucked a piece of hair behind her ear.

"I mean, they're working. And they should have packed a lunch. Like, that's on them if they didn't." Dex responded confused.

"Oh," she replied, her hopes made higher.

"Plus, I mean, I was kind of just hoping for the two of us?" He scratched the back of his head even though he wasn't itchy. "I mean, if that's okay?"

"Oh no- it's totally okay," Cassandra replied. Damn, she thought. That was too fast of a reply. What the hell was going on? To be honest, it was the same thought that both fop them had. It didn't seem to make sense. They had begun to know each other, but this seemed different in a way. Perhaps they were just making things too complicated. This was simply another way to get to know each other. That's all. They had agreed to that much. The problem was that the more time they spent together, the more they knew of each other. Eventually, that excuse would run out and they would have to make some decisions.

"Right. Ralph's Kitchen?" Dex asked.

"I was hoping for Giorno's again," Cassandra said with a smile.

"Dude, you have expensive tastes," he complained.

"And you better get used to it," she said.

"Interesting," Dex smirked. "That implies the possibility of future dates." Dex's eyes went wide. Why did he just use that word?

"So is this, um..." she looked at him. "Is this a... an actual date then?" Well... crap, Dex thought to himself. He had painted himself into another corner. He looked at her. Slightly dilatated pupils. Increased breathing and reddening of the cheeks. But even above that, there was something else. It was hope. For some reason, Dex felt that she was feeling hopeful. Just freaking say it, he thought to himself.

"I would very much like this to be a date," he said shyly. Cassandra smiled.

"That would be... nice." She replied. They both walked smiling back into the comic shop. There were only a few customers in the shop, simply browsing various items.

"So when The Green Goblin threw Gwen Stacy off the bridge and Spiderman went to save her, he never knew if he actually killed her which still haunts Peter Parker to this day." Neil was explaining.

"And this is one of his driving forces, right?" Morgan asked.

"Yes, exactly. The same thing happened with Kyle Raynor and when his girlfriend got fridged by Major Force."

"But fridging is a sexist trope and lazy writing," she added.

"Exactly," Neil replied. They looked up. "Hey. What did you learn?"

"It's possible that Dex is a target for the machine or he's found others to power it, but he's probably got it running on low power using his charged blood.," Cassandra explained.

"Fun times," Neil said rolling their eyes. "So, what's the plan?"

"As it stands," Cassandra explained, "we only have a few days to figure out Niall's plan. His M.O. in the past was to cleanse the world. However, he apparently had also been experimenting with positive and negative energy. So those competing forces could have him unbalanced."

"Well this just keeps getting better and better," Neil said with a fake smile.

"We keep an eye on Dex. Like one of us with him at all times. We keep an ear to the ground because eventually he'll make a move. And when we does, we stop him."

"It's not a vision or anything, but I have this feeling he is going to do something soon," Morgan said grimly.

"Cool, cool, cool," Dex replied. "So, I'll always have a buddy with me. Sounds fun, I guess."

"It'll be fine," Cassandra said. She turned to Morgan and Neil. "We're going to go get some lunch. And we'll see you back at home later for dinner. Don't forget: It's Taco Tuesday."

"So long as you make some fresh Pico, we'll be fine," Neil said.

"This is why I call them Guac," Morgan added, smiling at Neil. "Because they're so extra." The group laughed and Dex and Cassandra headed towards the truck. Digging out the keys, Dex unlocked Cassandra's door, opening it for her. He handed her the keys and walked around back. Dex noticed Cassandra lean over and unlock his door. Dex smiled to himself, content with her kindness. When he climbed in the truck, he politely asked for no music to be played.

"Is my music really that terrible?" She asked with a laugh.

"No," he responded with a smile. "I just don't want to know what happens next is all. I want to actually be in the moment for once and enjoy life as it happens."

"Sounds good to me," she replied as she pulled away from the comic shop.

Lunch was enjoyable to them for the simple reason that they did not talk about the current state of The Order or the upcoming eschaton that they all knew in the back of their minds was coming. After all, if the end of all things was coming, it certainly was nice to have a few last moments of normalcy. They both, however, felt a sense of unease with everything. After all, they did not know what the future was going to hold for them. No one did for once. All they knew was that some kind of cosmic deadline was inching closer and closer to them, determined to find them. These moments of getting to know one another helped. Perhaps that was what it was all about after all. More so than any earth-shaking revelations, they were, essentially, living like they were dying. While a terrifying prospect, it did lend itself a sort of freedom with the urgency of it all.

"If we're still here in a week," Dex said smiling, "I'd like to take you back to Giorno's." It was the dark specter that was hanging over them. Dex was simply the one to give it a proper name.

"I'd like that," she said smiling sadly.

"I'm going to get the chicken parmigiana this time," Dex said. "It looked amazing."

"It really was. Maybe I'll try the lasagna."

"Well then," he said taking a drink of his soda, "looks like we better make sure to stop the end of the world then." They moved closer to each other in the booth, each one afraid for the future, desperate for a real connection. She placed her head on his shoulder.

"This is... nice," she said quietly. "No other cares. Just two people." He reached up and put his arm around her, holding her close.

"Yeah. It is." Time slowed; the only passage of time marked by their breathing. "If I lay here," he sang softly. "If I just lay here. Would you lie with me and just forget the world?"

"Yeah," she said quietly. "I think I could do that."

"What happens next?" he asked her.

"I don't know," she answered in a worried voice. "I don't really want to know, to be honest." She looked at him. "But we can't stay here. We have to go home- we have to keep moving forward." I know. They paid their bill and got in the truck.

"Hey," Cassandra said on the way to the door, "can you drive?"

"Yeah," Dex responded. "You okay?"

"Yeah," she said, tucking her short black hair behind her ear. "I was just… I was comfortable at the table. That's all." Dex could fell his face redden.

"Okay. That's fine. That means you're in charge of music then."

"I can handle that," she said with a smile. They got in the truck but instead of pressing shuffle, she decided to take command.

"What are you doing?" Dex asked confused.

"Even if the future is set, we don't know what it is. So, I'm going to make my own future." She looked at Dex. It began to rain. "I'm going to make sure there's the best possible future." Dex started the truck as the song began, driving off into the rain to the guitar.

"This is a good choice," Dex said with a laugh.

"I thought it was appropriate for the day," she replied smiling.

"Breathe in for luck. Breathe in so deep. This air is blessed you share with me."

"Dashboard Confessional is a classic band," Dex said.

"Absolutely," Cassandra agreed.

"My hopes are so high that your kiss might kill me. So won't you kill me so I die happy?" She laid her head on his shoulder once again, sighing contently. Dex felt whole, as if the world was finally complete. The song reached its crescendo as they approached home.

"Hands down this is the best date I can ever remember." She turned the song off as they pulled up.

"What are you doing?" Dex asked.

"I don't want the song to be over. Not yet. Just trust me." She looked at him, her eyes gazing into her soul. "Do you trust me?" If Dex was being honest with himself, he had trusted her ever since he met her in a dream what seemed like an eternity ago.

"Yeah," he said. "I do." He turned the truck off. She continued the song as they got out of the car in the pouring rain.

"I'm going to make sure my destiny is one that I want," she said, laughing and pulling his hand to the front porch, playing the song once more.

"And the streets were wet. And the gate was locked. So I jumped it and I let you in."

They reached the door, both soaking wet with the rain, baptized by the realization that they could help shape their own futures. She placed his hands on her waist, placing her own hands around his face.

"And you stood at the door with your hands on my waist. And you kissed me like you meant it." The rain seemed to hang in the air. Or maybe they just didn't care that it was raining. All that mattered was this moment-this one shining moment where nothing else mattered. Cassandra pulled him close to her, their lips touching slowly and softly at first. It was the first time in a long time Dex had felt another person's lips on his own. This moment was perfect.

"And I knew that you meant it. That you meant it."

Chapter Sixteen

"Honey!" Neil said loudly, walking in the door with Morgan, "We're home!" There was silence. They looked at Morgan. "That's suspicious." Suddenly, they heard a sound of shushing.

"That's very suspicious," Morgan said. She pulled out a ponytail holder and began to tie her hair up.

"Okay," Neil said smiling. "Get it, girl." They channeled energy to their hands, ready for a confrontation. Slowly, they crept into the kitchen and found nothing. Neil pointed to the living room and they made their way there. Suddenly, there was a loud sound.

"Kiss, kiss. Fall in love!" The television was on, playing Oran High Host Club. Neil sighed and powered down.

"Damnit, Dex," Neil sighed. "Stop leaving the tv running when no one is watching."

"Dude!" Dex shouted. "You're interrupting the theme song!" Neil and Morgan looked over the couch, absolutely dumbfounded by what they saw.

"Oh my," Morgan whispered. They saw Dex and Cassandra lying on the couch. They were... they were cuddling?

"I'm sorry," Neil said with a laugh, "but what is going on here?" They both looked at Neil confused. They turned to look at the tv, and then back to Neil.

"She's never seen Oran High Host Club," Dex answered confused.

"Yeah," Cassandra added, equally confused. "Dex was telling me how awesome this show is, so we started watching it." She looked to Dex. "You were right. It's an interesting play on the harem anime type."

"Oh, if you like subversion then wait until we watch Puella Magi Madoka Magica. Absolutely stunning!" She smiled at Dex who smiled back. Neil looked around, confused.

"Am I on crazy pills?" they asked, turning to Morgan. "Babe, did I miss something here?" Morgan said nothing, but slowly raised her phone and took an obvious picture with the flash. Cassandra laughed.

"Morgan! Really?"

"No, this is adorable and this moment needs captured," she defended. Cassandra looked at her watch.

"Yeah. I gotta go finish getting dinner ready anyway." She looked at Neil and Morgan, then planted a quick kiss on Dex's lips. She said nothing and got up to go finish preparing dinner. Morgan trailed behind her, almost giddy for the gossip. Dex smiled and sat up, turning the tv off. Neil sat down next to Dex. They closed their eyes, making some calming motions with their hands. His eyes snapped open and he punched Dex in the arm.

"Ow!" he said, rubbing his arm. "What the Hell, bro?!"

"Oh and you didn't think to tell me any of this?!" Neil yell whispered at Dex. "Your best friend for all these years and you didn't think to say anything?!"

"Dude," Dex said defensively. "It just kind of... happened today."

"What do you mean it happened today?" Morgan asked Cassandra in the kitchen in her own yell whisper. Cassandra sighed, dicing some tomatoes.

"Okay, so after you both left, I said we should get lunch but he wanted to go to HQ and you know that part because we ran into you both there."

"Right," Morgan said. "I'm just confused about how we got from there to you both cuddling on the couch watching a romance anime! I mean, I don't know much about anime but I know that one for obvious reason," she said, dismissively waving her hand. "So, spill it!"

"Dude, we went to go get lunch at Ralph's Kitchen," Dex said with a sigh to Neil.

"I am familiar with this part, yes," Neil said, "but the question remains..."

"Because I officially made it a date, Neil." Dex was quiet for a moment.

"Like, I actually called it a date. Like an honest date. Like, between two people." Neil put their hand over their mouth.

"I am so proud of you," they told Dex.

"Well it was about damn time," Morgan told Cassandra, stirring seasoning into the meat.

"What is that supposed to mean?" Cassandra asked.

"Girl, please," Morgan responded. "You stayed with him, like, all the time when he was in a coma. I was damn near smothered by how thick the tension was."

"That... is... a gross overstatement," Cassandra said, embarrassedly.

"Sure, Jan," Morgan retorted. "Okay. So official date for lunch. Then what?"

"We... we kind of talked about the end of the world..." Dex told Neil in an embarrassed voice.

"You are so good at flirting," Neil said laughing. "Teach me thy ways, oh master of smooth talk."

"Dude- come on. I mean... look all of the prophecies have been stopping in like five days from now. That's not a terribly comforting sign. So, I mean, I don't know. I just wanted something normal and nice." Dex smiled to himself. "And she's nice."

"So, because the world may end, you decided to date her?" Neil was beyond confused.

"No," Dex explained. "I... I'm tired of being controlled. I'm tired of things being out of control. I totally get that there are things that are, like, preordained or whatever. But I'm going to work inside of that. It's no reason to not live my life." Dex smiled. "She kind of helped me realize that."

"This is, like, the weirdest date I have ever heard," Morgan told Cassandra, pulling the tortillas from the oven.

"It was actually the most authentic date I've ever had," she replied smiling, getting Neil's Pico out of the fridge.

"Then what?" Morgan asked. "You don't go from that to cuddling without..."

"I played his own game against him," she interrupted, smiling. "You know that whole weird music dropping future hints to him?"

"Yes," Morgan said dryly. "I am vaguely aware of this fact."

"Well you showed me that it can be controlled. Which, I'm assuming, is part of some grand, cosmic plan, but whatever. The point is... I guess it's like a haiku."

"I'm getting lost," Morgan admitted, "but I love the enthusiasm." Cassandra sighed.

"I haiku follows a set pattern of syllables: five, seven, five. It has to have that scheme to be a haiku, so it needs to be planned out, right? But in the confines of that plan, you can do whatever you want. And it still plays a part in the plan."

"Okay, I guess that makes sense," Morgan admitted. Cassandra shrugged.

"So that's what I did. I chose the song to shape the destiny."

"What song did she pick?" Neil asked.

"Hands Down by Dashboard Confessional," Dex said dreamily.

"O-M-G," Neil squealed. "So romantic. Go on."

"It started to rain," Cassandra told Morgan, who was totally engrossed.

"And?" she asked.

"So then she stops the song when we get home, wanting to wait to finish it," Dex told a captivated Neil.

"It was raining," Cassandra said, her mind going back to the memory. "We ran to the door soaking wet, but I played the song again."

"Then we stood at the door with my hands on her waist," Dex told Neil.

"And I kissed him like I meant it," Cassandra said.

"And I knew that she meant it," Dex concluded. Across the distance, Dex and Cassandra sighed happily. Neil and Morgan hugged Dex and Cassandra, respectively. Finally. After all the bad news as of late, something to be happy about. Something joyful. Perhaps, they all thought, this was the secret to life. After all, each of them was familiar with tragedy in their own right. All four of them each had terrible things happen to them. Their tragedies were as unique and different as each of them. Yet in the midst of that, they had managed to find one another. Not only that, they had decided to forge ahead with new bonds bound in each other. Their shared bonds creating a joyful experience for one another. In the midst of everything going on, the love in their life had increased. It didn't make the pain of the past any better. It didn't help with the fear and terror of an unknown future. It helped. It was the silver lining in an otherwise oppressive and dark cloud. In the end, wasn't that the true meaning of life- to find joy where you can with those you love?

"This Pico is amazing," Neil told Cassandra.

"Thanks. I used my mom's recipe."

"She was an amazing cook," Neil said suppressed.

"No she wasn't," Cassandra laughed. "She bought stuff like this. It was a joke."

"My mom never even let me cook after the toast incident," Dex laughed.

"You burnt something once, didn't you?" Morgan asked.

"Oh, he tried to make us toast once and this dumbass buttered the bread before he put it in the toaster." Neil pointed to Dex. "I one hundred percent approve her decision to have you not burn the house down after that one."

"Okay good to know I'm not the only one," Morgan added. "Tried to make me and my brothers' breakfast. Good lord- I can still smell the smoke." Everyone turned to look at Neil. They looked at them, holding a chip full of Pico in front of their face, his mouth open, waiting to eat.

"What?" they asked, chip still in front of their face. "My parents never taught me to cook. I'm self-taught. And Dex can confirm that."

"Can confirm," Dex said, nodding his head once.

"I ain't ever burned anything," they said defensively, point the chip at each of them.

"I'm legit just glad Morgan and Cass moved in. I don't have to cook all the time now."

"I cook!" Dex replied while Neil finally enjoyed their chip.

"Putting mozzarella on Spaghetti-O's and calling it baked ziti doesn't count, honey," they replied.

"You didn't..." Cassandra said in a slightly terrified voice.

"I... I mean..." Dex was trying to defend himself.

"Oh, this is amazing," Morgan responded, laughing.

"Then he ate them out of a mug because someone," Neil motioned their head towards Dex, "didn't do the dishes the night before." Morgan threw her hands in the air.

"And it gets better! I didn't think it could, but it did." She started a slow clap. "Well done, Dex. Well done indeed." Even Cassandra couldn't help but laugh.

"Honestly, I just came out to have a good time and I feel so attacked right now," Dex said with insincere disgust. The group burst out laughing.

This was the new "new normal" for them. It wasn't as if they forgot what else was going on around them. After all, with the deadline fast approach, they actually were working and investigating. They spent the next few days talking to The Four individually. There just weren't many leads. What they gathered was that Niall convinced Jude that the world needed fixing. He gave Jude access to his network of Vampires, Corrupted, and Grafters. What he didn't tell Jude was that he knew he was going to fail. The only reason Niall would have worked with anyone was to use them. Niall decided that manipulating Jude into essentially beta testing his machine was the best way to see how it really worked with no danger to himself.

When Dex had heard this, he felt the old familiar rise in anger well up inside of him. How many people over the years did Niall sacrifice to achieve his goals? Dex reasoned that, on some level, Niall's goals were noble. After all, who can honestly say that fixing the world isn't a noble endeavor? He also felt, however, that there was more to this than meets the eye. It seemed too standard for Niall. The more Dex read and learned about him pointed to some kind of inflated view of himself. He viewed himself as the only one capable of saving the world. The idea of a global cleansing, however, seemed beneath him. It didn't, in Dex's mind, match his actions or what he was learning of him.

All in all, everyone was rather happy, even with this supposed deadline fast approaching. To live one's life in the face of such uncertainty boldly was the only natural response. It was as if they knew the world was ending yet were too busy planting trees to allow themselves to be affected. The only concern was that happiness can lead to a false sense of security. Had he been paying more attention, he may have noticed the song that was playing as he drifted off to sleep that night. *"Do you realize that you have the most beautiful face? Do you realize we're floating in space? Do you realize that happiness makes you cry? Do you realize that everyone you know someday will die?"*

The day began rather normal. Neil and Dex arrived home from working a shift together at The Cathedral of Heroes. Morgan and Cassandra were going out for a girl's evening, leaving the other two at home.

"Dude we need to throw a party," Neil suggested.

"Pretty sure our girlfriends would kill us if we messed up the house. Also: who are going to invite? The Four?" Dex asked.

"Oh I would love to see Adrian do Jager Bombs," Neil said laughing. "I would literally pay good money to see that."

"No one even really likes that drink," Dex said slightly disgusted.

"Well fine," Neil said pouting. "But you and I should party. Or something."

"I mean, we could order pizza and watch anime and play Smash Bros?" Dex suggested.

"You're terrible at Smash," Neil said dismissively.

"Yo!" Dex exclaimed. "I'm sorry Xir I only spam Kriby drops when I'm losing. What was that?"

"Oh!" Neil replied. "Are you approaching me? Instead of running away you're coming right to me?"

"I can't beat the shit out of you without getting closer," Dex responded, narrowing his eyes.

"Ho-ho! Then come as close as you like!"

"You damn nerd," Dex said with a laugh. "I'll order the pizza. Set up the game. Switch while we wait, anime while we eat."

"Good plan. But don't forget cheesy bread, please."

"Like I would forget that," Dex said, sounding all offended. Dex ordered the food, paying over the phone. "Dang they must be busy," he told Neil. "About an hour for delivery."

"That's fine," Neil responded. "Plenty of time for some good matches." They started stretching their arms. The two friends sat down, playing the game and laughing. About a half hour into it, Neil got up.

"Dude. We need some party music. This party sucks without music." They connected their phone to the wireless speaker.

"Please. No dubstep," Dex asked kindly. "My head can't take that today."

"Oh fine you big baby," Neil said frowning. "Andrew W.K. then?"

"I can jive with that," Dex said.

"Awesome. I have a whole play list of his songs. Aaaaand shuffle."

"Wait, what?" Dex said. Something was... not right. The electronic rhythm started followed by heavier tones.

"This is your time to pay. This is your judgment day. We made a sacrifice and now we get to take your life." No, no, no, Dex thought. This is all wrong. The doorbell rang.

"I'll get it," Neil said, dancing towards the door. A terrible feeling of déjà vu swept over Dex.

"No," he whispered. "What happens next?"

"Mmm?" Neil turned and looked at him.

"You better get ready to die. You better get ready to kill. You better get ready to run 'cause here we come. You better get ready to die."

"It's not working," Dex said in a panicked voice, his head hurting. "Why isn't it working right?"

Neil gently opened the door. Dex turned to look, time slowing down. Several shots rang out, hitting Neil in the chest.

"Aw, beans," he said sadly. "I'm Johnny Storm." A man took a step in, placing a gun to Neil's forehead, pulling the trigger one last time. The blast knocked them backwards. Neil fell, dead before they even hit the ground.

"No!" Dex screamed in rage and loss. Instantly, he powered up to fifty percent, his wings glistening. He flew towards the door, his hand outstretched. He summoned an unsheathed Ruach to his hand, instantly igniting it with a flame of energy. "No!" he screamed again, readying a killing blow. The man pulled a sword out from under his long black coat. Stepping calmly to the side, he sliced off Dex's left hand, causing him to drop Ruach. He grabbed Dex's right hand, his left-hand slamming Dex into the wall by his neck.

"Hello, Dex Machina." The man blinked with an emotionless face. "My name is Niall."

"You... you killed Neil," Dex said struggling to breathe.

"Yes," Niall replied, still showing no emotion. "I had my reasons."

"I'm going to kill you," Dex said, tears of rage and grief cascading down his cheeks.

"Perhaps," Niall added, cocking his head to the side. "Perhaps not. At least not today." Niall's hand glowed with a mixture of golden and purple energy, washing over Dex. Where his left hand used to be felt like it was in an agonizing fire. "There," he said calmly, his voice showing compassion but his face still showing no emotion at all. "I have healed your hand. Please cause it to grow back. It's rather embarrassing to see a Conduit with so little control. Now," the pale blonde man said, "I'm going to let you go so we can discuss things. If you promise not to attack me, I can promise to help you see Neil again." Dex stopped moving.

"You're going to kill me? Is that it?" Dex asked.

"Far from it, Dex Machina. I don't want to kill you. I want to bring Neil back to life for you." The sentence hung ominously in the air. It was possible, as Dex knew, but it seemed that it wasn't a great idea. Dex understood all the moral implications, but he looked down and saw Neil's body riddled with holes, blood pooling beneath them. His best friend, his sibling was dead. It wasn't right. It wasn't fair. He had already lost so much. What would be so bad about helping one's own sibling. Dex looked at Niall, his eyes burning with hatred and rage. He dropped down to ten percent so he could work on regrowing his hand even though it was painful.

"Fine," Dex said through gritted teeth. With that, Niall released his holds on Dex. He slid down the wall a few inches, coughing to take in some fresh air and rubbing his throat, landing on his knees over Neil's lifeless corpse, covering himself with a mix of his own blood and Neil's. "Let's talk." He got up and walked towards the couch, his eyes filling with tears once again as he looked at Neil. I'm going to fix this, Dex told himself. I'm going to fix everything. If he was thinking clearly and if his mind wasn't clouded by grief and loss, he would have done one thing and noticed something else. First, he would have worked on contacting Cassandra telepathically. He knew she was strong and their new bond made the connection even stronger. Yet he was so blinded by Neil's death that he wasn't thinking clearly. Second, he would have noticed Niall stopping down to pick something up off the floor. Yet even in his state, he was likely to think whatever he stashed in his coat was of little consequence.

Dex sat down, looking at the ever-growing stump of his left hand. It was painful business growing new skin and bones, but it was a necessary pain. He looked over at Niall, who sat down opposite him with a flourish of his coat. He tried to read him, but he found it rather difficult. He wore a simple white polo shirt under his long black coat and a pair of blue jeans. His golden blonde hair was wild and unkempt. It was as if he didn't care what he looked like. His facial expression never changed. That was the most unnerving thing, Dex decided. His voice held regular tone, betraying his emotionless veneer, but he carried himself anyway as if nothing mattered. That was all Dex felt from him- a gaping hole of nothingness.

"I imagine," Niall began, "that you have several questions."

"Well you're good at understatements," Dex snapped back.

"And you're terrible at humor," Niall quickly retorted. "We can do the typical quips and banter or we can just eschew all of that and get down to business. Your choice, but time is not something I want to waste."

"Why did you kill my parents?" Dex asked quietly.

"Really?" Niall asked with a surprised voice, his face still not matching his tone. "That's where you want to start with all of this?"

"Now who's wasting time?" Dex shot back at him. Niall laughed, his face still the same emotionless void.

"Fair enough, I suppose." He sighed. "I killed them because they wouldn't help me. I needed them for my machine. It was still theory then, but Jude helped me prove it. Using three Conduits will augment my own power greatly."

"And then you can kill all non-gifted humans," Dex added.

"That was the original plan, yes," Niall conceded, "but I've changed my mind." He stared at Dex, his cold, lifeless eyes boring into Dex's very soul. "I want to destroy all of existence now."

"That's a rather big leap," Dex said, raising an eyebrow. "Mind if I asked what changed?" Niall pulled a small, black leatherbound book from his coat.

"I grew tired of this."

"Then stop reading it," Dex offered. "Don't make a plan to destroy existence because you're not fond of reading."

"You are your parents' child through and through," Niall said in a mocking tone. "They thought they were funny, as well." Control, Dex thought to himself. Control your emotions. Focus on healing your hand and then take him out. "My Gift of Prophecy is rather simple," Niall continued. "Every night, I spend approximately fifteen minutes in a trance like state, furiously scribbling notes in journals. Once that is done, I have a dimly lit mirror with which to see the upcoming day." He laughed. "It's not very helpful, knowing what terrible things are going to happen and knowing that you can't stop them."

"Why couldn't you stop them?" Dex asked.

"Because I would often write how I couldn't involve myself in the events," Niall replied simply. "A perfect record of war and death and terrorism and here I was powerless to stop them from happening. Of course, I understood then that there was a grand plan. I understood that God was ultimately in control of such events, both the good and the bad." He looked at Dex in the eyes again. "I found all of this unsatisfactory. I grew to hate God's plan. At first, I thought a cleansing would fix the world. Yet living in a broken world seemed to be a part of the plan." He shrugged. "The only true choice I could make that I could say was even my own was to destroy everything."

"You know," Dex countered, "some might say even that was a part of the plan." Niall cocked his head to the side quizzically.

"Perhaps," he said quietly, "but perhaps not. After all, there are now only two outcomes. Either I succeed and prove my own agency over God's predestination, or I fail and die. Either way, I'm freed from someone else's control."

"Well that just sounds like suicide by cop but with extra steps," Dex added dryly.

"And this brings us back to your dead friend," Niall said coldly. Dex flinched, recalling the death of Neil.

"How so?" Dex asked bitterly.

"You're a Healer," Niall replied plainly. "Raise him."

"I'm pretty sure no Prophet told me this was going to happen," Dex answered.

"And I'm pretty sure my partially powered machine is purposefully creating problems for prophecy. You won't get the answers you seek from them. Time to make your own decision." He slipped up, Dex thought. He revealed that his machine is complete and is being powered, possibly by two Conduits. But he's not using it on himself. He's just using it to stop people from finding him out through the Prophets.

"So, I do this and then what?" Dex asked. "I'm so moved by your plight that I willingly get into your machine?" Niall laughed.

"Please don't flatter yourself. I no longer need you for my machine." This meant one of two things, Dex reasoned. Either he was going to go after Jules or he found other unnamed Conduits. "Look at your left hand, please." Dex looked down. He had almost forgotten the pain in his hand, but there was no pain. His hand had been fully regrown. "The human body is remarkable," he said breathlessly. He stood up suddenly and walked over to Neil's body. "Come," he instructed.

Dex moved on some unknown instinct, doing as Niall commanded. I mean, how bad could it be? This was what Dex was thinking. After all, Niall was correct that there wouldn't be any Prophets to confirm or deny it should or shouldn't happen. So what was the harm in it? Why shouldn't he save Neil?

"You start by doing a regular healing," Niall instructed.

"Why are you doing this?" Dex asked through tears. "Haven't I suffered enough?"

"Exactly!" he replied firmly. "Exactly! Haven't you suffered as a puppet long enough? The Order lied to you because that's what they do. God has used you yet tortured you all along the way. I'm not trying to hurt you, Dex Machina. I'm trying to set you and everyone else free." He gently and tenderly, with a lover's care, placed Dex's hands on Neil's body.

"Tell the body to heal itself. It knows how, it just needs your guidance." Dex closed his eyes, crying. His hands felt warm as he felt the energy flow into Neil. "Good, good," Niall said happily. "That's it. That's the easy part. Command the blood back in as well," he instructed. And just like that, Neil's body was healed. "Wasn't that easy?" Dex nodded. "Now, restarting the heart is also simple. It brings life to the body, but not the soul, so they are not resurrected until the end." Niall looked at Dex with his blank face. "Please proceed." They look like they're sleeping, Dex thought to himself. They should wake up. Yes. They always sleep too much. Dex just needed to wake them up. He placed his hands over Neil's heart, shooting healing energy into the body.

There was a gasp as Neil's eyes flew open, taking a deep breath into their body.

"Neil..." Dex said breathlessly, weeping openly.

"Hey, hey," Niall said embracing Dex. "It's okay. It's okay. We're almost done here." He grabbed Dex by the shoulders. "Are you okay?" There was concern in his voice, but not on his face. Dex wiped his eyes and nose with his left hand, still crying.

"Yeah," he said weakly. "Yeah. I'm okay. It's just shocking."

"I know," Niall said sympathetically. "I know. But we're almost done, okay? All we have to do it grab his soul from the other side and put it back. It's easy. You focus your energy on his essence."

"Their," Dex corrected them, touching Neil's face gently. "Please use their preferred pronouns."

"That doesn't matter," Niall snapped at Dex. "All that matters is that you finish this. You want him back, right?" Dex nodded.

"I do, but they matter to me. And they want to be referred to as they." Dex looked at Niall. "So it does matter."

"Fine," he snapped at Dex. "Whatever. Put *their* soul back in *their* body. Happy now?" No, Dex thought. He wasn't happy. He was mad. Neil was important to him. He was important enough to get their pronouns correct. Wait, he thought. He doesn't actually care about me. He sure as Hell doesn't care about Neil. The Four? Morgan and Cassandra? Now they cared. And Dex was sure they wouldn't want Dex or Neil bullied by this guy.

You idiot, he said to himself.

"Cassandra?" he reached out telepathically. "I can't say much. I need you both home. Now. It's an emergency."

"Understood," she replied. "We're on our way." Dex turned to Niall.

"You don't care about them or me," he told him. "You only want what you personally want. And Neil wouldn't want it to go down like this," he said standing up. He turned and looked at Neil's soulless, breathing body. "I'm so sorry, my friend. This is wrong. And I can't do it. I hope You'll forgive me one day." Niall sighed.

"Okay," they said, also standing up. "I really did try." He pointed a hand at Neil, filling their body with golden and purple energy. Neil sat up, shaking.

"What the f...."

"What did you do?" Dex demanded, grabbing Niall, his body going to twenty-five percent power.

"I did what you refused to do," he responded, headbutting Dex with a powered-up strike. "What you were too weak to do." Dex grabbed his nose, healing it. "You want *them* dead so badly? Then do it yourself." Niall turned and looked at Neil. "Kill him Neil. I'm leaving." He turned and ran out the door.

"You coward!" Dex screamed after him. Niall didn't hear him, as Neil stood and sent a blast at Dex, knocking him back a few feet.

"Crap!" they explained. "What's going on? I can't control my body!"

"Niall is controlling you," Dex said summoning Ruach to his hand once again. "Try to fight this programming!"

"What the bloody Hell do you think I'm doing?" they yelled at Dex, chasing after him, firing off blasts as they went. Dex was able to easily deflect the blasts. "One minute there's darkness and peace and I wake up to this?"

"Yeah," Dex said grimly. "You kind of died."

"I kind of what?!" they asked, missing a shot and shooting the tv. "Damnit. Now we need a new tv."

"I'd settle for you not trying to kill me for right now," Dex replied.

"Well I would settle for a lot of things, yes," Neil responded, "and that would totes be at the top of the damn list." Neil placed his hands back to his left side, gathering up energy. "Aw beans..." they said sadly. "You need to knock me out or something!" they instructed Dex.

"I got this," Cassandra said with a terrified Morgan in tow. "Sleep," she commanded. Neil crumpled to the floor, the energy they were collecting disappearing with their sleep.

"Explain, now," Cassandra demanded.

"Short version: Niall killed Neil, tried to convince me to resurrect them and when I didn't, he resurrected Neil and programmed them to try to kill me."

"I'm sorry- what?!" Morgan yelled, running over to Neil. Cassandra ran over, placing Neil on their back.

"Morgan, stand back. I don't know how bad this is." She placed her two hands on the side of their head, closing her eyes. She grimaced.

"Good lord," she said in a shocked voice. "It's like a spiderweb in here. I have to cut these threads one by one. This may take a little bit."

"Dex, are you okay?" Morgan asked.

"Yeah I'm fine," he said sadly. "I lost a hand but it grew back." She blinked at him.

"Okay. We're going to need a full debriefing after Neil is safe," she said.

"Morgan, write this down: 612 Wharf Avenue. It's some address that's imprinted in these commands." Morgan pulled out her phone and jotted the address down, sending it in a group text to everyone.

About fifteen minutes later, Cassandra sighed.

"Okay. I got them all. Damn- that guy was good at this."

"We can marvel at his handy work later," Morgan said impatiently. "Wake them up! Please!" Cassandra touched Neil's forehead and their eyes blinked open.

"No stay back!" they screamed. "I'm dangerous!" They curled up in a little ball, crying softly. Morgan held them in her arms.

"Hey! Hey!" she said in a soothing voice. "It's okay. You're fine now. You're back." Dex placed a hand on his head, closing his eyes. This was a line. This was a line that should never have been crossed.

"Cassandra? Grab a bottle of white wine and four glasses, please." He sighed and crouched down to Neil. "Hey buddy. You okay?"

"I mean, I'm kind of messed up right now, so if you could fill us all in that would be super helpful."

"Yeah, dude," he replied, smiling slightly. "Let's go sit down at the table. I'll explain."

"Excuse me," a confused voice said from the doorway. "Sorry. I got lost, but here's the pizza you ordered."

"Oh hot damn- pizza," Neil said, standing up. They walked over and grabbed the boxes. "Thanks. Did you get a tip?" The pizza deliverer nodded, slightly confused. "Awesome," Neil said. "Have a nice night." They closed the door and walked the box over to the table.

Dex poured everyone a glass of wine and began to recount what had happened. There were tears all around, which was to be expected. It was another in a string of horrible events that the four of them had to deal with.

"Well this is worse than a worst-case scenario," Cassandra said plainly. "We need to find him and stop him. Like, now." Morgan closed her eyes, her face twisted in concentration. She began to sweat, a small bit of blood trickling from her nose.

"Babe: what are you doing?" Neil asked.

"I'm... pushing... through... his...machine..." she said in a pained voice. "I... need... to... confirm... something...." She gasped and opened her eyes, raising a shaking hand to her nose, gently wiping the blood. "I did it," she said with a smile. "I beat that bastard. I know where he is."

"Where is he?" Dex asked in a dark, low tone.

"You already know. He wanted us to know."

"612 Wharf Avenue," Cassandra said. She laughed and shook her head. "Oh, he is clever. He left that knowing we would find it."

"What's the plan?" Neil asked, still pale from the encounter. "What are we doing? Calling The Four?" Dex shook his head.

"No," he said. "I'm going to finish this." Cassandra calmly sat her glass down after finishing it quickly and slapped Dex on the back of the head.

"Ow!" he exclaimed, rubbing the back of his head. "What in the..." she spun his chair around to face her.

"You listen here, Dex Machina. *We* are going to do this *together*. You understand me? An attack on one of us is an attack on all of us. You aren't running off for some personal vendetta and get yourself killed!"

"And I don't want any of you killed!" he yelled back. He looked at Neil, his eyes glassing over with tears. "I... I can't go through that again. He turned and faced Cassandra. "I've lost more family than I should have already."

"Bold of you to assume I'm intending to die. No: we're going to burn his plans to the ground. But we're going to do it together." She gently grabbed his head, placing her forehead on his. "We're a family. We look after each other."

"Is this when I do the Ohana quote from Lilo and Stitch?" Neil quietly asked Morgan. "Because I feel like I'm supposed to." Morgan laughed and cried, hugging Neil. Dex tried not to smile, but he knew Cassandra was right.

"I made reservations Giorno's," He said weakly. "Don't go dying because you said you'd pay this time." Cassandra tenderly kissed his forehead.

"I wouldn't dream of doing that." Neil left and came back with a bottle of whisky and four shot glasses.

"Well I don't know about you all, but a potential suicide mission needs a right proper drink." He passed everyone a shot.

"To us," Neil said, raising their glass.

"To the future," Morgan said, raising her glass.

"To teamwork," Cassandra said, raising her glass. Dex looked around. This was his family, and he was going to protect them all.

"To the end," Dex said, raising his glass. They downed their shots, tapping their glasses three times on the table afterwards. "Tomorrow, we finish this."

Chapter Seventeen

There was a knock on the door.

"Come in," Neil said quietly. It was Dex.

"Hey, buddy," he said shyly." Can I come in?" They shrugged and grunted a noncommittal grunt. Dex slowly and cautiously walked over to a desk chair facing their bed. He stared at his long-time friend. Their eyes were forlorn, thinking of the events of the evening. There was a mix of fear and sadness emanating from them. They sat in silence for a few moments, simply looking at one another.

"Please don't ask me what I saw when I died," they finally told Dex.

"Dude, I wasn't going to," he said honestly.

"Because I honestly don't even remember it," they continued, the words pouring out of their mouth.

"Dude: I seriously wasn't going to ask."

"It was dark," Neil continued, obviously feeling like the story needed to be told. "Then there was light. And that's when I can't remember what happened. I just know..." they sighed, holding back tears. "I just know that I was happy. Like, actually happy. I was at peace." They wiped a tear from their eye, smudging their eyeliner a bit. "There was, like these three voices that spoke as one and they... they apologized or something. I don't know. Something about how this wasn't supposed to happen and still more work." They threw their hands in the air with a laugh. "That's when I got jolted back to life, I guess." Dex moved and sat next to Neil. They placed their head on Dex's shoulder and he instinctively wrapped an arm around them. Neil looked up at Dex and said, "This all sucks."

"It powerful sucks," Dex agreed, holding them tight. "I'm so sorry." Dex's eyes started to well with tears of his own. "I... please don't hate me." Neil looked at him confused.

"Why on earth would I hate you?" They asked.

"Because I didn't bring you back. I wanted to. I really, really wanted to. But I couldn't do it."

"Oh, honey," Neil responded with a laugh. "I would never be mad at you for that. You did the right thing."

"Yeah, well, Niall made a very convincing argument about why I should do it."

"Then why didn't you?" they asked. Dex looked at Neil with a laugh.

"He kept getting your pronouns wrong. Then he went off about how it wasn't a big deal. That's when I knew he was full of it."

"Oh, that pretentious..." Neil closed their eyes and took a deep breath in, stabilizing themselves on a fake surface. "Honey, I am so glad you didn't listen to him. Because I would have kicked your ass if you took marching orders from someone like that."

"That's exactly what I thought," he replied with a laugh. He looked at Neil. "So, you aren't mad or hate me?"

"No, sweetie. You did the right thing." They sighed, running their hand through their hair and then rubbing their neck. "I couldn't and wouldn't fault you for doing what's right." Neil looked at Dex and smiled. "You get that from your mom." Dex smiled.

"Thank you," Dex said, lightly kissing Neil's shock of black hair. "I love you, buddy."

"I know," Neil said. "I love you too, man." Suddenly, Neil looked around. "Wait. Where are the girls?" Dex laughed.

"Oh, you're going to love this," Dex said, getting up and walking over to the window. Neil followed him.

"Well damn," Neil said blushing. "Not gonna lie- I kind of want Morgan to step on me."

"Dude!" Dex exclaimed with a laugh. "TMI!" He looked back out the window, focusing on Cassandra. The two were outside sparing with one another. Cassandra had her collapsible staff while Morgan was dual wielding a pair of batons.

"Really?" Cassandra asked Morgan. "Ophelia?" she took a quick jab at Morgan who jumped back, knocking the staff away wither her left stick.

"Yeah," she answered, taking a defensive stance. "I mean, that was a lot of the training to be honest. She's kind of... I guess philosophical is the right word for her." Cassandra went on the offensive, trying to a high attack and then a low attack. Morgan blocked the high attack, but the low swing hit her leg, getting her off balance.

"I literally have no offensive powers," she said, catching her balance. "A girl has to be able to defend herself." She lunged at Cassandra with a left then right blow.

"No, I totally get that," she said. "But Ophelia? She taught you how to fight?" Morgan stood up and put her hands on her hips.

"Girl, we went over this. Yes." Casandra put her staff by her side.

"And you're coming with us tomorrow?" She asked.

"I'm not going to sit by doing nothing while you all go off and fight for me."

"You don't have to come, though." Cassandra said in a worried voice.

"Look," Morgan said, "My mind is made up. Period."

"And this is why we've been out here sparing. Because..."

"Because I'm going." Morgan sighed. "I've lost one family already. That was their choice. I'm not losing another family. That's my choice." Cassandra understood, but she was still very concerned.

"Morgan," she said hesitantly, "we could... we could die doing this. This is obviously a trap." Morgan closed her eyes and took a deep breath.

"Okay. First, I obviously know that. I'm not about to send you all off to die without me." She made sure to place special emphasis on the word family. "Second, I'm pretty sure I can unbalance the plan. I mean, usually Prophets don't go on missions, so my very presence could tip things in our favor. Third, I'm not some dainty little girl that can't fight." Cassandra smiled. By all accounts, she knew Morgan was right. Morgan knew she was right, too. Cassandra put her staff away, collapsing it back in on itself. She walked over and hugged Morgan.

"Solidarity, sis." Morgan hugged her back. This was the moment she had been waiting for her entire life. To her, it wasn't just the found family that made her feel whole. Sure, that was nice, but her experience with families taught her that families were temporary. She no longer thought that with this family. No: her joy was in the fact that Cassandra had given her the one thing she always wanted and was denied for many years. She had finally been acknowledged as a sister. This is why she decided to fight for this family. They both knew her and loved her. That love and acceptance was worth fighting for. Cassandra felt her crying and pulled away for a moment.

"Honey," she asked concerned, "what's wrong?" Morgan smiled and wiped tears away.

"It's stupid," she said, slightly embarrassed.

"No," Cassandra demanded. "Tell me. What's wrong?" Morgan laughed again.

"I've always wanted a sister," she finally said. "And... I've..." she couldn't help but cry a bit harder. "I've always wanted to *be* a sister." Realization spread across Cassandra's face. She couldn't help shedding tears of joy.

"You are my sister," she said through the happy tears. "Whatever happens tomorrow, don't you ever forget that, okay?" Morgan nodded, wiping her eyes and smiling.

Dex left Neil's room, retiring to his own room. He spent some time cleaning and sharpening Ruach. Once he was done, he gave the blade a few slashes, the familiar sound of the wind filling his ears, bringing peace, comfort, and memories of his past. There were only two outcomes for tomorrow. Either Niall would succeed in destroying the world, or he wouldn't. Dex had no way of knowing what the cost of either would be. Truth be told, he didn't care. All he knew was that he had to try.

Perhaps, he thought, that this was all part of a plan. He could not help but keep returning to this idea over and over again. Schemes and plans seemed to be a part of his life. He hadn't even had time to properly digest the truth about his parents. Yet in the end, that kind of didn't matter to him. It wouldn't have changed the fact that they cared and loved Dex. It was possible that it influenced how they raised him, but in the end, he felt like he had turned out alright. His feelings weren't directed at them so much as it was directed at The Order. They had taken him in and accepted him, yet they withheld information from him. He understood, logically, the reasoning behind it. That doesn't mean he had to like it. He sighed, knowing what he needed to do.

"Hello?" Jules said over the phone rather confused.

"It's Dex," he said politely.

"Is something wrong?" he asked in a concerned voice.

"No," Dex said in a reassuring voice.

"Is it Niall? Dex, please tell me what happened." Dex hesitated. It has to be this way, he thought. Dex needed to be the one to do this. After all, this is what The Order wanted.

"We know where he is," Dex answered finally. "We are going to end this tomorrow."

"Dex, please," Jules pleaded. "Let The Four handle it. We have more experience with this sort of thing."

"Isn't this what you wanted?" Dex asked. "You wanted this. You wanted us to deal with the traitor. That was just the tip of the iceberg."

"We didn't know he was involved in this," Jules said honestly.

"It doesn't matter," Dex stated sharply. "This is our fight. We are finishing it." There was a brief pause.

"We?" Jules asked, slightly confused.

"This isn't some vendetta I have against Niall," Dex said. "This is about justice. This is about doing what we're supposed to do- about doing what's right."

"You're not going alone," Jules said. "Why?"

"Because at the end of the day, I'm not him. He killed Neil, Jules. He made a rather convincing argument as to why I should resurrect him."

"Neil is dead?" Jules asked alarmed.

"No. When I refused to bring them back, he did it himself."

"Why didn't you do it?" Jules asked.

"I would have been doing it for the wrong reasons," he answered. "I'm not God. I don't want to be God. I just want to make the world a better place. If that goes along with God's master plan or whatever, so be it. But I'm going to do this thing my way- the right way." There was another pause.

"I could easily alert The Four and we could stop you."

"True. And Adrian could probably figure out where he's hiding. But you won't do that."

"Why do you think we won't do that?" Jules asked.

"Because at the end of the day, you either know I'm right or you have faith in us. Or both. I don't know. But I know you know that this whole system of The Order needs an overhaul." Dex took a deep breath. "This world needs a better system in place. And we're going to give it to them."

"As usual, Dex Machina, I am proud of you. I never doubted for a moment that you would make the right choices. Go and do what you need to do."

"Thank you," Dex said. He paused, just for a moment. "Jules?" he said cautiously.

"Yes?"

"It wasn't your fault. What happened. Not with Niall or my parents. I need you to know that. It wasn't your fault."

"Thank you, Dex Machina," Jules said, his voice cracking slightly. "I appreciate that. Please give my best to the team. And please contact us afterwards."

"I will," he replied. "Good night." He hung up the phone,

Down the hallway, Morgan was laying with Neil on their bed. She was holding him. She understood that Neil was still shaken up after what happened. Dying and being resurrected would have that effect on anyone, she supposed.

"Neil?" she whispered in their ear from behind.

"Yeah, babe?" they responded.

"I'm going to be there with you tomorrow," she said plainly.

"I know," Neil responded with a smile.

"What do you think is going to happen?"

"Honestly I should be asking you that question," they replied with a laugh. "You're the one who can see the future."

"But I can't see this at least," she hesitated, afraid of finishing her thought.

"Just say it," Neil said with a laugh. "I feel the same way." They turned around, facing her. "It's okay," they reassured her.

"I don't want to," she finally said, slightly ashamed. "I don't want to know what happens tomorrow. I'm afraid, Neil. My stomach is in knots. I... I can't even sleep." Neil gave Morgan a light kiss.

"Whatever happens tomorrow, we will be there together."

"Do you think you can change fate?" she asked them.

"It's hard to say," they replied with a sigh. "On the one hand, no. It's already set in stone. On the other hand, even when you do see the future, you don't see everything. I'm not saying that we have much control over the future, but I'm saying what we do does matter to us. It at least looks to us like we influence the future. And truth be told, that's enough." They smiled at her. "I mean, you're proof of that. You've taken destiny by the horns a few times. You as your real, authentic self, shows us that we have a part to play in the grand scheme of things. Even if it's a part of a plan, we can still deal with it our way. I guess it has to do with how we perceive time and stuff. And if we have the drive to do what we need to do." She smiled and brushed the black, curly hair from his eyes.

"You're sweet," she said.

"And you're amazing," they added.

"I don't want to leave," she said sadly, tears in her eyes. "I'm not ready for this to be over." Neil understood that she wasn't just talking about leaving their room. She wasn't ready to for life to be over.

"Neither am I," they said with a laugh. "So, let's not let it be over. Deal?" She kissed them again.

"Deal," she said smiling.

"Stay with me tonight," they said. "Nothing hinky or anything like that. Just... we don't have to let this end. I want to hold you all night. I don't want this to end, either." She smiled and nodded, plugging her phone in and playing a song. "Oh, good Lord!" Neil said with a laugh. "Dex got to you, too?"

"No," she protested with a laugh. "I'm making the destiny I want."

"I mean, that just sounds like a way to go along with destiny but with extra steps," Neil said with a laugh.

"Hey! Don't knock the system!" The guitar started soft, but fast, followed by drums and classic pop punk drums and riffs.

"You're playing Blink 182 and you expect me to believe that Dex hasn't gotten to you?"

"Shut up!" she said with a laugh, snuggling closer to Neil. Let's just listen to it and go to sleep, okay?"

"Deal, babe," they said, giving her a goodnight kiss.

"I haven't been this scared in a long time. And I'm so unprepared, so here's your valentine. Bouquet of clumsy words, a simple melody. This world's an ugly place, but you're so beautiful to me." With that, they feel asleep holding each other, not caring about the future because they had each other.

Dex, meanwhile, sat at his computer, looking at the address. He was attempting to formulate something when there was a knock on the door. He turned to look, seeing Cassandra standing in her doorway, obviously ready for bed.

"Oh. Hey Cass. Come on in." She came in, sitting on his bed closest to him.

"What are you doing?" She asked, slightly confused.

"Well, I'm too worked up to sleep right now, so I pulled up some pictures of the address. Turns out it's an old dilapidated cannery on the river." He turned back to the screen. "I'm trying to get a feel as to what to expect. I need to see how much space there is. Obviously, we'll see some resistance because he will want protection, but..."

"Dex," Cassandra said, her voice full on concern. "What's really going on?"

"I told you," he responded, slightly annoyed. "I'm trying to make a plan."

"I thought your go to plan was to improvise?" She said with a laugh.

"Everyone else plans. Might as well join them. I mean, I'm not really wanting anything to happen to anyone." He turned and looked at Cassandra. "He's not going to hurt any of you."

"The bravado is adorable," she told him, "but we need to do this together. So," she stood up, grabbing another chair and sitting next to Dex saying, "let's plan together." Dex smiled and nodded.

"Here's what I've gotten so far. The machine is at least partially operational. It's what he's using to mess up prophecy. But it may not be perfect, so he may be using the water to keep it cool. Maybe."

"That's a lot of maybes," Cassandra admitted.

"It's... it's kind of all I have right now," Dex admitted, embarrassment in his voice. "That and the fact that I think we can expect the same amount of resistance that we did at the castle. At least number wise. It'll be a grab bag as to who actually shows up there."

"That's a good point," she replied encouragingly.

"But there is, like, literally no good spot to launch an attack. I can't see the inside. We don't know how sturdy the structure is and..."

"Hey. Hey." Cassandra interrupted I'm a calming voice, holding his hand. "Relax, okay? It's going to be fine."

"Your optimism is endearing," he admitted, "but if we just knew for sure..."

"But we can't know for sure. We never can. Even when we know the future, we only get parts. We just have to roll with it." She gently kissed the back of his hand. "It is what it is." Dex gave a disappointed laugh.

"You know, I used to love that saying before it came to dominate my whole life." He gently rubbed the back of her hand with his thumb.

"If you want me to make up some crap response about duty and honor, I can do that. I just thought the truth was better"

"No, it is," Dex told her. "It really is. Especially when it comes from you," he said, smiling and tucking her hair behind her ear.

"Oh, good Lord," she said with a playful laugh. "You have, like, this endearing quality to flirt while facing danger, don't you?" Dex smiled coyly.

"I mean, I feel like that's one of my lovable qualities if I'm being honest." He tossed his head to the side, throwing imaginary bangs from in front of his eyes. Dex smiled sadly and sighed. "I'm just a little concerned about tomorrow," he said truthfully. "If we could just see the future..."

"Then we'd be no better off," Cassandra interrupted him. "Their prophecies are just guidance. That's it. And to be honest, we're not doing too badly right now. We have direction. We have guidance. You want to know how it will end. And we can't know that."

"He's very dangerous," Dex replied grimly. "His face... it shows nothing. Like, absolutely nothing. He cares for nothing- not even himself. That's what makes him dangerous. He killed Neil. He cut off my hand. I had to throw out a perfectly good outfit because I got covered in blood. He's just..." Cassandra put a finger to Dex's lips, causing him to be quiet.

"Hey. We'll deal with this. We got this." She gave Dex a reassuring hug. He held her tight, at least taking comfort in her strong arms. He sighed deeply, losing himself in her embrace.

"Whatever happens tomorrow, it will happen with us together," she said tenderly kissing his cheek.

"I'm not losing you. I'm not losing anyone else."

"Good. I mean, you're a Healer so it's kind of, like, your job," she said laughing.

"Thanks for the added pressure," Dex said cynically.

"I didn't mean..." Cassandra began.

"No, I know," Dex interrupted, "but you're right. It is my responsibility. And, if I'm being honest, that weighs on me." Cassandra looked at Dex. In speaking about healing, it was as if a weight fell on Dex. He was over encumbered with the weight of the responsibility of it all. Niall had experience on his side. Dex had a team. Yet with a team came certain risks- namely the risk of losing teammates. Dex had lost his parents. He had lost the way his life had been. He had lost his innocence with the deaths of Mary and Jude- both of which he felt rather responsible for. He had lost what he knew of his parents. He had lost Neil. Loss seemed to be interwoven into Dex's life. Here he sat on the precipice of a battle that would literally decide the fate of all existence. Yet in the midst of this, he was worried about losing his team- his new family. Cassandra finally understood what Dex's kryptonite was- loss.

She grabbed Dex by the hand and led him to the bed, sitting down next to him. She wrapped his arms around her and had him hold her.

"When my dad left, I thought the world was over. I blamed him for... for everything. I blamed him for my mom getting sick. Like, if he had just been there, I thought that would be enough: that would make her better." She moved some hair from in front of her eyes, tucking it behind her ear.

"All I had was anger and resentment. I hated him for what I thought he did. Even when I learned what he had been through, I was still mad." She tilted her head to look at Dex. "I thought we were going to die on that boat, Dex. I honestly thought we were goners. And all I wanted was my mom to hold me and tell me everything was going to be okay. But I knew she wasn't there. So, I decided to get my dad back." She placed a hand on Dex's face, rubbing his cheek gently. He closed his eyes and listened to her. "I realized that in order to move into the future, I would have to be informed by my past. If I wanted that relationship, then I needed to let the past inform what was going on, but not rule it. We cant's change the past, Dex, but it doesn't have to determine our future."

Say it, you damn coward, he thought. Tell her. Tell her the truth.

"I'm afraid I'm not strong enough to save you," he said honestly. "Neil died, Cass. My parents died. If I was stronger, if I was actually worth a damn then I could have saved them all."

"Dex," she said pleadingly, "it happened. I know it affected you. I don't want to minimize those feelings. I'm saying use those feelings to shape the future you want. Even if it is a part of fate, you have choices to make that matter to you. You don't have to be strong enough to protect us. We are doing this together." She smiled lovingly at him. "You're a good man, Dex Machina. I don't know if you hear that enough, but it's true."

"I'm just a simple man trying to make my way in the universe," he said with a light smile. "Truth be told, I'm nothing without my team. I need them to keep me grounded and kicking my butt every so often to get back on track." Cassandra smiled.

"I will always be there to kick your butt when you need it," she said, giving him a light kiss. But then she sighed. "But it's late," she said sadly. "We should probably get some sleep."

"You're probably right," Dex replied equally sad. He went to say something but stopped.

"What's wrong?" Cassandra asked. Dex sighed and smiled.

"I just want to make sure that we're still on for Giorno's later." She smiled.

"Yeah. Yeah, we are. My treat."

"Then we'll be fine. Because I'm looking forward to it." He lightly touched her face, inching it closer to his own and kissed her. If Dex was being honest with himself, he would admit why he was kissing her with such passion. He was afraid it was a good-bye kiss. They said good night to each other and each laid down in their own beds. With every fiber in his being, as he lay there, he worked on a plan to leave early. He wanted to face Niall alone, without endangering his family. If he arose before dawn, he thought, he would have the element of surprise. It was the surest and best way to keep his team safe. It was logical. He didn't have to worry about them getting hurt and he could start at full power and go in guns blazing.

But no matter how much he wanted to do that he knew he couldn't do it. He knew in his heart that he couldn't. If he did, he was giving into his fear of loss. He was saying to himself that he didn't trust them. Worse, he was saying that he didn't trust himself to be able to help them. Cassandra was right, he decided. He couldn't hold on to the fears of the past. He had to do this with them. At the end of the day, what he needed was family. Because of how important family was to him, he was going to do everything in his power to make the future bright. He wasn't going to shoulder the responsibility on his own. No- for the first time in a very long time, he knew that he wasn't as alone as he thought. He had more than Neil now- he also had Cassandra and Morgan. The future, he decided, was theirs to make.

Chapter Eighteen

"Breakfast is the most important meal of the day, so eat up!" Neil had outdone themselves this time, making quite a spread for breakfast. "We have eggs and bacon and sausage- all good for protein. I also made potatoes because, you know, carbs are important too. Oh! And everyone needs at least one glass of orange juice- vitamin C and all that jazz." Dex, Morgan, and Cassandra sat at the table. Morgan was smiling, having helped Neil create the spread before them and feeling rather proud of the potatoes that she worked so hard on. Dex and Cassandra were simply amazed at the size of meal they created in such a short time.

"Teamwork makes dream work," Morgan said smiling, scooping some crispy potatoes on her plate.

"I'm impressed," Cassandra said, grabbing some eggs and bacon. "You two have really outdone yourselves."

"Well we need to make sure we have a good healthy breakfast. It kick starts the metabolism and will grant us the energy we need for today's activities." Neil was very proud of this meal. It was their way of showing his friends how much they loved them. They shot a smile over to Morgan, thanking her for her help.

Suddenly, Dex picked up his glass of orange juice and drank it down quickly. Wearing a grimace on his face, he slammed the cup somewhat gently down on the table. Morgan and Cassandra looked at Dex confused while Neil rolled their eyes.

"What?" he asked in a voice that seemed to suggest everyone should know. "I don't really like orange juice. Plus, now I can have coffee."

"Then I'm making your plate and you better eat it all!" Neil shouted him. He didn't head for the counter where all the prefilled coffee cups were sitting. Instead, he went to the snack cupboard.

"I've been wanting to try these for a while now," he said, grabbing a fresh box of coffee cups.

"You've been holding out on us, Dex?" Cassandra asked with mock hurt.

"Hey: I didn't say I wouldn't share. I got it a bit ago and I haven't tried it yet." He held up the box as if it was some sort of sacred relic. "This is a pecan bourbon flavored coffee. I wanted to try something different." He placed the cup in the machine, carefully setting his mom's old Ziggy mug under it. The smell of pecan and bourbon filled the air- two of his dad's favorite things in the world. He took the mug back to his seat, inhaling the scent. He took a sip. With no sugar or cream, there was still a hint of bitterness, yet it was underscored by the other flavors. It wasn't sweet by any stretch of the imagination. It was different. The flavors worked with the bitterness to create something new.

The meal was simply amazing. It filled their souls. Their conversations, while important discussing tactics and plans, were still lighthearted and filled with love. Even though they were going through something serious, even though they felt the weight of what was about to happen, they felt content in this moment. Even if the worst was to happen, they would be together and they all decided that would be enough. Dex looked at his watch.

"I think it's time to get ready," he said in a resigned voice. Neil put the leftovers away and Morgan went to do the dishes.

"No," Cassandra said with a sad smile on her face. "Leave them. We'll do them when we get back here, okay?" It took a moment, but Morgan understood what Cassandra was really saying. Her eyes starting to well with tears, she nodded and smiled. Each retired to their rooms to pick the perfect battle outfits.

Morgan went with a simplistic look. She took a pair of leggings that were green with red roses running up them. She wore a crop top black hoodie and sensible sneakers. Her brown hair was tied up in a dancer's bun to keep it from her eyes. She put on red eyeshadow and a matching lipstick. She looked at herself in the mirror. She felt strong, yet feminine. She sighed, thinking the night she spent in Neil's arms. She awoke to their smile and it was the happiest she had felt in a very long time. She decided that nothing was going to take that away from her.

Neil spent a lot of their time in front of the mirror, examining their body. There were no holes. They had no scars from when he was murdered. Good, they thought. I don't need a reminder of that. And I'm certainly not letting any of my team feel like that. Their goal was to dress for speed and agility. They grabbed a black muscle tank top with white skinny jeans and a large yellow belt. They grabbed their Chuck Taylor shoes and began to tie them. Their hair was tied back in a flowing, curly ponytail. They accented the look with purple eyeshadow. This was who they were. If they were going to die again, they would do so proud of who they were.

Jeans. Spaghetti strap tank top with a light cardigan. Running shoes. Subtle but natural make up. Cassandra usually was not one for frills most of the time, especially not when there was going to be a battle. This was too important for her to get hung up on what to wear. She fancied herself as a leader, so she needed look and feel as if she could handle any situation that would come up. She herself, she thought, was responsible for keeping her team not only alive, but successful. She had spent much of the evening after she left Dex's room thinking through her team's abilities. She understood what they could do in a fight and began working on how they would be the most effective. She took a deep sigh, looking into her mirror. She thought of her mom and how proud she would be of her. Her dad always told her she had her mother's eyes. In this moment, it was a great comfort knowing that in some way she was there with her.

For Dex, there really was only one option of what to wear. After all, he had been on what he felt was his own bizarre adventure. His black shirt with the kanji for "menacing" would do perfectly. To be honest, he didn't really care what pants he wore. His dad always wore jeans, so that was good enough for him. Same with his tennis shoes. He just didn't care what he was wearing. He wasn't going to church or anything so he didn't need to dress up. No- the only important part of his outfit was his shirt because that was what most people would see. His shirt showed what he wanted to be- menacing. More important than his clothes was the care and attention to Ruach. Never did he ever dream that he would actually wield the blade in battle, yet here he was again getting ready for war. As he changed his shirt, he looked at his torso and arms. For some reason, he did have some slight scaring which was strange because he had healed Neil perfectly. He deduced that, because it was his own body, perhaps it was his subconscious sending him a message. Perhaps, he thought, that he needed to be reminded of all his battles. There was a faint line around his wrist where he healed his hand. His arms had lines on them from cuts- each scar telling a story of where he had been. They were his memories. Each mark left a literal impression on him. If he could learn from these pains and these hurts, perhaps he would be able to do better in the future. All he had to do was carry the pain with him and learn from them.

They reassembled in the living room, each ready and armed for the daily activities. Everyone looked apprehensive. Cassandra spoke up.

"Here is the plan. There are multiple points of entry to the warehouse. I'm going to try to psychically cloak us. There is no effective cover, so we're going in the front door."

"Bold strategy: let's see how it plays out," Neil said.

"We're going in with the goal of not being separated," she continued. "Chances are they will try to break us up to pick us off. We have no back up," she said looking at Dex, "unless..."

"I spoke to Jules last night. They offered to take over the mission. I declined. They wanted us to do it, so we are doing it. And I have no other contacts, so yeah: on our own." Cassandra nodded.

"I thought as much. So, in the event that you get separated, let us know where we are and we'll come find you."

"If I can see you, I can heal you," Dex reminded everyone. "So please help me maintain line of sight to you, okay?"

"So, I can't exactly force myself to see the future," Morgan said awkwardly, "but I can still get flashes. And if I try, I can force a flash. It's not that painful- just, like, a minor headache."

"If we need them, we can use them. Thanks, Morgan," Cassandra replied smiling. "Is there anything else we need to know before we head out?" Dex sighed.

"Yeah," he said in a serious tone. "I've got a few things. First..." he paused, thinking how best to say what he wanted to say. "First things first: no dying, okay? Like, I'm not allowing it. Second, this guy is more dangerous than you can imagine. Don't believe what he says. Don't believe what he promises you. He killed two Conduits by himself in the past. So be careful. Third, no matter what happens today, I want- no. I need you all to know how much I love each of you." He smiled at them. "We've got this."

"We're driving there," Cassandra said. "We need to arrive outside the building and not the inside. We will need to be on the lookout for anyone tailing us." They all nodded. "You all ready?" she asked.

"Absolutely not," Morgan responded. "So let's do this. And we're taking the truck, for some reason. I don't know why, but I know we are."

"Well who's going to..." Cassandra began. She was interrupted by Neil.

"I call the truck bed!" they took Morgan by the hand and headed outside. Dex shrugged and followed them outside. Once outside, he turned to look at the house. This was the only house he had ever known. He grew up here. He lost his parents while living here. He wondered if this was the last time he was going to see it. No, he thought. We'll be back here soon. Dex climbed in the driver side and Cassandra sat next to him. She gave him a knowing nod as he went to start the vehicle. Cassandra turned around and opened the back window.

"You both doing okay back there?" she asked Neil and Morgan.

"We're good," Morgan answered.

"I picked out the song," Dex said suddenly. "I thought it was appropriate for us- for all of us together." Dex had come to peace with his decision to not go it alone. From the beginning, he realized how much he needed Neil. Now, he understood how much he needed Cassandra and Morgan as well. It started with the sound of an electronic heartbeat. *"This is gospel for the fallen ones, locked away in permanent slumber. Assembling their philosophies from pieces of broken memories."* Dex understood, and he believed that they did as well, that they were more than the sum of their past. They were who they were and they were bound together. And that would be enough for them.

"The gnashing teeth and criminal tongues conspire against the odds, but they haven't seen the best of us..." Neil smiled looking around them, their hair blowing in the wind. They smiled at Morgan, who smiled back. They looked at Cassandra, lovingly holding Dex's hand. This was their family, and they knew their family could great things.

"This is gospel for the vagabonds, ne'er-do-wells, insufferable bastards. Confessing their apostasies, led away by imperfect imposters." Morgan had been through Hell and back, never really feeling like she belonged anywhere. That was gone now. She knew where she belonged, and nothing was going to take that from her.

"Don't try to sleep through the end of the world and bury me alive, 'cause I won't give up without a fight..." Something worth fighting for. Cassandra looked at Dex, who wore a serious look as he drove down the road. She looked in the review mirror. Her sibling Neil and her sister Morgan were laughing, enjoying the freeing ride. This is what she had been waiting for. Since her mother died, she had been looking for the next family to be a part of, to defend with her life. She thought The Order would be that family. To an extent, it was. After all, it led her to these three people.

Something like a large bird flew the opposite direction of the truck, getting behind them.

"Dex," Morgan said in a concerned voice, "we've got company."

"Damn: that was fast," Cassandra said grimacing.

"What have we got?" Dex asked, focusing on the road.

"Looks like a Horned Devil," Cassandra said, sticking her head out of the window.

"Dex!" Morgan shouted. "Dodge right!" Dex instinctively jerked the wheel a bit to the right, narrowly missing a large fireball heading towards the truck. Dex looked at his side mirror. Behind them, was a large humanoid shaped being with twisted ebony horns from its head. It flew on leathery bat-like wings which kept its orange and red hued body aloft, its pointed tail following behind it. The fiend narrowed its gaze, watching them speed away. It held one of blood red clawed hands in the sky, producing another fire ball, tossing it almost effortlessly towards them.

"Move left!" Morgan instructed, keeping an eye on the monster. Dex got too excited, cutting the wheel too hard. Thankfully, the road was empty as Dex momentarily lost control, sending the car into a donut. The others held on; their balance suddenly thrown off. As fate would have it, the car performed a perfect circle, allowing only a narrowing gap between the demon and themselves. Dex pushed the peddle to the floor and Neil got on their knees.

"Oh I don't think so," they said with a cocky grin. Their held their left hand up, producing a ball of positive energy in a light blue hue. They simply flicked their wrist, tossing the ball of energy at the demon, who easily avoided it. "Wait for it," they said. Then suddenly, Neil picked up their right hand with something like a long, silvery strong coming out of it. After the ball was behind the demon, they pulled their right hand, causing the ball to move backwards towards them, hitting the demon in the back. There was an inhuman screeching of pain as the demon crumpled to the ground. "You good, boo," Neil yelled at Dex. Cassandra looked worried.

"A full-fledged demon," she said shaking her head. "This guy is connected as Hell..."

"I'm assuming most demons don't work well with humans?" Dex asked, making a turn down a back alley.

"Typically, no," she answered. "They serve their own needs. I'm not sure what they would have to gain from working with Niall."

"Show of force, most likely," Dex surmised out loud. "Like, they could show off and get more Grafters." They pulled into a parking garage and Dex shut the car off.

"Okay," Cassandra said after everyone was out of the truck. "We're right next door to the warehouse. Morgan: did you get anything yet?" She shook her head and closed her eyes. After a moment of pain, she responded.

"Lots of opposition out front, she said, shaking the headache from her head. "A couple Werewolves and Vampires. Mostly Grafters and Corrupted. The Werewolves are positioned on the left and right sides of the building."

"Stealth is not an option, correct?" Neil asked. Cassandra shook head with a troubled look.

"I have, like, half a plan," Dex said suddenly. "Let me go in first. Like last time, but flashier. And from above." Cassandra looked confused. "Look," he said continuing. "I can start at fifty percent power. Then I'll be able to fly up and do a ground attack. That will let you guys come in from a side and take out one of the Werewolves, right? And I'm fairly confident that I'll be fine till you all come in."

"Are you sure you want to start off with that much power?" Neil asked. "You won't, like, run out of energy or anything?" Dex shook his head.

"At that level, I should be good. My body will be constantly healing itself, so I won't burn out. And the higher I go, the more it works. It'll work," he said optimistically. Cassandra nodded.

"It's the best chance we get for a surprise round. You all ready?" They all nodded. Dex closed his eyes, encasing himself in energy and emerging with a pair of shimmering wings. This was only the second time the others had seen him transform. They looked at him with a sort of awe and terror filling them.

"See you soon," he said, his voice filled with power. He winked at them.

"Wait!" Cassandra said. Dex turned back around to face her. She pulled him close and kissed him, energy emanating from his lips into hers. "Be careful," she said. He nodded and flew off, a few feathers falling off, surrounding his friends.

Once Dex reached a good height, he looked down to the scene that Morgan had described perfectly. His eyesight was enhanced to where he could easily make out individuals.

"We're going in on the left side," Cassandra told him in his mind. "It's closer to us."

"Got it," Dex replied. "Wait for the boom and then head on over." He got in what appeared to be the center, gathering energy into Ruach. He closed his eyes and took a deep breath. He rose higher, his blade and his wings shimmering with energy. In a flash, he turned, plummeting head-first towards the ground, gathering both speed and more energy. Some of the enemies looked up with terror in their eyes, but it was too late. He landed with a loud boom, creating a crater and taking out several enemies with the positive energy that flowed out of him due to his landing.

"Hello," he said rather politely. "I was wondering if you all would like to surrender?" There was a great roar as they all descended on him, a mass of limbs and negative energy and claws and fangs. Dex spread his wings, knocking some of them over. With a powerful push of his wings, he was once more in the air. Tucking the wings closer to him, he performed a corkscrew like maneuver holding his sword pointed in front of him. It was then he heard the animalist howl of the first Werewolf. Suddenly, it stopped. A large bright beam of energy shot out from the ground in Dex's direction. His friends had entered the battle.

It was all a blur of blood and violence. Dex reacted even faster during the battle than he thought possible constantly healing his team of every injury no matter how minor while still battling his own enemies. Morgan proved Ophelia's training to be quite effective, using her batons to both defend and attack. Neil was living their best life as if they were a character in a video game, dispatching foes with ease. Cassandra moved with grace and elegance, clouding the minds of her foes and gaining an advantage on them. When all was said and done, they stood over their fallen foes: some living and some not so fortunate. Dex looked around at his team, bloody and bruised and took care to make sure they were all back at one hundred percent before they continued. Morgan had a strange look on her face.

"He's alone in there," she said suddenly. "He's waiting for us." Cassandra closed her eyes. After a few moments, she opened them again.

"He's in there, alright. I'm picking up two other lives, but something is off about them. I don't understand it: it's like nothing is there. The lights are on, but no one is home."

"He must have found two other Conduits," Dex said, his anger rising. He gently folded his wings in behind him. "We have to go save them." The team agreed, and they entered the front door. The smell of mold and mildew was prevalent. The warehouse used to be used for shipping up and down the river but now stood as a worn-down reminder of better times. There was suddenly a sound like the crackling of a speaker coming on. A knot developed in the pit of his stomach. It's him. It has to be. Morgan looked to Cassandra, who readied her staff. Neil lit his hands up. Dex scanned the area to see where the sound was coming from, to no avail. There were hidden speakers everywhere. Dex sensed no danger. This wasn't a trap. No; it was a welcoming. The haunting piano music started slowly and pointedly. Niall's voice followed, singing.

"All around me are familiar faces, worn out places, worn out faces..." Neil sneered.

"Oh he would, wouldn't he?" they remarked with a dismissive laugh.

"Let's keep moving," Dex said. "We need to find him. Now." They continued walking towards the back of the building, assuming that he was near the back.

"Hide my head I want to drown my sorrow. No tomorrow. No tomorrow." They kept walking, the haunting song surrounding them. Finally, they made it to a large area with a machine with two obscured figures in the tubes, suspended in the liquid in large tubes, moving back and forth like leaves in the wind. Niall sat there, at a piano, finishing his song, staring at them, expressionless save his voice.

"And I find it kind of funny, I find it kind of sad. The dreams of which I'm dying are the best I've ever had. I find it hard to tell you. I find it hard to take. When people run in circles it's a very, very... mad world..." His voice, not his face, was filled with happiness.

"Welcome, friends. I'm so glad you could come to the end of the world."

"Why that song?" Cassandra asked him. He shrugged.

"Because it's good. Because it's a cover. And sometimes, something new has to come to make something old better." Dex looked back at Neil, their face a mask of rage and sadness and fear. The light surrounding their fists pulsated with the beating of their heart and it was doing so at an alarming rate.

"You need to let them go," Dex said in a forceful voice, unfolding his wings once more.

"No thank you," Niall said politely. "I've been warming it up for a while, and it's almost ready to go."

"Not possible," Dex said. "There are only two bodies in there. Let those two go and we can work something out."

"It is possible," Niall said, tilting his head slightly to the left. "Oh," he said, his voice dripping pity. "You didn't realize, did you? You finished the machine for me."

"I would never do that," Dex said defiantly.

"Not willingly, no," Niall confirmed. "But you did lend a hand." He pressed a button on a remote control, illuminating one of the tubes. Dex took a step closer, the other tubes still obscured by darkness.

"Is that...?"

"Yes," Niall replied. "Your hand. I need a piece specifically from you, when your body was flooded with healing energy. In my studies, I found that the same principles that lend itself to healing Vampires can do much, much more. In effect, it does the job I need of a full Healer Conduit, and then some." Dex felt sick to his stomach.

"Let the others go," he said through gritted teeth, his eyes a flame with raw power and rage.

"No. I've been looking forward to this. I need you to understand how right I am- how nothing matters in life. So, I'm going to break you." The click of the lights coming on reverberated across the room. Dex fell to his knees.

"You son of a..." Neil fired a large blast at Niall through their own tears. Niall's hand became engulfed in purple negative energy. He harmlessly caught the blast, crushing it.

"No..." Dex said softly. "Please. No."

"Did you never wonder what those Grafters were doing there that day, Dex Machina? Did you think it was coincidence? Fate? No. I sent them. Because I needed some of their bones." Dex sat there, shaking and depowering on reflex and guilt. Inside the other two tanks were the fully formed bodies of his parents. Morgan and the others ran towards Niall, ready to attack. Niall calmly put a hand a hand up and said, "No." They froze, their bodies psychically locked in place.

"Give me a minute," Cassandra said in the team's minds, "and I'll have us unlocked. It's simple enough. It just takes time." Dex didn't hear her. He heard nothing. He felt nothing. He cared about nothing. His parents. Not only were their bodies fully healed, but he could tell they were alive.

"You did this, Dex Machina. By your hand and your blood, you brought them back. I told you: it is very simple for us to raise the dead. I used your blood to help grow new bodies." He placed a hand on the ground, sending a web of positive and negative energy shooting out the way they had come in. He walked over to Dex, placing a hand on his shoulder. "They just don't have their souls. Their bodies work well enough, though. All those life functions still going." Niall sighed. "The lights are on but no one's home."

"Why?" Dex asked in a meek voice. "Why did you do this?"

"I needed them. They wasted their lives. I didn't think that they should waste death, too." He grabbed Dex's head and pointed it towards his parents. "Look, Dex. I said look." Niall struggled to keep Dex's head straight, eventually forcing Dex to see his handy work. "This is what happens to us, Dex. We die. It doesn't matter what we have done or what we have said. When God says it's time, it's time. Don't you see, Dex Machina? Nothing matters. Nothing matters at all. That's why it has to end, Dex. It's the only logical mercy- to hasten the inevitable." Niall looked up at his machine. "Soon, Dex Machina. Soon it'll all be over."

Dex stood up, his eyes red from crying, his nose a running nightmare. He placed his hands on the tubes containing his parents. I should be happy, he thought to himself. I'm with my parents. They're right here. Oh man- all the things we can do now! I can bake with Mom! I can watch Star Wars with Dad! It'll be perfect. He smiled as he looked at them.

"Mom. Dad. I'm here," he said in a whimper.

"Dex! They're gone!" Neil shouted.

"No!" He protested. "They're right here."

"Dex," Cassandra said. "They aren't fully there. You know that."

"No," Dex said crying. "No, they're back. Look! Mom! Dad! Say something." He stood there in silence, with Niall looking on. "Please," he begged them.

"He's still going to destroy the world, Dex," Morgan said. "You won't see them alive again. If you love them, then honor them. Live like they taught you to live." He hit their tubes with his palms, expecting a reaction. Put your hands on my, he thought. Please. Give me a sign. I'm begging you. But there was nothing. They really were gone, weren't they? This life of their bodies- it was a false life. They weren't alive. They couldn't feel. They couldn't love. They were finally, Dex realized, gone.

But I'm not, Dex thought. I'm still here. I'm still alive. I still feel. And they are with me, always. No matter what, they are always with me. It was time, Dex thought. He could almost hear his parents singing the words of Brendon Urie.

"If you love me let me go..."

It happened in a moment. Faster than he knew he could move, Dex drew his sword and transformed, gaining his angelic wings. One strike. It was horizontal- the same type of strike that took his parents from him the first time. This time, it was releasing them in peace. The tanks shattered, engulfed in positive energy, destroying all organic matter in them. His parents, finally, were gone. Gone, but with him in a different way. For the first time in a long time, Niall's face moved. It began as a twitch, the muscles unused for years. His face slowly contorted into one of rage and hatred.

"NO!" he screamed.

It was then all hell broke loose. The energy that Niall sent out earlier was meant to heal and resurrect his agents. They all came bounding in, ready for revenge. Cassandra had finally freed the others from Niall's presence, placing certain mental blocks to prevent Niall from doing that again. They stood there; weapons ready. Morgan pressed a button on her batons and they split, being two handles now. They had transformed into nunchaku, being whipped around her body with speed and skill.

Niall went all out quickly, his body completely transforming. Niall was longer standing before Dex. Instead it was a being of pure nothingness. He was humanoid in shape, but completely white. He had no discernable features anymore. He was simply a being of nothingness with six large, black leathery wings coming from behind him. He moved with incredible speed- speed that Dex had only seen while training with Jules.

Niall's hands transformed, turning into sword like limbs, impaling Dex over and over again over his body. Dex thought he heard his friends scream for him, but they were busy with problems of their own. He did everything he could to keep up with the wounds forming on him, but they were too much. He looked over to the rubble of the machine and he remembered. My parents. He turned and faced Niall, glaring at him. No. Not today.

"You fool," Dex said in a maddening laugh. He looked at the blankness that Niall's face had become, smiling. "This isn't even my final form."

The explosion was instantaneous. Sending Niall backwards and destroying the remnants of the machine once and for all. The enemies stopped and stared as did his team.

"Dex?" Cassandra asked in a bewildered voice.

"Yes," he said, his voice carrying a new weight. "It's me." His clothing had changed. He now wore black pants and boots with no shirt. Instead, he wore a blood red leather trench coat. Six pure white wings stuck out from Dex's back, creating holes in his jacket. His hands were wrapped in white bandages as if he was training. Above his head floated something like a multicolored gyroscope covered with eyes and something like a fire burning in the center as the rings moved around. He had no eyes, only pieces of what looked like burning coals where his eyes should be.

"Well," Niall said in a distorted voice, "I see that you have chosen to be a slave to God's will.

"No," Dex replied. "I'm just doing what's right- what's decent. If that makes me a tool to be used, then so be it if it means I get to stop you."

"This only ends in one way," Niall mocked. "I know because I've already written it."

"Then don't tell me," Dex replied. "I hate spoilers." Their movements created a rush of air, blowing Dex's team and their enemies.

"Come on, you apes!" Cassandra roared at her team. "You wanna live forever?" She screamed a battle roar and charged back into the fight, flanked by Morgan and Neil. Somehow, Dex was able to keep tabs on his team, healing them with barely a movement as they fought. No. Not only healing them but giving them more energy. Their muscles were full of the boost he was giving them, giving them the edge that they needed.

Dex and Niall moved too fast to be seen by human or demon eyes. They were a flurry of color and energy, stopping only a few times so their images could catch up with them.

"We're evenly matched, Dex," Niall said in a mocking tone.

"No," Dex chided him, "we aren't."

"And what makes you so confident in that?"

"Because I believe it."

As Niall twisted in rage, Dex brought Ruach down with the sound of a hurricane. Niall fell to the ground in two parts. He glided over to his friends who had already dealt with half of their foes.

"Surrender now or keep fighting. The choice is yours. This fight is over either way." One by one, their enemies laid down their arms. Dex looked at Cassandra, his gaze as intense as the sun.

"Call The Four. They can deal with this." She pulled out her phone and called her father. Within moments, The Four came with reinforcements ready if needed to collect those responsible.

"Oh dear God," Rhianna said, looking at Dex.

"He chose wisely," Jules said with a smile.

A few moments later, it was all over. Just like that, it was done. Dex slowly floated back down to earth, transforming back to normal as the reinforcements arrived to take people into custody. His team ran to him.

"Dex!" Neil shouted. "Holy crap! What was that? You looked like an anime character!"

"Yeah," Dex said sheepishly. "Sorry. I guess our final forms are based on our subconscious or something."

"Dude: you are Goku," they replied with a laugh.

"Are you okay?" Morgan asked in a concerned voice.

"Yeah, Morgan. I'm fine. You all okay? Need any more healing?"

"I think we're okay," she replied. Cassandra walked up and slapped Dex on the back of the head.

"Ow!" he said with a laugh. "What was that for?"

"Together," she replied enunciating each syllable. "Together. We were supposed to take him on together."

"We did!" Dex defended. "We totally did! It's not my fault he did a mass heal and resurrection. You all were perfect! I have no idea what would have happened if you all weren't here. My guess is he would have ambushed me before I even got in here." He grabbed her hands and looked in her ice blue eyes. "I literally couldn't have done this without you."

"Don't," she warned. "Don't try to get on my good side with flattery. You had me worried sick there for a moment. You should have transformed sooner. You wouldn't have been hurt as much. You should have..."

"You're right," he said softly. She was taken aback by this.

"I am?"

"You are. But... I think it needed to happen this way. I mean, I think it was supposed to work out like this. And I'm fine. Look! Even my shirt is okay. Which is good because I love this shirt." He hugged her. "And you all are safe. Other than me having to kill Niall, I see this as a win. But that's a trauma to deal with for another day." He grabbed her and kissed her deeply. "Tomorrow, the sun will come up like it's supposed to. We don't know what else will happen, but we'll be together. And that will be enough for me." He kissed her again deeply.

"Dude," Neil said in their minds. "Adrian is, like, right there." They quickly disengaged, blushing. Adrian looked like he wanted to say something, but Rhianna elbowed him in the side to shut him up.

"So what now?" Neil asked pointedly, looking at Morgan.

"No," she said. "I'm not going to try to see the future anymore. I'll just wait to see what I see. Let's handle it that way." She shrugged. "I like surprises."

"Shoot. I'm down with that," Neil said putting their arm around her.

"Actually," Adrian said, "what will happen is that as soon as we have a new Council, they will debrief you. And then we can get back to business as normal." The four of them gave him a strange look. They looked at each other, silently, discussing and weighing their option. Finally, they all nodded in agreement.

"Hard no," Cassandra finally said. Adrian looked shocked.

"I'm sorry," he said laughing, "but what?"

"We pass," she said.

"Young lady, this is not the time..."

"No- it's actually the perfect time," she interrupted. "We aren't going to be under a Council again."

"A new day is dawning," Dex said with a smirk. "So, we have a counteroffer. We'll be the new Council." The Four, other than Ophelia who was engrossed in reading a collected edition of The Future Foundation, looked shocked and surprised. Dex looked at them all. "We all agree. It's that or we walk. And to be perfectly honest, we are fine with that option." They all collectively shrugged. The Four had their own silent meeting with a lot of furrowed brows.

"Honestly," Ophelia said out loud, "it's not that big of a deal. It's going to happen anyway, so might as well get used to it." The other three looked at her. "What?" she asked. "The machine is gone and I don't mind spoilers." Jules sighed.

"I supposed this is something that you all won't waver on?" he asked hopefully.

"Nope," Morgan answered. "It is what it is."

"It is what it is," her team echoed.

"Well, I for one will agree to this," Jules said with an unsurprised smile. "And I am sure my associates will as well. Please join us tomorrow for lunch so we can discuss the future."

"No," Dex said suddenly. "Cassandra is taking me to Giorno's tomorrow for lunch. It's her turn to pay."

"We will set up something eventually," Neil added. "Morgan and I will look at the chore wheel and the schedule and see when we're free. And then we can work on reform. Sound good?" Adrian went to speak, but Rhianna cut him off.

"Yes," she said. "I think it sounds perfect." She smiled at them, proud of her students. They were beginning to understand. The role of a teacher is not to just teach, but to equip their students to lead the future.

"So, we're going to Ralph's Kitchen for a late lunch now," Morgan said. "Till next time, whenever that will be," she said with a smile. The four of them turned and headed to Dex's truck.

"And we're really going to let them leave?" Adrian asked. "We're going to just trust them?"

"We have since the beginning," Rhianna said. "Nothing has changed."

"No," Jules said with a smile. "Everything has changed. He was right: tomorrow is a new day. Now the rest of it can finally begin."

Dex and his team- no: his family- got in his truck. He turned the key and the engine roared to life.

"I have the perfect song," he said with a smile as the pop punk guitar started playing. They drove off towards Ralph's Kitchen, smiling and excited for what's next- the freedom that the future offered them, content with the plan and their part in it for once.

"Throw it away. Forget yesterday. We'll make the great escape. We won't hear a word they say. They don't know us anyway. Watch it burn. Let it die. 'Cause we are finally free tonight."

Dex looked at his family: Neil and Morgan cuddling in the back. Cassandra holding an arm in triumph out the window as they drove into the future, her face wearing a beautiful smile. He was happy. He was actually happy. Not only that, but they were happy and that meant the world to him.

"Tonight will change our lives. It's so good to be by your side but we'll cry. We won't give up the fight. We'll scream loud at the top of our lungs and they'll think it's just 'cause we're young and we'll feel so alive."

Perhaps, Dex thought, this was what he had been waiting for. For the first time in a long time, he was actually excited about the future. No. Not excited, but rather looking forward to it. Yes, it's most likely that this was all a part of some grander plan, but that didn't matter to him in this moment. In his mind, he was going to do everything possible to make it the best future. He owed it to his family. He owed it to himself. So they drove onward, ready for tomorrow with only a hint of what was to come, but it didn't matter because they had each other. And for once, all of them were content with the past, the present, and the future.

Deus ex Machina Playlist

The songs featured in this work were created by amazing artists. Please support their official release.

1. Wish You Were Here by: Pink Floyd
2. Eclipse by: Pink Floyd
3. Float On by: Modest Mouse
4. Make My Story a cover by: Johnathan Young Ft. SixeenInMono
5. Yoshimi Battles the Pink Robots, Pt. 1 by: The Flaming Lips
6. Cruel Angel's Thesis a cover by: AmaLee
7. Where is My Mind? by: The Pixies
8. Pinch Me by: Barenaked Ladies
9. All These Things That I've Done by: The Killers
10. Tonight, Tonight by: The Smashing Pumpkins
11. M&M's by: Blink 182
12. Time After Time a cover by: Quietdrive
13. Dakota by: A Rocket to the Moon
14. Chasing Cars by: Snow Patrol
15. Black Rain by: Blink 182
16. 99 Red Balloons a cover by: Goldfinger
17. Chemical Bomb by: The Aquabats
18. Helena (So Long & Goodnight) by: My Chemical Romance
19. Manic by: Coleman Hell
20. Wake Me Up When September Ends by: Green Day
21. Move Along by: The All-American Rejects
22. Believer by: Imagine Dragons
23. Sakura Kiss a cover by: AmaLee
24. Do You Realize?? by: The Flaming Lips
25. Ready to Die by: Andrew W.K.

26. Going Away to College by: Blink 182
27. This is Gospel by: Panic at the Disco
28. Mad World a cover by: Michael Andrew featuring Gary Jules
29. The Great Escape by: Boys Like Girls
30.

Thank You

I would like to thank my wife, who put up with me writing this for hours on end. I would like to thank my children for inspiring me to write something they can hold on that is a piece of me when I'm gone and for constant inspiration. I would like to thank God for all they have done for me. Thank you to my friends who played Dungeons and Dragons with me and listened to me rant about anime. Thank you to all my family who has supported me over the years. Thank you to the dream I had that inspired this story and the many sleepless night I spent thinking about how it would come out. Thank you to the wonderful musicians whose work played a pivotal role in crafting this tale. Thank you to the authors who inspired me throughout my life. Most of all, thank you, dear reader, for taking the time to read a piece of my soul.

Author's Note:

Well. Here I am about four years later and not during a pandemic. I decided I needed to sit down and properly edit this thing for a rerelease give that this trilogy has a name now. Most changes were cosmetic. There are some other slight changes, but none that affect the story in an impactful way. The scene that changed the most was dance scene as I felt I needed to do it more justice. Other than a few odds and ends, the story remains fundamentally the same. I have even kept the original thank you unchanged as a monument to the time in which it was written. I hope to see you all for some Dramatic Irony when it's done.

www.ingramcontent.com/pod-product-compliance
Lightning Source LLC
Chambersburg PA
CBHW060628310726
48982CB00003B/714
* 9 7 9 8 2 1 8 3 6 9 7 5 0 *